Seeing Stars

Seeing Stars

Christina Jones

ISIS
LARGE PRINT
Oxford

Copyright © Christina Jones, 2005

First published in Great Britain 2005
by
Piatkus Books Ltd.

Published in Large Print 2007 by ISIS Publishing Ltd.,
7 Centremead, Osney Mead, Oxford OX2 0ES
by arrangement with
Piatkus Books Ltd.

British Library Cataloguing in Publication Data
Jones, Christina, 1948–
    Seeing stars. – Large print ed.
    1. Caterers and catering – Fiction
    2. Country life – Fiction
    3. Love stories
    4. Large type books
    I. Title
    823.9'14 [F]

ISBN 978–0–7531–7856–0 (hb)
ISBN 978–0–7531–7857–7 (pb)

Printed and bound in Great Britain by
T. J. International Ltd., Padstow, Cornwall

For Berkshire's original JB Roadshow: Del, Dolly, Richard, Dave, Snib, Alan, and the late David "Totty" Tinson — Soul-singer and front-man extraordinaire.
Thanks for the memories.

Acknowledgements

Many thanks to all at Piatkus, especially my brilliant editor Gillian Green; to my agent Sarah Molloy; to Vivid for another wonderful cover design; to all my friends in The Romantic Novelists Association; to Mags and Wendy for keeping me going; to Rob and Laura for being them; and to my Dad for his Oscar Wilde "looking up at the stars" take on life.

Prologue

"Amber Parslowe! You can't do this! You're a northern lass! You've never been further south than Rhyl in your entire life."

Amber nodded sadly. It was true.

"Listen, Amber, you do clubbing in Manchester and shopping in Liverpool and hen nights in Blackpool. You can't go south. You'll be like a duck out of water."

"Fish," Amber muttered over the rim of her glass. "And no I won't."

Her friends, Emma and Jemma, Kelly and Bex, crowded round the wine bar table, ignored her.

Jemma leaned forward. "Look, we're not stupid. We might be Oop North but we still know all about the global village and stuff — but hell's teeth, there are limits!"

"Exactly what I was going to say." Bex interrupted loudly. "Amber, listen to us. We're your closest friends. We've known you since forever. We've your best interests at heart here."

Emma wasn't going to be left out. "And not to put too finer a point on it, if you're serious about this, then you must be totally barking. I mean, why go *south* to do *this*? Even if you don't want to leave England with your family — although God knows why not — and

1

you really don't want to stay here, which we find very hurtful, you've still got plenty of choices."

"Yeah — you could get a job on a cruise liner and travel and get paid at the same time." Kelly's eyes were dreamy. "Or move to London as an au pair, or live by the sea as a beach bum, or — well, millions of things."

"The world's your, um, thingy. You could do, well, *anything*. Anything rather than this."

They all stared at her, willing her to change her mind.

"Are you going to let me say anything at all?" Amber grinned at them.

Bex shook her head. "Only if it's to say you're not going. There's still time to say no. We really don't want you to go anywhere. We'll miss you. Why don't you stay here, get a nice little flat in that new warehouse complex thingy —"

"They're luxury loft apartments for the rich kids," Amber chuckled. "I couldn't even afford the front door key to one of those!"

"OK," Bex conceded. "But what about a flat-share? Or bedsit?"

"Please," Amber shook her head. "If I could even afford to do that I'd have already done it, wouldn't I? Wouldn't we all?"

They nodded. They were all in the same boat.

"OK — but what about shopping? I bet you haven't even thought about shopping!" Kelly almost choked. "What on earth are you going to do about shopping? There won't be any shops, or wine bars, or clubs or well, anything, will there?"

2

"Or nail bars and hairdressers!" Emma flicked her dead straight glossy fall away from her eyes.

Jemma looked horrified. "Ohmigod! Yes! Amber, have you even considered not having a hairdresser? You won't be able to get your bone-straight blonde highlights and lowlights done in some hick-stick place, will you? If there is a hairdresser — which I doubt — it'll be someone called Cynthia who still does bubble perms and mullets and uses hood dryers."

"And work?" Emma butted in again. "Have you actually thought about where you'll work? It'll be all farming and wellies and mud and cack. You won't be able to sign on with an agency and pick and choose your office jobs there. You'll probably end up serving in the village post office — if they've got one and then only if you're very lucky and the postmistress hasn't got several hundred inbred relations waiting in line to grab the opportunity."

"Or mucking out pigs."

"Or driving a tractor."

"Exactly." Jemma sat back. "Listen to us, Amber. We care about you. We, um, love you. You're only twenty-seven, and you're a townie girl through and through. Listen to what we're telling you. Who, in their right mind, would choose to leave town and go and bury themselves down south in some godforsaken village when they've got everything they need right here on their doorstep?"

Amber tried to stop the flow. "What if I said I'm bored with all this? Oh, not with you, not ever, but with all this . . ." she waved her arms vaguely round the wine bar. "What if I said I wanted a change — just for a little while? I've temped for the last five years since we all got made redundant from Bellamy's — and to be honest, one admin desk, one reception area is much like another . . . And now, with what's happened . . ."

They all looked at her in sympathy. OK, life had dealt her a bit of a double-handed punch recently — but even so . . .

Kelly shook her head. "Still don't see why you have to go and bury yourself in the country. What do you know about actually living in the *country*? I mean, the country's fine for — well — looking at once in a while, but no one wants to live there, do they?"

"Amber does."

"Amber's completely crazy, then."

Amber laughed and rather unsteadily raised her umpteenth glass of Chenin Blanc. "Nice to know I've got the wholehearted support of my dearest friends. But seriously, this is what I want to do. I'm really looking forward to it."

They all stared at her.

Bex still wasn't convinced. "OK then, this place you're going to? Is it scarily remote? Like Wales or Cornwall?"

Amber drained her glass. "I've never been there, remember? But it's in Berkshire. Almost civilised. They have huge towns like Reading and Newbury and Bracknell and Ascot and —"

"Reading? Isn't that close to London?"

"Close-ish, I think."

Jemma looked more cheerful. "Oh well, maybe it won't be *too* bad then . . . And this village — is it near Reading and Newbury and wherever else you just said?"

"Not that close, no. The nearest places are called, um, Winterbrook and Hazy Hassocks and — oh, yes — Bagley-cum-Russett . . ."

Emma was clearly appalled. "Dear God!"

"When are you going?"

"Next week."

"And you're going to be living with someone you've never met?" Kelly's slender eyebrows skittered upwards. "Some mad old bat?"

"My Gran's best friend from when they were young, yes. She's always written to us, sent us cards and postal orders on our birthdays and at Christmas, that sort of thing. She's been like a sort of surrogate long-distance grandmother. She wrote to us when Gran died and we've been in touch ever since. And I'm only going as a lodger — not as some sad Jane Austen type companion."

Bex was clearly still not impressed. "Jesus, Amber. You're really going to live with a wrinkly, in a village, with no job, no shops — and no men?"

"After Jamie the last bit will come as something of a blessing." Amber continued to grin. "I've had enough of two-timing, spineless, commitment-phobic men to last a lifetime. In fact it's one of the main reasons I'm going."

They all pulled sympathetic faces. Jamie had broken Amber's heart, everyone knew that, but was that really any reason for her to up sticks and bury herself in the middle of nowhere with some very, very old lady she'd never met?

Normal women would make do with getting roaring drunk and then indulging in a bit of retail therapy before dusting off their stilt-heels and finding another, far better, man.

"I'll give you a month at the most," Kelly smiled. "Then you'll be back."

"A week. She won't last more than a week."

Amber said nothing. What was the point? She'd made up her mind. It was all her parents' fault anyway. Well, and Jamie's of course. But mostly her parents.

Like all her friends, she was a SLAHWP: Still Living At Home With Parents. The lack of well-paid jobs and crippling house prices, and the fact she spent every penny of her salary before it arrived in her bank account, had seen to that. So when her parents decided to take early retirement and, overexcited by the surfeit of Change Your Lifestyle programmes on the television, chose to sell up and move to rural Spain, she'd been left with few choices.

At first she'd thought she'd move in with Jamie. They'd been together for nearly two years. It made sense.

Jamie, however, had nearly passed out at the suggestion and muttered feebly about being far too young to settle down and not being ready for that sort of commitment and, well, to be honest, Amber living in might just cramp his style, because — er — she wasn't actually the only woman in his life. He'd hoped she wouldn't find out this way, of course, but . . .

Renting was out of the question on her own; house-shares were few and far between. Her much-younger twin sisters, Coral and Topaz, at sixteen, had been thrilled at the thought of living in a tumbledown goat shed about three million miles into the hinterland of Andalucia and attending the local college and learning Spanish and being able to chat up waiters. Amber, who felt that luxuries like electricity, running water, drainage and a roof were fairly important, was simply horrified.

Then she'd had the letter from Gwyneth Wilkins, her grandmother's friend.

Why didn't Amber come and live with her for a while? Maybe just for the summer? Until she could sort out what she really wanted to do with the rest of her life?

Amber, still smarting from Jamie's rejection and deception, and her entire family's embracing of the Spanish peasant lifestyle, had thought about it for all of two minutes and then said yes.

Her friends all looked at her sorrowfully.

Kelly pushed another bottle across the table. "Well, when it all falls apart, don't say we didn't warn you."

"It's not the other side of the world," Amber said. "You could always come and visit me."

"Get real!" Bex frowned.

Jemma patted Amber's hand kindly. "Yeah, well — we might . . . One day . . ."

Emma sighed. "And what's this village-that-time-forgot called?"

Amber filled her glass again and smiled.

"Fiddlesticks."

CHAPTER
ONE

Dark Side of the Moon

Wincing at herself in Chrysalis Cottage's bedroom mirror, Zillah knew that unless she could lose two stones in three days, then Saturday night was going to be a total disaster.

Oh, why did her reflection never match her imagination?

At least they agreed on the clouds of dark-brown hair and the black-lashed dark eyes and the tanned skin. Where they started to fall out was over the wrinkles and dimples and folds and cellulite and yes, damn it, the sheer middle-aged avoirdupois.

Of course, the looking glass in her bedroom was less than flattering. It always had been. It wasn't her, it was a flaw in the bevel, honest. The mirror stubbornly refused to see her as the taut-skinned, firm-jowled twenty year old she knew she was inside, and spitefully insisted on giving her the full-on, fifty-something, outward truth.

It also delighted in giving her several chins, ridiculously shortened bulbous legs, three spare tyres and a bottom that protruded like a Volvo estate's parcel shelf.

However, on this occasion, maybe the mirror had a point. Maybe skin-tight lime-green spandex really wasn't her thing.

In fact, skin-tight lime-green spandex surely wasn't anyone's thing?

How many years had she been through this rubbish? How many years had she sworn never, ever again? How many years had she then been swept up in the general village excitement and thought what the heck? How many years had she actually itched to say that maybe there was something more than a little odd about celebrating someone who *might* just have lived umpteen hundred years ago and who, even if he had been canonised, which was doubtful, was clearly insane?

Oh, sod Gwyneth for suggesting the spandex. Sod Fiddlesticks for being so bloody archaic. And even more, sod mad old St Bedric for having his Eve in flaming June.

And now she had to get out of this darn thing and — ooooh! Great. Crotch poppers undone and one arm free. Now for the other — ouch — no chance.

In the middle of her gyrations, Zillah caught sight of the alarm clock on her bedside table. Crikey! Where on earth had the time gone? Now she only had an hour before she was due at work and there were millions of things to do before then and — oooof! — she simply had to get out of this stupid outfit and —

With mounting horror, Zillah came to the conclusion that second-skin spandex and the hottest morning of the year were not a great combination. No matter how much she tugged and wriggled the stupid outfit wouldn't budge. In fact it seemed to cling even more tightly, nestling into sweating nooks and crannies she'd not even noticed before. The more she struggled the more the damn stuff squelched and snuggled.

After a further ten minutes the situation really was getting seriously scary. Exhausted, every inch aching, she was alone in her bedroom encased in a shiny chin-to-knee body suit that The Only Gay in the Village would die for, and was probably about to expire from dehydration.

Maybe she could hop to the window and shout for help across the village green.

Stumble-trip-hop — sod it. Hop and hop and — hallelujah!

Help came mid-hop.

"Zil! Yoo-hoo! Are you upstairs?"

Joy, oh joy! Big Ida from Butterfly Cottage next door. At the foot of the stairs.

Zillah stopped writhing. Big Ida was OK. Big Ida and a gaggle of chums wasn't.

It was yet another problem with living in Fiddlesticks. No one locked their doors and everyone just wandered in. Now she'd probably got half the village in the hallway and she would have to waddle out on to the landing to greet them looking like something left over after a wrinklies fetish festival.

Bugger, bugger, bugger St Bedric!

"Yes — whoomph — I'm up here, Ida." Despite the years of living in Berkshire, Zillah's soft Cornish accent still came to the fore in moments of stress. "Aaah . . . Won't be a — oooh — minute . . . I'm just trying to — aaah . . ."

"You all right, duck? You sound a bit breathless — 'ere, you haven't got someone up there with you, 'ave you?"

"I wish . . . No, I'm all alone. Oooomph . . . Erph . . . Are you?"

"What? Alone? Yes — Zil, you sure you're all right?"

"I — erk — yerp."

The upside, Zillah thought, was that at least Big Ida didn't have a clutch of Fiddlestickers in tow. The downside with Big Ida as rescuer was that Zillah'd probably end up without any skin, but what the heck — she'd just have to hope Big Ida would be gentle with her.

Big Ida, nearly six feet tall and built like John Wayne, had apparently done a Charles Atlas body-building course in her youth and the rudiments were still with her some six decades later.

Ida sounded as though she was all ready halfway up the stairs. "I only popped round to say we're putting the kettle on for elevenses in Gwyneth's. We thought you'd like a cuppa before you go to work — and anyway, Gwyneth's like a hen on pins over this Amber arriving today and you know you always manage to calm her down."

Zillah pulled a face which owed nothing to the vice-like grip of the spandex. Gwyneth Wilkins, her other octogenarian next-door neighbour, had talked about nothing but Amber for days now. For her own reasons, Zillah really, really didn't want to hear any more about Amber's imminent arrival in the village. Not now. Not ever.

"Zil? Can you 'ear me?"

"Yes . . ." Zillah puffed. Forget Amber, she told herself, there are more urgent and immediate problems to address here. Oh, sod it, she'd have to risk the skinning. "Ida, be a dear and — errumph-oooh — give me a hand here. I'm in the bedroom . . ."

Big Ida wasted no time in thundering up the stairs.

"Blimey, Zil. What do you think you look like?"

"Probably like an overweight middle-aged woman stuck in a stretchy thing. Don't laugh . . . Ow . . . It's not funny."

"I ain't laughing. It ain't no laughing matter, duck." Big Ida, looking for all the world like Les Dawson in drag, hitched up her massive bosoms beneath her floral wrapover pinafore and pursed her lips in disapproval. "Aren't you a bit long in the tooth for that sort of get-up? Is it for work?"

"Whooomph . . . yes to the first, no to the second. Gwyneth picked it up at a Hazy Hassocks jumble sale. She said — ooooph — that as everyone has to wear green on St Bedric's Eve she thought it would be lovely with one of my long skirts over the top, but — oomph . . ."

Big Ida shook her head. Her steel-grey pudding basin hair didn't move. "That outfit weren't meant for someone of your size, Zil. You shouldn't 'ave even tried to squeeze yerself into it, duck. You know how Gwyneth tends to lose 'er head when she thinks she's got a bargain. That's like trying to get a quart into a pint pot. If you ain't careful you'll cut off your circulation."

"Thanks so much. I've managed to undo the poppers but now I'm really stuck. Look, do you think you could just grab the sleeves while I sort of tug it over my head because it hasn't got a zip or anything and — ouch!"

"Stand still," Big Ida grunted. "Brace yerself against the dressing table and don't be such a baby."

Zillah braced. There was a brief undignified and extremely painful tussle.

"You-didn't-use-talc-first-did-you?" Ida panted.

"Nooooo — ouch. And how do you — ow! Blimey — careful! — know about talc?"

"My godsons told me," Ida gritted her teeth for the final heave. "They had a bit of a thing for spandex last Christmas. It's crushed velvet this year. Catsuits. Nice."

Zillah nodded. Big Ida's godsons were always at least one dainty step ahead of the fashion police.

With a wrench and a squelch, Zillah and the bodysuit finally parted company.

As Ida, still clutching the lime-green spandex, rocketed backwards with the propulsion, Zillah whizzed forward into the dressing table with a clatter. Owing to her now being practically naked, this hurt. A lot. And her eyes and nose were running and every inch of her generous flesh smarted as if she'd been body-waxed.

"Thanks, Ida," she sniffed, blindly rummaging for her dressing gown. "And I'd appreciate it if you didn't mention this to anyone."

"You know me, duck." Ida picked herself up from the bed and adopted a pious smirk. "I ain't no tittle-tattler."

Yeah, right, Zillah thought, still sniffing. It'd be all round Fiddlesticks by lunch time.

It didn't even take that long.

By the time she'd showered — very gingerly — and dressed in one of her trademark long flowing skirts and a baggy T-shirt, and fastened her damp hair up with a haphazard collection of combs, and stepped over the broken-down fence which separated her cottage from Gwyneth's, the bodysuit incident had already passed into rural myth territory.

Gwyneth Wilkins, sitting on a kitchen chair outside her front door with two cats on her lap and a large dog of dubious origins snoring across her sandals, and expertly shelling peas into a battered colander at her feet, grinned at her.

"That all-in-one thingy not much good then, duck? Ida said it were like trying to get the peel off a green banana with gloves on."

Zillah lowered herself carefully, because of the soreness, onto the front-door step and glared across at Big Ida who was sitting innocently on the worn and weathered bench fastened to the front of Gwyneth's Moth Cottage and which looked as if it might not quite manage to support Big Ida's bulk for much longer.

Judas.

"It wasn't a great fit, no. I must have put on a few pounds. Sorry, Gwyneth, it was very kind of you to think of me. I'll have to find something else. Maybe I could wear what I wore last year or dye one of my dresses?"

"Maybe — although you've had some disasters with dye in the past, haven't you, duck? The last time you tried it you didn't add enough salt and it ran all down your arms and legs and everyone thought you'd got some lurgy. Still, as long as it's green. You know it has to be green for St Bedric's."

Zillah nodded. She knew. On account of St Bedric's assertion that the moon was made of green cheese. Of course.

"I'll go and get the tea, shall I —" Big Ida peered at them from beneath her steel grey, pudding-basin fringe "— now that young Zillah has finally joined us?"

Gwyneth nodded. "You know where everything is. Oh, and bring a bowl of water out for Pike, will you, duck?" She indicated the dog. "And some biscuits — for us as well as 'im. The cats have got their stuff in the shed."

Big Ida eased herself to her feet. The bench instantly sprang back to horizontal as she lumbered into the depths of Moth Cottage.

"Why is it always you that has to do elevenses?" Zillah hissed at Gwyneth. "Ida's so tight. She never offers tea when we're in hers — and after all, she only has to step over the fence."

Gwyneth shrugged and whizzed another podful of rattling peas into the colander. "Zil, duck, Big Ida and me have lived next door to one another for the best part of sixty years. She's always been careful with the pennies. She ain't going to change now, is she? And she only has her pension to live on."

"So do you," Zillah said quickly. "Well, apart from your little jobs on the side — and we all know you get paid peanuts for them. Still, having a lodger will help out with the finances a bit, won't it?"

Gwyneth looked shocked. "Eh? What lodger?"

"This, um, your friend's granddaughter." Zillah rolled the name round her mouth then spat it out like a bad taste. "Amber."

"Oh, I won't be asking young Amber to pay for her keep — wouldn't dream of it. How could I, Zil? She hasn't got a job and being a youngster I doubt if she has any savings. No, the invite to stay here weren't never financial. It was because the poor lass really didn't have anywhere else to go and I thought she might enjoy a bit of a change from city living."

Zillah gave a hollow laugh. "Fiddlesticks'll certainly be that — but I really think you should take some money from her. You're far too soft. You can't afford to feed both of you and all the animals on your pension."

"I'll have to take on some more little jobs then, won't I?"

"You'll kill yourself if you do. You're over eighty. Get this Amber to earn her keep. She's not coming here on holiday, is she?"

Gwyneth smiled gently. "No, of course not. And I'm sure she'll look for work when she's settled in. Give her a bit of time, Zil. She's bound to find it all a bit strange to start with. After living in the city this may come as a bit of a shock."

Shock? Zillah stared out into Gwyneth's narrow front garden, a tumble of head-high lupins, foxgloves and delphiniums leaning together in a haphazard rainbow arch almost hiding the path. Opposite the gate the rest of Fiddlesticks arranged itself neatly round the village green, which was scorched to dusty gold and shimmered beneath the sun.

The green was criss-crossed with sandy pathways, dotted with willow trees, and had a rustic bridge over a fat brown-bedded stream. Apart from the distant disembodied voice from someone's radio and the constant flute of bird song, Fiddlesticks was silent and sleepy in the heat of a perfect June morning. Butterflies preened themselves on the abundant buddleia bushes as bees bumbled and fumbled in and out of the blossoms, heavy and drowsy with pollen-dusted legs.

Zillah shrugged. "Shock? She'll think she's landed in paradise. And right on her feet if you're going to let her stay for months without paying a penny. She's, er, going to ring you when she arrives, is she?"

Gwyneth nodded. "Ah, she's going to ring on her mobile thingy when she gets close to Reading station. It could be any minute now."

Zillah sucked in her breath. She wished Amber would never ring. Never arrive. She knew what would happen when she did.

Still, looking on the bright side, this city-girl Amber might take one look at a horde of villagers dressed in green and eating verdant cheese and singing inebriated praises to a saint who probably never existed, and flee back to where she'd come from.

Zillah really, really hoped so.

CHAPTER
TWO

Starlight Express

It wasn't anything like Amber had imagined it would be. Of course she was out of practice, probably never having done this for — what? — oh, at least seventeen years, but even so she'd had her memories, her expectations.

She sighed heavily. Like so much else in her life recently, this had been one huge letdown.

Having only taken short local commuter trips for years, she'd really been looking forward to this long journey. Those "let the train take the strain" adverts were always full of relaxed, happy commuters reading broadsheets and doing complicated things on laptops in huge comfortable seats with acres of space between them, and a smiley flunky serving coffee and, well, she'd just expected so much more from this rail journey which marked the end of her old life and the start of — well, who knew what.

"Ooops, sorry . . ." Amber muttered for the umpteenth time. "Sorry."

She peeled herself away from a heavily perspiring businessman who was jammed into the airless vestibule alongside her and about 500 other sweaty people as the train rattled relentlessly southwards.

Of course she should have pre-booked a seat. Her parents, before they'd rolled away from the house for the last time in their piled-high camper van, had said so. Her sisters, Coral and Topaz, dressed in shorts and T-shirts and espadrilles all ready for their new life, had clambered into the back of the van and said that without booking a seat Amber would probably have to stand for the entire journey.

Overcome by a sudden and unexpectedly violent wave of homesickness at watching her family's departure, Amber had grinned bravely through her tears and said she'd be fine. Who else would be daft enough to want to spend over four hours on two different trains in the middle of summer heading for the wilds of Berkshire? She'd have the pick of seats. In fact she'd probably have both the entire trains to herself.

She hadn't even managed to get into a carriage on either of them. Having stood in the restaurant car corridor all the way from Manchester, she'd been wedged into her current crowded cubbyhole since Birmingham.

The sweltering confines were made even more uncomfortable by the concertinary bit between the compartments suddenly swaying without warning which meant everyone catapulted together, and also by people who were lucky enough to have seats in some distant carriage selfishly wanting to use the one and only lavatory, which happened to be somewhere behind Amber's right shoulder and her eight bags and three suitcases and —

"God! I'm really, really, sorry," Amber muttered again, trying to unstick her arm from someone's cheek. "Oh, was that your toe? Sorry . . ."

If only there was something solid to hang on to. Something that wasn't fleshy. Something that meant this non-stop colliding of skin-on-skin could be brought to an end.

The perspiring businessman lurched against her again as a large woman in an even larger T-shirt tried to haul herself towards the lavatory.

"Sorry . . ." Amber said again as the large woman elbowed her in the chest. "Look, let me just get out of the way and — ouch!"

The businessman looked innocent. Amber glared at him. God, how much longer was this going to last? She'd been on this train for ever. She hadn't sat down for hours. Why, oh, why, had she ever agreed to do this?

The goat shed in Spain began to look really appealing.

"Didcot Parkway!" A nasal voice intoned across the tannoy. "Didcot Parkway next stop!"

Amber perked up. Didcot Parkway. That sounded pretty. Maybe she'd get a glimpse of countryside there. All chocolate boxy and flowery and green and gentle. What was that poem she'd loved at school? About a country station in midsummer? Adelstrop. That was it . . . all willow-herbs and billowy haystacks, whatever they were. Didcot Parkway had to be something like that. Rustic and peaceful. With fields and trees. And maybe loads of people would get off there and maybe she'd find a seat and —

Nope.

The run-in to Didcot Parkway looked like Beirut on a bad day and there were another six million people on the platform clearly all expecting to squeeze on to the train.

The doors opened allowing a gust of hot air into the tiny corridor. A stampede of sticky humanity billowed in after it.

The doors slammed.

"Reading next stop!" The nasal voice sang happily through the tannoy. "And please stand well away from the doors!"

Amber pulled a face. One out of two wasn't bad. She was pressed right up against the door, true, but she definitely wasn't standing. Now wedged between the businessman and a couple of lads in baseball caps and Man U shirts who'd clearly had more than their fair share of recent vindaloos, her feet were at least six inches off the ground.

"Excuse me!" Amber yelled at the businessman who now had more bits of his body pressed against hers than Jamie had ever achieved in daylight. The noise from the concertinary bit of the train made normal conversation impossible. "How long before we get to Reading?"

The businessman was glistening all over like a disco ball and managed to drag his eyes but not the rest of him from her cleavage as he yelled back. "About fifteen, twenty minutes, I'd say . . ."

"Thanks." Hallelujah. She might just survive after all. "Oh, sorry — excuse me, I just need to get my phone out of my bag and — bloody hell!"

"Sorry . . ." the businessman looked embarrassed. "I didn't expect you to fumble *down there*."

"I was not fumbling," Amber hissed, trying not to breathe in too much of the second-hand curry fumes to her right. "I was putting my hand into my bag. Just because your groin got in the way doesn't mean — oh!"

"Sorry . . ." the Man U curry-eaters grinned sheepishly at her from beneath the peaks of their caps and shoved their hands deep into their pockets.

Jesus. This was worse than that lap-dancing club she'd accidentally stumbled into with her friends after a night on the town and too many tequilas where several drunken stag-nighters had mistaken her for the star turn.

She managed to push her hand into her bag without arousing anyone else and after a lot of rummaging clutched her mobile and the post-it note with Gwyneth's phone number on it. The businessman, the curry-eaters and the large T-shirt lady all watched her with interest as she held the phone above her head and started to punch out the numbers.

CHAPTER
THREE

Full Moon Fever

Outside Moth Cottage, Zillah tried hard not to strain her ears for the phone ringing. It was ridiculous, she knew it was, but Amber arriving in Fiddlesticks could be the worst thing that had ever happened to her. Well, almost the worst thing. The second worst definitely.

She knew it was silly to worry, but the arrival of a new woman, especially a young one, in Fiddlesticks, was bound to attract everyone's attention — especially Lewis's — wasn't it?

"Er . . . sorry," she looked across at Gwyneth. "What did you say?"

"I said that's something I'm really looking forward to."

"What? Sorry, Gwyneth, I was miles away."

"So I noticed," Gwyneth chuckled, shaking the empty pea shucks on to a sheet of newspaper. "I was just saying I'm looking forward to having young Amber here with a mobile phone. I've never had a go on one. I want to learn to text."

"You have to text someone else with a mobile," Zillah said gently. "And you don't have any friends with one, do you?"

"No. Bugger. Don't know why you ain't got one. I could text you, then."

"I only live next door, and why would I want a mobile phone? Everyone I want to talk to is within shouting distance."

"To be honest, why does anyone want one, duck? Who do they talk to? And why? It's a mystery to me. You can't tell me all those people you see with 'em clamped to their heads in Hazy Hassocks and Winterbrook used to spend that long on the phone at home or down the call-box." Gwyneth paused in her shelling to peer at a handful of peas. "Thought they might be maggoty, but they're not . . . Ah, and yes, I do know someone with a mobile, so there. Lewis has got one, hasn't he? I could text him."

Zillah sighed. Oh yes, Lewis had a mobile phone. And probably every woman in Berkshire had his number.

She nodded. "Of course you could. He'd probably love it. Mind, you'll join the long, long list of females sending him strange and clearly exotic messages by the way he hides them from me when I'm at his place, but I'm sure he'd be delighted to hear from you."

"Of course he will. He's a nice boy."

"Hardly a boy." Zillah raised her black eyebrows. "He'll be thirty next year."

"He don't look it though, does he? Bless him. Such a handsome lad. Thirty . . . my, my — where does the time go? It seems only five minutes ago he was a babe in arms. Mind, in my day any young fellow worth his salt would've been married and fathered at least half a dozen kiddies by the time he was thirty."

"Lewis'd run a mile from the first and has probably already achieved the second." Zillah stared up at the flax flower sky. "What would I know?"

"There, there. Don't get upset." Gwyneth balanced the colander on her knees and leaned down to pat Zillah's plump shoulders. "He might be a bit flighty, but you know underneath it all Lewis is honest and hardworking and friendly and always kind and helpful and —"

"Mmmm. Very helpful. Especially today. You didn't have any trouble persuading him to collect her, did you? This Amber? From the station?"

Gwyneth machine-gunned an entire pod of peas into the colander with scary accuracy. "I asked him if he'd mind and he said he was free and he'd be pleased to do it. Why? Have you got a problem with that, young Zillah?"

"No." Zillah quickly shifted the cats and picked at a threadbare patch on her long skirt. "No, of course not. If she hasn't got a car it'll be murder trying to get here by bus, and a taxi would cost a fortune from Reading — but, well . . . she's young, free and single, isn't she?"

"Ah, the last two as far as I know. And youngish. She was twenty-seven last birthday."

"Oh, God. And is she pretty?"

Gwyneth shook the remaining empty pea pods onto a sheet of newspaper among the tumbled nasturtiums at her feet. "I've never met her, have I, Zil? Mind, if she takes after her Gran she'll be a real stunner. Jean broke umpteen hearts when she was a lass. And little Amber was a bobby-dazzler when I last saw a photo."

26

Zillah groaned. "And when was that?"

"'Bout twenty-five years ago."

They laughed together. Gwyneth's laughter rang more true.

"Have I missed a joke?" Big Ida emerged from the doorway of Moth Cottage, carrying a tray with three mismatched cups, an earthenware bowl of water and two plates of biscuits.

"No, duck, only young Zil here getting herself into a panic that Lewis will decamp with Amber en route from Reading."

Big Ida handed round the teas and placed the bowl of water and Bonios in front of the slumbering dog. "Crikey Moses — that's a definite in my book. Lewis is a bit of a gigolo, after all. Don't know why you asked him to collect her from the station. Asking for trouble, that is."

"Don't be daft, Ida," Gwyneth said quickly. "Zillah don't want to hear that sort of thing. Did you bring out any custard creams? Ah good, there's nothing better for dunking, I don't think."

Pike crunched Bonios at the speed of light then slurped messily at his water bowl, and the cats shoved their heads under his dripping jowls to join in. Silence reigned as custard creams were dunked and devoured.

"And what time is . . . is Amber actually arriving?" Zillah took a swig of tea and asked the question with a nonchalance she was far from feeling.

Gwyneth wiped her mouth. "Could be anytime now, I reckon. But you know what the trains are like."

They all nodded. Not that any of them really knew from experience. Late-running trains were like motorway grid-locks and binge drinkers causing weekend mayhem, and unfaithful footballers — something they heard a lot about on the news and read about in the papers. All a bit exciting and rather pleasant in a safe voyeuristic way as none of it had actually reached Fiddlesticks yet.

Zillah really, really wanted to change the subject away from Amber's arrival even if it meant discussing a doubtful saint and his ludicrous centuries-held beliefs. "So, apart from my costume, are we all ready for St Bedric's, then?"

Big Ida eased custard cream crumbs into her mouth with a large grubby forefinger. "Ah, all done. Should be a good 'un this year if this weather holds. We needs a clear sky to get the full effect."

"No worries on that." Gwyneth creakily put down her colander and her mug and stretched. "We're in the middle of an Azores high according to the wireless. Oooh, I'm getting stiff. Maybe I should join the Hazy Hassocks keep fit class . . ."

Despite her misgivings, Zillah grinned at the idea of Gwyneth — four foot ten in her stockinged feet, and about as broad as she was high — leaping and stepping and stretching and skipping.

"Don't you laugh, young lady," Gwyneth said sternly. "You know me and Big Ida have already had a go at kick boxing and Tai Kwon Do and we did OK. I'll have you know at eighty I'm fitter than most people half my age, but sitting in one position for any length of time just plays 'avoc with me knees. Maybe I'll pop into Winterbrook and see about buying meself a leotard."

Zillah bit her lip and said nothing.

"I'd join you," Ida said, "but they never do 'em in my size. I'd have to wear me vest and knickers. Anyway, more importantly, the pub's doing the food for after, on Saturday, is it? Timmy Pluckrose 'as got the message this year, has he? Proper St Bedric's Eve food — none of that foreign stuff on sticks he tried to fob us off with last year? Even if it were green it weren't *right*."

"I'm sure Timmy's got the message, yes," Zillah said shortly. "He's contracted the catering out to Hubble Bubble. You know, Mitzi Blessing and her herbal stuff, in Hazy Hassocks, this year."

"Oh, nice idea," Gwyneth sucked damp custard cream from her fingers. "Young Mitzi's cornered the market in old-fashioned cookery stuff. She won't make no mistakes. She'll be just right for the first of our big astral celebrations. I hope she remembers to make a proper St Bedric's cake. With green cheese."

Mitzi Blessing, Zillah thought, hadn't simply cornered the local foodie market, although of course there were still those who were a bit reluctant to indulge in her kitchen-witch dishes thinking that some of the more, well, magical results after eating them smacked of paganism; Mitzi had also cornered the Life After Fifty market too.

Zillah and Mitzi, being much of an age, had become good friends, and Zillah envied her not only the up-and-coming herbal cookery business, but also her ability to sort out other people's lives — not to mention her gorgeous and much younger lover.

As far as Zillah was concerned, Mitzi had it all.

"I'm sure she will. Timmy says she's got it all in hand." Zillah still looked slightly mutinous. "Although why there was so much fuss about his kebabs last year, I can't imagine."

"Because it weren't traditional food, that's why." Ida guzzled the dregs of her tea. "We've always had green cheese for St Bedric's. It don't do to tamper with the old ways. And giving people things on sticks when they've 'ad a pint or two is a recipe for disaster. I'm surprised they didn't 'ave someone's eye out. You can't go messing about with the old traditions. Mind, you wouldn't understand, being a newcomer."

"I'm not a bloody newcomer. I've lived in Fiddlesticks since 1976."

"Newcomer, as I say," Ida sniffed. "You has to be able to trace your ancestors back to the thirteenth century like we can before you can say you really belong."

"Ida!" Gwyneth shook her head. "Zil's part of this village just like we are. No one bothers with all that old feudal stuff any more."

"Well, they should," Ida huffed. "The moon and the stars don't never change, do they? Year in, year out they're always the same. St Bedric was the first one to point that out round here. And it'll be a full moon on Saturday which is just how it should be. It's what St Bedric's Eve is all about, after all."

"Is it?" Zillah raised her eyebrows. "I thought it was like all the other things we do here under the guise of celestial celebrations — an opportunity to get roaring drunk and behave badly. And maybe I can't trace my family back through the Fiddlesticks charters, but I intend to have a good time on Saturday night anyway."

Well, as long as Amber stayed as far away from Lewis as possible.

Big Ida replaced her cup on the tray. "Course you will, my love. We all will. And even if you don't *belong* here as such, me and Gwyneth are damn lucky to have you as a neighbour ... Now I'm off to feed me chickens and see if they've provided me with an egg for me dinner."

They watched as Ida lumbered through the delphiniums and stepped heavily over the tumbledown fences towards her own garden.

"Was that an apology for calling me an incomer?" Zillah squinted at Gwyneth.

"About as close as Ida gets to one, I reckon. She really should think before she speaks — but like her being careful with her money, she ain't going to change now. Her heart's in the right place."

"So's yours. And I'm lucky to have both of you. I wouldn't have coped when I first came here without you."

Both she and Gwyneth sat silently for a moment, remembering.

"Ah, yes duck, but things have changed so much since those days, haven't they? You're fine now. And Lewis has —"

Zillah didn't want to talk about Lewis. Not any more. And she certainly didn't want to think about the past, and the awfulness of her life when she'd arrived in Fiddlesticks. Not today. Not when everything was going so well.

She stood up quickly. "It's time I was getting ready for work, anyway. It's going to be another scorcher. Pity I've got to be shut in the pub for hours."

"Get away with you." Gwyneth rolled the newspaper round the pea pods and reached down for the colander. "You love your job. And your boss loves you."

Zillah pulled a face. "Oh, please don't start that again."

"You could do a lot worse than Timmy Pluckrose. He's got a lot to offer a girl. A nice little pub, a pot of money in the bank and all his own teeth."

"And that last bit is more than you can say about most men in Fiddlesticks. We're in serious danger of becoming another Eastbourne."

"That's why we need youngsters like you and Lewis to stay on and regenerate the village," Gwyneth chuckled. "Which is what, according to you, he's aiming to do."

"Thanks for reminding me." Zillah, as always amused that Gwyneth saw her as a mere slip of a girl despite being in her fifties, gathered up her skirts and stepped over the low rickety fence separating her cottage from Gwyneth's. "Ah well, better go and slap on the barmaid face and sort out yet another bosom-revealing top — that's if Ida had left me any skin worth revealing. I'll, er, pop round later to see if Amber has arrived safely, shall I?"

"You mean to give her the once-over? Or more likely to make sure young Lewis hasn't kidnapped her to add to his harem between Reading and here?"

"Something like that," Zillah sighed.

"Zil, love, you shouldn't worry about —" Gwyneth stopped and cocked her head towards the cottage's dark hallway. "Oh, is that my phone?"

They both listened to the shrill trilling echoing from Moth Cottage.

"Ah," Gwyneth raised her eyebrows at Zillah. "It is. Blimey O'Reilly, Zil, this could be her, couldn't it? Young Amber? To say she's on her way here. I'll have to ring Lewis and let him know he'd better make tracks for Reading. Ooooh, mind out of the way Pike, lad, I'm all of a tither and pop!"

Zillah watched Gwyneth and Pike trot excitedly indoors to answer the phone call, then walked into the cool gloominess of Chrysalis Cottage with a very heavy heart.

CHAPTER
FOUR

Goodmorning Starshine

Having eventually catapulted stickily from the train and negotiated Reading station's lifts, stairs, ramps and turnstiles with the help of a stocky girl with a lot of nose studs and tattooed biceps like Arnie, who had hefted the towering trolley one-handed, Amber blinked in the dazzling sunshine.

Not for the first time that day she wished she hadn't left her to-die-for designer sunglasses tucked away in one of the heavily-zipped holdalls.

Her mountain of luggage had been deposited outside a small newsagents and she perched on the nearest suitcase to wait in a prominent position at the entrance to the station's concourse as Gwyneth had instructed.

Some local taxi driver was going to pick her up shortly, Gwyneth had said. Well, no she hadn't said he was a taxi driver as such, but that's what she must have meant. And she'd called him Lewis.

They must refer to people by their surnames down here, Amber thought. Would he be like his namesake, Morse's sidekick? She decided he would: a sort of ruddy-cheeked, middle-aged rustic who probably ran the local garage and taxi-service and was the funeral director as well. With a tweed jacket with leather patches on the elbows and possibly a cap and a pipe — oh, yes — definitely a pipe.

Well no, maybe not the jacket and cap, Amber rethought, as perspiration started to prickle her scalp. It must be in the 90s. Even if he was in his dotage and thin-blooded, with these temperatures Lewis would probably be wearing a sweat-stained singlet and reek of sheep and other strange countrified odours.

During the shouted and rather odd phone call to Gwyneth which she'd shared with the businessman, the large T-shirt lady and the curry-eaters, Amber hadn't managed to ask how she'd recognise Lewis. And Gwyneth hadn't described him at all. She'd simply asked Amber what she was wearing so that she could write it down and pass it on to Lewis so's he'd recognise her.

Gwyneth had clearly taken down Amber's answers then chuckled throatily down the phone. "And you've got long blonde hair? And you're very pretty?"

"Well, my hair is longish and blondish, yes — but pretty?" Amber had stopped. She was OK-ish. Passable. With make-up and her hair done she could almost look glamorous. "No . . . no, I wouldn't say pretty. Just — well — normal. Like most people . . ."

"Don't be coy, duck," Gwyneth had chuckled. "If you takes after your Gran then you'll be a proper bobby-dazzler. And believe me, if you're wearing, er, let me see, a short denim skirt and a vesty thing and pink suede slouch boots — whatever they might be and I must say I can't wait to find out — then Lewis will spot you a mile off, duck. Take care of yourself, and I'll be seeing you really soon. I'm looking forward to it."

"So am I," Amber had muttered, because it would have been rude not to. "And thank you."

So here she was, very hot and very tired, waiting for Lewis the taxi driver like a modern-day David Copperfield, another book she'd done at school and really loved, and convinced now that he was not only the local jack-of-all-trades but also some sort of ancient lecher. He was probably going to try and grope her legs and peer lasciviously down her top and — oh well, Amber sighed. After the intimacies of the train journey, she felt she could cope with anything. And she'd simply slap him if he got too frisky.

She still wished they'd arranged to have name cards like at airports so there'd be no mistake.

It was so hot. The sky was brazen. The sun bounced relentlessly from the rooftops, dazzled from shimmering cars, and scorched the ground. Amber wondered if she could leave her heap of worldly goods and nip into the newsagents for a bottle of water. No, on second thoughts, probably not. She really hoped Lewis wouldn't be long.

Reading, or what she could see of it from the station's entrance, looked promising though. Everyone was dressed glossy-mag fashionably, and there seemed to be a mass of shopping opportunities along the not-too-distant maze of city centre streets.

If Fiddlesticks really proved to be the end of the world then Reading would definitely offer some salvation. There was clearly shopping and possibly clubbing to be had, and maybe, when she'd fully recovered from Jamie being a two-timing spineless commitmentphobe, there may even be men, or at least a man, who might make her forget all the heartache.

Blimey! Talk of the devil.

The man thrusting his way through the crowds towards the station was absolutely stunning. Amber peered into the quivering brilliance. Was he real? Surely not. Maybe he was a mirage? After all, she'd been standing here for ages in the broiling sun.

Mind you, he looked real enough.

Amber smiled to herself as he came closer. Yep. Definitely real. If this was an example of Reading's male population, then Jamie's memory would be wiped out in a nanosecond. She squinted again, unable to believe her eyes.

This devastating vision of male beauty was a true havoc-maker.

All female — and a few male — heads turned as he walked across the mock cobbles towards the railway station's entrance.

Tall, lean, tanned, tousled layers of longish brown hair, huge dark eyes . . . Amber drank him in. If only Jemma and Emma and Kelly and Bex could be here now. They'd rate him way, way off their male-lust Richter scale.

His T-shirt was much washed and thin and couldn't disguise his superb body; his faded jeans were second-skin-tight and torn in a sort of well-worn way that not even the top designers could achieve.

Blimey again — he was fit!

It was exactly as if her mother's long-adored Jim Morrison poster had come to glorious living, breathing reality.

And — blimey yet again! — he was walking towards her!

"Hi," he grinned at her, his eyes flicking over her in a practised way. "You must be Amber. Gwyneth said you'd be waiting outside the shop. Jesus! Is all that luggage yours? How long do you reckon on staying?"

Amber opened her mouth but no sound emerged. His voice was deep and warm and hinted at laughter. It was also soft-edged and southern. What on earth would she sound like to him? Foreign? Harsh? Northern-shrill?

"I'm Lewis Flanagan," he held out a slender brown hand. "I think you're expecting me."

Oh no she wasn't. Far, far from it. Too stunned by his beauty to remember the niceties, Amber ignored his hand and tried to kick-start her brain. Her accent was the least of her problems right now.

"Er — um — yes. That is . . . No . . . I mean . . . This is my luggage — er, the heavy stuff, like the telly and things, went separately and, er, yes, I'm Amber Parslowe."

"Nice to meet you," Lewis grinned again. His teeth were very white and — endearingly — slightly crooked. "I can manage the suitcases in one trip — do you want to hang on while I bring the truck down here for the rest?"

"I, er, think I'll be able to carry them."

"Great. It's not far. If you take the holdall and those squashy ones, and all your glossy magazines and —" he laughed "— that industrial size vanity case thing. I'll do the heavy stuff. OK?"

Amber nodded. Intelligent words seemed to be way beyond her capabilities. Instead she watched as Lewis made short work of hefting her bulging suitcases away up the cobbled incline, her heart sinking to the bottom of her pink suede slouch boots.

She might fancy Lewis like mad, but there had been no reciprocal spark in his eyes, his smile or his body language.

He'd been friendly and polite — and totally disinterested.

Maybe he was gay, Amber thought, as she heaved the holdall strap on to her shoulder and followed him beneath the glare of the unrelenting sun. And then again, maybe he wasn't.

Oooh, damn. There was nothing more humiliating than being rebuffed before you'd even got past the opening flirt.

The truck, parked at the top of the cobbled incline in a no-waiting area, turned out to be a sort of minibus painted in bright primary colours and with the words "Hayfields Tribe On Tour" embossed across the sides.

Amber looked at it in trepidation. Was it some sort of tour bus? Was Hayfields the rustic equivalent of Cold Play? Clearly Lewis's resemblance to Jim Morrison wasn't merely a coincidence. She was probably going to make her entrance to Fiddlesticks knee-deep in discarded groupies.

"OK?" Lewis made short work of stacking what was left of her life's possessions in the minibus. "Hop in quick then. The wardens are shit hot round here and I don't want another ticket."

Amber hopped in quick and almost hopped out again. The front seat scorched her bare legs and the inside of the van was stifling. It was clearly too much to hope that there was air-con. It was not only hot but also very scruffy, being filled with empty coke cans and screwed-up sweet wrappers and several grubby T-shirts. Someone had scrawled 'haYFieLds rOCkS' on the dashboard in scarlet felt tip and a total disregard for either upper or lower case, and a similar hand had added 'sO DoEs lEWis' with a lot of hearts and kisses underneath it.

Maybe she'd been right about the groupies.

While she was still struggling with her seat belt and her make-up case and her zillions of magazines, Lewis had roared into reverse, negotiated a scary amount of traffic and was driving away from the station. He had, she was miffed to notice, not even glanced in the direction of her rucked-up skirt.

The city centre roads were like a maze, with vehicles coming in all directions, but Lewis was clearly used to driving in the area and, with an apologetic look at her, merely kept up a stream of non-stop staccato conversations on his hands-free mobile which shrilled into life the minute he switched it on.

"Sorry," he mouthed across at her as one call followed another. "Work."

Despite Amber being able to hear both sides of the rapid conversations, they all sounded as though they were in code. Nothing made much sense. However, the name Jem cropped up in most of them.

Work my eye, Amber thought darkly.

No wonder he hadn't given her more than a cursory glance. Lewis only had eyes for Jem.

Was that short for Jemma, like her friend back home? Or Jemima? Or maybe it was just a lover's nickname? Whatever. It was obvious that Jem was the love of Lewis's life. Sod it.

Within minutes the multiple lanes of fume-belching traffic in the town centre had been left behind and they were tearing along a dual carriageway towards what looked like real countryside.

Even though the phone was now switched off, with the windows open and the radio blaring, conversation was a non-starter. Lewis didn't seem inclined to talk to her anyway. As the sweat trickled between her breasts and beaded her upper lip, Amber stared out at the unfamiliar scorched fields and dry dusty trees and tried to swallow her mounting wave of homesickness.

She'd love to ask him about Fiddlesticks, and what Gwyneth was like and what sort of band Hayfields was. Although that last one was possibly self-explanatory. With a name like that, they had to be Country and Western. Her absolutely least favourite type of music. Lots of gingham and boots and wailing about broken hearts and lonesome train whistles and men who knew how to be men.

There was possibly even bloody line-dancing. And Jem was probably a blonde and buxom Fiddlesticks' answer to Dolly Parton.

She blinked back a rare tear and suddenly wished she was sitting cramped in the camper van with Coral and Topaz and her parents. They may well be going to live in the dark ages in a strange country, but at least they'd be going together.

For the first time in her twenty-seven years, Amber was alone. Without friends or family. She'd wake up every morning and see only strangers. It should have been a spine-stiffening moment of glorious self-discovery, but it wasn't.

Oh, for goodness sake get a grip, she thought. Now's not the time to be wallowing in self-indulgent loneliness. She was a grown-up. She was simply going to live in a new place for a while and it would be exciting and uplifting. It would. It really would. Think about women like Ellen MacArthur, sailing single-handedly round the world, alone at the mercy of the wildest oceans, facing all manner of terrors. On her own.

They'd left the main road behind and were now hurtling along narrow, high-hedged country lanes which all looked the same. The occasional small cottage or imposing house swished past and out of sight, leaving nothing but sweeping fields and hills and clumps of tired trees.

"OK?" Lewis looked across at her quickly, raising his voice above the radio. "Not too hot?"

She shook her head. She felt as though she was melting and knew her make-up had run and her hair was clinging in sweaty rat's tails, but she was damned if she was going to show how miserable she was.

"I'm fine, thanks. Er — Reading looked lively. What's the nightlife like? Any good clubs?"

Oooh — how bad had that sounded?

"Not that — I mean . . . I just wondered about —"

"Reading's got some great bars and clubs — not that I have much time for that sort of thing, but you might enjoy them. Anyway, we won't be long now," Lewis grinned. "Everyone's dying to meet you. You've been the main topic of conversation in the village for weeks."

Amber smiled weakly. "I hope they won't be disappointed."

Damn! Why had she said that? It sounded like a major fishing for compliments remark.

"They won't be," Lewis said gallantly, clearly trying not to laugh. "Trust me. Oh, sorry . . ."

Mercifully the phone interrupted not only the embarrassingly awful conversation but also a particularly sad song on the radio.

"Hi," Lewis said. "Fern? Not problems?"

"Only the usual. Jem can't bear to be apart from you for a minute, as you know. Wants to know how long you'll be and if Amber is pretty."

Lewis laughed. "Tell Jem not to be so nosy! And I'll be a few minutes. We're just skirting Bagley-cum-Russet now so we'll be in Fiddlesticks before you can blink. I'll drop her off at Gwyneth's and come straight over. OK?"

"OK," Fern chuckled. "I'll pass it on. Ta. See ya."

Amber tried to look disinterested. Who was she to interfere in what was obviously a very under-the-thumb relationship? She was off men anyway, wasn't she?

"There." Lewis switched off the radio. "Or rather, here . . . This is Fiddlesticks."

They'd hurtled round yet another cloned, high-banked lane and into a sort of clearing. There was a circular green, parched beneath the midday sun, with a shallow, fat, brown stream and a lot of drooping shimmering silver trees and a pub on one corner, a small shop on the other, a church which looked like it should belong in Lilliput, with a handful of red-brick houses and whitewashed cottages dotted around the circumference.

Amber swallowed. "Er — this bit looks very pretty. Like a picture on a calendar. What's the rest of it like?"

"What rest of it?" Lewis grinned as he screeched the minibus to a halt outside three ramshackle cottages almost hidden behind a rainbow explosion of flowers. "What you see is more or less what you get. This *is* the village. A few cottages round the green, a couple of streets of houses at the back, and the council estate on the Winterbrook Road, the church, the pub and the corner shop. Oh, yes, there's a bit more new residential stuff for the incomers behind the pub — and a couple of lanes which lead to Hazy Hassocks and Bagley-cum-Russet, two farms and a few more biggish houses, but other than that, this is the lot. Hardly a metropolis. Still, you'll probably find more of what you're used to in Reading. Welcome to Fiddlesticks."

Amber looked at him in disbelief, but knew he wasn't joking. Her friends had been right. This truly was the back of beyond.

Oh, God. What the hell had she done?

CHAPTER
FIVE

Give Me the Moonlight

"What the heck is this supposed to be?" Billy Grinley waved his glass under Zillah's nose, taking the opportunity to leer down her cleavage across the gleaming bar of The Weasel and Bucket. "How many years have you been serving me, Zil? Since when have I been drinking halves of diet Coke? Blimey, love, get a grip — you're miles away."

"Sorry, Billy. Sorry . . ." Zillah took the offending glass, managing to avoid Billy's hopefully groping fingers, replaced it with a pint pot and started to yank at the Andromeda Ale pump.

Various other lunchtime customers at the bar had watched the exchange with interest and were now keen to add their own pertinent opinions.

"No wonder she ain't concentrating, she's thinking of old St Bedric's Eve and what to wear on Saturday night, you mark my words. Gels is all the same when it comes to clothes."

"It's not just the gels. Let's face it, we're all a bit stumped when it comes to the wearing of the green. It don't flatter the majority. No wonder Zil's mind is on St Bedric's."

"I don't reckon she's thinking about Saturday night at all. I reckon it's because it's so bloomin' hot. Don't know why Timmy don't get air conditioning like they've got in Tesco. Mind, I likes to see young Zil in them vests . . ."

"Mebbe she's got a man on 'er mind. Is that it, Zillah? You thinking of the love of yer life, duck?"

"Oh, yes. Of course. Let me think — who is it today? Pierce Brosnan? Johnny Depp? Jude Law? Little Leonardo? I'm spoilt for choice. None of them will leave me alone for a minute." Zillah flashed them her second-best barmaidy smile and wished they'd all shrivel up and disappear. "Right — who's next?"

Lunchtime at The Weasel and Bucket was always a rumbustious affair. Due to the majority of Fiddlestickers being either retired or in part-time employment, the pub was the midday meeting place of choice. In the evening, it was packed with customers from all the neighbouring villages too. Some of the regulars, like Billy Grinley who drove the bin lorry and had finished work by noon, were middle-aged. The majority weren't. And as they were in the main lonely and slightly deaf, as soon as they got together they all yelled happily at each other non-stop without ever listening to the replies.

Zillah always thought the clientele suited The Weasel and Bucket admirably, being sort of ancient and dark and gnarled and unchanged for centuries. Timmy Pluckrose, the pub's current landlord, had resisted the trend for wide-open drinking spaces and light bright eating areas. So the huge fireplace, the inglenooks, the uneven polished floors, the odd corners, the rickety tables and chairs, the tiny leaded windows covered in ivy, and the low beams which all had "duck or grouse" signs pinned to them, hadn't altered in living memory.

"Billy giving you trouble, Zil?" Timmy Pluckrose, tall, thin and balding, appeared from the kitchen. "I can always bar him you know."

"As if," Zillah grinned, dropping lemon slices and ice cubes into three glasses of house gin and low-cal tonic for the elderly Cousins Motion. "You've never barred anyone in your life. And I gave him the wrong drink so he had every right to grizzle."

"Did you?" Timmy's pale eyebrows arched towards his non-existent hairline. "Not like you. Are you feeling poorly?"

Poorly didn't even come close. It was nearly one o'clock. Amber would have arrived at Reading station. Lewis would have met her.

"I'm fine," Zillah lied, then smiled at two of the three ancient Motions. The male third had slipped off, clearly unnoticed by his cousins, to the gents for a crafty fag. "Not having a sandwich today, ladies?"

They shook their heads in unison.

"Go on," Timmy wheedled. "I can do you a nice bit of ham off the bone and some mustard."

"We're not paying your inflated prices, Timmy Pluckrose," Constance made a prim moue with thin lips made even more mean by a slash of unflattering crimson lipstick. "A fortune for a couple of slices of white loaf and a scrape of marge and a bit of ham you can see through — I don't think so, thank you all the same."

"You get crisps and a salad garnish as well. Tasty, well balanced and healthy-ish, not to mention exceptional value for money. And the surroundings are second to none. You could go and sit out the front in the garden in this glorious sunshine, beside the stream, and watch the world go by . . ."

"No thank you — ouch!" Constance stopped and glared at her younger cousin. "Why did you jab me like that, our Perpetua? I know money slips through your fingers like water but we are not — definitely not — eating out again."

Perpetua, grey and wispy, half Constance's height and a quarter her width, stood on the tiptoes of her sturdy sandals and whispered urgently in the area of Constance's ears. As Constance's ears were always hidden by a glazing of fat, lacquered, bleached curls it was a wonder anything penetrated.

"Ah . . ." Constance nodded slowly. "Ah, right." She beamed at Zillah. "We've changed our minds. Three rounds of ham and mustard, please. We'll take one for Slo even though he says the ham gets stuck in his dentures but it's no good giving him cheese because of the flatulence and anyway he's been so good about giving up smoking that he deserves a bit of a treat although I'm a touch worried about the amount of time he spends in the lavatory these days — can't be too careful with your prostate at his age. We'll be out in the garden."

Mrs Jupp from the corner shop pushed her pointed face over the bar top. "Now that the flaming Motions have made up their flaming minds, I'll have two pints of

Pegasus Pale please, Zillah. Some of us is sole traders and only has our lunch hours. We can't —" she shot a cutting look at Constance Motion "— all swan out of work as and when we choose."

"Come along," Constance gathered her cousin to her, "don't rise to her bait. We know that some of these *small* business people are simply envious of the nature of our business empire. Of course, all it takes is damn hard work and —"

"What it takes in your case madam, is a flaming business what's been set up for a couple of generations handed to you three on a flaming silver plate along with a bucketful of inherited money," Mrs Jupp muttered as the Motions filed away. "Hard work my eye!"

Timmy frowned as the Motions pushed two-abreast through The Weasel and Bucket's door. "What was all that about? Not the spat with Mrs Jupp, that's ongoing. Their change of heart over the food, I mean. Not that I'm complaining of course, but I wonder what Perpetua said to change old Con's mind?"

"No idea," Zillah blew strands of hair away from her sweating face as she heaved at the Pegasus Pale pump. "But whatever it was it seems to have caught on . . ."

As the Pegasus Pale foamed merrily over the top of the glasses, Timmy and Zillah watched as at least a dozen customers, gathering up their drinks and snackettes, followed the Motions and headed for the beer garden.

Mrs Jupp's nose wrinkled like an inquisitive kitten's as she paid for her two pints. "I'll just go and find out, shall I? I quite fancy having me lunch in the fresh air.

I'll have one of your pasties, Timmy, if you don't mind. Zil can bring it out when she fetches the sarnies for the flaming miserable buggers."

"Yes, milady," Zillah muttered as Mrs Jupp clattered out of the door.

Timmy paused in the kitchen doorway. "When you've got a minute, Zil . . ."

"Sometime next year, then," Zillah hissed as she attacked the next order of three pints of Andromeda, a half of Hearty Hercules and a bitter lemon with a dash of Worcester sauce.

In fact it was about ten minutes before all the customers had been served, by which time Timmy was just putting the final prettying touches to the lunches arrayed across the kitchen table.

The Weasel and Bucket's spotless kitchen was the only part of the pub that had been dragged into the twenty-first century. Timmy was very proud of his granite and stainless steel and multitudinous gadgets, not to mention his lunchtime snacks and rather more adventurous evening menu. Not that the Fiddlestickers had ever really got to grips with blanched leeks, sweated onions, sun-dried tomatoes, balsamic vinegar or lemon-drizzled sea bass, being steak and kidney pie and chips people to a man, but visitors from Hazy Hassocks and Bagley-cum-Russet, or even Winterbrook, certainly appreciated them.

Timmy looked at Zillah with some concern. "Are you sure you're OK? If you're feeling off-colour you know you can go home. I can manage."

"I told you I'm fine," Zillah slid the plates of sandwiches up her left arm and took Mrs Jupp's pasty in the other hand. "It was just a simple mistake. It's so damn hot and you know what Billy's like — can't keep his eyes or his hands off the merchandise."

"Hmmm," Timmy snorted. "Not that I can blame him — you look good enough to eat."

"Oh, come on! At my age I'd be far too tough and gristly for him," Zillah smiled gently. "Or anyone else for that matter. I'm way past my best-before date."

"You haven't even reached it yet. You're the funniest, kindest, most beautiful woman in the world and why some man hasn't snapped you up I have no idea. Well —" he paused in slicing a lump of buffalo mozzarella "— apart from the fact that your heart clearly belongs elsewhere, of course."

Zillah smiled at him. If only he knew.

Timmy was such a nice man. He'd make her Mrs Pluckrose tomorrow, she knew that. He'd give her a wonderful life. Shame there was no spark whatsoever. Shame that he was spot on about her heart.

"Are you sure you're not coming down with something?" He looked at her in concern. "Is that a rash on your arms?"

Smiling, Zillah shook her head. Big Ida's ministrations in removing her from the spandex had left large swathes of her skin looking and feeling like sunburn. She felt it might inflame Timmy's latent passions a touch too much if she told him about it. "Probably just a bit of prickly heat. Now let's go and feed the starving hordes before Constance stomps back in here and starts quoting the Trades Description Act."

As she walked outside, the midday sun momentarily blinded her. The heat rushed up from the parched grass and almost choked her. It felt like being immersed in a bath of hot treacle. Across the road the cottages slumbered, the village green shimmered in the broiling heat, and the stream which usually gurgled and bubbled through it before roaring under the road to reappear in a crystal torrent along the front of The Weasel and Bucket, was sluggish and slothful.

All the Fiddlestickers were huddled beneath the huge umbrellas, clutching their glasses and staring across the green.

Sliding three plates of sandwiches in front of the Motions, Zillah caught an eye-watering whiff of Marlboro Full Strength emanating from Slo's Fred Perry tank top. As he'd promised Constance and Perpetua that he'd given up smoking on New Year's Eve she was amazed that neither of them seemed to have yet sussed his secret. Maybe it was working with all that embalming fluid, she thought. It probably deadened the olfactory nerves.

The Motions ignored the sandwiches and remained, well, motionless, their eyes all fixed on the green.

Zillah, long past expecting anyone to say thank you, smiled at them anyway and wove her way between the trestles, kicking up little clouds of dust from beneath her sequinned flip-flops.

"Pasty, Mrs J." Zillah slid the plate in front of Mrs Jupp who was sharing her rustic bench with four other villagers including the one-eyed churchwarden, Goff Briggs. "I'll just make a bit of room . . ."

None of them spoke or even acknowledged her as she cleared a space among the glasses. She simply sighed and after pushing strands of wayward hair back into her various combs and fanning her face, Zillah picked up a double handful of empties.

"I ain't quite finished with that, duck." Without taking his eye from the green, Goff Biggs snatched back his glass and guzzled the dregs. Only then did he look first at the table then at Zillah, his head, by necessity, askew like a parakeet. "Ah, that pasty smells good. Is that for Mona?"

Zillah had always thought Mrs Jupp was aptly named.

She nodded. "Timmy can do you one if you like."

"Ah, it'd go down a treat with a bit of piccalilli, thanks Zil, love."

"You're welcome." She paused. "What on earth is going on out here? Why is everyone watching the green? Have I missed something?"

Goff gave a throaty chuckle and closed his one eye in what passed for a wink. "Ah, you could say. We're just waiting to see what happens next."

"What happens next where?"

"Over the road. At Moth Cottage." Goff crinkled his eye. "Goodness me, gel — with that snazzy city piece who's moving in next door to you. With Gwyneth. Lewis has just dropped her off — and enough luggage for a good dozen people."

So that's what Perpetua had reminded Constance about. Amber's arrival. Of course, that would be Breaking News in Fiddlesticks — an event not to be missed.

Zillah shivered suddenly. "And, um, what did she look like? And, er, did Lewis, um . . .?"

"Lewis helped her with her bags and stuff," Mrs Jupp joined in at that point. "As you'd expect, him being a proper gentleman even if he does look like one of them flaming scruffy long-haired rock and roll people. Then he jumped back into the van and took off. Anyway, Zillah, we're not interested in Lewis — even if you are — so don't interrupt."

At least Lewis hadn't hung around. Zillah clung desperately to this morsel of comfort.

"But what did she — Amber — look like?"

"Phwoar!" Goff's eye watered lasciviously. "Legs up to 'er armpits. A little skirt no more than an inch wide — and boots! Pink boots! And long blonde hair — blimey . . . She looked like that Middle-Eastern woman."

Zillah shook her head in non-comprehension.

"He means Jordan," Mrs Jupp spat in disgust. "Silly old devil. And no she doesn't. She's much, much prettier than that. She'll turn a few 'eads in Fiddlesticks and that's for sure."

"Bet young Lewis has got her in his little black book already," Goff gurgled, helping himself to a hefty chunk of Mrs Jupp's pasty in his excitement. "He'll be all over her come St Bedric's Eve, you mark my words."

Mona Jupp, so intent on not missing a thing across the road, didn't even notice her pasty had mysteriously diminished.

"Zillah!" Constance's voice screeched imperiously across the solid, broiling, dizzy dazzling garden. "Could we have some more mustard for Slo, please?"

Zillah, tearing her eyes from Moth Cottage, turned back towards the pub like an automaton, and completely ignored her.

CHAPTER
SIX

Fly Me to the Moon

"There you go then, duck," Gwyneth said happily, stepping over the sprawl of bags, cases and holdalls. "This is your room. All your other stuff arrived yesterday. Big Ida got it all upstairs — you can arrange it as you wish."

"Oh, it's lovely. Really lovely," Amber peeped over Gwyneth's head at the top of the narrow, twisty, dark-green staircase. "You've gone to so much trouble for me — thank you so much — it's a wonderful bedroom."

And it was: cream and pale blue and girlie, exquisitely pretty, with a low sloping ceiling and a glorious panoramic view of Fiddlesticks' village green through the sash window.

And very, very tiny.

Which figured.

Amber had been stunned at how small Gwyneth was — almost as broad as she was high with her head not quite reaching Amber's shoulder — and how minute the cottage's downstairs rooms were, so she really should have been prepared for her bedroom to be on a similar scale.

But of course she hadn't been.

Where on earth was she going to put her mountains of clothes and bags and shoes and make-up and CDs and DVDs and magazines and books and stereo and portable tv-cum-dvd player and ceramic hair straighteners and other vital life-paraphernalia?

Apart from a beautiful flounced and sprigged three-quarter bed, there was an elderly single wardrobe and a matching two-drawer chest, and that was it.

"Why don't you have a freshen up first?" Gwyneth patted her arm. "It's so darned hot and that train journey must have taken it out of you. Then we'll have something to eat before you even think about unpacking. The bathroom's along here. It's quite new. We didn't have indoor bathrooms for ages in these cottages and Dougie Patchcock, he's the local builder, duck — 'e did a smashing job on the conversions for us. Mind, we've all still got our lavs in the garden."

Amber performed a sort of pincer movement with Gwyneth at the top of the staircase and another door was opened.

"It used to be part of my bedroom," Gwyneth said proudly. "But you'd never know, would you?"

"Um, no. Not at all . . ." Amber blinked again. The bathroom — minuscule sink and Gwyneth-sized bath — was about the size of a coffin. No loo, no shower, no window other than a skylight in the sloping ceiling directly above the bath. "Um . . . it's lovely. And the loo is where?"

"Downstairs. Just outside the back door, duck. Big Ida's is still right at the bottom of the garden but I had mine moved into the old coal house. We've got all mod cons here. There's plenty of hot water in the Ascot. You just turn that knob on there and make sure the pilot light is on. Like I said, all mod cons. I'll see you downstairs when you're ready."

Half an hour later, having made the most of the miniature bathroom, which had been lovely really as the plentiful hot water was silky-soft and Gwyneth had left some gorgeous gardenia-scented bath salts and a big fluffy bath sheet, Amber pulled on a pink vest and short white canvas skirt from her nearest bag and tugged out a pair of sandals. Then, ducking her head, she carefully negotiated the stairs, trying not to fall over several cats and the large and lolloping dog.

"Better?" Gwyneth beamed in the gloom of the oddly-shaped kitchen. "Oh, don't you look puckie! I've made some lemonade, look — you must be dry as a bone — and the food's all ready. We can start the unpacking later. This must all seem very strange to you."

Amber nodded. Strange and a bit scary. In fact, there had been a moment when Lewis had deposited the last of her luggage at the top of Moth Cottage's staircase and leapt back in the Hayfields van with no more than a cheery grin, that she'd wanted to beg him to take her back to Reading station. Or Heathrow. Or the nearest town. Or anywhere with a bit of twenty-first century civilisation from where she could return to her friends and/or family and not be left alone in this stunningly pretty but exceptionally isolated place.

But Lewis, no doubt with the ever-demanding Jem on his mind, hadn't even given her a backward glance, let alone a chance to plead for a return trip, and had roared away round the village green's dusty single-track road and out of sight.

Watching Gwyneth move nimbly around the kitchen, which appeared to have no modern appliances or gadgets whatsoever, Amber gave herself another mental talking-to. She really had to stop being such a wimp about this. Yes, it was strange and naturally unfamiliar, but for goodness sake — wasn't this exactly the sort of thing she'd wanted? She'd never, as her friends had pointed out, been far away from home except for holidays, and she was rattling towards thirty, for heaven's sake — surely she had to make some life-changes, experience different things, before it was too late?

And it was only a couple of months in a southern village after all. It was hardly a solo Himalaya-trek, or moving away to live on the other side of the world for ever.

"Go and sit yourself in the garden," Gwyneth said. "Get comfy and I'll bring the dinner out." She stopped. "Sorry, duck — I suppose you'll call it lunch, but we still mostly have our dinner midday here, with a bit of tea late afternoon and supper later on."

Amber smiled. "Gran always had her dinner at midday, too. And after all, the people who dished up the meals at school were called dinner ladies, so dinner is fine by me — but please let me help you."

"Won't hear of it," Gwyneth said stoutly. "I've got it all in hand and you're a guest. But a word of warning, duck. If you wants to have a bit of peace for a few minutes, I'd sit out the back rather than the front. Sit in the front and every man and 'is dog will come and give you the once-over."

Knowing that she definitely wasn't up to that sort of scrutiny just yet, Amber gave a grateful smile and accompanied by the dog and a posse of cats, ducked out of the back door.

The garden was adorable. Like something out of a picture book. It matched the rest of Moth Cottage exactly. Long and narrow, with tiny well-worn brick paths wending between raspberry canes, strawberry beds, vibrantly stuffed flower borders and equally well-stocked vegetable patches, overhung with stunted apple and cherry trees, and with a rickety trellis smothered in fat creamy roses at the far end.

Beneath the trees, Amber was delighted to see two deck chairs set on either side of a very elderly table with odd legs. Real deck chairs like she used to slide into on sand-encrusted childhood seaside holidays, slung with faded striped canvas on splintery wooden frames and those strange notch contraptions that her Dad used to have so much trouble putting up.

How long ago all that was. When she had been very young, before Coral and Topaz had been born, and a week in Blackpool was as alluring as Mecca and twice as exciting. She swallowed the lump in her throat and lowered herself gratefully into the seat.

Kicking off her sandals, she wriggled her toes in blissful freedom. Oooh, but it was so hot. Hotter than ever. Even hotter than it had been on the train — God, how long ago that seemed too. Was that really only this morning? It could have been in another lifetime.

Wearily, Amber leaned her head back and allowed the drowsy warmth to wash over her, while the pungent scent from the herbs and flowers soothed her more effectively than any essential oils. One of the cats jumped onto her lap and she stroked it idly, as the other curled on her bare feet. The sky was vividly blue through the dappling of the trees, the sun almost directly overhead smothering the riotous rainbow of the garden in molten gold, dazzling and dizzying.

She'd have to text her friends and her parents later — which was another thing: there was only one single electrical socket in her bedroom so charging her mobile would prove tricky if she needed to dry her hair or watch telly or listen to music at the same time — and tell them that she'd arrived safely, and about Lewis of course, and about this strange antiquated village, and how lovely Gwyneth was even if she did look like an elderly *matryoshka*, but right now all she needed was food and drink and sleep.

"Here we are, duck — no, shove over, Pike, it's not for you — I've brought you animals some water and some more Bonios. And I see the cats like you — that's a really good sign." Gwyneth trotted from the dim quarry-tiled kitchen, ducking beneath the overhanging branches, and placed a massive tray on the table. "I hope this will be all right. We'll have to sort out your likes and dislikes later. Plenty of time for all that."

Amber opened her eyes, struggling to sit upright without disturbing the cats, and blinked at Gwyneth. "Oh, wow. Thank you so much. This looks wonderful."

"Mostly from the garden," Gwyneth said proudly, pouring lemonade from a jug clunking with ice cubes. "Well, the salad and peas and potatoes. And as I don't eat meat, the goat's cheese came from Mona Jupp at the corner shop — we always do a trade: I get milk and cheese from her goats, she gets eggs from my hens. There's a lot of the old barter and swap mentality here in Fiddlesticks. Go on, duck, dig in."

"Thank you — I don't know where to start. It's all fantastic." Suddenly extremely hungry, and having moved the cats, who now swished grumpy tails, Amber happily piled her plate. "And you've got hens? Chickens? Here?"

"At the bottom of the garden. The run's behind the trellis. I'll introduce you to them later on. Me and Ida — she lives in Butterfly Cottage, the third in the row — we've always kept hens. Our girls are all good layers."

"And you're a vegetarian?"

Gwyneth nodded through a mouthful of salad. "Mmmm, yes. Me and Big Ida are very involved in various animal charities. I love animals, duck. All animals. Animals is better than most people. You won't mind not eating their flesh while you're here?"

"No . . . Not at all. Do you know I'd never thought of it like that. Eating animals, I mean . . . I suppose I should have done. But the stuff we had at home, well, it just never seemed to have ever belonged to something alive."

It was like a whole new world. No meat. Eggs that came from real hens and not just in neat little boxes. Vegetables straight from the earth.

At home, all food appeared from the weekly supermarket shop, most of it ready processed to be microwaved as and when needed, because everyone in the family worked and socialised at different times, and they never sat down to eat together except on Christmas Day. And at home the garden was a triumph of decking and gravel and a few easy-to-tend shrubs in strategically placed pots. At home both cooking and gardening were looked on as irritating necessities to be dealt with as quickly and easily as possible.

At home . . . feeling suddenly overwhelmed, Amber swallowed her goat's cheese quickly and put down her knife and fork. Home no longer existed. She had to forget about home right now. She'd have to do a Scarlett O'Hara and deal with it later.

"OK, duck?" Gwyneth leaned across the table and patted her hand.

"Mmmm, oh, I'm sorry if I seem ungrateful — it probably sounds daft, but I was just feeling a bit homesick."

"Understandable, duck, I know. But you'll soon settle in. Have you 'ad enough to eat? 'ere have some more peas."

Amber sighed. She was being pathetic again. "Sorry, yes and thank you. This is all so delicious. I don't think I've ever had real peas before." Amber picked up her fork again.

"That's a good girl, you eat up. You'll feel better when you've had something to eat and drink and a bit of a sleep."

While they ate, Gwyneth chattered about her youthful friendship with Amber's Gran, and about the village and its seemingly zillions of inhabitants, and about various upcoming social functions and a lot about the moon and stars, and strangely about someone called St Bedric.

Amber let it all drift over her in a contented way. There'd be plenty of time to meet the Fiddlestickers in the next few weeks. She'd never remember the names anyway.

". . . so, have you got anything green to wear for Saturday night, then Amber, duck? I really should 'ave checked before you arrived 'cause I know you'll want to join in."

Green? Green was so last year.

"We all have to wear green on St Bedric's Eve," Gwyneth continued. "Saturday night, it is. St Bedric's is always fun. Luckily you've arrived bang in the middle of the really good astral celebrations."

For the first time Amber felt a slight pang of unease. So far Gwyneth had seemed so — well — normal. But despite her apparent youthful outlook, she was after all extremely old. Could she possibly be suffering from some sort of dementia?

"Have I?" she said carefully. "That's lovely. But I've never heard of St whatever his name is."

"St Bedric's our patron saint and he was the first person to point out the moon is made of green cheese."

Oh, pul-ease. Amber laughed. "But it isn't."

"No, we know that. We're not daft, duck. But 'undreds of years ago people didn't know that, did they? They were scared stiff of the moon and its powers. People and animals are still affected by the moon, even now, but then it was regarded as an all-powerful deity. Everyone was terrified. Scared for their very lives. St Bedric was a kindly soul who took the fear away. Made people's lives happier. That's why we celebrate 'im and why we wear green. To honour him and the cheese thing."

"Oh, I see," Amber said. "I think . . . But surely, what with space exploration and everything, no one these days can possibly believe that the stars and moon can harm them or make any difference at all to their lives, can they?"

"Don't you sound so doubtful, duck. Everyone in Fiddlesticks knows that the moon and stars can change things. Make things happen. You wait and see."

Amber smiled kindly. She didn't want to upset Gwyneth. "Er — right. I'm not sure I've got anything green to wear, though — but I'll have a look when I unpack." And if the whole village was going to be skipping around like something out of the *Faery Queen* come Saturday then Lewis might be there too which would be a mega plus. "Um, does everyone get involved in these starry things, then?"

"Ah. Everyone. All through the summer right up to September. There's Cassiopeia's Carnival, and Leo's Lightning and Plough Night and oh, loads of them. Then at the end we have a right old shindig come the Harvest Moon — which sets us up proper for the winter."

Amber tried not to laugh. Her friends simply wouldn't believe it. Or maybe they would. They'd warned her that life would be very different Down South, hadn't they? Maybe though, she thought drowsily, she wouldn't tell them that in two days time she was going to be baying at the moon. She'd keep that bit of information to herself. She'd simply go along with the partying and try not to giggle.

After all, there was no chance that the moon and stars could make one jot of difference to her future, was there?

CHAPTER
SEVEN

Blue Moon

Annoyingly for Zillah, despite living next door and her best spying efforts, she didn't actually get to meet Amber until St Bedric's Eve.

Admittedly it was a mere thirty-six hours since Amber had arrived in Fiddlesticks, but the damn girl had been kept more firmly under wraps than a royal wedding dress.

Gwyneth, with, it seemed to Zillah, quite unnecessary determination, had explained that Amber was tired after her long journey and needed to unpack and settle in and adjust to her new surroundings, and that she'd have enough time to explore the village and meet everyone come St Bedric's.

"But I'm not everyone," Zillah had protested. "Come on, Gwyneth. You've been like a mum to me ever since I moved in and we've always shared everything. I only want to say hello . . ."

"Sorry, duck. I wants to let young Amber take this at her own pace. I may not 'ave 'ad a lot to do with youngsters but I like the lass, and I want 'er to be 'appy here. I want her to stay — and right now I reckon this is the last place on earth she wants to be. She's not only homesick — although she's trying 'ard not to show it — but this is like living on another planet to her. From what she's told me it seems city living is light years away from what goes on here." Gwyneth had grinned at this point. "Mind, she's taught me 'ow to text. Fiddly job that is, and all. It took me ages but I sent a message to 'er mum and dad en route to Spain to say she'd arrived safely. Ain't that amazing?"

"Absolutely bloody incredible," Zillah had muttered, slamming the door to Chrysalis Cottage behind her.

Even Big Ida, the fount of all gossip, hadn't had a great deal to add.

"I ain't seen much more of her than you 'as, Zil. Just a quick glimpse when I snook round to borrow a cup of proverbial sugar . . . What's she like? Well, she seems friendly — and she's pretty enough, the little bit I've seen of 'er. Very brown. Uses fake tan, Gwyneth said. Gawd knows why, mind. And she wears ever such short skirts. Like the kiddies wear. No more'n a few inches long." She'd pursed her lips. "Didn't young Lewis tell you all about her, then?"

"Not a lot, no. I . . . I haven't seen much of him. He came into the pub last night but we were busy and he — he — didn't say anything about Amber really. And I, er, didn't want to pry. Didn't want him to think — well . . . you know. Mind you, he was with Fern and Jem, and of course when he's with Jem no one else gets a look in."

Big Ida had snorted loudly. "That may well change if Amber sets 'er cap at him. She's a right little glamour puss. She'll turn a few 'eads and no mistake. Funny voice, though. Like Coronation Street. Doubt if that'll put 'em off, though. Young Lewis, with 'is reputation, could be heading the queue. Anyway, we'll all get to see a bit more of her tomorrow night, won't we? Gwyneth says she's really looking forward to celebrating St Bedric's."

Everyone, Zillah thought darkly, was probably looking forward to meeting Amber more.

And now it was St Bedric's Eve morning in The Weasel and Bucket, and Zillah, having found a long floaty green dress circa 1972 in the "can I bear to part with this?" heap at the bottom of her wardrobe to take the place of the limegreen spandex, was deciding if she should wear her hair up or down, and which of her pairs of dangly earrings would look best with the hippie frock.

The pub was empty. It really wasn't worth opening up at all in the day time on St Bedric's Eve. Not even the regulars put in an appearance. Everyone was saving themselves for the evening.

Timmy Pluckrose was in the pub's kitchen with Mitzi Blessing from the neighbouring village of Hazy Hassocks, unloading the St Bedric's Eve food and there was a lot of laughter escaping through the open doorway.

Mitzi, Zillah's age and very sparky, made everyone laugh, Zillah thought as she tidied the pristine bar top for the umpteenth time. Mind you, she'd probably laugh if, like Mitzi, she was lucky enough to be sharing her life with a drop-dead gorgeous man several years her junior.

Zillah paused in realigning a row of Paris goblets which had never been used in all her years in the pub and smiled as Mitzi, looking like a teenager in faded jeans and a white T-shirt, emerged from the kitchen. "All sorted?"

"Yep, all under control. Timmy's happy with the spread. Enough traditional herbal-based goodies in there to intoxicate the whole of Berkshire and a few neighbouring counties as well — and all livid green, as ordered. But blimey, it's sooo hot."

"Have a drink before you go. You look as though you could do with one. You must have been up all night cooking that lot. Something long and cool?"

"Thanks, Zil." Mitzi hauled herself onto one of the high bar stools. "I really should be getting home to clear up the debris, but a lime and soda with an entire floating iceberg would be lovely."

"Coming up. Can't you get someone to help you now your Hubble Bubble Country Cooking thing has taken off so well? What about your daughters? Couldn't they lend a hand?"

"Both too loved-up to be any use at all." Mitzi tucked some strands of streaked red hair behind her ears and grinned. "Can't prise either of them apart from Brett or Shay long enough to hold a decent conversation, let alone get them to do any work. No, seriously, Doll's still working at the dental surgery and her baby is due in two months, and Lulu is about to take her RSPCA exams, so I wouldn't dream of asking them to take on anything else — but you're right about needing help. I've got more bookings than I can handle. I'll have to advertise — especially if I'm going to be doing food for all your astral shindigs this summer as well."

Zillah reached for the ice bucket. She was delighted that Mitzi's business was such a success; that she was so ecstatically happy in her new relationship. It proved that there was life — and love — and hope for the over fifties. Maybe it would be her turn next.

Mitzi peered at her. "You're looking a bit down, though. How's everything going? Really?"

"With St Bedric's?"

"With Timmy. With Lewis. With life in general."

"The first still proposes on a daily basis. The second spends a lot of time avoiding me in case I say something he doesn't want to hear. The third is about as humdrum as ever."

Mitzi giggled.

"Fine for you to laugh." Zillah expertly foamed soda over a heap of ice cubes with one hand while dispensing lime juice with the other. "Your life is about as good as it gets."

"True . . . oh, thanks, Zil — that's great. What? On the house? Thanks even more, then." Mitzi gulped at the glass. "Oooh, that's better. I thought I was going to melt. And yes, OK, my life is great now — but this time last year I was really stuck in the doldrums: divorced, living alone, doing a job I'd done since I left school. Same old routine, with no chance of any of it changing anywhere on the horizon . . . But you never know what might happen — look at me now."

"Hmmm." Zillah propped her elbows on the bar. "Maybe I should eat some of your 'Find Me A Man — Quickly' cakes or something."

"Just say the word."

Zillah's dark eyebrows shot upwards as rapidly as a pair of homesick angels. "No way! I was only joking. I had enough dabbling with that sort of thing in my hippie youth in the seventies, thank you very much. And anyway, you know I don't believe in all that hokum."

"Oh no," Mitzi smiled, "that's right. I forgot. Being a Fiddlesticker you only believe in the stars granting wishes and the moon making magic, don't you?"

"I don't believe in any darn magic. Like luck, you have to make it for yourself. There aren't any herbs or sprites or incantations that can give me what I want. I gave up wishing and hoping a long time ago ... Oh, don't take any notice of me. Most of the time life is rosy. I'm just a misery at the moment."

"Any particular reason?"

Zillah decided that Mitzi really didn't want to hear about her nebulous worries over Amber's arrival in the village. "Not really. Nothing important. Just something that's cropped up that reminds me of mistakes I made a long time ago really ... Sort of afraid of history repeating itself ... Brought back things I'd rather forget. Just silly stuff."

Mitzi looked concerned. "Want to talk about it? Properly, I mean. A girls' night out sometime?"

"Maybe," Zillah nodded. "Yes, that'd be nice — although I'd probably bore you to tears because what I said earlier is true. I've spent most of my adult life wanting something I can't have — and nothing you could concoct, or calling on all the celestial goddesses at the same time, can make it happen. One day I'll simply accept that this is all there is to the rest of my life and make the best of a bad job."

"And would that include accepting Timmy's proposal?"

"Probably."

"Then don't." Mitzi finished her drink and placed the glass on the counter. "Don't ever settle for second-best. It'll never be good enough. And not fair to either of you."

"We can't all be as lucky as you."

"Luck had sod all to do with it," Mitzi said robustly, sliding from the bar stool. "As you just pointed out — we make our own luck. However, magic — now that's a different thing all together. Just say the word my dear, and I'll fetch me cauldron round and me pointy 'at and me magic wand and a few toads and newts and —"

"Get out, you daft bat!" Zillah laughed, chucking a bar towel at Mitzi.

Mitzi stooped to pick up the towel and chucked it back. It missed Zillah and draped itself artistically round the Andromeda Ale pump.

They both shrieked with laughter.

"Girls, girls . . ." Timmy stuck his head out of the kitchen door. "What unseemly behaviour! Remember, neither of you will see your first half century again . . ."

"Bugger off, Timmy," Mitzi said cheerfully. "At least we're young at heart — and we've both still got all our hair."

"Ouch," Timmy grinned. "I must remember to tell that man of yours tonight that he's got himself involved with a very cruel and heartless woman."

"He'd never believe you," Mitzi smiled. "And we're not going to be here tonight. Joel's taking me to dinner in Cookham Dene. It's our anniversary."

"Is it?" Zillah restored the bar towel to its rightful place. "I thought you two only met in autumn last year?"

"Oh, we did. It's not that sort of anniversary . . . Far more intimate . . . See you . . ."

Zillah watched as Mitzi practically undulated out of The Weasel and Bucket's door. Lucky, lucky cow, she thought wistfully.

"Want to come and inspect the food?" Timmy asked, patting her hand. "The cake is out of this world."

"OK." Zillah gently removed her hand from his. "Why not? I might even gorge myself on a huge chunk tonight and do a bit of moon-wishing."

"You don't need to," Timmy looked at her. "Say the word, Zil, and I'd make all your wishes come true."

CHAPTER
EIGHT

Bad Moon Rising

The dusk hung heavily over Fiddlesticks in a lilac heat haze. The lights from the pub and surrounding cottages fanned out across the village green, causing leaping shadows to turn the willow trees and benches and rustic bridge into slumbering prehistoric beasts.

The moon, the reason for the village's excitement, was suspended in a perfect white-cold circle against a black sky, reflected in perfection in the darkly sluggish stream and adding a wide swathe of silver to the illuminations.

Amber took one look at the apparently zillions of people gathered on the village green and almost turned tail up Moth Cottage's path. If it hadn't been for Gwyneth standing sturdily behind her, she might well have managed it.

It wasn't just the vast crowd of strangers, or the fact that they were actually going to be doing something really odd concerning the moon, not to mention an ancient myth, and worship someone who probably hadn't ever existed — although all that smacked of acid-fuelled paganism in her book — it was the ocean of unrelenting *green* that was really scary.

Everyone, absolutely everyone, was dressed in some verdant shade. It simply wasn't normal.

"OK, duck?" Gwyneth whispered somewhere beneath Amber's shoulder blade. "No need to be shy. I'll introduce you to everyone. You stick close to me and you'll be fine."

Gwyneth was wearing a green paisley shirtwaister — well, shirtwaister was a bit of a misnomer due to Gwyneth being box-shaped with no discernible ins or outs — a green beret and a pair of green leather gloves. None of the greens matched.

"Um, what exactly do we have to do?" Amber asked as Gwyneth shepherded her across the dusty road and into the middle of the crowd. "Is there a sort of programme?"

"No, duck. Well, not really. Once the formalities is over it's just a big free-for-all. A party, you know? Eating, drinking, chatting, meeting old friends."

OK, Amber thought, a party I can cope with. I think. "And the formalities?"

"Well, Goff Briggs raises his glass of Emerald Elixir to the moon and does the usual thank yous to St Bedric for freeing us from fear for another year, then 'e throws it open to the floor so to speak. You can have a go if you like. Well, if there's something you want sorted special like."

Amber blinked. "Sorry? You mean *talk*? Out loud? To the *moon*?"

"Ah now, you may scoff but you just wait. There's a lot of people, people who live in the twenty-first century and hold down all manner of responsible jobs and that, who still aren't averse to 'aving a big bite of Lucky Cake and making a green-cheese wish for summat they need on St Bedric's Eve. Sometimes, when life ain't going the way you want, there are *other methods*, if you gets my drift."

Amber nodded. Paganism and ritual sacrifice and all sorts of things she shouldn't be dabbling in, as she'd thought. Green-cheese wish for pity's sake!

"And this Goff person? Is he your, um, vicar?"

Gwyneth shook her head. "Churchwarden, duck. The vicar from Hazy Hassocks, he oversees us in Fiddlesticks and six other rural parishes and 'e always says 'e's too busy to do St Bedric's. Between you an' me, I don't think 'e approves."

And who could blame him?

Much to Amber's relief, there were several pockets of people on the green who looked as though they may be under pension age. And several who were definitely young. Sadly they all had rather old-fashioned hairstyles and the green outfits let them down badly, but it was reassuring to know she wasn't the only person under thirty in the whole of Fiddlesticks. Maybe she'd meet some of them in the pub later. Maybe Lewis would be there.

There was a sudden roar from the direction of The Weasel and Bucket followed by a thunder of applause.

The first virgin meeting her doom?

"Timmy and Zillah bringing young Mitzi's food out," Gwyneth said reassuringly. "It always goes down well. Oh, watch out, duck — 'ere comes the 'ordes."

There was then a really weird few moments when masses of odd-looking old people, all dressed in green, of course, swarmed round them and shook Amber's hand and told her she was a proper little bobby-dazzler and right puckie and a little sweetheart and how quickly she'd settle into village life and wasn't she excited about St Bedric's and wasn't it lucky that she still had lots of astral festivals to look forward to through the summer.

Amber had smiled and smiled and smiled, and the names — Mona Jupp, Billy Grinley, Mr and Mrs Tuttle, Bernie Someone, Jackie Someone-Else, Dougie Patchcock, Constance and Perpetua Motion, and a thousand others — slipped through her memory like quicksilver.

"There, duck!" Gwyneth tapped Amber's shoulder as the crowds fell away for a minute. "Look! There's Zil. Outside the pub. She's our other neighbour — lives in Chrysalis Cottage — I told you about her, remember? She's really looking forward to meeting you tonight."

Amber squinted. She could just make out a woman with a lot of dark hair and a long green dress busily arranging food on the tables outside The Weasel and Bucket. Her heart sank. Gwyneth had said Zillah, the other neighbour, was a youngster: Amber had hoped for someone of her own age to play with. Zillah must have been as old as her mother. At least. Still, that was probably positively juvenile to Gwyneth.

"Oh, hello, Ida." Gwyneth's voice was raised above the roar again. "Wondered where you'd got to. Don't you look chipper?"

Big Ida Tomms, who lived in Butterfly Cottage at the end of the row and who had terrified Amber the previous day when she'd loomed like a monolith over the garden fence, tramped across the green, elbowing people out of her way, beaming at them both.

"'ello Gwyneth. Young Amber. You looks lovely."

"So do you," Amber said quickly because to be honest the sight of Big Ida, dressed from head to toe in a far-too-tight, far-too-short, bottle-green, panne velvet with her pudding basin hair tucked into an acid-green, satin snood, was truly jaw-dropping.

"Thanks," Big Ida preened. "Borrowed this off one of my godsons. The all-in-one, I mean. Even they don't wear snoods. Is that a nightie you've got on?"

Amber shook her head. The green-beaded, chiffon, baby-doll top was one of last year's cast-offs which had somehow accidentally found its way into her luggage. She'd teamed it with a pair of down-and-dirty green ripped jeans which she wouldn't have been seen dead in back home. No doubt, down here, the ensemble would be considered cutting-edge catwalk.

To be honest, her wardrobe was causing her some concern. Due to the lack of space, she'd relegated most of it, still unpacked, to Gwyneth's garden shed and was hoping to exist on what the fashion pages always referred to as "capsule". It was going to take forever to get used to only having one of everything.

"It's very à la mode." Ida scratched beneath her snood. "And the green flippy-floppies are lovely."

"I found her those," Gwyneth burst in proudly. "Didn't I, duck? In the shed. From me jumble buys. Just the ticket."

80

"Perfect," Amber assured her as they were suddenly buffeted by a crowd of villagers heading towards the rustic bridge. "Oh — what's happening over there?"

"That's just Goff getting ready for 'is big moment. He 'as to stand on a trestle being a bit of a short-arse and hopefully someone will have given him a microphone this year. He was 'oarse for a fortnight after last St Bedric's . . ."

Gazing at the gibbet-like structure being erected beside the stream, Amber still doubted that any of this was happening. It was just too surreal. She couldn't wait to phone her friends and give them all the gory details. In fact once she'd recharged her mobile she'd probably admit that they were right and she'd been wrong and could they come and rescue her as soon as possible.

The dearth of electricity in Moth Cottage meant that the phone had taken a bit of a back seat — the hair straighteners and television got first dibs at the socket until she'd managed to buy an adaptor — and she was also mindful of Gwyneth's electricity bill. She really must remember to charge the phone in the morning and discuss finances with Gwyneth again. There was no way she was going to live with Gwyneth without contributing something to the coffers.

Mind you, if tonight was anything to go by she wasn't going to be staying long — definitely not for the whole summer — but even so, she'd have to pay her way. Which might prove difficult as she had no income and her savings were probably even less than Gwyneth's.

"Crikey Moses! Don't the Hayfields' youngsters look lovely?" Big Ida boomed. "Look at Fern! She's even dyed her hair green this year! And is that Lewis with her?"

Amber immediately stopped worrying about high finance and peered into the gloom for some sign of a rock band — or, to be honest, the luscious Lewis and, she supposed, Jem. It was always a good idea to size up the opposition. The peering was hampered by the heat haze now being accompanied by swirling piquant smoke from a series of small bonfires along the edge of the green, and the crowds alternately appeared and disappeared from view.

There was no sight of anyone even slightly resembling Jim Morrison.

"Are we having music?" Amber said hopefully. Well, even if it was Country and Western it would be *something*. "From Hayfields?"

"Shouldn't think so," Big Ida chuckled. "There ain't one of 'em as can hold a note let alone a whole tune."

Definitely Country and Western then.

"And what are all the little fires for?" Amber bent down to Gwyneth's ear. "Are they barbecues?"

"No, bless you." Gwyneth yelled back. "They're all part of the ritual. We sets fire to green broom and bracken on St Bedric's. They drives away any bad sprites."

Of course they do, Amber thought. Silly me.

"Here we go!" Big Ida bellowed. "Just in time!"

The throng, as if choreographed by Busby Berkeley, flowed into place round the stage and gibbet. Goff

Briggs, green polo shirt, green cords, his head askew beneath a green baseball cap, clambered up and clutching a chalice in one hand, raised his arms aloft. Everyone cheered and clapped.

Blimey, Amber thought, it's like something out of *The Wicker Man*.

"We call on St Bedric," Goff bellowed, "to smile down upon his children."

"No microphone again," Gwyneth muttered. "Poor bugger."

Goff held the chalice towards the moon and howled something about Emerald Elixir, the bringing of good luck and the granting of wishes.

Silence fell as he glugged at the chalice, swayed a bit, and his head dropped forwards.

Crikey, Amber thought, has he been poisoned?

"What's in that goblet?" She asked with some concern. "It's not lethal, is it?"

"Depends on your idea of lethal," Gwyneth hissed. "Crème de menthe, chartreuse and lime juice — all green, see duck? Emerald Elixir . . ."

"Purges the pants off you," Big Ida added thoughtfully. "I never touch it."

Goff, his face now as green as his ensemble, slowly raised his head again, and wiped slurry-coloured froth from his lips.

There was another round of applause, then Goff kicked off again, more unsteadily this time, shrieking various strange incantations and lots of thank yous — much like a late-night radio phone-in — and then launched into what sounded like an epic poem.

Amber caught the words "Bedric" and "thee and thou", "green" and "cheese", "fear" and "no fear" and "wishes" and "thank you" again a lot and that was about it. Nothing rhymed. The villagers seemed to know it all off by heart and droned along in unison.

Everyone, simply everyone, was staring up at the moon.

Amber simply stared at Goff Briggs.

He only had one eye! She hoped someone whose green-cheese wish wasn't answered wouldn't rush at him in a fit of pique and gouge out the other one.

"Now bring on the Lucky Cake!" Goff yelled. "Let's all make our wishes!"

Yet more foot stamping and clapping and hollering followed this announcement.

Amber shook her head. It was the maddest thing she'd ever seen. Quite, quite insane.

A tall, thin, bald man was wheeling a huge green cake across from the pub on what looked like an operating trolley. A knife glinted in his hand.

Maybe this was the time for the sacrifices?

With less than ruthless efficiency, Goff staggered down from his podium, seized the knife, and started hacking at the cake. Everyone surged forward, holding their hands out for a sliver.

"Ida'll get ours," Gwyneth informed her. "She's great at barging 'er way through. You should see 'er on pensioners' bargain day at Big Sava in Hazy Hassocks."

Even though she hadn't touched a drop of alcohol — yet — Amber began to feel quite intoxicated. Maybe the scent of the burning broom and bracken was making her squiffy? It seemed a mere matter of moments before everyone had a piece of green cake and amid a great deal of laughing and shrieking, quite sensible-looking people were lifting their slices towards the moon and making wishes. Out loud. Without looking the least bit embarrassed.

Ida handed her a slice, and on inspection, despite its livid colour, it looked like a feather-light cheesecake. Amber nibbled a crumb. Blimey! It was delicious.

"Young Mitzi has certainly got the gift," Gwyneth mumbled through her mouthful. "She says she'd never cooked before she started this herbal magic stuff — but you'd never know, would you? Go on, duck, eat up and make your green-cheese wish."

Amber grinned. Why not? What harm could it do?

She took another mouth-watering bite and looked up at the moon. Could she really do this? Talk out loud? To the moon? Still, everyone else was, and no one had laughed — yet. "OK — not that I believe in any of this stuff for a minute, of course, but — I wish that — oh . . . I wish that my life could get, well, sorted . . ." She stopped. Maybe that was a bit vague. "I wish — I wish — that being in Fiddlesticks was meant to be. That being here is the start of the rest of my life and that it doesn't just keep drifting. Oh, and that something wonderful is just around the corner . . ."

Maybe that was far too many wishes. And wasn't it all a bit me-me-me? Maybe she should have simply wished for world peace and prosperity? Maybe St Bedric wasn't going to grant wishes to the self-obsessed.

Not that she had too much time to think about it.

"Amber, duck!" Gwyneth swallowed the last morsel of her cake and waved. "If you've finished wishing, I've got someone here who wants to meet you."

CHAPTER
NINE

By the Light of the Silvery Moon

"I've been *so* dying to meet you. I've heard so much about you. Well, I mean, Lewis told us all about you when he'd picked you up — oh, does that sound tacky? Sorry . . . well, you know what I mean — and then everyone's been talking about you being here — and to have someone new *and* young in Fiddlesticks is so amazing that I'm surprised the bloody *Winterbrook Advertiser* hasn't got hold of it for the front page." The curvy girl with shaggy day-glo green curls, tight green shorts, an Ireland rugby shirt and mile-wide grin paused for breath. "I'm Fern."

Amber grinned back. "I'd almost guessed. Something someone said earlier about the hair . . ."

Fern patted her curls. "Sprayed on about half an hour ago. Might be all over someone's pillow in the morning if I get really lucky. Do you fancy a drink?"

Amber nodded. The evening seemed to be growing even hotter and the thought of something long and cool was irresistible. Everyone else was already stampeding towards the pub. And, not that it mattered of course, but Fern had been with Lewis, earlier hadn't she? Which meant that he might still be in the pub. And it would only be neighbourly to thank him again for collecting her from the station, wouldn't it? Even if he was with the ever-present Jem.

She looked at Gwyneth. "Is it OK if I —?"

"Course it is, duck. You run along with young Fern and 'ave a good time. Me and Ida will have a nice cuppa in a minute, but you need to get out and socialise. The door'll be on the latch if you're late coming home."

Amber smiled her thanks. Coming home . . . Hmmm. Maybe . . . Maybe Moth Cottage was going to be home — at least for a little while — anyway it was the only one she had now and she did love it and Gwyneth and Pike the dog who slept on her feet and the cats and the hens.

Thank goodness her friends couldn't tune into her thoughts. Barking they'd said she was, and now, having made a green-cheese wish and considered, without a second thought, that dark-ages Moth Cottage was actually *home* they were probably right.

Fern linked her arm through Amber's and led her towards the pub. There were small pockets of people dotted around the green still chatting, laughing, gazing up at the moon, and dozens of children splashing in and out of the stream and dangling over the rustic bridge, their parents smiling on fondly without any hint of nanny-state concern for their safety.

"I bet this all seems odd to you," Fern said as they slithered off the green and crossed the road, kicking up puffs of dust. "You being a city girl."

"Odd doesn't come close," Amber grinned. "I've never seen anything like it in my life."

"Get used to it. We have all sorts of get-togethers like this through the summer nights. Personally I reckon most people just join in for the eating and boozing, but in the olden days, well, they really did worship the stars and the moon. And —" Fern paused and looked at Amber almost seriously "— things have happened here, you know. And not just in the past. Recently. As a result of the star-wishing and moon-baying."

"Get away."

"No, really. Some really impossible things have happened with no rational explanation after Fiddlesticks astral parties. I don't reckon anyone should scoff. There's more stuff going on out there —" Fern gestured vaguely above her head "— than any of us understand."

"You mean little green men — oh, ha-ha, very appropriate for tonight — and all that?"

"No," Fern giggled. "But seriously weird things have happened. Oh, maybe some of them would have happened anyway, without the intervention of Cassiopeia or Andromeda or St Bedric or whoever — but until someone proves that it's all hokum then I'll happily go along with it."

"As long as all your dreams come true?"

"Something like that," Fern laughed. "And you'll get used to it. I promise. By the Harvest Moon shindig at the end of September you'll be calling on all the ancient goddesses to make things happen and be as addled as the rest of us."

By the Harvest Moon shindig, Amber thought, I probably won't even be here.

"Maybe . . ." She looked at Fern. "And as you clearly believe in all this, did you make a green-cheese wish tonight?"

"Course. The same one as last year and the year before that and the year before and . . . St Bedric must know it off by heart by now. Ah well, maybe one day the damn man'll come to his senses and realise that there's more than one woman in the bloody world."

Aha, Amber thought. Another Lewis-devotee. Another Jem-rival.

She recollected that Fern had been on the phone to Lewis during the van journey from Reading station. She'd mentioned Jem a lot during the calls. She'd also mentioned Hayfields. Maybe Fern was part of the band? The Dolly Parton lookalike singer? She certainly had the chest for it.

Goodness, there was so much to catch up on.

The Weasel and Bucket was packed to the doors. Outside, villagers had taken all the trestle tables and benches and most of the parched grass. The food tables had a four-deep crowd on each side. Just as well, Amber reckoned, that thanks to Gwyneth's substantial tea she wasn't feeling peckish. Every so often someone emerged triumphant from the scrum with a plate piled high with green goodies and scuttled off to a vacant space.

The roar of splintered conversations rose and fell in the drowsy heat. Huge moths bumbled and fumbled round the illuminated pub sign and hundreds of white fairy lights were threaded through the trees.

It was ridiculously pretty.

"Grab a patch of grass if you can find one," Fern advised. "Spread yourself out a bit. I think we've missed out on the food but I'll go and barge my way through for the drinks. What are you on? Spirits? Minerals? Wine or beer?"

Amber looked at the crowd in the pub. If Fern ever got served at all it'd be some sort of miracle. "Whatever you're having as long as it's alcoholic — twice . . . Not that I'm an alkie dipso, you understand, but it might be a good idea to stop having to go back in there again. And whatever you get, can I have lots of ice, please. Here, I'll pay."

"No way. My shout. I got paid my monthly pittance today. And you're a sort of guest. And my new best friend."

Within a nanosecond Fern's day-glo curls had disappeared into the throng.

Amber found a vacant bit of grass and sank onto it, drawing her knees up to her chin. Fern considered they were friends, did she? After less than half an hour? This was something new for her: all Amber's previous friendships had been formed through years at school or work. She'd never made an instant friend before. Still, she could certainly do with a friend right here and now in Fiddlesticks, and Fern was certainly — er — friendly.

But Fern wasn't like any of her friends back home.

While the St Bedric's Eve costume could simply be an aberration and the rest of Fern's wardrobe might well drip with Names, Amber somehow thought not. And she clearly didn't give a fig about dieting or exercising, and her hair-style was about two decades out of date — she'd probably never heard of ceramic hair straighteners and she had no streaks or highlights or anything remotely stylist-created beneath all that green — and her smudgy eye make-up was very last year, and her nails clearly had never seen a French manicure.

And yet . . . Amber nodded slowly — and yet there was more life, more vitality, more natural beauty, more down-right earthy sexiness to Fern than anything she and her city friends could concoct with all the salons and glossy magazines and glamour aids in the world.

How very weird.

Aware that people were staring at her with open curiosity, she smiled vaguely in their direction. The one-eyed churchwarden smiled back. His teeth were green. And a stout woman with an elaborate swirls and whorls Mrs Slocombe hairdo in rigid blonde — one of the Motions, Amber seemed to remember from the earlier introductions — shook her head as if finding Amber wanting in some way.

Maybe she should have had "Yes, that's right — I'm Amber. From Oop North. I talk funny but I'm friendly" tattooed across her forehead.

"Oh, sorry . . ." someone loomed out of the darkness and trampled on her feet. "I didn't see you down there. Oh — oh, er — you're Amber aren't you?"

"Yes," she peered upwards. Clearly she didn't need the tattoo. "Sorry, I don't . . . Oh, yes, you must be Zillah. Gwyneth's neighbour. She pointed you out earlier. It's lovely to meet you."

Zillah, with her abundant dark hair and big gold earrings and a gorgeous Bo-ho frock, both hands filled with a clutch of empties, didn't look as if the feeling was mutual. "Are — er — you enjoying yourself?"

"Yes, thank you. I've just been saying to Fern —"

"Fern? You're with Fern?"

Amber nodded. "She's gone inside to get some drinks."

"Right." Zillah sketched a smile which merely stretched her lips but did nothing for the wariness in her brown eyes. "OK, well as you can see I'm very busy — maybe we can have a proper chat later. Um — nice to have met you at last."

Frowning, Amber watched Zillah collect some more glasses and then shove her way into the pub. Very pretty woman but oddly not very friendly ... Ah, well — she'd been warned that southerners weren't as open and chatty as their northern counterparts. All that reserve and stuff, no doubt. Maybe Zillah'd loosen up a bit when tonight's mayhem was over.

Zillah elbowed her way through The Weasel and Bucket's merry throng and plonked the empty glasses on the bar. Timmy winked at her. She didn't wink back.

Well, at least she could stop torturing herself with imagining what Amber would be like. Now she knew. And it didn't help one little bit.

"Hi, Zillah," Fern yelled along the bar. "Where's Lewis?"

"Over there." Zillah nodded her head in the direction of the dartboard. "Talking to Slo — and probably giving him an illicit fag while Constance and Perpetua are outside."

"And Jem?"

"Over there as well. Naturally."

They both looked. As the crowd parted for a second they could see the tiny table by the dartboard. Lewis, standing up, had his back to them, leaning down towards the elderly Slo who was blissfully wreathed in cigarette smoke. They were both rocking with laughter. Jem — tiny, reed thin and dark, also facing away from them, also laughing — was, as always, holding Lewis's hand.

"I won't interrupt — but if you get a moment, tell him I'm outside," Fern said. "With Amber."

"Mmmm, OK. Mind you, I doubt if he'll be interested." Zillah slid behind the bar and ignored the dozen or so people who all immediately screamed "When you've got a minute, Zil, love!" "I've just met her. She seems a bit vacuous to me. I'll admit she's very pretty, though. Lewis didn't say she was that pretty."

"Probably didn't notice," Fern sighed, fanning her face in the intense heat. "After all, as every woman in the world hurls themselves at his feet, he's spoilt for choice. And I don't know what vacuous means but I guess it isn't complimentary. Anyway, can we have four big glasses of house white and four pints of Andromeda and two pints of lime juice and soda with ice, because it'll save us having to come back and wait forever to be served — oh, no insult meant there, Zil. I know you're working as hard as poss — oh, and a tray, please."

"If you drink that lot you'll both be sick," Zillah said shortly, reaching for the wine glasses and the Jacob's Creek. "Which won't endear you to anyone, will it? And who's paying for all this?"

"Me. Why?"

"Because I wondered, that's why. As Amber is clearly happy to sponge off Gwyneth for the duration of her stay, I wondered if she'd at least had the decency to put her hand in her designer pocket and pay for the drinks."

"She offered, I refused." Fern frowned. "Blimey, Zil, that's a bit harsh. I'm sure she'll stump up when it's her turn. Strewth, it's so hot in here! And so many people — I don't know why Timmy didn't get more staff on tonight."

"I'm quite capable of coping with this lot — bugger and sod!"

Both Zillah and Fern watched a good half pint of Chardonnay gush merrily across the bar top.

"I wouldn't have minded working behind the bar tonight," Fern said, mopping up the wine with the sleeve of her rugby shirt. "Or you could have asked Amber. I'm sure she's looking for work . . ."

"One barmaid with shaky hands is all I need." Timmy, his face gleaming with sweat and the glow that only a constantly ringing cash register can bring, beamed along the bar. "And much as I'm sure your cleavage would be universally admired, Fern, I do need someone who can add up — and you've got your hands full with Hayfields."

"True," Fern grinned, grabbing the tray. "But I do get some evenings off. Still, the offer's there — you know where I am if you need me. But Amber might honestly be —"

"Over my dead body," Zillah muttered, still mopping spilt wine with angry vigour. "What use would someone like she be in a village pub? Anyway, she's not staying long, is she? Gwyneth said she was finding it all a bit strange. She'll be back to the bright lights before she's even had time to unpack if you ask me. Next!"

Amber, having been mercilessly cross-questioned by the elderly lady with a lot of lacquered curls, who she thought may have introduced herself earlier as Cornucopia, looked up in relief as Fern arrived with the tray.

"Thank the Lord for that. I've been grilled better than a charcoaled steak. And everyone keeps laughing."

"Not at you," Fern reassured her, placing the tray carefully between them and sinking to the ground. "It's because of the St Bedric's food. Hubble Bubble. Mitzi Blessing cooks — er — herbal dishes. She uses this old-fashioned recipe book and puts all sorts of funny natural substances in her recipes, and they all have sort of — well — magical properties apparently. And they make things happen."

Amber shook her head. How gullible could you be? Magical cookery? Asking the moon to make things happen? It was really, really sad how backward these rural places were. Emma and Jemma and Kelly and Bex had been right — this was like something out of the dark ages. And she'd never go along with all this witchy magicky stuff — never.

Still, everyone did seem a bit — well — spaced out.

"You mean they're *stoned*? All these old people?"

"Pretty much, yeah." Fern handed Amber a glass of lime juice. "Cheers!"

Amber drank greedily. The whole place was mad. Completely insane.

"So?" Fern raised her eyebrows over the rim of her glass. "Have you and our Zillah had words?"

"No — well, yes, but only passing introductory sort of words." Amber sighed. "I was just going to ask you if she had a problem with me. I met her for the first time just now and she really didn't seem to like me at all. Why are you smirking like that?"

"I don't smirk, I smile winningly. But I bet it's got something to do with Lewis."

"Why? What — you mean . . .? She's another one of Lewis's women? She thinks that I'm after him?"

"She thinks everyone's after him. She's very protective. And you're new here and very pretty and sexy and — oh, I don't know. Zillah seems to have this thing about Lewis being a bit — er — casual with his love life, and it seems to scare her every time someone new comes on the scene. She's practically phobic about it."

Amber shook her head and started on the wine. "Sad . . . And I know she's attractive and all that, but isn't she a bit old for him, anyway?"

"Oh, God! Zil's not one of Lewis's women!" Fern trilled with laughter. "She's his mother!"

CHAPTER
TEN

Moonlight Shadow

"Surely that's even more dubious?" Amber said. "She's his *mother*? I've heard all about Andromeda and Cassiopeia and Orion and Pegasus and the like since I got here — but no one mentioned Oedipus."

"Who's she?" Fern was taking mouthfuls from each glass and was currently halfway down her lager. "Nah — I'm not really that ditzy. And it's not like that. Zil just gets hung up over Lewis being less than committed to anyone. No idea why. She goes spare every time a new woman comes on the scene — like she knows he's going to do his love 'em and leave 'em act and takes it personally. I honestly think she'd like to see him settle down — but he shows no sign."

Amber bristled. "Huh. And she thinks I'm going to be the next on his list, does she? That I'm some desperate piece from the frozen wastes with my morals round my ankles? That her son is so damn irresistible that I'm going to hurl myself panting in his direction? And that he'll dally with my affections for a while before adding me to the heap of broken-hearted damsels?"

"That's about it," Fern giggled.

"Well, she needn't worry about me. Has Zillah never heard of women with gumption? Women who take control of their own destinies? Women who can make choices? Women who can say no?"

"Oh, I'm sure she has — it's just that when Lewis is around even the most together independent ladies seem to forget that this is the twenty-first century."

"For heaven's sake!" Amber snorted. "How sad is that! Of course he's a great looking bloke, but he's not the only man on the planet. I, for one, intend to remain immune. Zillah need not worry about my heart being rendered into a million pieces by her cavalier son."

"Hah!" Fern rattled the remaining ice cubes in her lime and soda. "Famous last words."

There was absolutely no need, Amber thought, to mention that no matter what she felt about Lewis, he clearly had no more interest in her than he had in taking up macramé. In fact, considering the way he'd behaved on the Reading journey, he'd clearly far rather be fashioning pot holders out of string. It was the sort of snippet a girl should keep to herself.

Fortunately at that moment, a crowd of villagers started a loudly discordant impromptu singsong and there was a burst of hand-clapping and foot-stomping. Sadly several of them, clearly fortified by their green cheesecake, were also attempting to salsa. The number of people sprawled on the ground hampered any flamboyant moves and the lack of organised music meant they were all dancing to different rhythms. It was pretty scary.

Why on earth wasn't there a band? There was food, drink, moon-baying and dubious substances in vast quantities: music, Amber felt, would have made it into a real party.

As the dancing gaggle swept past them and on to safer territory on the village green, she clutched her glass of wine and leaned towards Fern. "Read my lips: I Do Not Fancy Lewis."

"Yeah, you do. Everyone does. And Zillah knows it. And it bothers her big time."

"But what about Jem? I thought, Lewis and Jem were, well, together."

"Oh, he lives with Jem — but that's not the same at all for God's sake."

Amber groaned inwardly. Jem was a live-in lover. Well, that was Lewis off-limits then. She'd never been a man-stealer. And surely that made Zillah's attitude even more weird. Most mothers, in her experience — especially two-timing rat Jamie's harridan of a mother — had always been delighted that their sons *weren't* about to make honest women of their never-quite-good-enough girlfriends.

"And is Jem in Hayfields?"

"Oh yeah," Fern nodded. "We all are."

As she'd thought. "So why aren't you all providing a bit of yee-haw tonight? It is Country and Western, isn't it?"

"Uh?" Fern frowned. "You've lost me now. Is what Country and Western?"

"Hayfields."

"Hardly. Hayfields is a house. Well, it used to be — it was a big farmhouse, a couple of centuries old. It's all been converted to flats now, of course, but we've still got several acres of land so the grounds are lovely. We all live there. What on earth made you think it had something to do with music?"

"You mean it doesn't?"

Fern shrugged. "We have our fair share of parties, and we've got some musical instruments kicking around, and the stereo is always on. Is that what you meant?"

"No, I just thought . . . the Hayfields van and the scribbled messages and everything was all so rock'n'roll . . . and the way Lewis looks . . . and . . ." She stopped. "And I didn't realise that you lived with Lewis."

"I don't. Lewis lives with Jem. I live with Win. Win's stayed at home tonight with Martha to watch something on the telly."

Now she really was confused. "So, Hayfields is flats, you all live there, it's nothing to do with music. So what is it? What do you do?"

"You'd better ask Lewis," Fern giggled, swirling rapidly melting ice round in her glass. "It'll give you something to talk about. He's just come out of the pub."

Amber couldn't see Lewis at first because Goff Briggs, clearly overcome by a herbal fancy, had attempted to wink with his good eye and tumbled from his rustic bench. The two elderly Cornucopia women were trying to haul him to his feet. All three of them were chuckling raucously.

It simply wasn't what you expected from the older generation.

Then she spotted him. Despite her recent protestations she felt her stomach do a wanton somersault. Oh God, he was gorgeous.

He'd made concessions to the wearing of the green, by adding green patches to the knees of his tight faded-to-grey black jeans and had a slender green bracelet around one wrist. His thin T-shirt might well have been green once too but the colour had long since disappeared. He was, quite simply, the most beautiful man she'd ever seen.

Knowing she was also looking for Jem, Amber was surprised to notice that Lewis was not accompanied by some sort of supermodel but by a lanky, cadaverous, elderly man wearing a green tartan suit and a furtive air.

"Who's that with him?"

"Slo," Fern said. "One of the Motion cousins. He bums fags off Lewis. The other two cousins —" she indicated the mêlée round Goff Briggs who had promptly slid from his bench again "— think Slo gave up smoking at New Year and he's terrified of them — well, of Constance in particular. Which is understandable."

"*Slow?*" Amber laughed. "Really? Slow Motion?"

"S-L-O — Sidney Lawrence Oliver — either his parents were as mad as hatters or they really didn't realise. Still, it's quite a good name for an undertaker."

"No way!"

"True," Fern nodded. "Their fathers were brothers, funeral directors, each of whom had one child: Constance, Perpetua and Slo — the Cousins Motion.

None of them married and they've carried on the family business. I guess it'll die with them as there are no baby Motions, but despite all three of them being geriatric they're still going strong at the moment. No one round here gets despatched by anyone other than the Motions."

"Talk about something else, please," Amber groaned. "Let's do life rather than death."

"OK. But I think it's important you know who's who in the village as it's going to be your home."

"Is it?" Lewis smiled down at them — a very *brotherly* smile — pushing his hair away from his eyes. "Oh, good. Fern, can you keep an eye on Smoky Slo for me for a minute while I go back into the pub for Jem?"

Fern nodded. Slo grinned at them both with badly fitting dentures and sat awkwardly on the grass behind them as far out of Constance and Perpetua's vision as possible. Amber, realising that she'd been holding her breath while Lewis had been so close, finally exhaled. Oh sod it. She was not going to fancy him. She really wasn't.

With a hacking cough and a lot of rasping, Slo lit the dog-end of the cigarette he'd been secreting in the recesses of the tartan suit. Wreathed in fumes, Amber fanned the smoke away.

"Enjoying yourself, duck?" Slo wheezed over her shoulder. "Good do, old St Bedric's. Mind, I prefer some of the others. The moon-talking is OK, but you gets real magic from the stars. You'll love Cassiopeia's Carnival Night — that's a really special one. One year, I wished on a shooting star and you'll never guess what happened — aaargh . . .” The story was interrupted by a burst of coughing. “Erg-spluff — that’s better . . . Lewis is a good lad; he knows it’s murder for an eighty-a-day man like me to be deprived of me fix.”

“Takes one to know one,” Fern muttered, “only in Lewis’s case his addiction isn’t nicotine.”

Amber simply wondered how quickly Slo would become a customer of his own family company. Maybe Cassiopeia had magicked up some sort of bronchial protection.

“There they are!” Slo gasped wheezily, treating Amber to another blast of spit and badger-breath. “Young Lewis and Jem!”

Amber looked up again. Even if Jem was a Keira Knightley clone, she could cope with it. She knew she could.

“Budge up.” Fern nudged her. “Make a bit of room for Jem.”

Jem, holding Lewis’s hand, and dressed almost identically, had negotiated the crowds in the dusky heat and beamed down at them.

“Jem’s been dying to meet you,” Lewis looked deep into her eyes. “Jem, this is Amber.”

Amber read the message and took a deep breath. “Er — hi, Jem. Lovely to meet you, too. Come and sit down.”

Slo, lighting another cigarette from the butt of the last, had already made a space.

Smiling broadly, Jem sat between Fern and Amber.

Lewis challenged Amber with his eyes again. “Jem isn’t very co-ordinated and he doesn’t speak, but he communicates perfectly — as you'll soon find out. And he can hear and understand everything. Everything. As well as you or I. OK?"

Amber felt a lump of shame building in her throat as she nodded and smiled again.

Jem was a young-old man, short and bird boned with a pixie face and a shock of dark hair. His eyes were alight with pleasure and — a glint of mischief?

Fern was laughing. "No way, Jem! Amber is not going to be the next on his list. She's just told me that she doesn't fancy him."

Jem turned and looked at Amber, shook his head and winked at her.

"Behave," Lewis laughed, sitting beside them and handing Jem a glass of beer. "You're worse than my mum."

Amber didn't say anything at all. How could she have got it all so very wrong? How could she have thought Lewis was merely a self-obsessed, sex-mad, drop-dead gorgeous himbo, only interested in notching up yet another conquest?

How could she not adore him even more now? Oh, damn it.

"Hayfields," Fern said kindly, "is nothing to do with music. We're not a Country and Western band —"

Jem put his beer down and played air guitar with a flourish.

Fern flapped his hands away. "Give over for a minute, Jimi Hendrix. I need to explain to Amber what Hayfields is all about. She's a bit — er — confused. Hayfields is a halfway house. It's what we do. There are a dozen residents and a dozen of us. Martha is the House Mother so she takes over on our days or nights off. Otherwise we live in self-contained flats on a one-to-one basis with the residents. It means they can live normal lives."

Jem giggled and pulled a face.

"Oh, shut up," Lewis said cheerfully. "We have a great time. Even if your cooking is better than mine."

Jem laughed and made a finger-down-the-throat gesture at Amber.

"Really?" she smiled at him. "Is his cooking that bad?"

Jem nodded vigorously and pointed at her.

"Pack it in," Lewis said. "She's not going to cook for us. You don't need anyone else spoiling you rotten."

"And neither do you," Fern added. "You've got a queue of ladies a mile long waiting to cook your breakfast."

Jem sniggered.

"SLO!" Constance Motion suddenly roared across The Weasel and Bucket's garden. "Did I see a cigarette glowing over there? Are you SMOKING?"

Slo quickly dropped his cigarette in his beer glass and shook his head. "No way, our Con. Of course not. I'm a non-smoker now. You know I am. It was Lewis."

Jem's eyes opened saucer-wide in indignation.

"A bad influence, as always," Constance stood up and beckoned. "You come over here and join us. I've told you before about hanging around with those *young* people."

"Sorry," Slo mouthed as he groaned to his feet.

"It's OK," Lewis grinned up at him. "She scares the shit out of me, too. See you later."

Jem by now was jigging with impotent fury and tugging at his hair.

"Don't worry, Jem." Lewis touched his shoulder. "I don't mind getting the blame. I'm used to it. What? No, I don't think so — even though I must admit setting fire to Constance's wig does have a certain attraction."

"Lewis doesn't even smoke any more," Fern whispered to Amber. "Slo hides his cigarettes all over the show so that Constance doesn't find them during the body searches."

"But surely no one should be encouraging him to smoke?"

"Give over! He's nearly eighty. He's smoked since he was eleven. When he stopped smoking he was so bloody miserable — and by God he has enough misery living with Constance and Perpetua — what extra harm can it do him now? And anyway, Lewis's is only one of his stashes. Lewis, even though he doesn't like anyone to say it, is a pretty good guy."

Jem nodded and held up both thumbs in agreement.

Fern returned the gesture. "Anyway, have you got the Hayfields picture now?"

"Full frame," Amber nodded. "And I wish someone had told me before."

"Sorry, I just assumed Gwyneth had told you — and then it seemed so funny that you thought we were a band." Fern peered into the array of empty glasses. "Oh dear, we seem to have drunk everything and I'm ready for a refill. Anyone else?"

They all nodded. Amber fumbled in the pocket of her jeans and pushed some notes at Fern. "No, please — this really is my round."

"OK, thanks — if you're sure . . . I'll just take pot luck." Fern scrambled to her feet. "Hopefully they haven't drunk the pub dry — yet."

Jem waved happily as Fern picked her way across various prone Fiddlestickers, then nudged Amber and pointed at the moon.

She leaned towards him. "I made a green-cheese wish tonight — did you?"

Jem nodded, then gestured towards her with a thin and twisted forefinger.

"What? Oh, what did I wish for? Am I allowed to say?"

Jem nodded vigorously.

Amber, aware that Lewis was watching the interchange with interest, grinned. "Well, I wasn't sure what I should wish for. I mean I've only just arrived here and I didn't really understand about St Bedric — but even though I felt pretty silly doing it, I made a wish that my life would get sorted out. Here. In Fiddlesticks. Does that make sense?"

Jem nodded again.

"Not that any of this makes much sense to me. I've never seen anything like it. Everyone talking to the moon. Completely barmy . . ."

Lewis looked at her over the rim of his glass. "Well, it figures. Where do you think the word lunacy comes from?"

Clever sod, Amber thought, before smiling at Jem again. "OK, so I've told you my wish. What about you two?"

"No way," Lewis said. "My wish stays secret."

Jem frowned at him and shook his head.

Amber shrugged. "Never mind him then. What about you, Jem? Did you wish for something nice?"

Jem nodded and turned his head to stare at the crowds outside The Weasel and Bucket. He studied the groups carefully, then pointed at a family of mother, father and two children sitting at one of the tables.

Amber knew she mustn't get this wrong. She felt she'd managed OK so far. "A family? You want to be part of a family?"

Jem shook his head and hugged Lewis's arm.

"Ah, OK — Lewis is your family. So . . ."

Jem pointed at Lewis, then again at the family group, moving his finger through the air until it reached the man. Then he smiled at Lewis.

Amber bit her lip.

Lewis sighed and came to the rescue. "Jem has never known his parents. And don't flinch like that — I'm not being brutal. It's a fact — Jem knows about his past. He's happy with it. We get on so well because we're honest. For as long as we've known each other Jem has been fascinated by family stories — you know, cosy groups, continuity, happy ever afters . . ."

Jem beamed broadly and nodded.

"Sounds great," Amber said softly. "I like those sort of stories myself. And having a family is pretty important as I'm just discovering. You take them for granted but then when they're not around . . ."

Jem patted her hand gently in sympathy. Amber returned the gesture.

"What Jem wished for," Lewis shrugged, "wasn't for him. He reckons he's got everything he wants. He wished for me. The same St Bedric's wish he's wished for the last three years. Ever since we've known each other even though I tell him not to bother."

Jem smiled and indicated that Lewis should continue.

"What he wished for was that I could find my father. He knows Zillah is my mother and can't understand why I don't have a dad like in his favourite stories."

"Oh, right . . . And is that likely? I mean —"

"About as likely as hell freezing over."

"But surely, if you want to meet him, can't Zillah, your mother . . . I mean —"

"Zillah won't even tell me his name," Lewis said coldly. "I doubt if she knows it. She's always refused to tell me anything about him at all. Apart from Zillah, I have no family at all. And, whatever Jem thinks, I have no interest in knowing about them. Especially not about my father. Not now, not ever. And I hope, if you intend staying here and getting involved in the village gossip, you'll remember that."

CHAPTER
ELEVEN

Midsummer Moon Madness

Midsummer morning dawned hot and gauzy, still and silent. Watering the drooping plants in her front garden before the heat of the sun scorched them further, Zillah thought Fiddlesticks looked like a film set.

Such a shame the rest of her life couldn't have been scripted to match: with high passions, nail-biting moments and a crescendo of cliff-hanging tension before the final satisfying dénouement, leading, of course, to the happy-ever-after ending.

Ah well, she thought, chucking the final silver arc of droplets across the multicoloured star petals of the mesembryanthemums, she'd had some of it, hadn't she? Even if it was years ago. Most of it, in fact. All played out in glorious Technicolor and surround-sound.

Honestly, if truth be told, the only bit missing from her personal epic was the happy-ever-after. And how many people really got those?

"Morning, Zil!" Billy Grinley leaned from the cab of his bin lorry and flashed a lascivious smile. "Hot enough for yer? I'll be finished by eleven this morning. See you in the pub?"

"Oooh, let me see — yes, probably — unless someone rich, famous and gorgeously handsome makes me a better offer in the meantime."

"Can't do the famous," Bill leered, "but I've got a nice bit salted away in the Nationwide and the 'andsome bit goes without saying. I'd show you a good time, Zil love. Just say the word."

"The word being no?"

"Get away with yer! I'd make you smile a lot more than that long streak Timmy Pluckrose! You think on it, duck. You could be the third Mrs Grinley this side of Cassiopeia if you plays your cards right."

Zillah watched the lorry choke away in a cloud of dust. Mrs Grinley? Mrs Pluckrose? She certainly wasn't short of offers. Billy was a non-starter of course, but maybe she really should think about accepting Timmy, despite Mitzi's exhortations to the contrary.

No . . . she shook her head. How could she? How could she marry anyone? Ever?

With her long skirt swishing the tops of the scarlet geraniums, she headed back towards her front door and the first boring task of the morning's boring housework.

Fiddlesticks was yawning and stretching and coming to life all round her, although next door the curtains were still pulled in Amber's Moth Cottage bedroom even though Gwyneth had been up since first light as usual.

"She'll still be asleep, duck," Big Ida loomed across the box hedge, a muck-and-straw-encrusted egg in each hand. "Them city girls don't keep country hours like we do. She's a lovely lass, though, don't you think? Even if she does go a bit heavy on the powder and paint. Fitted in nicely with the youngsters, I thought."

Zillah nodded. Amber had certainly done that. Since St Bedric's Eve, Amber seemed to have fitted into the village very nicely indeed.

"You were a bit hard on her, Zil, I reckon. And you was wrong about her becoming Lewis's latest fancy — 'e don't seem interested in 'er at all."

No, he didn't. Zillah grabbed a crumb of comfort from that. And she refrained from reminding Big Ida that it was in fact she who had first said Amber wouldn't be safe within a mile of Lewis's lecherous clutches.

"Timmy got a bit of a do on tonight, 'as 'e? At the pub? For Midsummer?" Big Ida started to walk up her path. "Or is he saving it for the next lot of proper star magic on Cassiopeia's?"

"Probably," Zillah shrugged. "There's nothing official planned for tonight. Fiddlesticks doesn't do a lot for midsummer, does it? Not like some places. Not so soon after St Bedric's. I doubt if many'll turn up so hopefully I'll have a quiet night."

Ida looked as though she was about to juggle the eggs, then thought better of it.

"Me and Gwyneth won't be 'aving a quiet one — and that's a fact. We've got a bit of a animal rescue job on this morning — cats kept in cages out Bagley way — buggers probably selling the poor little things on for breeders or worse; then we're doing the security and car parking over in Hazy Hassocks tonight, remember? Tarnia Snepps is 'aving one of her parties. Not for midsummer mind, a bit of a celebration after 'er

Marquis making it on to the birthday honours for 'is so-called charity work — at bloody last."

Zillah grinned. Everyone in the area knew how hard Hazy Hassocks' odious self-appointed lady of the manor Tarnia, and her even more odious husband, had smarmed and blagged to claw their way into the realms of the regally honoured. It had come as something of a relief when the news had finally been broken.

Tight fisted as a street fighter, Tarnia Snepps employed pensioners at a pittance to carry out the menial tasks at her thrashes. Gwyneth and Big Ida were usually top of her list.

"Must get on. I'm all behind the cow's stump this morning," Ida nodded. "Mind, I'm surprised to see you here today, young Zil. I thought as you'd 'ave been off with the rest of them old 'ippies last night."

"Last night?"

"Ah — they went off in droves from Winterbrook, so Goff Briggs said. Down to Stonehenge. For the sunrise this morning. You know — the Summer what's-it-called — oh, yes — solstice."

Solstice.

Zillah felt the shiver snake along her spine. God — it was still there. After all these years.

One word that could freeze the present and whisk her back to the past: a past more real, more vibrant, than anything that was happening, could ever happen, now.

One word, a host of memories: like snatches of certain songs and the feel of sun-warmed grass beneath bare feet and the scent of bonfire smoke on chill

114

autumn evenings and the wonder of night-time snow tumbling from a black sky and dancing naked in gentle summer rain.

The memory of a laughing voice whispering her name.

The word that could break her heart.

". . . Zil? You OK, duck?"

"Er? Oh, yes — sorry — miles away . . ."

And years. In another time. Another life.

Amber mooched round the village shop, smiling at things like hairnets and rain-hoods and packets of American Tan tights and single glass marbles and little pots of bubble mixture complete with plastic wands. She wondered if Jem might be amused by one of those, or would he be insulted? Probably, she decided, seeing as he drank pints and liked heavy metal and had a wicked grown-up sense of humour. And, as Gwyneth had attempted to explain, Amber gathered that Jem's particular type of cerebal palsy only affected his growth and co-ordination and speech and physical stuff like that. His intellect, as Lewis had made sure she understood, was as sharp as hers.

And anyway, would buying presents for Jem be interpreted as a chance to see Lewis? Mmmm, probably.

Putting the bubble mixture down, she then picked up a bottle of own-brand shampoo, a litre of mucous-green bath foam — pine and tropical wisteria — and an unfortunately phallic deodorant. She was beginning to accept that Mona Jupp only stocked one of everything. There was no choice. Mona Jupp held a bigger retail monopoly than Procter & Gamble.

Yes, there was no doubt that she was getting used to the shop, and the pub as the only source of entertainment, and the fact that the villagers thought the heavens could answer all their problems. Fiddlesticks had a drowsy magic — whether celestial or more earthy she wasn't sure — of its own, which meant Amber hadn't charged her mobile since she arrived and strangely no longer needed to have her call-fix. Nor had she unpacked her laptop, so her promised emails to her family and friends were still waiting to be written. The sleepy self-contained attitude of Fiddlesticks was certainly casting a spell on her.

As was Lewis — but she wasn't going to think about that right now.

It was really odd just picking up shampoo and deodorant without agonising for hours over which one was the latest must-have. And sort of liberating, and certainly timesaving — although, Amber thought as she queued behind several elderly people in sturdy sandals, that was something she truly didn't need to save. She had far too much time on her hands at the moment.

What on earth did everyone find to do all day? Those who didn't vanish off to Winterbrook or Reading each morning on the single-decker green and cream bus that looked as if it belonged on a 1950s advertising hoarding. How did Gwyneth and Ida and even youngish people like Zillah seem fully occupied each day by menial tasks and chatter? Would she ever get used to the laid-back pace of life in Fiddlesticks?

"Missing the hustle and bustle of the city life, are you?" Mona Jupp enquired perceptively, prising the bottles from Amber's fingers and playing the till keys with a Liberace flourish. "Must seem strange to you. You wants to find yourself a flaming job." Amber blinked. That was pretty harsh. True, but harsh nonetheless. And where exactly? Certainly not here. Sooner rather than later she'd have to travel into Winterbrook on the twentieth-century coach, register with an agency and see what happened. Maybe receptionist and admin jobs here would be more — er — fun than back home?

"Do you take Visa? I mean, credit cards?"

Mona affected an entrepreneurial simper. "I know what Visa is. We've taken credit cards for ages — since last year. We've even got chin and pip."

"Sorry?"

"Pip and chin. You know — the latest card security thingy. Now — what else can I do you for? Stamps?"

"Stamps?"

"Do you want stamps? For your letters to them up North and your mum and dad in Spain? We even do flaming airmail forms for them what lives abroad. We're very New Millennium, you know."

Stamps? Letters? Amber didn't think she'd written a letter since post-birthday and Christmas thank yous as a child. And how on earth did Mona Jupp know every last detail of her life? The village grapevine was certainly alive and well and living in Fiddlesticks.

Why not write letters, though? Electronic communications had ground to a halt, and she had plenty of time to put pen to paper.

"Er — yes. OK. Thanks. Ten stamps and a couple of airmail letters, then. And some writing paper and envelopes, please."

Grinning at this retro step and imagining Bex and Kelly and Emma and Jemma's reaction when they received A Proper Letter, she handed her Visa card across the counter and jabbed in her PIN.

Mona Jupp, having punched and swiped in vain, was now brandishing the card in triumph. "Won't flaming go through!"

"What? It must go through."

"Says declined on here," Mona beamed. "And this machine's never wrong. Declined, it is."

Amber, very aware of the Fiddlestickers' delighted massed gaze on her back, tried to shrink into her hair. Oh, God. Had she paid off the balance last month? Had she made a payment at all? There had been so much going on before she left home — she'd last used the card for her rail fare which had been just after the girls' night out to say farewell.

The perspiration made her palms itch. "Er — sorry . . . Um — I think I might have forgotten to pay it."

The Fiddlestickers rustled in glee behind her.

"Have to be another card or flaming cash, then," Mona Jupp smiled with more than her share of teeth. "This your only card, is it? You have got cash? Enough cash?"

118

"Er — yes it's my only card because I cut the others up when I left my last temping job and — er — and I think I've got enough money . . ."

Had she? After a lot of argument and persuasion, she'd managed to get Gwyneth to accept some money for her keep yesterday and there'd still been money in her purse — hadn't there? Amber emptied the contents of her purse onto the counter. Mona swooped down and counted the coins with Fagin-like relish.

"There — this lot is mine and this —" she pushed two coins back towards Amber "— is yours. Like I said, you'll have to get yourself a flaming job."

Watching as Mona bagged up the purchases in a flimsy pink striped carrier, Amber wanted the floor of the shop to open up and gulp her into oblivion. How embarrassing was this?

"Jobs is all on the board," Mona Jupp advised almost kindly. "Outside. Some of them have been there some time and the best ones have probably gone. You'll have to check the dates — I don't always take the postcards down on a regular basis."

"Er — right . . . thanks . . ." Head down, Amber scuttled past the queue and burst out into the cheerful sunny morning.

Oh God, oh God, oh God.

Humiliated beyond belief, she squinted at the noticeboard. The majority of the advertisements were yellowing and dog-eared and were business cards for taxi firms or take-aways. There didn't seem to be an awful lot of jobs on offer unless you wanted to be an

Avon lady or work on commission for various double-glazing firms.

"Sorry," a cheerful voice spoke over her shoulder. "Can I just reach over for that drawing pin there? Thanks. Were you putting on or taking off?"

"Neither," Amber said sadly. "Just grazing."

"More in hope than expectation, then," the pretty fifty-something woman in the faded jeans and yellow T-shirt with hair in vivid red layers beamed at her. "Mona Jupp isn't exactly up to speed on employment matters. Money is a different matter though. She'll be after my fifty pence for this like a shot."

Amber watched as she pinned her postcard neatly over one advertising chiropody for all in the comfort of your own home, dated 1998.

Cheerful and hardworking assistant required for Hubble Bubble Country Cooking. Parties catered for. No function too small. Traditional recipes. All fresh herbal ingredients used. Various hours and good salary for right person. Contact Mitzi Blessing — Hazy Hassocks 501.

Amber removed the card and grinned. "Er — do I need to phone?"

"You're interested in the job?"

"Very."

"Oh, right — how, um, handy. Actually I've never employed anyone before so I don't know what I'm supposed to ask you."

"I've never worked in catering before either so I'm not sure what I have to do," Amber said reassuringly. "But I'm hardworking and honest and clean and I do so need a job."

"And I do so need an assistant," Mitzi nodded. "Could you start immediately?"

"This minute."

"Shall we go over onto the green?" Mitzi shot a glance at the knot of Fiddlestickers who had emerged from the shop and who were now clearly intending to add this conversation to their morning's entertainment. "And sit on one of the benches for some privacy?"

They did. It was gloriously hot, and the willow trees hardly shivered their drooping silver foliage. The stream ran like crystal over its soft brown bed, and children were paddling and clutching fishing nets.

Amber sat on the nearest bench and wondered again why everything in Fiddlesticks looked like an advertisement for The Perfect Life in the mid-twentieth century.

"That's better." Mitzi kicked off her espadrilles and wriggled her bare toes in the sun. "So, do you know anything about what I do?"

"Only that you're a friend of Zillah's, and you did the food for St Bedric's and it was fantastic although I never tasted it except the green cheesecake because it had all been snaffled and everyone giggled a lot afterwards. And that several people have said you cook from old-fashioned recipes using herbs and things and that it might involve some sort of — well — witchery."

"That about sums it up," Mitzi chuckled. "And yes, my grandmother's recipes do have some surprising results. Although before it scares you off completely, I am definitely not a witch . . . well, not a nasty, cackly, old hag-type, anyway."

Hmmm, Amber thought. So there might be an element of witching involved somewhere, then? Not, of course, that she believed in any of it — and she really, really needed a job. "Er — do you know anything about me?"

"Only that you're staying with Gwyneth for the summer and you're from up north and that Gwyneth was your gran's friend."

They smiled at each other. It seemed enough to be going on with.

"Right then," Mitzi smiled happily. "How are you fixed for tonight? I'm doing a big party in Hazy Hassocks and I desperately need some help."

"With cooking or waitressing?"

"Neither tonight. Just setting stuff up, making sure the waiting staff Tarnia has employed take the right dishes out at the right times, keeping the plates heaped, all that sort of thing."

Amber nodded enthusiastically. "Sort of menial? Great, I can do that — although I'll be happy to tackle cooking and waitressing as well."

Mitzi smiled. "I'll certainly need you to help with both in the future, and preparation and deliveries — but I've got everything in hand for this one. And I didn't know how to cook until I started Hubble Bubble so don't worry if you don't know Job's tears from grated cyclamen bulb — all the recipes are written down and you'll soon pick it all up. Will the minimum wage do until we see how you get on?"

"Perfectly, thanks." Amber wasn't sure if she could manage on the minimum wage — it would be far less than she was used to, but her lifestyle was so curtailed in the village that she'd damn well have to cope, wouldn't she? At least, for now.

And this was just so opportune. It had been meant. It really had. She'd asked St Bedric to sort her life out and he had. Maybe the village *was* weaving some kind of magic around her — it must be — because she actually wanted to stay. She stopped. She was clearly getting far too comfortable with the Fiddlesticks mindset of allowing celestial magic to take control. This would have happened anyway. It had nothing to do with green-cheese wishes — or did it?

"Shall we say a month's trial on either side?" Mitzi continued. "I don't know how long you're intending to stay here, of course and —"

Amber sighed. "Neither am I. At first I thought it would only be for a few weeks, then I fell in love with — er — the village and wanted to stay for ever, and then I thought it wouldn't make financial sense to stay and — I'm still not sure . . ."

"You'll know in a month's time," Mitzi lifted her face to the sun. "One way or the other. Believe me. This place has a magic of its own. It'll enchant and entrance you."

Oh, dear. Amber looked doubtfully at Mitzi. She'd seemed so normal. Now she was another one talking about magic as if — as if it were *real*.

"Do you believe in magic? Truly?"

"Oh, yes. Well, in magical properties in the elements and in herbs and stuff, at least. And don't look like that. I'm not away with the fairies. You'll soon find out that there are more things governing our lives than those we can see and touch. After all, don't you think us meeting like we did was just a touch of midsummer magic?"

"Coincidence," Amber laughed. "Chance. Definitely not because of the summer solstice or because I made a green-cheese wish or anything . . ."

"Cynic. And you admit to making a St Bedric's wish, so you must have thought —"

"I only did it because everyone else was and because I didn't want to upset Gwyneth. I didn't really believe it for a minute."

"You'll see," Mitzi grinned. "My elder daughter Doll didn't believe in magic at all until something inexplicable happened to change her life. You'll be the same — I'll put money on it. Now, I suppose we ought to get back to business. Gwyneth is helping out at tonight's party, so you can get a lift over with her and Ida, and I'll meet you there at around six-thirty. Oh, and what about suitable clothes? Black skirt and white shirt and comfy shoes? I should supply them, I know, but I'm not that organised and —"

"I think I can dig out something along those lines," Amber assured her, relieved to be back on subjects she understood. "And I'll try really hard not to let you down. Thank you so much."

"Don't thank me too soon," Mitzi beamed. "You haven't met Tarnia Snepps yet."

CHAPTER
TWELVE

Stars Look Down

Whatever else Amber may have been expecting from her first night's employment, it certainly hadn't included having Lewis as a chauffeur.

Not having given any thought to how they'd travel to Tarnia Snepps' party, the Hayfields van turning up outside Moth Cottage came as a complete surprise to her — but not to Gwyneth and Big Ida.

"Neither of us drives, duck, so Lewis always obliges," Gwyneth puffed happily, using Big Ida's cupped hands as a leg-up and catapulting into the van. "Hello, Jem."

Amber, trying to look nonchalant, clambered in behind her under her own steam. Unfortunately, the clambering was made less than elegant by Pike lolloping in over the top of her and plonking himself on Jem's lap.

"You'll have to sit in the back," Lewis grinned over his shoulder at her. "Sorry."

"'S OK," Amber said, wishing that her black skirt wasn't so short or her white shirt so tight or her sandals so spindly.

The sandals were not a good choice, she knew. Her feet would be screaming before the evening was half over. Sensible shoes, as prescribed by Mitzi, simply weren't in her wardrobe. The only flat things she had, apart from the pink slouch boots, were trainers and they, with the skirt and shirt, made her look as if she were going to a schoolgirl fetish party.

At least Lewis looked more friendly than he had the last time they'd met. She'd never ask him anything about his father again. Once bitten and all that.

"Hi, Jem."

Jem, now practically hidden beneath a mountain of doggy fur and lolling pink tongue and dribbly jowls, struggled out, turned, and gave her a true reprobate's wink.

Yep, the bubble mixture would have been a *huge* mistake.

Lewis smiled at her through the driving mirror as they rumbled out of Fiddlesticks. "Great news, you getting the job with Mitzi Blessing. You'll have a blast with her. She's cool. I used to fancy her daughter."

"Which one?" Gwyneth edged forward on her seat. Her legs didn't touch the floor and protruded in front of her at right angles. "The bohemian one or the nurse?"

"Both," Lewis grinned. "But thanks alledgedly to Mitzi's herbal recipes they're now both spoken for and permanently in lurve. No doubt everyone's told you about her hedge witch cookery? And what it can do?"

"Sort of," Amber nodded. "Not that I believe it any more than all the astral stuff."

Jem snorted and raised his eyebrows.

"Start believing," Lewis advised cheerfully. "People have had all sorts of magical experiences after eating Hubble Bubble recipes. And as we're rapidly approaching Cassiopeia's Carnival, when you get an evening off I'll explain the Fiddlesticks celestial stuff properly if you like — just so you don't make any mistakes."

Amber met his eyes. "OK. It's a date."

"Oh, no," Lewis swung the van away from the Bagley-cum-Russet turn and towards Hazy Hassocks. "It certainly isn't one of those."

Jem and Big Ida chuckled.

Sod it, Amber thought. How *needy* had that looked? "No, of course it isn't. I mean, not a going-out-together sort of date. I know that. I'm not daft. It was just a figure of speech. I meant, yes, thanks I'd love you to explain the star stuff sometime and — oh!" She caught Lewis's eye in the mirror again. He was laughing. "Very clever . . ."

"I thought so," Lewis looked innocently at her. "One-nil to me."

Behind her hessian curtains, Zillah watched the Hayfields van drive away from the cottages. Strange how quickly things could change. How silly had she been? It no longer worried her that Lewis and Amber were in the van together. Well, they were more than adequately chaperoned after all, but even if they'd been alone, Zillah didn't think she had much to concern her.

Certainly the panic she'd felt about Amber's arrival had subsided considerably. Whether Amber fancied her son wasn't clear, but Lewis had shown no interest at all, and as far as Zillah was concerned, that was all that mattered.

Also delighted that Amber was going to be working for Mitzi and therefore not freeloading on Gwyneth's generosity, she'd now changed her mind about Amber on all counts. She'd been wrong about her and she didn't mind admitting it.

Amber had proved to be a far more pleasant and feisty young woman than Zillah had expected. It was totally unreasonable, she knew, to imagine that every girl would be like she'd been so many years ago: silly, vulnerable, naive, trusting. Girls were different these days — far more grown up and worldly wise. No, Amber wasn't going to make Zillah's mistakes. She didn't need Zillah's protection.

It was just that Lewis was so like his father.

Oh, God — Zillah pushed the feelings away.

No point in going down that route. She had to get ready for work. But the memories, so carefully buried for so long, had emerged and engulfed her all day.

If only Big Ida hadn't mentioned the summer solstice.

Mitzi was waiting for them outside the ornate electric gates.

"Welcome to Tarnia Towers."

"Crikey!" Amber blinked at the outrageous OTT house in the rosy glow of midsummer evening. "It's like *Footballers Wives!*"

"It's the absolute worst of tacky tat taste that money can buy," Mitzi agreed cheerfully. "Tarnia thinks it's classy. And if you think this is bad, you wait until you see inside."

Gwyneth, Pike and Big Ida had trundled off towards the field earmarked for car parking; Lewis and Jem had whizzed away in the Hayfields van, laughing together. Whether or not they were coming to collect everyone at the end of the evening Amber hadn't asked. It seemed enough to be going on with that she was meeting Lewis in The Weasel and Bucket next Saturday for her instruction in celestial magic.

As they scrunched up the vast curl of the shingled drive, Amber gazed at the veritable army of people swarming everywhere, and at the seemingly endless sumptuous swathes of land surrounding the house. "She must be rolling to own all this! And all these people . . . Are they the guests?"

"Goodness no. These are simply the minions employed by Tarnia to make the party go with a swing. She never lifts a talon herself."

"Oh, right — and oh, wow!" Amber almost clutched Mitzi's arm in excitement. "She's got a fairground!"

"Just for tonight. It's not a permanent fixture. She's also got a zillion-pound fireworks extravaganza — supplied by The Gunpowder Plot, who are the biggest pyrotechnics company in the south of England, run by a bloke called Guy Devlin who is simply sex on legs and who Tarnia fancies the pants off, poor sod — and a . . ."

Amber didn't hear the rest of the line-up. She was far too entranced by the fairground: old-fashioned traditional rides in deep colours and burnished gold. It was so beautiful. And nostalgic. None of the hi-tech, white-knuckle rides that seemed to grace every

130

fairground these days. It was like looking at a picture book: there was a helter-skelter and a big wheel and a ghost train and hurricane jets and a caterpillar and oh yes, oh joy — galloping horses!

The huge roundabout with its intricately-painted horses suspended on their barley-sugar, twisted brass rods, stood silent and still in the evening sun, glowing like a casket of jewels, a thousand glass prisms reflecting rainbows of sparkling light.

"Petronella Bradley and Jack Morlands's Memory Lane Fair," Amber said softly, reading the lettering on the deep-red trucks. "Oooh — lucky buggers, whoever they are. Imagine spending your entire life travelling from place to place with all that beautiful stuff and having ultimate freedom and — oh, crikey — what the heck's that thing over there?"

"A showman's traction engine," Mitzi grinned. "Have you never seen one? No, I suppose you wouldn't have — amazing monster isn't it?"

"Awesome . . . And is that a sort of organ beside it? That ornate thing? Behind the stage? I remember seeing something like that at Blackpool Tower ballroom when I was a kid . . ."

"That's a fairground organ. The engine drives it — it's a fantastic sight — and the sound is wonderful. They both belong to Flynn and Posy Malone from Steeple Fritton — not far away from here. When Posy and Flynn got married last year they went to church on the engine — all decked out in flowers and ribbons. Brought Steeple Fritton to a halt, I can tell you."

Amber grinned to herself. This was so cool. They'd never had anything like this back home.

"And the stage? Are they putting on a show?"

Mitzi pulled a face. "Ah now — the stage is for the Bagley-cum-Russet can-can dancers. I had a bit of a hand in that. One of my Baby Boomers — long story, so many people over fifty on the scrap heap with years and years of useful life ahead of them and nothing much on the horizon and I found myself being one of them, and well, someone had to do something, so I did — I'll tell you all the gory details one day. Anyway, she had always wanted to be in the Folies Bergère, but at fifty-two it was a bit of a non-starter for her. So we advertised and found a few other like-minded high-kickers in Bagley-cum-Russet and the troupe was born."

"Incredible."

"Oh, it's all pretty incredible round here," Mitzi chuckled. "Now for the most incredible bit of all. Meeting Tarnia."

The inside of the house, as Mitzi had predicted, was even more amazingly bad taste than out. Amber blinked in the miles and miles of marshmallow pink and white hall. There was a burnished and filigreed *Gone With The Wind* staircase and statues and fountains and pink maribou-trimmed mirrors everywhere and a stained-glass window which dominated the stairwell.

"Who's that?" Amber peered up at the primary coloured panes of the immense window. "Stevie Wonder?"

"We're not entirely sure. My money's on Martin Luther King — or Lionel Ritchie."

132

Could be, Amber thought, still squinting upwards. Hmmm — probably not Stevie Wonder on second thoughts. No sunglasses.

Mitzi grinned. "Actually, originally the window depicted the entire Beckham family, but when they unexpectedly added little Cruz to their entourage Tarnia commissioned the addition and sadly there was an accident with Victoria's head during the refurb. The replacement simply didn't cut the mustard, apparently looking far too much like Anne Robinson before the facelift, so Tarnia went for — er — well, whichever gentleman you now see before you. Ah, and here's the lady herself."

Victoria Beckham? Anne Robinson? Amber really wouldn't have been surprised to see either of these redoubtable women shimmying down the curlicued staircase. This place was simply surreal.

"Hello, Tarnia."

Tarnia Snepps was everything Amber had expected and more. Stick thin, very Botox'd, all-over woodstain-orange tan, short black hair with frosted pink tips and the most amazing leather mini dress in gold and white stripes.

"I didn't know you'd taken on help," Tarnia Snepps frowned at Mitzi. "I trust this won't mean your prices will be increased to cover?"

"Of course not," Mitzi sighed. "Not that you'd notice a few hours at minimum wage, I'm sure. This is Amber. She's staying with Gwyneth Wilkins in Fiddlesticks and is going to be helping me for the summer."

"Lovely to meet you," Amber held out her hand, still not sure if she was more stunned by Tarnia or the inside of the house. Both were pretty terrifying.

Tarnia took her hand and shrieked with laughter. "That accent! You're not from round here, are you?"

"Eeeh, you're on the ball, luv. Well spotted. I'm from ooop north," Amber went into her best Peter Kay routine. "On't trip of a lifetime to see how t'other 'alf lives. It's a reet treat t'be 'ere, luv."

Mitzi was giggling.

"Yes, well," Tarnia bared her teeth. "Nice to have you here, I'm sure. Mitzi will show you where everything is and tell you how I expect my staff to behave."

"I'm sure she will," Amber resumed a more normal voice. "And you certainly know how to throw a party. Congratulations on the honour, by the way."

"Thank you," Tarnia simpered, her trout-pout not moving. "Marquis and I have always worked extremely hard for our little community."

Mitzi sniggered.

Amber bravely tried to ignore the sniggers. "And your husband has been knighted for services rendered, has he?"

Mitzi giggled.

"Not exactly, no." Tarnia's rigid gaze flickered slightly. "Apparently you need to be a slip of a girl and sail single-handedly round the world, just the once, or win Olympic golds to get that sort of honour without even trying. My poor Marquis, slaving his fingers to the bone for the common people for years and years, merely got an MBE."

134

"But that's really good," Amber said. "Isn't it? And if he's a marquis already . . ."

"She calls him that," Mitzi hissed, her shoulders shaking with mirth. "It's made up. We still know him as Snotty Mark round here."

Amber grinned. Tarnia didn't.

"Mitzi and I have known one another from schooldays," Tarnia grated. "Sometimes she feels it's amusing to remind me of that fact. Illustrating, of course, that while I've moved on she's remained firmly rooted in the playground. Now, if you'll excuse me I have important meeting and greeting to attend to."

"Superb," Mitzi chuckled as Tarnia furiously click-clacked away across the tiles. "Absolutely superb. Now, Amber my love, let's get to work . . ."

The sandals had been discarded within an hour. Amber, in a pair of trainers borrowed from a cupboard under Tarnia's kitchen staircase which were just a bit too small, promised Mitzi she'd find something more suitable for their next sortie. Streams of pretty waiting staff of both sexes flowed in and out of Tarnia's spacious never-been-cooked-in kitchen, bearing away piled-high plates of Mitzi's creations. Amber seemed to have spent hours on a treadmill circuit from the fridges and freezers and table. In the too-tight trainers, her feet were killing her.

"You must have spent weeks preparing this," she puffed to Mitzi in a lull. "Do you do all the cooking yourself?"

"At the moment, yes. It's been a bit of a trial and error experiment. I started off at home, but due to health and safety regulations and all sorts of hygiene laws and EU directives, once I made Hubble Bubble a commercial venture, I had to find proper premises. Currently I'm operating from a small hut on Hazy Hassocks High Street. Beside the library."

Amber looked at the umpteen empty Tupperware boxes strewn across every surface. The labels intrigued her: Midsummer Marvels; Dreaming Creams; Summer Surprises; Full Moon Fricassees; Solstice Supreme — and then some dishes clearly prepared for the announcement of Marquis's honour: Celebration Cakes; Royal Risotto; Tansy Titles . . .

"And they're all *magic*? Surely not . . . I mean, aren't they just old country recipes. How can they be magic?"

"Depends what you understand by magic," Mitzi shrugged. "They're all from my grandmother's cookery book. They all use herbs and natural ingredients which can, if combined properly, apparently cause all sorts of things to happen."

"But if you don't believe?"

"You don't have to believe. The effect is the same."

Blimey . . . Amber shook her head. No doubt Lewis would tell her the same about the stars on Saturday. It was all rubbish, of course, but if the shrieking and laughing and general merriment outside was anything to go by, Mitzi's cooking had certainly made the party go with a swing.

"So?" Mitzi looked hopefully. "Have you enjoyed it so far?"

136

"Loved it," Amber nodded. "Have I been all right?"

"You've been brilliant. No one could have worked harder. And this was a bit of a baptism of fire — most of my functions are much smaller. So — are we in business?"

Amber grinned. "Too right we are."

CHAPTER
THIRTEEN

Starlight and Sweet Dreams

"So, which of the local brews haven't you tried yet?" Fern leaned across the table in The Weasel and Bucket and ticked them off on her fingers: "Andromeda Ale? Hearty Hercules? Pegasus Pale?"

"I haven't tried any of them, at least not knowingly and while conscious," Amber pulled a face. "I've told you I'm not really much of a beer girl — and don't go all beady on me. I'm certainly not going to start now, so don't even try. I'll have another glass of Chardonnay, please. Small. Very small. I'll need to keep a clear head tonight."

Fern giggled. "Because of Lewis?"

"Because of the star stuff."

"Yeah, whatever . . ." Fern pushed her way through the Sunday evening crowd towards the bar and laughed with Timmy as he served her.

It was a blessing, Amber reckoned, that this was Zillah's Sunday off. OK, she'd been much more friendly recently, but somehow it would have been too embarrassing spending an evening with Lewis — however much of a non-date it was — with his mother in the audience.

She'd rooted around in her still-unpacked bags and come up with what she hoped was a suitable outfit. Her jeans were designer worn and torn, her flimsy camisole top was a wisp of pink and cream chiffon that weighed nothing and had cost almost a month's salary in the New Year sales, and her sandals were again stilt high and sparkly. She'd managed to get her hair to dry bone straight in the sun in Gwyneth's garden and her make-up had taken forever.

Gwyneth had said she looked like a model straight off the telly, and Fern had whistled and declared the whole thing far too Uptown Girl for words. To a man, The Weasel and Bucket regulars had stared at her, open mouthed, and continued staring.

She hoped Lewis would feel the same way.

"This'll have to be my last drink." Fern plonked a pint and a wine on the table. "I'm sitting in with Jem tonight as well as Win. He's cooking lasagne for us all and I've got to supervise. I trust you realise," she added, "that you're very honoured to be seeing Lewis without his sidekick."

"I wouldn't have minded Jem being here. I think he's great and —"

"Hey." Fern grinned. "I know. Don't get defensive. And it's Lewis' night off anyway."

"And you don't mind?" Amber took a mouthful of wine. "About him — well, meeting me? Tonight? I mean, it's not a date and I know you fancy him and —"

"*What?*"

Amber smiled. "You can't deny it. You told me you fancied him when we first met — on St Bedric's Eve. With the Lucky Cake thing. You said you'd made it your green-cheese wish — again. You said something along the lines that it was the thing you'd been wishing for every year and that one day he'd realise that you existed and —"

"Not *Lewis!*" Fern hissed, blushing. "God, not Lewis! I didn't mean Lewis. Yes, he's beautiful and sexy and a fantastic bloke and all that, but he doesn't press my buttons in that way. I'm not in love with Lewis."

"You're not? Who, then?"

"Keep your voice down," Fern whispered, glancing towards the bar. "And if you promise, cross your heart and hope to die promise, that you'll keep it to yourself."

"Promise." Amber made all sorts of chest-crossing movements.

"Him." Fern jerked her head towards the bar. "Timmy. I've been mad about him ever since I came to Hayfields — but he's besotted with Zillah who doesn't give a fig for him. It's too Shakespearean to be true. Which is why I've been relying on the stars to sort it all out."

Timmy? Timmy Pluckrose? Amber managed to keep silent, trying not to look shocked as she squinted across the pub. Nope. However hard she tried, she simply couldn't see the attraction.

Fern sighed. "See — you don't understand. I knew you wouldn't."

"What makes people fancy other people is always a mystery," Amber said kindly. "Um — I take it he hasn't — er — reciprocated?"

"Well, obviously not. Oh, he's always really nice to me, and we have a laugh, but he never sees me as a *woman*. I mean while Zillah still keeps him dangling I

140

think there's still hope for me — but one day I'm sure she'll just give in and take the easy option and marry him, and then he'll never know what it could be like with someone who really, truly loves him and my heart will be broken for ever."

"Er — yes, I can see that . . . but — um — he's quite old and —"

"He's twenty years older than me, that's all. And what's age got to do with anything?" Fern took a frantic gulp of Andromeda Ale. "Love transcends age and creed and — oh, all that stuff. I know what you're thinking — that he's a tall, thin, bald, middle-aged man with very little going for him. Go on — admit it."

"No — well, um, yes."

"But I love him for all that! For it, despite it, because of it — I don't know! I just love him. I'd lie for him, cheat for him, steal for him — even bloody die for him. I love him that much. OK?"

Amber took a deep breath. She'd never, ever, loved anyone like that. Not unconditionally. Not with that intensity. Not even Jamie — especially not Jamie.

"But — does he even have an inkling how you feel?"

"Of course he doesn't!" Fern sighed heavily. "What would be the point? He's in love with Zillah."

Amber thought for a moment. "And isn't this what the star magic is all about, then? Sorting out tangles like this which seem insoluble? And isn't it what you've asked for over and over again? And nothing's happened. Which just goes to show that it doesn't work. What you need to do is the good old-fashioned earthbound stuff — you know, vamping, flirting —

letting him know that you'd be a much better bet than Zillah."

"No one ever said the star magic worked instantly."

"Flirting would be quicker."

"I can wait."

"But —"

"I believe the stars will sort it out." Fern drained the last of her pint. "I'm pinning all my hopes on Cassiopeia next weekend. And, even if you are my new best friend, if you breathe a word of this to anyone I will never, ever speak to you again."

Amber smiled. "It's safe with me. I think it's just a bit sad, relying on all that hocus pocus stuff."

"That's because you don't love anyone," Fern said as she stood up. "One day you will and then you'll understand that desperate remedies are called for when things don't pan out. Have a nice evening. See you tomorrow?"

Amber nodded. She was working for Mitzi again the next day, but only for the afternoon. "Tomorrow evening? In here?"

"Yeah, great." Fern cast a longing glance towards the bar. "At least I can look at him even if I can't touch. Such sweet torment . . ."

Amber watched Fern — all curves and curls and Matalan — bounce out of the door and into the musky dusk, then glanced across at Timmy again. She shook her head. How weird this love thing was.

"Anyone sitting 'ere, duck?"

Amber looked up. A stocky man with a bristly black moustache was leering down at her.

142

"Er — well, no — but I am expecting someone."

"Ah, yes. Lewis. And no, duck, there ain't nothing mystic about me." He held out a swarthy hand. "I'm Billy Grinley. Bin man at your disposal. I hears all the gossip in Fiddlesticks and surrounding area. A pretty little thing like you wants to be careful with young Lewis — he's a bit of a love rat."

"Not like you then, Billy." Goff Briggs lurched up to the other side of Amber's table and winked scarily with his one eye. "Don't listen to him, young lady. And whatever you do, don't invite him to sit at your table. You'll never get rid of him and — oh, hello Slo — come to join us?"

"Come to see if anyone's got a spare ciggie." Slo Motion, wearing a check vyella shirt and a Fair Isle tank top, with stripy braces over both despite the heat of the night, smiled with stained teeth. "And to say hello to this little minx."

Minx? Amber clamped her lips together.

"She's going to be doing a function for us tomorrow," Slo continued, his fingers twitching over Billy Grinley's packet of Bensons. "With Mitzi."

"Am I? I know we've got a private party booked, but I didn't realise it was for you. Is it for your birthday?"

"No, bless you." Slo lit the cigarette at the speed of light, coughed extensively over Goff, and finally blew a luxurious plume of smoke into the air. "Ooooh, that's better. It's a wake. For old Bertha Hopkins."

A wake? A funeral tea? Amber blinked.

"Ah," Slo continued, calmer once the nicotine had started coursing through his veins. "Mitzi does all our wakes — for them as doesn't just want to go down the pub or put on a bit of a spread themselves. You'll be sure to wear black, won't you? Old Bertha's lot hold all the traditional values dear to their miserly hearts. They don't want none of this all wearing bright colours and smiling and doing the hokey-cokey up the aisle after the coffin malarkey."

Amber was still stunned. She'd had no idea that Hubble Bubble catered for such a wide range of occasions. She'd only ever been to one funeral — her grandmother's — and she'd been absolutely devastated by it. Would Mitzi sack her if she cried over Bertha Hopkins?

"Anyone seen Zillah?" Yet another middle-aged man suddenly joined the group round her table. "Don't tell me it's her night off. Damn — I only comes in here to look at the barmaid." He stared down at Amber. "Blimey — you're a corker. You don't fancy popping behind the bar for a bit to gladden an old man's heart, do you, darling?"

"No she doesn't," Slo wheezed round his filter tip. "She's gainfully employed by young Mitzi Blessing and therefore subcontracted to us. She don't want to do no bar work . . ." He coughed spasmodically, then beamed at Amber. "This is Dougie Patchcock — local builder and handyman — or so 'e says. He's another one you'll need to keep an eye on."

"Do I have to join the queue to speak to Amber — or are you issuing tickets like the deli counter in Tesco?" Lewis grinned from behind Slo. "And I'll tell my mum of you, Billy Grinley — flirting with another as soon as her back's turned."

Amber grinned back at him, hoping the grin looked casually "pleased to see you" rather than the "bloody hell — he's sooo fit" that she felt inside.

She hadn't seen him since he'd dropped her off at Tarnia Towers. Annoyingly, at the end of the night Mitzi had bundled her, Gwyneth, Big Ida and Pike into her mini for the rather squashed return journey.

His eyes now flickered over her in a friendly appraisal but held nothing more than amusement. If she'd been expecting him to exclaim loudly and publicly about her appearance she was obviously going to be disappointed. Ah well.

However, every woman in The Weasel and Bucket, Amber noticed, no matter what their age, was staring at Lewis and having a discreet preen.

Each time she saw Lewis, Amber thought dreamily, was like the first time. The sheer breathtaking male beauty of him — the tight, faded jeans, the T-shirts, the tousled hair . . . Oh, dear.

She pulled herself together very swiftly.

Goff, Slo, Dougie and Billy reluctantly all made their excuses and left.

"I see you've already captured the attention of the Geriatric Degenerates. You only needed Timmy to complete the set." Lewis laughed. "What can I get you to drink? Another glass of wine?"

"Please — thanks — I think it's Chardonnay."

"House white then. A good choice. The red would dissolve squirrels' nuts. Won't be long."

And he wasn't.

"Thanks." Amber took the glass. "How's Jem?"

"Mad as a wet hen at being left behind. He'll probably add sennapods to the lasagne out of spite. He likes you. A lot."

"I think he's great, too. And — well, you and him — what you do . . . I think it's wonderful."

Lewis raised his eyebrows. "It's the best job I've had since I qualified, and the one I want to do for as long as possible — but I'm no Mother Theresa. It just works well with me and Jem — and yes, maybe some people do have misconceptions about social workers. But Jem is a real person, not a statistic, and his quality of life is as important as anyone's. The Hayfields set-up means that he can remain as independent as possible — and the fact that we're really good mates is a bonus."

Amber took a mouthful of wine. Lewis was still about as far removed from her idea of a social worker as it was possible to get.

"He's made you a present," Lewis continued. "Which he's going to give you next weekend when we do Cassiopeia. It's a surprise, he says — but as he works at the Winterbrook Joinery it's probably a safe bet to say it'll be wooden."

"I didn't realise that he went to work — I mean . . . Sorry, I don't want to say the wrong thing."

"It's OK. Don't worry about being PC," Lewis smiled. "I never do. He works part-time, supervised of course, but Jem's a stickler for detail and he's learned to do the most amazing fretwork . . . So — what else do you want to know?"

146

Amber almost choked on her wine. Too much . . . far, far too much.

"About the star stuff?"

"About the star stuff," Lewis agreed. "I don't answer questions about my private life."

Bugger.

"All of it, I suppose. I know it's part of the village tradition, and that life here is very different — I mean, I've even been writing letters instead of phoning, can you believe that? And I haven't bought a glossy mag since I got here, and as for shopping or clubbing . . . but worshipping the heavens just seems, well, so odd."

"Why? Rural communities have lived by nature for centuries. The mystery of the changing seasons impacted on their religious ceremonies, and as the moon and stars changed at the same time they were regarded as gods ruling the heavens and earth. Because it couldn't be explained, it was considered magical — and some of it has just stuck. Simple."

Amber leaned back in her chair. She really didn't care too much about the history; she just wanted to sit there, looking at him, listening to his voice. "Um, right — and yes, even we in the civilised world know about it being bad luck to look at the new moon through glass, and turning your money over on a full moon, and making wishes on the first star in the sky — but it's only like wishbones and lucky four-leafed clover and things. A bit of a laugh . . ."

"And it still is," Lewis smiled slowly. "It's basically all fun these days. But truly, some of the old magic remains. There are things that still can't be explained rationally. Come on."

He'd stood up. Amber frowned. Was that it? Five minutes max?

"I'll show you the sky," Lewis said. "And yes, I know you've seen the sky before, but this is different. Bring your drink — you might need it."

She smiled and followed him outside.

The night was almost dark, still, warm, sensuously scented with honeysuckle and jasmine and unseen roses.

The trestle tables outside the pub were all occupied and Lewis crossed the road onto the village green. Couples sat by the stream, the dog-walkers were out in force, and teenage shrieks and laughter echoed from beneath the rustic bridge.

The sky, so much bigger here than in the city, was darkly clear and studded with stars.

"You know something about the constellations? The Plough? The Bear? The Pole star?"

Amber nodded. "I'm no Patrick Moore, but yes, they're all words I know."

"OK, then, our main celestial celebrations in Fiddlesticks — at least, during the summer months — are for St Bedric, Cassiopeia, the Plough and the Harvest Moon. Cassiopeia's over there . . ."

"Oh, yes — right . . ." Amber held her breath. He was very, very close as he pointed upwards.

"And the Plough — over there. See?"

Obediently, she followed his finger to the next constellation.

"Mmmm, yes, now that one I do recognise. I always thought it looked like a dog when I was a little girl. I used to call it Trixie."

Lewis smiled at her. "I'd keep that scrap of information to yourself if I were you. That sounds a bit heretical to me. Of course there are zillions of stars, millions of constellations, but this isn't supposed to be an astronomy master class. It's to do with Fiddlesticks' customs."

Amber nodded. She wanted him to tell her about every one of the stars. In minute detail. Anything to keep him standing beside her for as long as possible, so close, almost touching.

He moved away.

"And, anyway, then there's the Harvest Moon shindig — which takes us into the autumn and winter skies, but we won't worry about them right now."

Oh, damn.

"So —" she sipped her wine "— what happens on each of the ones you've mentioned? The Fiddlesticks ones?"

"Cassiopeia's Carnival is for lost lovers really. It's like Valentine's night only more manic. There's a lot of hearts and roses and stuff — and lots of people wishing they could be reunited with other people; there have been several quite spectacularly awful pairings as a result . . . The myth goes that Cassiopeia was banished to the heavens for eternity by Poseidon because she was very vain and declared herself to be even more beautiful than his daughters. So she was left up there, alone, for ever."

Oh, dear, poor girl.

Amber peered up at the sparkling cluster again. "Er — she — it — doesn't look much like a beautiful woman to me."

"No, well, you do need a bit of imagination. But you're supposed to be able to see her chained up there, sometimes upside down, swinging around the pole and —"

"What?" Amber spluttered through her drink. "She's a celestial pole-dancer? How cool is that? She definitely gets my vote."

Lewis laughed. "Yeah well, after her, I guess Plough Night is pretty mundane — although earthy — and possibly self-explanatory. And Harvest Moon is a huge party to celebrate the end of the summer and stoke up a bit of astral warmth for the longer nights ahead."

"And everyone gathers out here on the green for all these, do they?"

"They're the biggies in Fiddlesticks, yes — but there are all sorts of minor astral myths also observed on a more individual basis."

"In the privacy of your own home or back yard?"

"We tend to have gardens down here rather than yards." Lewis's grin was cheerfully mocking. "We've never even heard of ginnels. But yes. There are those who put their faith in Pegasus who was supposed to let the moon sleep on his back, or Andromeda who was rescued by Perseus, or Hercules who sounds like a mass murderer to me, or Leo who always brings rain, or the Seven Sisters and oh, loads more. Anyway, is it a bit clearer now? Astral magic?"

150

"I think I can understand the why, although the how is still a bit of a blur."

"That's all down to unshakeable belief and something else that simply can't be explained. Magic . . . something way beyond our understanding."

Amber nodded slowly. "You mean it's a bit like Catholics asking the saints for favours — you know, St Jude and St Catherine and so on?" And at least now she understood why Fern would be wishing for Timmy on Cassiopeia's. "Ancient religion? A time-honoured belief in something unseen and more powerful than mere mortals can rationally justify?"

"By George, I think she's got it!" Lewis laughed, draining the last of his beer.

"And the St Bedric's thingy is repeated for Cassiopeia, the Plough and Harvest Moon here in summertime — although the wishes and rituals are different. Is that right?"

"Spot on," Lewis grinned. "Oh and — ouf! What the hell —?"

"It's Pike!" Amber laughed as the huge shaggy dog loomed out of the gloom and hurled himself delightedly at Lewis. "He clearly likes you."

"And I usually love him, too," Lewis said as Pike continued to gallop around them, waggling and snuffling excitedly. "But I'd prefer some warning of his approach — oh, hello Ma."

Zillah, all floating long Indian print frock, dangly ethnic earrings and flip-flops, appeared from between the willow trees. "Sorry, love — oh hi Amber . . ." The smile faltered a little. "Come here, Pike! Come here!

Come — oh, don't bother then. I said I'd take him for his last run. Gwyneth's round at Ida's with Mona Jupp, having her eyebrows threaded."

"Uh?" Lewis frowned. "What with?"

Zillah looked at Amber. "Men! Hopeless! Not *with* anything. It's an alternative to plucking, love."

"Why, in the name of God, would Gwyneth and Ida and Mona want to have their eyebrows plucked?"

"Threaded," Amber and Zillah said in unison and laughed.

Any remaining ice dissolved in that moment.

"Gwyneth said she and Ida and Mrs Jupp were being lab rats tonight for someone from Bagley-cum-Russet School of Beauty or something," Amber said. "I guessed she meant guinea pigs."

Zillah nodded, then winced as Pike lolloped away into the darkness towards the stream and there was a tidal-wave splash followed by a tirade of four-letter epithets.

"He's dampened someone's ardour," Lewis said. "Poor sods."

"That means I'll have to get him dry before he goes back to Moth Cottage," Zillah sighed. "Still, with Gwyneth being tied up with young Sukie — you know, Lewis, she's setting up business with Mitzi's ex-husband's second wife — from Bagley, who is probably as we speak giving Big Ida's toenails a French manicure, we might just have time to get the worst off him."

"Sukie?" Lewis frowned. "Ah yes, I remember Sukie . . . Dark hair, pale blue eyes, very pretty."

Amber decided she hated Sukie with a vengeance.

"Down boy," Zillah chuckled warningly. "Young Sukie is trying hard to get the mobile side of the beauty therapy business off the ground. She won't want any distractions of the type you have in mind."

"Spoilsport," Lewis laughed. "And as I recall, the second Mrs Blessing is pretty hot too ... Maybe I should consider having my eyebrows threaded. Or do they do full body massaging? Together?"

Amber added the second Mrs Blessing to her hate-list too.

"You are disgusting." Zillah shook her head in mock despair. "So, are you two coming back to mine? For coffee?"

"Yes, please," Amber said quickly. "That'd be lovely."

Well, it might be. And anyway, it would mean she'd be able to be with Lewis for a bit longer. The celestial celebrations lesson was clearly at an end.

"Yeah, thanks," Lewis smiled in the darkness. "Here Amber, hang on to the glasses. Ma can take them back to the pub tomorrow. I'll just go and get that reprobate hound out of the stream."

They both watched him disappear across the green.

"Have you had a nice evening?" Zillah asked casually.

"Lovely. I understand more about the astral stuff now. Not that I'm convinced about the magic, but —"

"Me neither," Zillah sighed. "Mind you, I've gone along with it because Fiddlesticks just sucks you into the mindset. But it's never done anything for me ..."

Amber looked quickly at Zillah. There was a dreamy expression on her face in the drowsy darkness, a sad wistfulness in her voice.

Was Fern not the only one pining for a hopeless, unrequited love?

Aha. Amber smiled to herself. Wasn't this just the sort of opportunity she'd been waiting for? To see if the star magic worked or not? And what about Jem's wish for Lewis to find his father? Why not have a go at that one, too? Lewis needn't know anything about it, need he? It wasn't really meddling, was it?

Amber felt a flicker of excitement. If only she could find out which of the Fiddlesticks men Zillah was carrying a torch for, she'd give Cassiopeia something to sort out next weekend. Fern, Zillah and Lewis — three wishes — even if finding Lewis's father, who had to be one of Zillah's lost loves, might just clash a bit with the current man of Zillah's dreams — but, hey, Cassiopeia could sort that out, couldn't she?

Amber beamed.

"Got him and he's bloody soaking," Lewis trudged back across the green, with Pike trotting unabashed by his side. "And he'd clearly put an end to a rather uncomfortable coupling under the bridge."

"Anyone we know?" Zillah pushed her cloud of hair behind her ears. "A nice juicy snippet I can pass on to Gwyneth and Ida?"

"Not really. Hardly love's young dream. A couple of chavs from the bungalows on the Hazy Hassocks road. Very rude — especially the girl — about Pike, very spotty and stark naked apart from their baseball caps.

154

Not sexy. Not sexy at all. And bloody angry at the disruption. Come on then." He fondled Pike's dripping ears. "Let's get you home . . ."

Chrysalis Cottage was a revelation. Amber looked around in amazement. It was exactly the same shape and size as Gwyneth's cottage, of course, but that was where the similarity ended. Moth Cottage was overcrowded, stuffed full of very large, very old dark furniture and fat chairs and cabinets covered in photos and knick-knacks and the memorabilia from Gwyneth's long life. Now that retro décor was so hot, Zillah's home would have had the lifestyle supplements slavering.

It was like stepping into a 1970s time warp.

The living room was all earthy, beige and chocolate brown, with rough hewn hessian and sequinned tapestries, and Indian rugs on the original polished floorboards. There was a long, low sofa smothered in embroidered throws and cushions in a mishmash of natural textures, and several bean bags and huge squashy floor cushions, and wooden beaded curtains in all the doorways, and the only illumination came from wine-bottle table lamps.

"It's fabulous," Amber shook her head. "Absolutely amazing . . ."

"Is it?" Zillah carried the cream and orange coffee set into the tiny living room. "Crikey. It's how it's been since I moved in. I've never wanted to change it. It wasn't the happiest time for me when I arrived in Fiddlesticks, and I poured everything into the cottage.

It eventually became my nest, my sanctuary, the only place I felt safe . . . I suppose I sort of atrophied back then. I tried to recapture the happiness I'd had — um — before. I mean . . ."

Quickly, Lewis stood up from the sofa where he'd been sprawled with Pike and several large towels and took the tray from his mother.

He gave Amber a sort of "please back off" look. "I've always loved it, too. I think it's cool. I hated leaving it to go to college. I was born here; it was the only home I've ever known — even now, the flat with Jem isn't my home. It's his. This is home."

"I'm not surprised. It's lovely. Er — is it okay if I have a look at your photos and your record collection?" Amber asked, really not wanting to rake over emotions Zillah would clearly rather forget. "You've got millions . . ."

"Help yourself," Zillah nodded, thankfully looking less upset and relaxing onto a beanbag. "I'm a bit of a hoarder. You won't find anything catalogued in alphabetical order, though, I'm afraid."

Amber took her tiny coffee cup and saucer and wandered round the room looking at the photos. Zillah hadn't really changed much; her hippie mode of dress now was simply a copy of her earlier style. God — she was beautiful, though. Like some wild gypsy princess. Oh, and Lewis had been soooo cute! There were pictures of him throughout babyhood, childhood, schooldays, and — wow! — looking suitably embarrassed, but still undeniably rock-star-sexy, in cap and gown at his graduation.

156

There were no pictures of anyone who could be considered Zillah's current love or Lewis's father or any men at all. No clues to give Cassiopeia a bit of a head start. Damn it.

Amber moved on to the vast record collection. All vinyl. Probably worth a fortune now.

"I'm trying to get then all on CDs," Zillah said. "My ancient stereo system will give up the ghost one day and I'd hate to lose them. The memories . . ."

Amber carefully looked at the LP covers. They were all late 1960s and early 1970s soul bands, some by people she'd heard of, like Otis Redding, Sam and Dave, Wilson Pickett, but most of them by obscure, at least to her, British groups: Simon Dupree and the Big Sound, The Alan Bown Set, Robert Plant's Band of Joy, Ebony Keyes, The Chris Shakespeare Movement.

Amber gently flicked through the shiny sleeves. "I'd love to listen to these one day . . . I used to go to a lot of Northern Soul clubs back home. It'd be great to hear the originals sometime . . . Oh, look there's one here stuck at the back of the shelf. It looks as though it's been here for years. It must have slipped down and got caught. I hope it's not damaged."

"Not that one!" Zillah said sharply. "Amber — leave it! Please!"

"Sorry." Amber quickly dropped the dusty LP back into its hiding place. "I didn't mean to —"

"It's OK," Zillah's voice was slightly husky. "Sorry . . . I shouldn't have shouted. It's just that some of those records are — er — have long been deleted.

They're collectors' items. I'm sort of hoping they'll be my pension one day . . ."

Lewis, with Pike now dry and very large and fluffy on his lap, was looking about as puzzled as Amber felt. "What was it, then? An original by Aretha or something? Is it going to be my inheritance?"

"Something like that," Zillah said, not looking at him, her fingers tracing the pattern on her long frock. "Not important. Now, anyone want more coffee?"

Amber nodded, turning away from the shelves. "Yes please, that would be lovely . . ."

What was it, she wondered, about "Summer and Winter" by Solstice Soul, that meant Zillah kept it not only hidden, but also clearly a secret from even her own son?

CHAPTER
FOURTEEN

Walking on the Moon

Next morning, the Hubble Bubble premises proved to be more or less what Amber had been expecting. The shed beside the library, as Mitzi had described it, had a corrugated tin roof, breeze block walls, a solid bottle green door and two small windows.

The only bit of light relief was the sign: chunky, irreverent and immensely colourful, it shouted *Mitzi Blessing's Hubble Bubble Country Cooking* in fluorescent pink lettering like three-dimensional seaside rock, the length and breadth of Hazy Hassocks High Street.

Hoping that her tied-back hair and outfit of black skirt, black T-shirt, opaque black tights — despite the temperature again soaring headily into the eighties and a pair of second-hand black Mary-Jane shoes donated by Gwyneth from her jumble finds, would pass muster for Bertha Hopkins' send-off, Amber pushed open the door with trepidation.

"Hello — can I help you — oh, hi Amber." Mitzi, also dressed in black, looked up from the laptop on the big white-scrubbed table and smiled in welcome. "Goodness you're early — you should have phoned — I'd have come to collect you. Oh, lordy . . . you didn't come on the bus?"

Amber nodded. "It was fine. Only took a few minutes. Some of the passengers were a bit odd though."

"They would be. A lot of them get on in Winterbrook in the morning and spend all day going round and round the villages. They look on it as a mystery tour. And they can be very territorial about strangers. Gwyneth should have warned you."

"She couldn't say much. She's had her mouth done. She just gave me the bus timetable and pointed a lot."

Mitzi pushed the laptop away. "She's had *what* done?"

"Her mouth. And her eyebrows. And her nails and some other stuff which she couldn't tell me about because she's had her mouth done last night. Lip filler or something, I think it was."

Mitzi laughed. "Before we get into 'There's A Hole In My Bucket' territory, are you saying Gwyneth has been *beautified*? At home? Oh dear — not by The Harpy? Oh, sorry, the second Mrs Blessing?"

Too late Amber remembered what Zillah had said about the connection between Mitzi's ex-husband's second wife and the beauty therapy business. "Oh, no — by someone called Sukie."

"Hmmmm. From Bagley? Yes, I know her. She's friendly with my daughters. Nice girl. Shame she's chosen to hitch her star to Jennifer's wagon. No — sorry, mustn't be bitchy. But why on earth would Gwyneth want to be tarted up?"

"I don't think she did particularly, nor did Big Ida or Mrs Jupp — they just offered themselves as guinea pigs.

I'm sorry, I forgot that the beauty therapy business was run by your — er husband's — um . . ."

"Oh, please don't worry about that. It's not a problem. They've been together for years and years. Being bitchy about her is just a bad habit, not a truly felt emotion any more. Jennifer's OK really, but she only decided to start her own business because I had. I'm amazed she didn't call it Copy Cat." Mitzi chuckled.

Amber had been rather surprised that she hadn't felt the urge to offer herself up for experimental treatment. Not very long ago she'd have killed for a proper facial or a decent manicure. Now, with her skin tanned from the sun rather than a spraying booth, and her nails cut short because it was easier, and her hair silky from washing it in soft downland water and letting it dry naturally in the gentle summer breeze, the temptations of the salon had receded into Her Other Life, along with the mobile and the need to shop for the latest must-haves every Saturday, or get legless on vodka kicks every Friday night.

"Mitzi!" The door flew open again. "I've lost my earring!"

Blimey! Amber blinked at the man standing in the doorway. He was totally gorgeous. Tall and craggy, with short cropped black hair, sexy eyes and a sort of dangerously beautiful Vinnie Jones look. And there was something else about him, too.

"Stop panicking," Mitzi grinned, fishing in the pocket of her neat black trousers. "Here — I found it when I made the bed this morning. I was going to pop it into the surgery later."

Open mouthed, Amber watched the handing-over of the diamond ear-stud.

"Thanks, angel," the man kissed her thoroughly. "I feel naked without it."

"As you spend most of your time in that state I'm surprised you noticed," Mitzi chirruped with laughter. "Oh, sorry — where are my manners? Amber — this is Joel Earnshaw." She winked. "My — er — dentist."

"You sleep with your *dentist*?" Amber was totally confused. "Er — well, I suppose it beats the usual ways of waiting for National Health treatment, but —"

Joel shook his head. "Ah, no, Mitzi is a private patient. I have altogether different methods for those on my NHS list."

Mitzi grinned. "Behave yourself . . . Amber, Joel is my dentist, but he's also my live-in lover. Not partner, you understand. Nothing so clinical."

Wow! Amber thought. How cool was that? Joel, totally fab, was probably a fair bit younger than Mitzi but they were clearly head-over-heels in love.

"That accent! You come from Manchester!" She smiled in delight. "I *knew* there was something . . ."

Joel nodded. "And you?"

"Stockport."

"Oh lah-di-dah. Very ooop market. But thank the lord for that! At last! Someone who speaks my own language! If I didn't have a multiple filling waiting in the chair with the Novocain wearing off as we speak, I'd whisk you off and catch up on tales from The Old

Country right now. We must make a date to meet up one evening really soon. Arrange it with Mitzi. Please. Lovely to meet you."

"And you . . ."

Joel and Mitzi exchanged a passionate farewell.

Amber turned away, discreetly, smiling to herself. No need for Cassiopeia's intervention for Mitzi there, then.

"Sorry about that," Mitzi looked anything but as Joel disappeared out into the High Street again. "Now where were we?"

Amber didn't have a clue.

"Maybe I ought to give you a quick guided tour," Mitzi said, "before we load up the van for today's function. Oh, and you look absolutely perfect, by the way. I'm so sorry — I should have told you it was a wake."

"Slo told me last night in The Weasel and Bucket. Do you do many?"

"Too many as far as I'm concerned," Mitzi pulled a face. "Not that I'll turn down the business, of course, but I do prefer happier events. Fortunately, I never met Bertha Hopkins so I don't feel so involved. When it's for someone that I know I cry all the time — really unprofessional I know, but —"

"I was worried about crying, too."

Mitzi chuckled. "Oh, good. Another softie. We can weep on each other's shoulders then while handing round the Mourning Mallows or the Tarragon Teardrops. Now, let me show you what Hubble Bubble is all about . . ."

The next half an hour passed in a blur of pots and bags and packets and jars of herbs, seeds, nuts, berries and flowers — some fresh, some dried, some frozen — all catalogued and labelled. And details of what each herb was capable of achieving. And a swift browsing of laminated recipes and suggested menus for various occasions.

Amber was still more than a little baffled — and still not quite able to abandon her scepticism. Old-fashioned stuff, yes; herbal, definitely; but magical . . .?

"I had no idea . . ." Amber shook her head. "No idea at all. And all these are — er — magical?"

"So far the effects have always been very — um — pleasing," Mitzi nodded. "And don't ask me to explain how I'm just thrilled that they are. For instance, for funerals I use things that assuage grief, bring hope, calm despair — borage, cherry, camphor, valerian, basil, blackberry, allspice — oh, loads of them. All from my grandmother's original cookery book."

"And you believe in them?"

"Absolutely."

As it would clearly be new-employment-suicide to laugh, Amber didn't.

Mitzi closed the largest refrigerator. "Now, what I thought was, if you enjoy it here, and you're still in Fiddlesticks at the end of September and want to stay, I'll enrol you at the FE college in Winterbrook to do your Food Health and Hygiene certificate — which means you'll be able to cook as well. Until then, because I'm pretty snowed under, once you've got the hang of it, how do feel about taking on a few parties on your own? We'll split the smaller ones and do the big ones, like Tarnia's, together. Does that sound OK?"

"That sounds just brilliant," Amber said. "Thank you so much."

"Do you drive?"

"I passed my test years ago and have driven on and off since — but I sold my car ages ago when I was made redundant from my permanent job, and never bought another one." Amber still gazed at the jars and boxes and files and folders, wondering if she'd ever remember what did what. "We went everywhere by cab or tram at home."

"You could borrow the van if you like," Mitzi said. "It's very tiny and you'll probably need a bit of practice but you'll need it when you're going solo. I should have thought of it before. I've got my mini and I bought the van earlier in the year for humping stock around, or when I needed to deliver lots of dishes to lots of places. It sits here doing nothing most of the time. Would you like it?"

"I'd love it! Thank you."

"I'll sort out the insurance for you," Mitzi nodded. "Great. It looks like we're in business then, Amber my love."

Fortunately, the Hubble Bubble routine was to arrive at the home of the deceased while the funeral was in progress and set up the food in time for the mourners' return. Amber had been absolutely dreading seeing the coffin and the hearse and the flowers and the heartbreak.

"There," Mitzi stood in Bertha Hopkins' back parlour, her head on one side. "How does that look?"

"Perfect," Amber agreed. "Just right."

White cloths with black bands, the delicacies all neatly labelled on plain white plates, the tables decorated with dark roses and ivy and tall black candles in silver sticks. Piano music tinkled tastefully in the background.

"I usually bring the CD player and have suitable music playing softly," Mitzi said. "It breaks the ice when they get back from the churchyard. Sometimes the family request the dear departed's favourites. Today, fortunately, I was given a free hand so I'm sticking with Brahms. I did one recently to a backing track of The Black and White Minstrels."

Music. Amber nodded. Good idea. That was the thing she'd thought was missing from the Fiddlesticks' shenanigans. The village green celestial celebrations would surely be just the place for suitable, lively music? And of course, since the previous evening and the discovery of Zillah's soul collection, she'd been unable to remove the greatest hits of Otis Redding from her subconscious. Dock of the Bay was becoming seriously irritating. It was too late to suggest music for Cassiopeia's, of course, but maybe she should mention it for one of the later ones.

Which reminded her.

"Er — exactly how well do you know Zillah Flanagan?"

"We're good friends — I've known her for a few years. We're much the same age. I like her a lot — we

166

have a giggle when we get together. Why? Oh, she's your neighbour now, of course."

Amber nodded. "Her cottage is amazing. And she's lovely — but, well, I think she's lonely — and now that everyone is trying to convince me that astral magic really works, I was thinking about Cassiopeia and the lost love thing and . . . "

"For God's sake, whatever else you're thinking of, don't try to star-wish her and Timmy Pluckrose together!" Mitzi shuddered. "A match made in hell. Smashing people, both of them, but totally wrong for each other. And I've already told Zil never to settle for second best."

Amber refrained from saying that she had very different plans for Timmy Pluckrose. "Oh, no — it was nothing like that. Actually, I was wondering if you knew anything about Lewis's father?"

"Nothing at all. Zillah's never mentioned him. I think he may have been a youthful mistake, maybe not even a long-standing boyfriend, just a fling — or maybe he was married — whatever, it's always been a no-go area. Oh crikey, Amber, you're not going to *dabble*, are you?"

"No — no, of course not. But everyone has been telling me how the stars can make impossible things happen, so I thought I'd put it to the test."

"OK," Mitzi perched against a rocking chair. "Now let me give you a bit of friendly — very friendly — advice. This magic stuff, whether herbal or astral, is not to be taken lightly. It's not a game. You have no idea what you may unleash. And seriously, if you're thinking of trying to conjure up some man from Zillah's past who she clearly wants to forget, simply as an experiment, then I must warn you against it, love. Honestly. And then there's Lewis to consider . . ."

As Amber hadn't considered much other than Lewis since they'd first met this wasn't difficult.

"No, really," Mitzi obviously saw the gleam in Amber's eyes. "He's grown-up, clearly extremely happy and well adjusted, with just Zil. He may have all sorts of issues about his long-lost father turning up."

"He has," Amber admitted. "He got quite angry about it. He says he doesn't want to know."

"There you are then, best leave it well alone. You can certainly wish that Cassiopeia will make some wonderful man come along and sweep Zillah off her feet and make her as happy as she deserves to be, but please lay off asking for Lewis's father to make an appearance, or pairing Zil with Timmy, OK? Too dangerous. Anyway, love, lecture over — and just in time. Looks like the funeral's over, too."

As Amber circulated with plates and napkins and a suitably sympathetic expression, it became clear that Bertha Hopkins had left no close relatives and that the assembled crowd in the back parlour were either friends of an age to enjoy a good funeral, or distant nephews and nieces all keen to get a share of the pickings, such as they were.

Slo, looking sombre and exactly like a Central Casting funeral director, helped himself to a Wild Endive Whirl from her piled plates. "Not a bloody tear from one of 'em. Disgusting. Me and the girls —" he nodded his head in the direction of Constance and Perpetua who were also dressed top to toe in Edwardian black outfits complete with veils "— worked the crowd as 'ard as we could — gave 'em the real tear-jerkers, all the dirges and that — and not so much as a snuffle. Bloody disgusting. We felt right failures, I can tell you. It ain't a proper funeral unless the congregation is all prostrated with grief."

Amber looked at the crowd round the table. They were all chatting merrily as if they were at a birthday party, drinking non-stop and laughing immoderately. It didn't seem right.

"Ask young Mitzi to slip 'em all one of the specials," Slo lowered his voice. "She makes 'em for us just in case it looks as if we 'aven't done our job proper. And —" he looked over his shoulder "— if our Constance or Perpetua asks, you 'aven't seen me, OK?"

He sidled round the outside of the room and sloped off into the garden.

Doing as she was told, Amber found Mitzi deep in conversation with two elderly ladies dressed in drooping frocks and crocheted cardigans and — surely not — cycle helmets draped in black crepe.

"My neighbours." Mitzi introduced them with a gentle smile. "Lavender and Lobelia Banding. Lav, Lob — this is Amber Parslowe. My new assistant."

They all shook hands, hampered more than somewhat by the Bandings having towering pyramids of food on two plates each, and Amber gathered from Mitzi's eye-language that mentioning the cycle helmets was a no-go conversational area and she'd make explanations later. Lavender and Lobelia, she explained, had been at school with Bertha Hopkins, hadn't seen much of her since, and were at the funeral simply to celebrate them outliving yet another contemporary.

Trying hard not to look at the cycle helmets, Amber passed on Slo's message about the specials.

Mitzi nodded. "Ah, my Teardrop Explodes. They never fail. Such innocent ingredients to the untrained eye — peach, sage and sunflower — but lethal in the correct combination. You'll probably need them in the future so watch and learn, Amber, love. Watch and learn."

Amber did. Emptying out some rather pretty little orange buns onto a plate, Mitzi circulated among the partying mourners, insisting that they should each have one at least.

Within minutes there wasn't a dry eye in the house.

Sobs and gulps and sniffles had completely replaced the raucous laughter and off-colour jokes.

"Blimey." Amber shook her head. "I don't believe it . . ."

Mitzi laughed. "Nor did I, the first time. But you will, love. You will. Like I said, it doesn't matter which magic you're using, it's damn powerful stuff — so use it with care . . ."

Still shaking her head, and handing out napkins for Bertha's nearest and dearest to weep into, Amber was crossing the room when she was stopped in her tracks by Constance Motion.

"Did you give him a cigarette? Our Slo?" Constance's brassy and exuberant curls were escaping wildly from beneath the brim of her top hat. She blocked out the light. "Is that why he's gorn outside?"

Amber shook her head and raised her voice above the wailing. "Not guilty. I don't smoke. If he's outside he probably just needs some fresh air. It's very hot, after all."

"Ah, that's his excuse," Constance's chins wobbled. "I'm not daft, you know. Coming back in the hearse he gave me all the old baloney about the smell of smoke coming from the crematorium."

"Well, maybe it did," Amber said as the Bandings caught up with her and snatched several Cherry and Camphor Cries from her plate and stuffed them into their pockets before scuttling back towards Mitzi. "It must be an occupational hazard."

"At a *churchyard burial*?"

Constance stomped away into the garden.

Through the tiny, much-curtained window, Amber watched Slo look over his shoulder in terror and beetle away into the shrubbery. Constance, her black riding habit billowing, had sighted her quarry and bored her way through a particularly unrelenting syringa. It was like a huge determined crow bearing down on a helpless piece of would-be carrion.

"Our Slo been caught with a ciggie, has he?" Perpetua, grey and wispy beneath her bonnet, popped up at Amber's shoulder. "Silly boy. It'll kill him."

"Does it really matter? I mean — at his age . . .?"

"Bless you, it won't be the fags that finish him off. It'll be our Constance." Perpetua trotted after Amber as she returned to the table and collected two dishes of Weeping Willow Waffles. "Slo has to stop smoking. Because of that business with Gertie Bickersdyke's funeral."

"Oh dear," Amber said politely. "Was she an avid anti-smoker, this Gertie — er —?"

"Bickersdyke," Perpetua finished. "I've no idea, but the family were very big noises in Winterbrook and they wanted her ashes scattered on the little ornamental pond they were having constructed in the Bickersdyke Memorial Garden."

"Ah, nice . . ."

"Should have been. Course, we had to hang on to Gertie in her box back in the chapel of rest until they were ready for her. Several weeks it took for the pond to be ready — trouble with the pond liner. It didn't go anything like that Alan Titmarsh said it would. No sooner did the water go in than it all seeped out again. Trying to cut corners never works. Anyway, Gertie was with us much longer than we'd expected. Not that we charged extra for the shelf-space, of course."

Amber's fixed interest smile was beginning to ache.

"Anyhow," Perpetua continued, her thin lips pursing together like two small slugs having a love-in, "come the big day, we had the local press and the town council and about three hundred members of the Bickersdyke family at the ceremony. And when our Connie opened the casket and said the prayer and the local kiddies orchestra struck up 'Cast Your Fate To The Wind' —

172

terribly off-key I must add, sounded like a castration —
and scattered Gertie's mortal remains to the elements it
were like emptying a bloody ashtray."

"No!"

"Yes! Dog-ends, dozens of 'em, bobbing along on the
top of the pond. It looked like the local lads had had an
all-night party. It only needed a couple of After Shock
bottles and a condom."

"Oh, dear ..." Amber chewed the inside of her
cheeks.

"So, once the hiatus had been smoothed over and
we'd fished the worst out and the Bickerdykes had
stopped crying, me and Constance had to go straight
back to the chapel of rest and check the others. Slo'd
used all of them as ashtrays. All of them. We lost no end
of business to the Co-Op after that got out, I can tell
you. We had to diversify to try and claw our way back
into the good books."

"Yes ... I can see that you might have to ..."

"So —" Perpetua fumbled inside a little black lace
reticule "— we always do a bit of networking at our
funerals. We have a couple of nice limos that can be
used for any festive occasion. And, at a push, the
hearse is handy for moving furniture. You might have
need of us some time. Have one of our business
cards."

As Amber had no intention of dying, ever, but not
wanting to hurt Perpetua's feelings, she smiled her
thanks and watched as Perpetua wraithed away to
spread joy elsewhere in the room.

She flicked the card over before shoving it into her pocket. It had a Hazy Hassocks address and phone number.

Constance, Perpetua and Slo Motion
Christenings, Weddings and Funerals Catered For
Let Motions Carry You From Cradle To Grave

Much to the amazement of Bertha Hopkins' still-sobbing nearest and dearest, Amber shrieked with laughter.

"Amber? Are you OK?" Mitzi pushed her way through the mourners.

"Never better," Amber sniffed happily. "Honestly. Oh, I love this place. It's magic."

CHAPTER
FIFTEEN

Twinkle, Twinkle Little Star

"Twinkle, twinkle little star," Amber trilled as she pulled on her second best jeans in Moth Cottage's tiny girlie blue bedroom.

"You sound happy, duck." Gwyneth poked her head round the door. "Lovely to hear you singing."

"Why wouldn't I be happy?" Amber hopped over her piles of clutter and hugged Gwyneth. "I love you. I love being here. You've given me a lovely home, not to mention the best food I've ever had in my life, and I've made friends with Fern and — um — well, with Fern, and I've got a job so I can pay you for my keep — and I'm going to use Mitzi's van soon so I'll be able to take you and Big Ida out all over the place — and . . ." She paused for breath and looked sympathetically at Gwyneth. "Your cheeks are still a bit rosy."

"Ah, it's stopped hurting though. Mind, the nails and that were fine. Even that funny stuff she squirted in our lips was good once the numbness wore off. Made us look like the Beverly Sisters. All told, young Sukie did a grand job at beautifying — but we felt the derma-blasting was a step too far for us at our age."

"At any age." Amber shuddered. "Are you putting anything on the sore bits?"

"Margarine."

Oh, right.

"Anyway," Gwyneth returned the hug, then perched on Amber's bed. Her legs stuck out straight in front of her as always. "I'm dead happy that you're happy, duck. And you'll have a lovely time tonight. Cassiopeia's Carnival is allus a good 'un. Shame young Mitzi isn't doing some food — that'd make it go with even more of a swing."

"Mmm ... So would some live music." Amber straightened her silver vest, checked her make-up in the tiny mirror, and flicked her hair silkily over her shoulders. "Don't you think?"

Gwyneth nodded. "You ought to ask Mitzi about that, too. I think some of the Baby Boomers she works with formed a chamber orchestra last year. Or were you thinking of something a bit more modern?"

Amber shrugged. "Well, I wasn't planning on turning Fiddlesticks into the next Glastonbury, but yes, I thought maybe a rock band of some sort. Not too youthful, of course — something for everyone."

"That'd be nice." Gwyneth nodded. "A bit of Victor Sylvester, maybe? And some James Last for the youngsters?"

Amber didn't ask. It was clearly a generational thing. She doubted if Gwyneth would have heard of Slipknot or the Flaming Lips.

"So, if we wanted music for — say — the Harvest Moon do, would I have to approach a committee or something? I mean, how are these astral celebrations organised? Who by?"

"Bless you, they sort of do themselves. They're centuries old, after all, and they've changed very little over the years. But Goff Briggs and Mona Jupp make a lot of the more earthly arrangements these days. You could start with them I suppose. The only problem would be money. The stars don't make Fiddlesticks any money. We couldn't afford the likes of Cliff Richard."

And thank the lord for that, Amber thought.

"No — I mean, of course I realise that they're not commercial ventures. But maybe we could have a bit of fund-raising or something if we wanted dancing? Do you think anyone would object to live music?"

"Can't see anyone in Fiddlesticks not wanting anything that would make it even more of a party, duck. Everyone likes a bit of a knees-up, don't they? Me and Big Ida did salsa lessons last year in Hazy Hassocks village hall and brushed up on our Charleston and there was a waiting list miles long. Mitzi's influence again — she's been like a breath of fresh air, that gel."

"Sounds like it. She was telling me about her Baby Boomers thing — how she's got everyone who thought they were surplus to requirements involved in activities and community schemes and stuff. She should be everyone's role model. I know Hubble Bubble is going to be huge — and she's so nice and down to earth with her magic ..." Amber laughed. "Oh, and on that subject, just so I don't make a complete fool of myself, what else goes on tonight that I should be forewarned about? Lewis said it was a bit like a mad Valentine's Day."

Gwyneth chuckled, the chuckle being cut short as Pike hurled himself at her. They both collapsed onto the bed. It took a few moments before she emerged spitting fur.

"Well, yes. That's about it, really. All hearts and flowers and love stuff. Sit Pike! Sit — oh . . . all right, then, don't. Oh — and did Lewis tell you about the balloons? No? Well, everyone has two silver balloons, one heart-shaped, the other a star — come to think of it, there must be a sort of fund for them because we allus has loads — and at around eleven o'clock, when the sky is dark enough and Cassiopeia's constellation is right in the heavens, we all makes our love wishes and let the balloons go floating up to her . . . 'course, they used to have doves and things I think in the olden days, before the balloons. I wouldn't have liked that. They'd have been so scared, poor little mites."

"Oh," Amber smiled. "That sounds wonderful. Not the doves — of course . . . but the rest of it. Especially the balloons."

"It is. The kiddies love it. And there's a lot of rose petals scattered and Timmy makes a Cassiopeia Cup — a sort of punch — and there's a barbecue for after. That's it really. Oh, and some people go off and make their own love wishes to Andromeda — but we don't take no notice of them. They're a bit fundamentalist, if you gets my drift."

"Andromeda has her own night doesn't she? Or so Lewis said."

"Ah, later in the year." Gwyneth struggled with the dog a bit more and lost. "She's an autumn constellation for the northern hemisphere. But she's a powerful lass, and the sad and lonely likes to get a bit of 'ead start."

Amber squirreled that piece of information away for later use. Just in case Cassiopeia didn't come up with the goods on the Timmy and Fern front tonight, of course.

She also decided she'd approach Mrs. Jupp or Goff Briggs once tonight's shenanigans were over, about the possibility of sorting out some live entertainment for future celebrations.

"Thanks. It all sounds wonderfully complicated as usual. So?" She grinned at Gwyneth. "Will I do?"

"Duck, you looks lovely. Like a film star. You won't need any help from Cassiopeia tonight, and that's a fact. You'll have everyone swooning at your feet."

An hour later, as the sultry July evening faded into a pink and lilac dusk, Amber's feet were still swoon-free.

Fiddlesticks was once more out in force. Amber, sitting at one of the trestle tables outside The Weasel and Bucket — tonight glittering beneath a thousand tiny pale-pink fairy lights — with Fern, gazed across the shadowy sea of now familiar faces, listened to the rise and fall of the soft, southern accents which had at first sounded so odd, and felt at home.

Weird — was this because of St Bedric? Because she'd asked him to sort out her life? Tonight, because of the fizz of magical anticipation and the party excitement, she really wanted to believe that it might be. But there was still the no-nonsense part of her that remained sceptical.

What it needed, of course, was absolute proof that this astral magic worked.

She tilted her head and stared up at the darkening sky. If she squinted she could just make out the stars beginning to show. Tiny white pinpricks of light against the lush deep blue velvet. Try as she might she still couldn't recognise Cassiopeia. She'd have to ask Lewis again to point her out before she started making her wishes.

"It's make or break for you tonight," she said silently to the heavens. "Because, honestly, I still think this is a lot of old hokum."

"Uh? Sorry? Did you say something?" Fern, burrowing into a packet of salt and vinegar crisps, asked across the table.

Amber shook her head. "I hope not! I was thinking, that's all."

"Dangerous at your age, dear," Fern giggled. "And despite your earlier denials, are you going to be wishing for Lewis to fall madly in love with you tonight?"

"No way," Amber pulled a face. "I've told you before — Lewis simply isn't on my agenda. No, I've got other plans for tonight — and don't ask. Secret. Top secret. Is it my round?"

"Yep, but I'll go — any chance to have a quick ogle at the delectable Timmy — and don't laugh."

"I'm not. Of course I'm not. I wouldn't. But actually, he's just coming out to clear tables, which means if you sit here you can ogle to your heart's delight and I'll go and get the drinks . . ."

Amber pushed her way into the pub. It was like walking into a very overcrowded rose-scented sauna.

Timmy had entwined yet more twinkling pink fairy-lights round everything, and big red heart balloons bobbed round the chairs and the walls, and even the beer pumps. Several bunches of aggressively pink plastic roses sprouted in unlikely places and there were further rosy nosegays on each of the tables.

Amber thought it looked wonderful.

Zillah looked even more so.

"Oh," Amber sighed greedily, "that dress is amazing . . ."

"Do you like it?" Behind the bar, Zillah smiled as she reached for four glasses with one hand and the Pegasus Pale pump with the other. "It's years old, but I thought it would do for tonight."

"It's perfect."

Long, sleeveless, low cut, close fitting at the top and floating down to the floor in multiple chiffony layers, it was a mass of tiny pink and cream sprigged roses. With dangly pink and silver earrings and her curls tumbling to her shoulders, Zillah looked like everyone's idea of a Romany Queen.

"Same again for you two?" Zillah called across several heads.

Amber nodded, raising her voice above the Weasel and Bucket's roar. "And one for Lewis and Jem. Fern says they won't be long. Oh — and they're bringing Win with them, too. So, whatever they all usually have. Thanks . . ."

"Make way for the workers," Timmy chuckled, powering his way through the throng, towers of empty glasses in both hands. "You look damn sexy, Amber. You'll have to keep well away from Billy Grinley."

"I intend to," Amber grinned passing the money over to Zillah and taking the tray. "And Slo and Goff and Dougie and everyone else."

"Including Lewis?" Timmy laughed.

"Oh, especially Lewis."

Amber glanced at Zillah. Had she heard that last bit? Probably not. She'd moved along and was busy serving a crowd at the far end of the bar.

"Actually —" Timmy plonked his empties on the bar "— I wanted to ask you something."

Amber's heart gave a little skip. Was he going to ask for some sort of intercession tonight? To admit he'd been secretly in love with Fern for years and now realised that his destiny wasn't with Zillah.

"Can you use a computer?"

Amber's heart resumed its normal rhythm. Bugger. She nodded.

"Great. There's not many round here as can, to be honest — and despite the IT classes in Winterbrook all I ever seem to get on search engines is a lot of irrelevant American stuff or porn."

"It happens all the time," Amber's arms were beginning to ache and the noise level was reaching danger decibels. "Do you want me to sort something out for you? Tomorrow?"

"Now, if you've got a minute."

"Now? Tonight?" She looked around the bar. "In the middle of all this?"

Tommy nodded. "Please. Before the Cassiopeia stuff really kicks off. It's important and I've made a real hash of things."

"OK, let me just go and dump the drinks outside and then I'll come back."

Having explained to Fern that she wouldn't be long, and wondering where Lewis and Jem and Win had got to, Amber pushed her way back into the bar.

"Through here," Timmy jerked his head from the kitchen doorway. "I've got it set up down here for the accounts and everything. Zillah usually does my computer stuff — but I can't ask her to do this."

The kitchen, all pristine and gleaming, was a direct contrast to the chaos in the bar.

The computer sat humming softly on a neat little pulldown shelf beside a state-of-the-art cooker.

"I've logged on," Timmy said. "And the printer's connected. What I want to find is a love nest."

No wonder he'd hit every porn site in Christendom.

Amber's heart sank. "Er — OK — for two people, I presume? You mean, a sort of romantic hideaway cottage or something?"

"Or a hotel. Or guest house." Timmy nodded. "I've been trying to sort it out all day. So's I can present it to Zil as a fait accompli tonight. But she keeps coming in and I don't want her to see what I'm doing. If you could just find somewhere that offers exclusive, expensive, romantic seclusion for a weekend — in this country because we'd have to get someone in to look after the pub of course — and probably in September once Harvest Moon is over, when we're quieter. If you could print out anything suitable with phone numbers, I'll ring them straight away."

"OK," Amber sighed. "I'll see what I can do. You go back into the bar and keep Zillah out of here for as long as possible."

"You're a star," Timmy gave her a hug. "I won't forget this."

Bugger, bugger, bugger! Amber cursed as she started to Google. It would take a hell of a lot more than a bit of haphazard astral-magic to sort this one out. So much for her trying to get Timmy and Fern together tonight, not to mention Zillah and whoever it was in Fiddlesticks that made her go all dreamy-eyed . . . never mind introducing Lewis's long-lost father into the mix.

It was clearly a recipe for disaster.

After ten minutes she had printed a list of suitable properties for Timmy. All promising weekends of everlasting love and luxury. All within a few hours' driving distance. All with phone numbers.

Amber surveyed the list and sighed again. She'd been tempted to sabotage the search and tell Timmy the computer had crashed or something — but she couldn't. It wouldn't be fair. Who was she to interfere in the course of true love, smooth or not? Mitzi had warned her against trying to pair Zil and Timmy off, but what could she do to prevent it? Cassiopeia might be able to sort out star-crossed lovers, but Amber felt it was way beyond her own remit.

Just as she was about to log off, she remembered her own quest for live music. With her laptop still not unpacked, why not make the most of having Google at her disposal? It would only take a few moments. Could she remember the names of those old soul bands on Zillah's LPs? She typed in various combinations with varying results, scribbling everything relevant on the back of a handy pile of paper napkins, then pushed them into the back pocket of her jeans. She'd ring them tomorrow and get some availability and prices.

"How's it going?" Timmy popped his head round the door. "Any luck?"

Amber waved the sheaf of printed paper. "More love nests here than anyone could ever want. Er — shall I switch the computer off now?"

"I'll see to it," Timmy was beaming ear to ear. It creased his thin face in a pleasant way. "Thanks a ton, Amber. I'll get on to these places straight away and tell Zil all about it at midnight. I can't wait to see her face."

Neither can I, Amber thought sadly, shoving her way through the crowded pub again and out into the garden.

"What on earth have you been doing in there?" Fern grinned. "Changing barrels?"

Amber felt unbearably disloyal. Oh, God . . . Poor Fern.

"Nothing much — just helping Timmy out with a computer problem. It's sorted now. Oh — you must be Win. Hello. It's lovely to meet you at last."

Win, tall and middle-aged, with a baby face, very auburn hair and a beatific smile, raised her gin and tonic. "Hello, Amber. Fern said you were pretty. And you are."

"Thanks. So are you. And that's a lovely jumper."

"Made it myself," Win continued to smile. "I knit a lot."

Looking round for Lewis and Jem, Amber scrambled back on to the bench.

"Jem's just gone to the toilet." Win nodded, enthusiastically sucking her slice of lemon. "With Mr Motion."

God — surely Slo wasn't trying to nick fags off Jem now, was he?

"And Lewis?"

"No," Win shook her head. "Just with Mr Motion. Lewis had to see someone. Ah — here he is . . . Hello, Jem."

Jem, holding Slo's hand, waved at them. They all waved back.

Slo made sure that Jem was comfortably seated before beetling away to find another nicotine stash.

Having taken a satisfying gulp from his pint, Jem tapped Amber on the arm and waved a tissue paper package under her nose.

"Oh — thank you. Lewis said you'd made me a present . . . It's really, really kind of you." As Fern and Win watched and Jem grinned, Amber undid the bundle of much-sellotaped tissue sheets with some difficulty. "I can't imagine what it is, but — oh, wow!"

She blinked at the tiny wooden star in amazement. Five pointed, each point made from a different wood, polished and varnished to bring out the beauty of the veneers, the whole thing was threaded on a slim leather necklace to make a perfect delicate pendant.

Amber was ashamed to admit she had been expecting something pretty clumsy and unrecognisable which of course she'd love, but this was something else.

"God, Jem, I don't know what to say. Thank you is totally inadequate . . . You are so clever. This is just exquisite . . ."

Jem beamed and hugged her arm.

"It's a pentangle," Win said. "A star magic symbol."

Amber sniffed back her tears. Jem pulled away from her, giggling, and took the pendant, indicating that she should bend her head down. Taking infinite care not to tangle the star in her hair, Jem slowly pulled the thin strip of leather round her neck so that the pentangle nestled just above her breasts.

They all stared at it and smiled mistily at one another.

"Thank you . . ." Amber took Jem's face between her hands and kissed him. "It's the nicest present I've ever had. It's beautiful. I'll always wear it. I knew tonight was going to be special but this . . ."

Jem, having happily kissed her back, now suddenly pulled away and started to jerk his head towards the pub.

"It's Lewis!" Win cried, waving her gin and tonic with enthusiasm.

Amber, despite herself, felt her pulse beat take an up-tempo turn. Maybe tonight, with all the love emblems and star magic and frivolity.

"Shit!" Fern groaned. "And double shit! He's brought someone with him."

CHAPTER
SIXTEEN

Wishing on a Star

The calypso syncopation of Amber's heart dropped to an adagio funeral march in less time than the click of a metronome.

Lewis, all faded denim and tousled hair, was manoeuvring his way through The Weasel and Bucket's trestles towards them, his arm round the shoulders of a very pretty girl.

"Hi," he grinned round the table, making swift introductions. "And this is Sukie."

Sukie? *Sukie?* Amber had heard that name recently, surely?

Ah, yes! Bloody Sukie the bloody mobile beautician who had practised on Gwyneth and Big Ida and Mona Jupp the other evening. The one Lewis had remembered was pretty stunning. The one she'd decided she hated.

That hadn't taken him long, then.

"Hello." Sukie smiled sweetly.

Sukie, Amber noted, was so clever at using her own expertise and techniques, that she looked as though she was wearing no make-up whatsoever. Her skin was slightly freckled and sun kissed, her short dark hair chopped into haphazard glossy layers, her lips pale and plump, her turquoise eyes huge and simply framed by lush black lashes.

It must have taken her *hours*.

And she wasn't even particularly slim — but her very old jeans and very new white T-shirt fitted perfectly and accentuated her curves in an irritatingly sexy girl-next-door manner.

Amber absolutely loathed her.

"Hi," Amber beamed through her teeth. "Lovely to meet you."

Win also was effusive in her welcome. Jem and Fern weren't.

"I see Jem's given you his present already." Lewis nodded towards the pentangle. "I knew he wouldn't wait until I got here. It looks even better on than off. Do you like it?"

"It's wonderful," Amber touched the tiny star. "So special. I love it. I've told him it's the nicest present I've ever had and that I'll always wear it. He's very talented."

Jem grinned at her and blew her a kiss, then immediately frowned at Lewis and Sukie.

"And you just missed my round," Amber said, smiling so hard at Lewis that her jaw ached, "so I'll get yours now — no, I insist. Lewis? The usual? And what would you like, Sukie? Just pineapple juice? Sure? OK."

Amber, valiantly trying to maintain the sunny smile, stomped away back into the pub.

Zillah, taking a much-needed breather in The Weasel and Bucket's doorway, had seen Lewis and Sukie arrive.

Bugger.

Just when she'd thought she didn't have to worry any more. Just when she'd convinced herself that Amber wasn't going to foolishly fall for Lewis's charms, but that maybe they'd continue their friendship and that things may or may not develop from there. She'd eventually reassured herself that Lewis wasn't interested in adding Amber to his list of love 'em and leave 'em conquests, and Amber, if she was hankering after Lewis at all, had been clever enough not to show it.

Ever since Lewis had reached puberty, and her beautiful child had grown into an even more beautiful man, she'd been terrified that he'd make some poor girl suffer the way she had. If he — and the rest of Fiddlesticks — thought she was a sinisterly overprotective mother, then so be it. She'd had her reasons.

Bizarrely now, Amber, Zillah thought, sipping her iced Coke in the stifling darkness, would have been exactly the sort of girl she'd like Lewis to settle down with. If only, of course, Lewis hadn't inherited every one of his father's womanising genes.

She swallowed. The memories still wouldn't leave her alone. She'd successfully buried them for so long, but now everything, from Big Ida's casual mention of the solstice, to Amber finding that long-hidden record, seemed determined to remind her.

And how genuine were her memories anyway? Oh, she remembered the searing hurt and heartbreak, the I-can't-live-without-him desperation of sleepless nights, and then the almost unbearable fear of being left, young, alone and pregnant — but before that, had it

191

really been as amazingly wonderful as her rose-tinted glasses would have her believe?

Yes, he'd been the love of her life. Yes, she'd adored him unreservedly. And he'd loved her once, hadn't he? Yes, surely the wild, mad, exciting, blissful things they'd done together hadn't simply been the stuff of dreams? It had been real, perfect, total bliss, hadn't it?

She'd been so lucky to know what it was like to love and be loved like that, to be young and crazy and unconventional, to have her heart loop the loop each time he smiled, or feel her body shiver each time he touched her.

She sometimes wished she'd never met him. But then, if she hadn't, she wouldn't have had Lewis . . . If only Lewis wasn't so like him.

"Okay, Zil?" Timmy, hands full of empty glasses, loomed up in the doorway. "You can go and sit down for a while, if you like."

"No, I'm fine. There's no time to sit down — as you well know. I'll be back in a minute."

Timmy smiled down at her and for an awful moment she thought he was going to kiss her.

"You work too hard." He held the glasses over his head as a crowd of youngsters in baseball caps and strange, bright-white, hooded tops surged in. "And maybe you were right about taking on some extra staff tonight. Constance and Perpetua are behind the bar at the moment as they were the only ones available but as they've never poured a pint in their lives it's not going to be a long-term thing. About five minutes at the most. I honestly hadn't expected it to be this busy —

can't remember Cassiopeia's being this hectic last year."

"It rained last year," Zillah reminded him. "We all made our wishes to dark clouds in our macs and wellies. The rose petals got trodden into puddles, the rain fused the fairy lights, the barbecue had to be indoors and the balloons disappeared towards Winterbrook on a stiff north-easterly."

"God, yes . . . Hell! Balloons! Where are the balloons?"

"In the cellar. With the helium. Don't panic — Goff and the boys have them all in hand. Your bit is the buckets of rose petals, the Cassiopeia Cup and firing up the barbie — as well as serving ten thousand customers, of course."

"No pressure there, then." Timmy turned back into the pub. "And — er — if you want to stay out here for a bit longer, it's fine by me."

"Are you trying to get rid of me?"

"As if," he grinned and then frowned as his mobile started a muffled ringing. "Oooh — er — that might be important and it's in my pocket and I'll have to answer it and I'd better go and yes, OK — hang on you lot, I'll be there in a minute — and, Christ, Perpetua, whisky is *not* sold in pint glasses! Hang on . . ."

Zillah watched his confused exit with amusement. He was a nice man. Such a nice man. Why, oh why, couldn't she love him?

"Sorry, oh — sorry Zillah . . ." Amber, head down, brushed against her. "I wasn't looking where I was going."

"And I shouldn't be blocking the doorway," Zillah sighed, draining the last of her melted ice cubes.

"Timmy insisted that I took a break, though. Now —" she gestured towards the trestle tables "— I wish I hadn't. Do you think it's serious?"

Amber shrugged. "Lewis and Sukie? No idea. I mean, he's clearly known her for some time because he said so the other night. But I — er — hadn't expected her to be with him tonight, though. She's — um — very pretty. Seems a nice girl."

"She is. Both of those. They always are. And then Lewis gets bored and moves on. Oh dear, the joys of motherhood . . . Anyway, I suppose I ought to get back to work. For the last half an hour Timmy has done nothing but hold furtive conversations on his mobile and keeps giving me silly looks . . . Men!"

"Don't say 'who needs 'em'," Amber said, looking round at the multitude of hearts and flowers, "otherwise this lot tonight will be pretty redundant. Oh, lordy . . ."

"What?" Zillah frowned, following Amber's gaze into the crowded pub. "What — ? Oh, bloody hell!"

Goff Briggs, accompanied by his coterie of Dougie, Slo and Billy, had just emerged from the cellar and they were all prancing round the middle of the bar, high as kites on inhaled helium, singing "It's Raining Men" in Donald Duck voices.

Laughing, Zillah shook her head. "Sorry love — but who needs 'em?"

The rest of the evening had been fairly weird, Amber thought. They all sat round the table, drinking, talking, and apart from Lewis and Win, none of them were

194

happy. Even Sukie seemed to sense the atmosphere, which wasn't difficult, as Jem made his feelings particularly obvious with flamboyant gestures and his own brand of signing and facial expressions, and constantly hugged Amber's arm while glowering malevolently at Lewis.

As the night darkened gently, more and more people gathered on the village green. Timmy and Goff — now looking rather shamed-faced — had set up a huge barbecue beside the rustic bridge and the charcoal glow joined the fairy-lights and the waning moon in illuminating the scene.

Children splashed in and out of the stream, the benches were all taken and Billy Grinley and Dougie Patchcock were in danger of taking off with massive armfuls of silver balloons dancing in the moonlight on twisted tinsel threads.

Lewis leaned across the table towards Amber. "Have you got your Cassiopeia wish ready, then?"

She looked at him with what she hoped was a superior and scornful expression. "Of course. Not that I believe in this nonsense, as you well know. But I intend to join in."

"So do I." Sukie smiled her gentle smile. "We don't do anything like this in Bagley-cum-Russet and I'm never averse to anything that might spice up my love life."

Everyone looked at her. No one spoke.

Really, Amber thought, what could anyone say to a remark like that when you were sitting with the most gorgeous man in the universe thigh-to-thigh next to you?

"Cassiopeia is up there," Win shrilled, gesticulating wildly across the heavens. "Isn't she, Fern?"

"Yup," Fern nodded.

"And she'll make someone fall in love with you if you ask her nicely, won't she?"

"Yup," Fern pulled a face at Amber. "Course she will — even if she takes a bloody long time about it."

"Don't swear," Win said primly. "You always tell me not to swear."

"Sorry," Fern said as they all made a move to stand up. "Right — it looks as though it's about to start. Timmy's circulating with the Cassiopeia Cup, and those buckets over there are filled with rose petals and oh . . . thanks."

Billy Grinley, looming over the table, clearly going for the best cleavage-vantage point, handed everyone two silver balloons.

Amber fastened Jem's round his wrist. "Then you can let them go when we're out on the green, can't you? And up until then you can hold Lewis's hand."

Jem nodded, grinning wickedly, and clambered slowly from the bench, managing to wriggle himself between Lewis and Sukie and slide his hand into Lewis's.

"Nice one," Fern looked at Amber. "And I bet I know what you'll be wishing for . . ."

"And I bet you don't," Amber sighed. "OK? So — what do we do now?"

196

"Follow the herd," Lewis motioned towards the green. "Goff will do his usual bit — then it's every man — or woman — for himself."

For such a tiny village, the crush on the green was amazing. Despite her scepticism and Sukie, Amber felt a frisson of excitement. Now, in the balmy darkness, with all the traditional accoutrements, it was impossible not to feel fired by some sort of pagan zeal. Maybe, just maybe, there was *something* in this astral magic.

With her silver star and heart bobbling above her, she followed everyone else, managing to find a space beside the largest willow tree. As Timmy, helped by Constance and Perpetua, hurled millions of rose petals into the air, Goff stood on the bridge and held his arms aloft.

The rose petals tumbled over everyone and everything like a pale pink scented snowstorm.

It was too theatrical for words.

"Fiddlestickers!" Goff cocked his good eye towards the assembled throng. "Lady Cassiopeia is ready to receive your wishes. She will work her celestial magic for you. Remember, as you wish, release your balloons, the star first to add light to Cassiopeia's eternal path in the heavens, the heart for the granting of everlasting love, second, and then afterwards — as always — you can refresh yourselves with a draught from Cassiopeia's Cup and there'll be plenty of food for everyone."

Everyone clapped and whistled.

"Now!" Goff jabbed a finger towards the stars. "Greetings to Cassiopeia!"

Everyone clapped and whistled again.

Amber, feeling slightly foolish, didn't.

She could just see Gwyneth and Big Ida and the others dotted around in the throng. Lewis and Jem were standing by the bridge. She couldn't see Sukie or Win. And there was Zillah, close to Fern. And Timmy, smiling soppily . . . Poor old Cassiopeia, Amber thought, having to sort out that one.

Tipping her head back, she stared up at the sky. The stars were extraordinarily bright tonight. Glittering, truly like diamonds, remote, mysterious, far more beautiful than anything man could produce. Nature certainly had the edge on humankind for producing spectacular effects, Amber thought dreamily.

And then suddenly, Cassiopeia, the celestial pole dancer, was visible.

Amber could see her!

A zigzag formation of five fabulous stars, larger than any others near her, brighter, more stunning.

"Now!" Goff screamed. "Now!"

Fiddlesticks village green was instantly silent. Heads tilted back. Mouths worked.

Amber took a deep breath and stared at the constellation. "OK — now I don't believe any of this, but if you can't beat 'em join 'em — so . . . Please, please will you sort out Zillah. She's had a bit of a rough deal as far as I can tell, and Timmy's not right for her — so if there's a man she really, truly loves can you somehow manage to bring them together? Er — thanks . . ."

Self-consciously Amber released her star balloon. It joined dozens of others wafting heavenwards. A cloud of silver misting slowly, hazily, towards the star clusters above them.

"OK, and having done that, could you also make Timmy fall in love with Fern, please? I know she's asked you for this herself, but maybe she needs a bit of help."

Amber released her heart balloon. Hundreds of other silver hearts wafted above the village. So many people, so many hopes and dreams.

"And," Amber finished. "If you've managed to take all that in, I wondered if you could make Jem really happy and find Lewis's dad for him. I know Lewis says he doesn't want to know but if it's *right*, then I hope you can. I'm not sure if this is what you do, of course, but it's worth a try. Cheers."

Feeling a bit silly, but also strangely refreshed and invigorated, Amber smiled to herself.

There! It was all out of her hands now. If there was anything at all in this astral magic, she'd soon find out, wouldn't she?

CHAPTER
SEVENTEEN

Moon Madness

"We could do with a bit of rain." Gwyneth kicked at the dry, dusty ground with the toe of her crossover sandal. Little puffs of earth landed on Pike's breakfast biscuits. It didn't seem to spoil his enjoyment. "Going to be an awful year for me runner beans if we don't get a drop soon."

"Maybe we'll have to bring our Leo's Lightning incantation forward a tad." Big Ida, sitting on the bench outside Moth Cottage in the early morning sunshine, nodded over her mug of tea. "I know 'e's not due 'til August, but needs must, eh?"

"Ah, but we've tried that before, remember? After the scorcher of 2003? We said a few words early on the following year asking Leo to bring us a bit of rain for the gardens, and what happened? The summer of 2004 was the biggest washout on record. Never stopped raining until September. You 'ave to be careful with Leo."

"Right enough," Big Ida swallowed a ginger nut whole without blinking. "But looking on the bright side, we all 'ad a lovely crop of runners in 2004, didn't we?"

Zillah, sipping her cup of tea alongside Gwyneth and Big Ida with the cats rubbing round her legs, let this multi-faceted meteorological, astrological, and horticultural conversation drift over her as she stared out across the village green. Runner beans were the least of her worries.

She had a far more pertinent problem. A hugely pertinent problem.

As usual, Fiddlesticks was misty and for once eerily silent after the excitement of the night before. The only evidence that Cassiopeia's Carnival had enchanted the village was the still steaming barbecue beside the bridge, heaps of trampled rose petals, and several sadly limp balloons hanging from the upper branches of the willow trees.

Both the postman and milkman had made their rounds more carefully than normal with less than cheery smiles, clearly nursing Cassiopeia Cup hangovers of massive proportions. The rest of Fiddlesticks was still sleeping off the excesses and dreaming sweet dreams of romantic fulfilment.

Zillah would have simply welcomed sleep, preferably dream-free.

Timmy's delighted midnight smile had meant she'd spent the remainder of the night wide awake, panic-stricken, pacing her living room listening to music she'd almost forgotten, reliving memories she so wanted to forget, wishing so much that she had someone to confide in. Wishing she knew what the hell to do now.

"Looks like Cassiopeia has worked for me, Zil," Timmy had said softly as they were clearing up after The Weasel and Bucket had finally shooed out the stragglers including the Motions, Goff Briggs and Billy Grinley and closed its doors.

Zillah, bone tired, hadn't even paused in whipping one load of glasses out of the washing-up machine and piling the trays with more.

"Has she?" She hadn't even stopped working to read the warning signs. "That was quick."

"Wasn't it?" Timmy had moved close behind her, bottling-up temporarily abandoned. "Zil, look at me."

She'd looked.

She'd seen a kind, nondescript man, his eyes luminous with love and she'd wanted to stop him then and there.

But she couldn't and hadn't.

"Zil, you know how I feel about you. No, let me finish . . . I love you, you know that. I know you don't love me — but I'll make you happy, I promise you. And you work so hard, so I've planned a little break . . ."

"Break?" she'd clung to the word. Maybe he was simply going to suggest she took some time off. "Well, I could do with a bit of time to myself but —"

"To *ourselves*, Zil. Just us. Together. Away from here. Away from everyone who knows us and the village nosey-parkering into everything. A few days together, in a little romantic hideaway in the West Country."

Oh, God!

"I know you're from Cornwall, so —"

Oh, God!

Timmy had smiled at her. "And I thought you'd always hankered after a bit of Frenchman's Creek, so I've phoned this place in Fowey and —"

202

No way! Not Cornwall! Not ever! Not with Timmy — and not on her own — just NO!

"We can't go away," Zillah had said, feeling the panic rising in her throat. "Not together. Not to Cornwall. Not both at the same time. I mean, who would look after the pub?"

"The brewery'll put relief people in. And it'd only be for a long weekend. Even if they were awful they'd hardly bankrupt us. See? There's nothing stopping us."

Oh, but there was. Cornwall was the last place on earth she wanted to go. Anywhere else might just be OK, with Timmy as a good platonic friend. But Cornwall with Timmy as a besotted lover? Her two worst nightmares. It simply couldn't happen.

"It's all booked, Zil." Timmy had resumed pushing colourful bottles of Irn Bru and WKD Blue into the fridge. "All paid for. In less than a twinkling, so to speak. Looked up on the Internet, contacted on the mobile, paid for on the plastic. Magic, eh?"

Magic, indeed.

Timmy had turned his attention to a selection of Vodka Kicks. "I thought we could go for four days at the end of September. After Harvest Moon. Plenty of time for you to plan your holiday wardrobe, eh?"

Zillah had grabbed handfuls of pint mugs and thrust them onto the overhead shelves. At least there was a bit of a lifeline. It was still only July. She had plenty of time to find a cast-iron reason not to go without hurting Timmy too much. Didn't she?

"Ah, you'll have to thank young Amber as well as Cassiopeia for pulling this off." Timmy had poured two glasses of house red and pushed one along the bar towards her.

"Amber? Why? What did she have to do with it?"

"Amber was a star. She looked all these places up on the Internet for me. You know how jackass-brained I am with technology. I'd never have found them in a million years. She got all the details of suitable venues and I rang them straight away. The one in Fowey was heaven-sent. Cassiopeia might have answered my wish, but I couldn't have done it without Amber."

Zillah had said nothing. She'd left the wine untouched. She'd decided to kill Amber.

Now she sipped her tea, her eyes gritty through lack of sleep, her brain churning. Pike, having finished his breakfast, nudged the cats out of the way and slumped onto her feet in the sun. Gwyneth and Big Ida were still mulling over the possibilities of making an early private plea to Leo for refreshment. All normal stuff. As it was nearly every summer morning.

Only this morning was different. This morning she'd have to make one of the biggest decisions of her life.

She stared out across the village green to The Weasel and Bucket, pretty as a chocolate box, swathed in a delicate rising heat-haze. The rooms in the ivied eaves had their blinds still drawn. One of those was Timmy's bedroom and if she said yes to him, she knew it could be hers too. Or maybe Timmy would want to live with her in Chrysalis?

God, no! That was unthinkable.

Chrysalis was her own shell, her haven. The place where she could be herself. She'd created it from love.

It could only be shared with love. And she didn't love Timmy.

But it wouldn't be fair to keep Timmy hanging on. She definitely wasn't going to Fowey and she'd have to tell him immediately, and then probably leave The Weasel and Bucket, maybe even move away from Fiddlesticks.

No, that was unthinkable, too. But then so was the alternative.

If she agreed to go away with Timmy, even if it wasn't Cornwall, she'd be agreeing to so much more. He'd love her, cherish her, give her security for the rest of her life. But she'd never love him in return. And even if he was prepared to accept that, she wasn't. Having loved once, she simply couldn't spend what was left of her life with a pale imitation. She'd rather live alone and just remember how it had been once when she was young.

Lots of women — and men — would be delighted to settle for companionship and security in their autumn years, but she simply couldn't.

She'd kill Amber.

"Is Amber awake yet?" She looked at Gwyneth. "I need to speak to her."

"She's up and gone long since." Gwyneth swung her legs backwards and forwards on the bench like a child on a swing. "Had a phone call from Mitzi at the crack of dawn. About work. Sadly, as young Mitzi hasn't got the van insured yet, Amber's had to go into Hazy Hassocks on the bus."

Usually the news that someone had had to take the round-village bus would have elicited all Zillah's sympathy. Right now, she felt Amber deserved it.

"Oh, right. Has she got a mobile with her?"

"No, duck, She don't use it no more. She says she can't see why she ever thought it was so vital."

Zillah shrugged. "OK. But when she gets back can you tell her I'd like to see her."

Gwyneth nodded. "About your Lewis being with Sukie last night, is it? Amber did seem a bit distracted when she came home after Cassiopeia's."

If only it was about something *sortable* like Lewis and Sukie. If only the clock could be turned back and all she had to worry about was Lewis's unsuitable liaisons. If only.

"Nothing to do with Lewis and Sukie," Zillah said shortly. "This is about something far, far more important."

Sitting on the early morning bus as it trundled through a myriad identical, sun-misted, green-tunnelled lanes, Amber felt as if she were in a time-machine.

A time-machine would be very welcome, to be honest. Something that could whisk her back — oooh, just a few hours to last night, to the moment when Jem gave her the pentangle. Just before Lewis arrived with Sukie.

Damn, damn, damn and sod!

She stared out of the windows at the bucolic beauty and sighed heavily. Lewis disinterested and unattached had been a challenge; Lewis disinterested and entwined round Sukie the Irish Witch was a kick in the teeth. Not that Amber was sure Sukie was Irish of course, but with that glorious Corrs colouring it was odds-on, surely?

Sod it!

And now she'd have to forget about it and concentrate on some silly coffee morning for Mitzi.

"Sorry if I've woken you, love," Mitzi had said breathlessly over the phone at about half-past five. "But I need you over here as early as possible this morning. Change of plan." Then there'd been a lot of muffled shrieking and laughing and staccato conversation in the background and Mitzi had giggled excitedly.

Amber could only imagine it had had something to do with the dead sexy dentist.

"Sorry," Mitzi had said eventually, sounding a little intoxicated. "Look, Amber, love, just get here as soon as you can. I'll explain then. No time now. Too much going on. Is that OK? Thanks, you're an angel . . ."

So Amber had washed, dressed quickly in her work clothes, rushed through mascara and lip gloss, screwed her hair up in a scrunchie, tugged everything out of the pockets of last night's jeans, grabbed her purse and her handbag, and had been at the Fiddlesticks bus stop within half an hour of the phone call.

The single-decker suddenly stood on its brakes and Amber found herself propelled forward. It was only her lightning reflexes that prevented her being hurled onto the lap of the man in front of her who had what she'd first thought was a dead mole tucked into the collar of his shirt, but which, after several minutes of the journey, she'd decided was back hair.

If her previous bus trip to Hazy Hassocks had been a bit odd, this one was far more disturbing.

The bus had collected little knots of people from hamlets and villages and simply at various spots along the road where would-be passengers waved their arms and leapt into the bus's path. The passengers all seemed to know one another and immediately picked up on conversations halfway through. And they had their own seats.

"You can't sit there, duck!" A woman dressed in a union jack two-piece and plimsolls screeched as Amber had found an empty space. "That's Sandra's seat!"

"Oh, right . . . sorry . . ." Amber had stumbled into another vacant seat further up the bus.

"Not there!" A middle-aged man who had one long eyebrow and bits of bloodied lavatory paper dotted about his chin, snapped. "Mr Emsworth always sits there."

"Right . . ." Amber had swayed even further along and looked hopefully at a vacant seat towards the rear. "Anyone sitting here?"

"Do it look like it?" Across the aisle, a box-shaped lady with post-menopausal acne and a moustache, pursed her lips. "It's empty, innit?"

As the bus turned a particularly sharp corner at that point, Amber found herself catapulted into the seat.

Mrs Spotty-Moustache glared across at her. "And don't sit by the window. Our Flintlock always sits opposite me. He gets on just afore Bagley and he gets travel sick if he can't see out."

Our Flintlock, thin and grubby and with a strange glint in his eyes, galloped onto the bus at the Bagley stop, scrambled over Amber and beamed at Mrs Spotty-Moustache. "Morning, our Peaches."

Peaches?

Amber tried not to breathe in as Flintlock and Peaches updated family information across her. Peaches clearly chewed recreational garlic. Flintlock probably hadn't been in close contact with deodorant since 1967.

By the time the bus reached the outskirts of Hazy Hassocks, none of the passengers had shown the slightest inclination to leave, and neither of the seats reserved for Sandra or Mr Emsworth had been taken.

"You could 'ave sat down there," Flintlock nodded down the bus, "if you'd wanted. Sandra's on holiday in Bulawayo and Siddy Emsworth died last Feb."

Amber stood up as the bus careered towards Hazy Hassocks High Street. Last time, she'd got off outside The Faery Glen pub and made her way to Mitzi's shed. It hadn't taken long at all.

"If you wants the library end, you don't want to get off 'ere," the woman in the Union Jack two-piece bellowed down the bus. "It's quicker to wait until you gets past Big Sava."

Amber sat down again.

Several shops including Big Sava flashed past.

"Missed it!" Peaches shrilled. "You should 'ave got off at the pub."

Amber pinballed down the aisle and fetched up by the driver. "Er, can you stop somewhere soon, please? Near the library?"

"We don't stop near the library!" the bus chorused.

"You'll have to wait until we reaches the dental surgery now, sweetheart," the driver grinned. "And a word of advice if you travels with us again — you don't want to take no notice of them back there. They're all barking."

Once safely on High Street terra firma with everyone on the bus waving to her as they sped away, Amber vowed never, ever to take public transport again. She'd have to hope Mitzi insured the Hubble Bubble van sooner rather than later.

The shed shimmered in the morning heat. The workaday traffic crawled along the High Street adding to the hazy effect. Amber, exhausted and irritable after a fairly sleepless night and the early start, tried the door.

It was locked. As there wasn't a bell or a knocker, she rapped smartly on the flaking green paintwork with her fist.

The door creaked open a fraction and Amber caught a glimpse of a thin, elderly face topped by a vibrant plastic cycle helmet.

"Yes?"

"It's me. Amber. Mitzi asked me to come into work early and —"

The door was pulled open.

"Hello, young Amber. Come along in. Do you remember me? We met at Bertha Hopkins' funeral?"

Amber smiled at the elderly lady. Vaguely. One of Mitzi's neighbours? Name escaped her. The cycle helmet never would. Mitzi had explained how the

Banding sisters had been told months ago, by her daughter's paramedic boyfriend, that cycle helmets could save lives, and had taken to wearing them constantly ever since, even though neither of them had a bicycle.

"Lavender Banding." She held out a wizened hand, liver-spotted and recently in close proximity with marmalade. "I'm looking after things this end while my sister Lobelia deals with the other things back at the house. Feeding Richard and Judy, things like that."

"Richard and Judy? Er — are they staying with Mitzi?"

"They live with her, silly."

"Er — do they?" Humour her, Amber thought swiftly, in case she reaches for the bread knife. "Really? I thought they lived in London."

"No, bless you. They've always lived with Mitzi. Well, since she rescued them from the garage, of course."

Oh, of course.

"And — um — Lobelia's feeding them? Can't they get their own breakfast then?"

"Of course not!" Lavender's cycle helmet nodded in scorn. "How are they going to get their little paws round the tin opener, for heavens sake?"

Paws?

Lavender chuckled. "They're very spoiled cats are Richard and Judy."

Amber breathed a sigh of relief. "Ah, yes, of course — er so Mitzi isn't here, then?"

"No. That's why I am. She's left you a list. She says it's only a very little soirée this morning and you're a capable girl and —" Lavender rummaged in her pockets and produced a much folded piece of paper. "Here we are . . . Young Mitzi said she's very sorry but she knows you'll understand."

Amber unfolded the paper.

Amber — sorry about this. Lav will explain. The van's parked out the back. Keys on the shelf above the microwave. Temporary cover note in the glove box. The food is on the third shelf down in the biggest freezer. Give it a couple of hours to defrost. There are chilled things in the fridge. All marked up for today's customer: HHLL. The address is in the diary. If you could get there about 10.30 to set up that'd be perfect. Thanks, darling. I owe you one.
Loads of love, Mitzi xxxxxx

Amber folded the paper again. OK, it all sounded straight forward and at least she had the van. She'd coped with more difficult things than this, and if — big if of course — she was going to make her permanent home in Fiddlesticks and her career with Hubble Bubble she'd have to go solo at some point, wouldn't she?

"Is it all straightforward?" Lavender peered at her. "Not too complicated?"

"No, it's fine, thanks. I'll just have to find what I need and get the plates and doilies and napkins sorted out. It shouldn't take too long. Er — do you mind

212

hanging on while I do it, then you can lock up behind me? Um — is Mitzi ill?"

Mitzi certainly hadn't sounded ill over the phone. If she'd taken to her bed it had to be more to do with that fabulous dentist than a virus.

"She's gone to the hospital but she isn't ill," Lavender chortled. "She's gone to be with her daughter, Doll."

"Her daughter? Goodness — what happened?"

"Doll started her pains in the early hours. She's having her baby. It's a few weeks early." Lavender beamed proudly. "We're going to be a grandmother!"

CHAPTER
EIGHTEEN

Seventh Star

"Can I come in?" Zillah popped her head round the door of the Hayfields flat. "Er — not interrupting anything, I hope?"

"Nothing carnal," Lewis grinned. "Unfortunately. Great to see you. This is a rare treat, Ma. Tea? Coffee? Something stronger?"

"If it wasn't ten in the morning I'd go for a double helping of the last, but coffee will be fine, thanks. Jem not here?"

"Just dropped him off at the joinery. His hangover was a corker. And in this heat I pity the poor bloke who's supervising him on planing and sanding this morning. Won't be long."

Zillah watched her son, long legged in denim, move with that heart-tuggingly familiar inherited stride into the small kitchen, then having cleared a pile of washed but unironed jeans and T-shirts to one side, flopped onto the sofa.

The flat, on the ground floor of Hayfields, was a bloke's paradise. Both Lewis's and Jem's clothes were strewn everywhere, lads' mags were discarded across the tables, beer cans and pizza boxes made an artistic statement by the fireplace, and the room was dominated by a plasma screen and dvd player, and a pile of silver stereo equipment that wouldn't have looked out of place in NASA. There were no feminine touches at all — no cushions or pictures or plants — nothing, which to Zillah would have softened the edges and made it a cosy home.

However, the sun-sprinkled view from the window across Hayfields' extensive and well-stocked gardens running down to the tree-fringed river, was sublime.

"Thanks love." She took the mug, not looking too closely. Neither Jem nor Lewis were too careful about washing up, despite the dishwasher installed in the tiny kitchen. She knew they relied on Fern, Win or Martha, Hayfields' House Mother, to pick up on the worst of their lack of domesticity.

"So? Is this simply a social call?" Lewis slumped onto the low sofa beside her with an easy grace. "Or have you come to check on whether Sukie stayed for bed and breakfast?"

Zillah sipped her coffee. "Don't be sarcastic."

Lewis raised his eyebrows. "Sarcastic? You've been the morality police for as long as I can remember. You must be the only ma in the world who actually wants her son to find a nice girl and settle down sooner rather than later."

She grinned at him. "Well, is she? A nice girl?"

"Very. I like her a lot. We had a great time last night. And disappointingly virtuous. I walked her home to Bagley as I'd drunk too much to drive, and left her with a chaste peck on her doorstep. We may or may not see one another again depending on who else crosses our paths in the meantime. We might meet up for a drink if and when we're both free. All very friendly and casual. There — full story. Maternal curiosity satisfied?"

"Not really," Zillah stared out of the window. "But it'll have to do."

"So, why are you really here?"

She told him. She'd realised as she'd walked from Chrysalis Cottage that he was the only person in the whole world that she could tell. She had plenty of friends, good friends, but no one else — apart maybe from Mitzi — who would understand. Of course she couldn't tell him why Timmy's choice of Cornwall made it a doubly awful idea, and hoped he wouldn't ask.

"Bummer," Lewis sighed when she'd finished. "But wouldn't you like to return to the land of your fathers? OK! I gather from the 'I'd rather pull my toenails out with rusty pliers' look that that's a no. Sometimes, I wish you'd tell me about Cornwall —"

"Nothing to tell," Zillah said quickly, "nothing at all. It's where I was born and I left and I never, ever want to go back."

They stared at one another for a moment.

Lewis shrugged. "OK — but I don't think you should be too hard on Amber in all this. It was hardly her fault. She only did what Timmy asked her. She's a newcomer so she doesn't know anything about the set-up between you, does she? And she certainly wouldn't know about Cornwall . . . She has no idea that you don't reciprocate Timmy's feelings, either. She probably thought it was a dead romantic thing to be doing — especially on Cassiopeia's."

216

"You would defend her." Zillah placed her empty mug strategically over a magazine cover displaying more of Jodie Marsh than she wanted or needed to see. "But, maybe you're right . . . Still, that doesn't change the situation, does it? What the hell am I going to do?"

"Tell him no," Lewis smiled at her. "Now — before he makes any more plans. Let him down gently, which you will anyway, but tell him. Thanks, and you're very flattered but you simply can't accept. He'll be hurt — but not half as much as he will be if you play him along and then tell him later. And if you accept this dirty weekend —"

"It's not a dirty weekend!"

"Whatever —" he grinned "— but if you agree to go then you'll be giving him false hope. Unless you're prepared to accept the whole package of course."

"I'm not. I can't. But if I tell him, then we can't go on working together, can we? He'll hate me and I'll just feel sorry for him and that'll be awful. He's so nice — he deserves more than sympathy and second-best."

"So do you. And Timmy's a great bloke — but given the choice I wouldn't want him as my stepfather. Far too straight. But honestly, Ma, you knew all this, didn't you? You didn't need me to tell you."

Zillah sighed again. Lewis was right. He'd voiced her own thoughts. She knew she'd have to tell Timmy and take the consequences — even if it meant leaving the pub.

"OK," she struggled to the edge of the sofa. "Thanks. You've helped a lot. A girl needs someone to talk things over with — even if she already knows what she's going to do. But I'm still going to ask Amber to keep her nose out of things that don't concern her."

Lewis laughed. "Treat her gently, then. I think there's a well-meaning and vulnerable lady hidden underneath all that slap and phoney celeb clone glamour."

Zillah raised her eyebrows. "Is that some sort of hint that you're not as disinterested in Ms Parlsowe as you pretend to be?"

"I'm growing very fond of her if you must know." Lewis gave her a challenging look. "We get on well and she's a friend — becoming a good friend — but how can it be any more than that? I've got as many issues with relationships as you have . . ."

"I'd noticed."

"Yeah, well — you know my reputation — none better. So many girls, so little time and all that . . . What do you want me to say? Amber is nothing special to me? Isn't that what you want me to say? She surely can't be your idea of the ideal permanent fixture? And what do I know about permanent fixtures anyway? Love 'em and leave 'em, that's what I do best." Lewis stood up and pulled a quizzical face at her. "Like mother like son, I guess. After all, isn't that what you did with my father?"

Amber was practically tearing out her scrunchied hair. The room was stifling, the food, so carefully arrayed, was becoming warm and runny, and the HHLL were, well, simply hell.

218

Having carried out Mitzi's instructions to the letter, she'd made several dummy runs round the quieter Hazy Hassocks roads, getting used to driving again, and found the Hubble Bubble van reasonably easy to handle and having had no difficulty locating the address, parking or unloading, the rest had so far been a nightmare of cliched proportions.

HHLL were Hazy Hassocks Literary Ladies. A writers' circle, they apparently met monthly in one another's homes to discuss their work in progress, the latest literary gossip, and, most importantly, those unfortunate members of the HHLL who weren't in attendance that day.

"Put the food in the conservatory, dear," today's hostess, a vision in lime-green Tricel, her pepper and salt hair held up in a scary number of diamanté slides, had looked down flared nostrils at Amber. "We'll be in the library until eleven. There are only four of us owing to holidays. A small but select gathering of our finest writers. You make coffee for four, and we'll come through for the nibbles when we're finished. You were told about serving us coffee at eleven, weren't you?"

Amber hadn't been, but she nodded.

"I must say I'm rather annoyed that Mitzi sent an underling. I'm the first of our little group to bring in outside caterers — quite a coup — and I had hoped for the organ grinder, if you get my drift."

Amber had already explained about Mitzi's happy and unexpected domestic crisis. The HHLL seemed to be of the opinion that Doll should have kept her legs crossed.

Now it was nearly half past eleven; coffee, which Amber had made in the DIY flat-pack kitchen, had been served in the library — a very small annexe to the living room with three bookcases, which was probably the dining room in real life — and still the HHLL hadn't appeared for nibbles.

The conservatory, a south-facing lean-to with a corrugated plastic roof, was like a sweat-box. Amber huddled into the one patch of shade, perspiration trickling under her T-shirt, praying that her deodorant was up to the job.

The Angelica Angels were wilting; the Saffron and Lemon Lumps had run into a dung-coloured mush; the Bronte Buns (Mitzi's interpretation of her grandmother's wisdom-giving recipe especially for the literary occasion) simmered.

So did Amber.

It was one of those moments when she wished she smoked. It would give her something to do with her hands. The insulated cool box which held Mitzi's pièce de résistance with a scribbled note: "*Ginger Janite Cake — this has been rechristened and reworked for the occasion. It was originally meant to produce total honesty and loosen inhibitions, but hopefully it'll simply enhance their literary prowess, although I may have overdone the bodhi leaves. Time will tell . . . To work properly they're supposed to chew the cake then spit it out but best not tell them that as it could lead to misunderstandings and a mess. Leave this right until last — and only give them a very small slice each — it's very powerful*" — had several ice packs. Amber knew that if the HHLL didn't show up soon she'd nick a couple of them and shove them down her T-shirt.

Amber surprised herself with the ease with which she now almost accepted that Mitzi's recipes might well have magical properties. Surely there were ancient tribes who still brought on hallucinatory experiences and mass trances simply by chewing leaves? Wasn't this the same sort of thing on a Berkshire basis?

She'd watch the effects of eating the Ginger Janite Cake on the HHLL with interest. The proof of the pudding might just sway her.

The sweat was now making her scrunchied hair itch, little rivulets trickled and settled under Jem's wooden pentangle, and beads of moisture had gathered malevolently on her upper lip. She scrabbled irritably in her bag for a tissue. God — what the hell had she got in here? Receipts and shopping lists and reams of paper but not a single tissue.

Ordinarily she'd use one of the Hubble Bubble dark-green paper napkins but Mitzi had warned that this batch were of an inferior quality and left a nasty stain when damp. It'd have to be kitchen roll pinched from the flat-pack kitchen, then, and plenty of it. Maybe it would be considered unprofessional, but it was all the HHLL deserved for keeping her in this sauna.

Then she grinned. One of the bits of paper, dragged from last night's jeans and pushed into her bag, had all the contact numbers for the soul bands she wanted to contact for Harvest Moon. If only she'd charged her mobile she could get that out of the way while she was waiting for the HHLL to emerge.

Oh, damn — now she'd have to wait until she got back to Fiddlesticks and she really wanted something to get her teeth into, especially as Lewis was no doubt romping at this very moment with the delectable Sukie. She needed something, well, challenging, to take her mind off that particular image — and hmmm . . . Amber remembered, as well as paper towels, there'd been a telephone in the kitchen, hadn't there?

Oh, what the heck.

Darting out of the patch of shade and through the intense heat of the lean-to, Amber poked her head round the library door.

The HHLL didn't break stride.

". . . and of course we all know how she got published, don't we?"

"Well, seeing that she can't string two words together it has to be a bung . . ."

"Bung? Her agent's sleeping with her editor, darling!"

"But they're both female."

"Precisely."

"Excuse me," Amber interrupted bravely. "How long do you think you'll be? Only the food is out and it's very hot in the lean-to —"

"Conservatory!"

"Er — yes, well — and I just wondered . . ."

"We're creative," a miserable woman with a little girl ponytail, sparkly jeans and a Barbie pink T-shirt which

222

would have looked lovely on someone four decades younger, said mournfully. "You can't rush creativity."

"Er — no. I don't suppose you can." Amber gave what she hoped was a charming smile in the direction of the HHLL hostess. "Um — please — would it be OK if I used your telephone for a moment? I'll pay, of course."

"Oh, you most certainly will. And yes, if you must, but do use the kitchen extension — I don't want you *prying*. There's a box on the shelf for the purpose of money — and none of the foreign currency like that bloke who came to check the drains diddled me with, thank you very much. But don't you have a mobile? Is it urgent?" Pausing for breath, the HHLL hostess drew her lips up to her nostrils. Affronted, they sprang apart. "Vital? Local?"

"No. Yes. Yes again, and absolutely."

The last one wasn't true but Amber no longer cared. Two out of three and all that.

"Very well, but make it brief and don't forget to pay and don't spend all day out there. We're nearly finished here and we'll expect you to circulate with the nibbles. I've paid for waitress service and I expect to get it."

Amber smiled her thanks and backed out of the room, but not before she caught the next slice of HHLL invective.

"Anyway, you do know that she's up for an award with her latest, don't you?"

"No!"

"Yes, indeed. I've got it on the best possible authority that her connections paid a fortune to the judges, of course."

"Well, they'd have to. It couldn't get there on merit. But — surely it isn't the one where —"

"Yes it is — four hundred pages of badly written crap about expat in-breeds conveniently living the life of Reilly on fresh air, for heaven's sake — not a job among 'em! — on a remote tropical island and they all have some sort of disability or terminal illness and half of them are related but they still all fall in love and then die in the most gruesome circumstances — and — and then she has the *temerity* to market it as a romantic comedy . . ."

The scorching midday sun shimmered across a still hungover Fiddlesticks as Zillah made her way towards The Weasel and Bucket. She felt truly awful. Doubly so now since she'd had the row with Lewis. Oh, God. How had it all got so out of hand?

Her long skirt dragged through the grass, the remaining moisture at the roots soaking the purple hem and making her toes slide inside her flat sandals. She couldn't remember ever falling out with Lewis before. Not over something major like this. He'd been such an easy child, they'd always been friends, there'd never been any of the real bust-ups which other mothers seemed to have experienced with their children. Not even when he was a teenager. Of course, there had been moments — but nothing like this.

Oh, why hadn't she been honest with him from the start?

Why had she assumed that he'd understand about his father? Why had she always thought it best that he hadn't known? Simply because she'd chosen to wipe it out of her life, she'd assumed that he would be happy with her decision. And it was one of those things — the longer you left it, the bigger it became, the more difficult to talk about.

Now, she realised, he'd been harbouring all the wrong impressions, seeing her as the villain of the piece: The dumper rather than the dumpee. Seeing her possibly as some sort of flighty floozy who couldn't, or wouldn't stay the relationship course. He'd probably built up this picture of his father, heartbroken at Zillah's defection, weeping nightly over an ancient dog-eared photograph, when of course it had been exactly the other way round.

"Hiya!" Fern, bare legged in a short tight white skirt and an even tighter black T-shirt, bounced up beside her. "I've been trying to catch you up ever since Hayfields. Have you been to see Lewis?"

Zillah nodded. She didn't want Fern's exuberant, vital company at the moment.

"Thought so." Fern continued to grin, all big teeth and bursting-with-vitality glow. "He had a face like a smacked arse when I passed him just now. Have you had a row?"

"No," Zillah sighed. "Not really. Look, Fern, I don't really want to talk about it, OK?"

"Whatever," Fern beamed. "Was it about him and Sukie? Because if it was —"

"Fern!"

"Sorry." She looked anything but. "Off to work, are you?"

Zillah nodded.

"Likely I'll be your first customer, then. I'm going to quench my thirst, too. The Motions have just collected Win so I've got a few hours free. It's her work day for cleaning their brass this morning — you know how much she loves cleaning. She'd do it for nothing, but we don't let the Motions know that, of course. Miserable as sin because she had too much to drink last night. I thought I'd be wrecked too, but I feel great — maybe Cassiopeia will answer me this year . . . Er — and perhaps I shouldn't be saying anything about it . . . Still, I had a great time. Did you? Oh, sorry again — you really don't want to hear all this do you?"

"Not really."

The Weasel and Bucket was waking up as they approached across the green. Timmy was unfurling the umbrellas over the trestles and looked up, grinning at them both.

"A sight for sore eyes! My two favourite ladies! Cassiopeia must have been working overtime last night."

Zillah groaned quietly.

Fern giggled. "You must have read my mind, Timmy . . ."

Zillah looked at her — did Fern fancy Timmy, then? Surely not. He was an entire generation older than her and she'd never given any indication . . . Well, she was always in the pub, of course, but that was because she had a healthy appetite for Andromeda Ale and anything else alcoholic, and it was the village meeting place and — Fern? Fancying Timmy? No, surely not.

Well, it certainly wasn't reciprocated, that was for sure. Poor Fern, poor Timmy, poor her — not to mention Lewis — what a stupid mess this love stuff was.

Zillah watched Timmy as he straightened up, surveying the tables, checking that everything was shipshape for his lunchtime clientele. Oh why, oh why couldn't she be going to give him the answer he wanted.

"OK, Zil?"

"Fine," she tried to smile, to look natural. "Just tired."

"Not surprised," Timmy grinned. "It was a late finish. Good night, though."

"Timmy — can we talk?"

"Course. Look, come on through to the kitchen and I'll pour you something awash with ice cubes before the ravening hordes start arriving." He stared up at the sky. "Forecast is for temperatures in the nineties today. Can't be far off that now."

"Any chance of a quickie before you disappear?" Fern chuckled.

"That would be liquid refreshment, would it?" Timmy beamed at her. "You wouldn't be proposition-ing me, by any chance would you?"

Fern blushed. "Me? Er — no — I mean, no — of course not. Er — I just thought if you and Zil were going to be talking I'd like to get my drink in first and —"

"Damn," Timmy gave a mock sigh. "For one minute there I thought my luck was in."

Zillah frowned. Was he *flirting*? With *Fern*?

What the heck was going on?

In the stiflingly hot kitchen, Amber replaced the telephone receiver, slipped far more coins than were necessary into the gruesome shell-encrusted money box — a present from Teignmouth — and sighed.

Well, that was that, then. Every one of the agents she'd telephoned, who represented the old soul bands on her list, had told her their clients were either dead, in detox, in prison, or ludicrously expensive to hire. Mona Jupp and Goff Briggs would never fork out even the merest fraction of the cheapest fee she'd been quoted for live music on Harvest Moon.

"What you want, doll," the last nasal voice with the irritating, rising-last-syllable inflection had informed her, "is a tribute band? We can do you a nice line in soul tributes? How d'you fancy Beano Dashington and the Flim-Flam Band?"

"Er — not a lot . . . Who are they tributing?"

"Geno Washington and the Ram-Jam Band, doll? For heaven's sake!"

Ah, yes, she'd heard of them. They were on her list culled from Zillah's LP collection. She'd already phoned their contacts. Still alive and touring but way,

way too expensive. And she couldn't, really couldn't, inflict Fiddlesticks with someone who wasn't anyone calling themselves Beano.

"They're very good, doll?" The nasal voice said inquiringly. "Beano is off the sauce now. And you can hardly notice his surgery. And the rumours about the drummer and the all-girl marching band in that caravan at Cleethorpes were exaggerated. What do you say?"

She'd said thanks but no thanks and hung up.

So, that was it. There was one number left on her list — but it was local. Winterbrook. Surely any entertainment agency working in a backwater couldn't offer anything better than those in London? She could hear the HHLL still chattering shrilly in the library. Oh, why not?

Shoving some more money into Teignmouth's gaping mouth, she punched out the final number.

"Retro Music and Theatre, Winterbrook, Paris, New York," a cheerful Berkshire accent informed her. "How may I help you, duck?"

For the umpteenth time, Amber explained her mission.

"Ah, right, duck . . . look, why don't you pop over soon as. I can show you the entire retro client list. I'm sure we'll have something to suit. Are you local now?"

"Yes, but I'm working. I'm free this afternoon though."

"Lovely. We're on the main drag. Next to the bank. Can't miss us. Knock three times and ask for Freddo,

OK? About three-ish? Great, duck. Look forward to it. 'Bye!"

"I say!" the HHLL hostess screamed from the hall. "I say! Waitress! We're ready now!"

The lean-to throbbed with midday heat. All four literary ladies were looking rather moist and uncomfortable. Two of them were eating the Bronte Buns with spoons.

"They've gorn orf," a chunky woman whose make-up had run into her wrinkles and stayed there, brayed, spraying the hostess with slurry. "I say, Georgette, they've gorn orf!"

Georgette? Amber blinked.

"It's not her real name," the little-girlie woman whispered. "Her real name is Doris. She didn't think Doris was literary enough so she calls herself Georgette Austen."

"Lovely. Most original. And is that the name her books are published under?" Amber smiled her very best professional-under-duress smile as Mitzi had shown her, while handing round napkins and the least lopsided of the remaining Angelica Angels.

"Books? What books? She's never had anything published."

"Hasn't she? Oh, but I thought . . . that is, I got the impression . . ."

"We're aspiring," the little-girlie lisped. "On the cusp. We've written several massively commercial volumes between us but as yet we're unpublished. It's all so unfair, of course. So many rubbish books out there by atrocious authors, when we're all talented and

230

write much, much better stuff — and so far not a sniff of interest."

"Not fair, no, I can see that," Amber murmured, circulating as obsequiously as the cramped space would allow. "Another Saffron and Lemon Lump, anyone? There's plenty here."

The HHLL looked as though what they really needed was an ice-cold plunge pool, but to give them their due, they munched on regardless.

As none of them seemed to be overtaken by wild urges to shed their clothes or anything over the top, Amber assumed that this lot of Mitzi's recipes contained subdued herbs suitable for soothing the fevered brows of unpublished novelists. Just as well, she thought. There was enough pent-up anger and resentment bubbling under those well-bred vowels without a bit of hedge-witchery thrown in to fuel the fire.

Glancing to make sure the plates were empty and the wine glasses filled — mean so and sos hadn't even offered her so much as a slurp of chilled white — she dived into the cool box for the Ginger Janite Cake and started to slice.

"No, no, no!" Georgette-Doris screamed. "Give it some welly, girl! Not little slivers like that! You've had the pleasure of my telephone and had absolutely nothing to do for hours — the least you can do is give us a decent chunk."

Gripping the knife and willing herself not to run banshee-like at Georgette-Doris's throat, Amber hacked the Ginger Janite Cake into four massive squares. Still smiling manfully, she handed it round, making sure the requisite napkin was folded neatly on the edge of each plate.

None of the HHLL said thank you.

Amber, her mind on the forthcoming meeting with Freddo in the sure and certain knowledge that his retro bands would be along the lines of Winterbrook's answer to the Wurzels, packed up the debris of the literary lunch as the ladies chomped and mopped. She wondered if she should mention to the HHLL that they all had green faces thanks to the less-than-perfect napkins and the heat.

Nah, she thought, stacking plates into the boxes, best leave it. It had all gone so well. Mitzi would be delighted. No hitches whatsoever.

"Tart!" The chunky woman suddenly screamed at Georgette-Doris. "Talentless tart!"

"Bitch!" Little Girlie rounded on Chunky. "Your last reading from your work in progress was remorseless drivel! My dyslexic grandson could have produced better."

"Whey-faced cow!" The up-until-then-silent fourth literary lady stamped a massive foot. "How dare you! We have to listen to you drone on and on about your turgid characters and we all know you'll never be published in a million, zillion aeons!"

"Sod you lot!" Georgette-Doris, her inner-bitch well and truly unleashed, shrieked, dabbing at her mouth with a napkin and emerging with emerald lips. "I'm the only one here with a modicum of talent. You all do commercial fiction. *I'm* literary . . ."

"Illiterate, you mean, you dozy bat!" Little-Girlie splattered crumbs of Janite cake over the lean-to. "And probably illegitimate to boot!"

"Whoo-wooo-wooo!" Chunky wailed. "Bitch, cow, bastard, tart! Unimaginative, boring, derivative — ouch!"

The large silent lady had punched her.

Little-Girlie and Georgette-Doris screamed with laughter and piled into the fray.

Amber, diving out of the way, hastily packed up the remainder of the literary lunch as the HHLL fought like hellcats on the floor of the lean-to. She imagined the Ginger Janite had been a touch too heavy on the bodhi leaves as Mitzi had anticipated.

"Er —" she coughed politely at the heaving, punching bodies rolling across the lean-to floor, "I'm leaving now."

"Sod off!" the HHLL snarled in unison, not missing a punch.

Amber, giggling, fled.

Shoving everything into the back of the van, she drove away from the demure semi as fast as residential double-parking would allow.

Still laughing, she stopped at traffic lights and peered up at the deep-blue sky through the windscreen. "I know you're up there somewhere, Cassiopeia, lass, even if I can't see you. Well, you're going to have to pull out all the astral magic stops to beat that bit of herbal witchery. So — what have you got up your celestial sleeve, eh? It's going to have to be pretty spectacular to convince me that star-wishing is more powerful than Mitzi's magic, I can tell you . . ."

CHAPTER
NINETEEN

Swinging on a Star

Darting in and out of The Weasel and Bucket with non-stop plates of food and trays of iced drinks, Zillah really didn't have time to dwell on anything other than the ever-demanding and steadily increasing river of customers. Timmy's forecast had been correct and Fiddlesticks shimmered in sky-high temperatures. The whole village seemed to have decided that after the excesses of the night before, preparing lunch or making their own cold drinks was way beyond them.

Repetitive cries of "When you've got a minute, duck!" and "Over here, Zil, love!" from both inside and outside the pub, meant she could concentrate on nothing else.

"Handy I turned up when I did this morning, wasn't it?" Fern beamed from behind the bar as Zillah rushed in with an order for the Motions. "I've always wanted to be a barmaid. Next!"

Zillah, balancing three pints of Hearty Hercules and a box of matches on the tray, shoved her way into the kitchen. "Three ploughman's for the Motions, please. Heavy on the pickle for Perpetua."

"Gotcha," Timmy grinned, working like summer lightning round his kitchen table. "Feeling better now, love?"

Zillah shrugged as she balanced the three plates on the tray and managed to get pickle on her thumb. Better? Not really. She'd probably alienated Lewis forever, and she still had to tell Timmy that the Fowey love-nest was a non-starter. Not that the latter, oddly, seemed to be bothering him much.

She backed out of the kitchen with the tray, manoeuvred her way through the jam-packed bar and out into the blinding reflected light. Negotiating the trestles was like an obstacle course, and only two of the Motions were in situ.

"Slo's slipped off to the lav," Constance informed the entire beer garden. "Call of nature — not a ciggie — we searched him before he went."

Zillah, who knew Slo kept cigarettes, lighter and Gold Spot hidden behind the gents' third cistern, said nothing.

She straightened up, pushing damp strands of hair away from her face. The stream reflected dancing crystal prisms of sunlight and young and old alike were cooling their feet in the flat brown water. She longed to join them; longed to be young and carefree again and run barefoot through damp grass at dawn and splash through the early evening shallows on deserted sunset beaches, and make love in dark and drowsy secluded places.

Oh, bugger it all!

Ignoring Billy and Dougie's insistent cries for refills of Pegasus Pale when she had a minute, Zillah slid her feet out of her flip-flops, dumped the tray on the nearest table, and trotted across the road.

Finding a patch of shade beneath one of the willows, Zillah sank down on to the soft short grass, bunched her long purple skirt above her knees, and slid her feet into the stream. Ooooh, bliss. The water was ice-cold, making her shiver with pleasure.

The waterfall of green willow fronds surrounded her, giving her much-needed seclusion: a moment of solitude and reflection. Despite the children with their fishing nets and their jam-jars splashing close to her, no one could see her. Not Timmy, not Fern, not the ever-thirsty Fiddlestickers outside the pub.

Zillah luxuriated in the cool green shade, moving her throbbing feet lazily through the translucent water. So? What on earth was going on?

When she'd arrived, with the annoyingly effervescent Fern, at The Weasel and Bucket earlier and had braced herself to tell Timmy the truth, it had all been rather odd.

"Tell you what," Timmy had said happily, "why don't we give young Fern here a try-out behind the bar as she's got a few hours to kill? We're going to be murderously busy today and —"

"But you've always said she'd be useless," Zillah had frowned. "Too dotty for words."

Timmy had shrugged, looking a bit perplexed. "I know, but a chap can change his mind, can't he? Not just a woman's prerogative, Zil, love. And you'll need a hand — you know I've been worried about you getting so tired lately. How about it, Fern? Shall we see how you get on?"

And Fern had dimpled and blushed and almost squirmed with pleasure about this about-face and said yes over and over again.

They'd agreed that it couldn't be a permanent fixture, of course, because of her job with Win at Hayfields, but on her evenings off, or the days when Win was doing her cleaning jobs, if and when it suited everyone.

Fern had practically danced on the spot and looked as though she was going to kiss Timmy and Zillah.

Timmy had looked as though he wouldn't mind at all.

And then, only after he'd given Fern a brisk and basic induction on the art of barmaiding with a lot of giggling, he'd grinned at Zillah and suggested they go through to the kitchen for their chat.

And he'd made them both iced coffee in tall glass cups and they'd perched on opposite sides of the vast spotless table and before she could say any of the words she'd been rehearsing so carefully he'd leaned forward and asked her if she'd spoken to Amber about — well — about her part in finding the Fowey love-nest.

And Zillah had said no, which Timmy had seemed relieved about, and he said that she had seemed rather annoyed about Amber and he'd hate for there to be more unpleasantness, so Zillah had assured him that she had no intention of being unpleasant, and Timmy had smiled again.

Then Zillah had bitten the bullet and said as he'd now raised the subject of Fowey . . . and haltingly she'd attempted to explain how much she liked him, how much she valued his friendship, but —

Timmy had stopped her at that point. "Please don't say the but bit, Zil, love. Let's leave it for a while, shall we? I don't want to rush anything. Oh, yes, I know I wanted to rush everything last night, but this morning — well, I've had time to think about it . . . I don't know why, can't explain it, but I feel differently this morning. More mellow. Less frantic. Must be the hangover, eh?"

And Zillah hadn't reminded him that hardly a drop of alcohol had passed his lips until the house red at closing time, but had silently thanked her lucky stars that she'd been spared from breaking his heart for a little while longer. One problem was more than enough to be going on with.

So she'd told him about the fallout with Lewis instead, and Timmy had been kind and gentle, as always, and leaned across the table again and patted her hand in a brotherly manner. And he'd suggested that maybe he should talk to Lewis, man to man, and Zillah had said no, she'd cope with it, but thanks.

And then Dougie and Billy and Goff had stomped into the pub and demanded serving and the village had cascaded in behind them doing the same, and Fern had shrieked for help, so they'd both reluctantly drained their coffee and prepared to go to work.

And that was it.

Now Zillah stared up at the cornflower blue sky, dappled through the willows, and wondered if Cassiopeia was looking down on them, hiding in her daylight haven, laughing at them as she played games with their star wishes.

"Oh get a grip," Zillah muttered to herself. "You don't believe in all that hokum, remember? You're in danger of becoming as addled as the rest of this star-struck village. If you want to change your life it's all down to you — not magic, not luck — just you."

She sighed. It seemed like a very lonely prospect.

Having returned everything to Mitzi's shed, scribbled a quick note about the HHLL, a warning about the inclusion of too many bodhi leaves in future dishes, and her best wishes on the imminent granny-hood, Amber splashed cold water on the bits of her she could reach, and still laughing intermittently, slid back into the van's scorching interior again.

Should she go back to Fiddlesticks and change or drive straight to Winterbrook and find Freddo and his Retro Musicians?

Winterbrook won.

Despite being a small country market town, Winterbrook, after Hazy Hassocks, seemed like being in the centre of Manchester again. People teemed and traffic snarled. And as Hazy Hassocks, after Fiddlesticks, had seemed like a cosmopolitan city, Amber was slightly overwhelmed. How quickly she'd forgotten what it was like to be choked by fumes and noise on a scorching summer day. How quickly had the pastoral silence and gentle air of Fiddlesticks become the norm.

She found the constant roar an assault on her senses and wondered how she'd ever been able to cope with this on a daily basis. It was scary how much Fiddlesticks now seemed like home. The occasional letters from Jemma and Emma and Kelly and Bex might as well have been sent from outer space. Their mutual points of contact were growing ever farther apart. Amber realised she was so busy with other stuff that she had no idea about the music charts, or the latest celeb gossip, the must-have fashions, or even which films or books were currently hot.

And, more to the point, she simply didn't care.

Retro Music and Theatre was, as Freddo had said, next to the bank. The name plate, along with several others, indicated that it was the world's superior entertainment's agency.

Although she was a little early, she knocked on the door.

"Yup?" A cheery voice echoed from the intercom beside her.

Amber jumped. She hadn't expected anything quite so advanced.

"It's Amber Parslowe. I rang earlier. About soul bands . . ."

"Ah, yes. The chick with the Boddington's accent. Come on up, chuck."

Hoping that the last bit of the remark had been jocular rather than mocking, Amber puffed her way up several dark, wooden staircases, past dingy doors announcing that they were fronting the establishments of debt collectors, private investigators, recruitment consultants, and financial advisors.

Retro Music and Theatre was right at the top.

"Come in, duck," Freddo chuckled as she tapped once more on the door — painted badly in silver and covered with stick-on gold stars. "Come straight in, the receptionist is at lunch. Still. Lazy cow."

Closing the door behind her, Amber blinked. The walls of the small and airless room were covered, floor to ceiling, with ancient posters and faded photos. Thousands and thousands of them. Freddo, it appeared, had contact with Cary Grant, Humphrey Bogart, John Wayne, Elvis, Katherine *and* Audrey Hepburn, Marilyn Monroe, The Beatles, Hendrix, Clark Gable.

"Through here, duck." Freddo's voice echoed from an archway into the next room. "Like I said, the receptionist is still at lunch."

Dazed, Amber crossed the room in three strides into an office decorated in much the same way with posters from cinemas and dance and music halls, the flyers promising a lot of be-bop-a-lula with Bill Haley, Gene Vincent and Little Neddy Small among starry others.

Two massive ceiling fans were working overtime. The crowded room was deliciously cool.

"By 'eck!" Freddo broke into theatrical northern once more. "You're a right bobby-dazzler and no mistake!"

Amber laughed.

Freddo, a sort of leathery, tanned, wrinkled 60s throwback with Peter Stringfellow hair and a matching grin, was lolling behind a desk piled high with higgledy-piggledy paperwork, three phones, a fax machine, two computers, an overflowing ashtray and several very dirty mugs.

Her mother, she realised, would have thought he was groovy.

"Sit down, duck — and I apologise for the piss-taking. The accent — it's lovely, really — but I used to do a bit of impressionist stuff in my heyday . . ."

Clearing a lot of ancient NMEs from the chair, Amber sat. "It's fine. I'm reet proud of being from ooop north. And your client list —" she indicated the reception area and the wall behind her "— is very impressive."

"Now who's taking the piss? OK, they're all for show — but it impresses the hell out of the punters, duck." Freddo roared with laughter. "Touché!"

They grinned at each other, friends already.

"Now." Freddo rocked dangerously on the two back legs of his chair. "You tell me exactly what you're looking for and when and why, and I'll come up with the goods. Just like that."

Amber frowned. "Was that an impression? I know — someone really, really ancient? Eric Morecambe?"

"Tommy Cooper," Freddo sighed. "Bless you, you're such a *child* . . ."

Amber went through the details again. All of them. And how she'd come by them and why she needed them and Harvest Moon, and Freddo leaned forward and listened, not interrupting.

"Sounds to me," he said, "that what you need is a sort of tribute soul band — no, don't stop me. You've probably already been offered dozens of tribute bands asking ludicrous amounts of money. They're all the rage these days, duck. But what I was thinking of was more along the lines of . . ."

He steadied the chair and delved into the piles of paper on his desk. Amber knew that he wasn't going to come up with anything useful at all, but she liked him, and she liked this room, and it was so nice to be sitting down.

". . . this!" Freddo flourished a dog-eared piece of paper under her nose. "These boys have been on my books for a long time. Always in work. Excellent musicians. All the boys played in original UK soul bands years ago when the genre was at its height. All defunct now, of course. Not really your top-notch chart acts, but some of them made records and they all had a massive following on the club and festival circuit. Real stars. They got together about ten years ago and haven't looked back. Been growing all the time. They do all the stuff you mentioned in their act. Bring the house down every time, they do."

Amber sat forward, intrigued. "And they're — er — affordable, are they?" She hadn't wanted to offend Freddo or his boys by saying cheap. "And available for the last weekend in September?"

Freddo scrabbled through the piles of paper again and emerged with a diary. "Bloody receptionist," he muttered. "Never here when you need her. My secretarial stuff needs a good seeing to too."

"Maybe when she gets back from lunch?" Amber ventured, thinking it would take an entire Brook Street army to bring about some semblance of order.

"She went to lunch in November 98," Freddo said mournfully. "I haven't seen her since."

Amber blinked.

"Oh, she's not gone missing, duck. She ran off with a magician who could pull budgies from up his sleeve and rabbits from his hat and — well, you get the picture . . . Affordable, did you say? Well, I'm sure we can negotiate a mutually agreeable fee if they're what you're looking for. Ah, right now, the boys are pretty booked up through the summer, but yes, it looks as if they'll be OK for your Harvest Moon thing. Shall I pencil it in?"

Amber nodded, deciding not to say that she hadn't actually mentioned paying for live music to anyone else in Fiddlesticks yet.

"Yes, please — thanks . . . er, that is — look, I don't want to be rude, but they must be pretty old and — well, I mean what guarantee would we have that they can actually stand unaided — let alone sing and play at the same time?"

Freddo chuckled hugely. "Clever girl! Always test the merchandise before purchasing! You wouldn't be looking for a job, would you?"

"Not at the moment, no. Thanks, all the same. So, do you have a video of — er — the boys or something?"

"I can do better than that, duck. I can give you a couple of agency passes to their next gig. Then you can go along incognito like, see if you like them and if they're suitable, and I'll arrange for you to go backstage and meet them afterwards too if you like, so you can get up close and personal. How's that sound?"

The up close and personal sounded a bit scary, Amber thought, but the rest was great. "Sounds brilliant. Thanks. Is the gig at a big concert hall? Theatre? In London? Soon?"

"Winterbrook Masonic Hall. Saturday week. Ruby Wedding Anniversary for Joyce and Brian Nixon."

Amber tried not to let her disappointment show.

"If they're that good — er — how come they're still doing local parties and stuff?"

"They're a working band, duck. They'll do anything, go anywhere — no gig too big or too small. You can't afford to turn down a booking in this game. Some other bugger'll be in there like a shot. All good PR. See — Winterbrook Masonic today — and maybe, just maybe, a slot on the nationwide Soul Survivors tour tomorrow."

"OK — yes, that makes sense. And — er — what are they called?"

"The JB Roadshow. They bursts on stage to 'Sock It To 'Em, JB'. Sensational stuff. It makes the hairs on the hairs on the back of your neck stand up and take notice, duck, believe me." Freddo had a further rummage on the desk. "Here — I've got their presenter here somewhere. Photos and all that. Prices. It's got all my contact details on too. And here's your passes for the Masonic Hall gig. Being a private party it's by invite only, of course — but you'll get in no trouble with these."

Thanking him, Amber glanced at the glossy presenter with some trepidation. "Er — they've been airbrushed, haven't they?"

"No. God's truth. These boys have worn really well. No rehab for them. They've got high on nothing but their music over the years, duck. The elixir of eternal youth. Not bad, eh?"

Not bad at all, Amber thought. Not that she believed they hadn't been touched up. For their age they all looked in reasonable shape. "Er — there's an awful lot of them . . ."

"The usual soul band line-up," Freddo assured her. "Singer, two guitarists — lead and bass, couple of saxophonists, trumpeter, drummer, keyboards . . . Gives the real gutsy big soul band sound."

Amber nodded. She assumed it might. And the JB Roadshow, photographed on stage, looked very impressive in their tight black flared velvet trousers and rainbow satin frilly shirts. Authentic, she guessed. Retro chic. Lovely.

If they could play as well as they looked, Fiddlesticks would adore them.

Freddo leaned across the messy desk and held out his hand. "Nice doing business with you, Amber, duck. Shall we leave it that you'll contact me to firm up or otherwise after the Winterbrook gig?"

Amber agreed that they would, shook Freddo's hand again, and reluctantly hauled herself out of the world's foremost entertainment agency and down the stairs into the frazzling heat of Winterbrook's town centre.

Pushing the JB Roadshow's presenter into her bag, she buffeted her way through the crowds towards the car park. It had been a really good day. Cassiopeia might not have had anything to do with it, but then she'd never expected her too. Hell — but it was hot! Hopefully Fern would be Win-free tonight and they could sit in The Weasel and Bucket's garden and drink long cold glasses of . . . "Oooouf! Sorry!" Amber cannoned into someone in the crush on the pavement. "Oh, bugger . . ."

"And great to see you too." Lewis glared down at her.

Amber, still on a high from Freddo, laughed. "You look really, really hacked off. Had a fallout with Sukie?"

Lewis growled something she didn't catch.

"Look — tell me to sod off if you like, but if you're not in a rush, do you want to talk about it?"

"Talking won't help. What I want is something cold," Lewis sighed. "Very cold."

"Like a paddling pool and an ice cream when you were a kid? Ah, yes — bliss. So — why don't you? There must be a park near here, surely? And an ice cream van. I'm not in a hurry to get back to Fiddlesticks either."

"Amber, go away, please." Lewis said gently. "I just want to be on my own, OK? I've got an hour to kill before I collect Jem from the joinery. I'm still a bit hungover from last night. And dog tired. I've spent most of this blistering day in the Social Services offices at Reading completing paperwork, sitting in on meetings, listening to more gobbledegook than any sane person needs in a lifetime, and I've had a row with my mother for about the first time in my life. What I don't want is to scamper about in a bloody park with a Mivvi pretending I don't have a care in the sodding world."

"I'll take that as a no, then."

"Yeah, sorry. As I said, it's not been a good day."

"It sounds pants, you poor thing." Amber smiled kindly, starting to walk away. "I won't make it worse by going all waggy-tailed on you. Far too irritating. Anyway, if you really don't want to talk about it, I hope things get better really soon. See ya."

"Amber . . . oh, bugger it. There's a park across the road. If you really don't have to dash off, actually I wouldn't mind unburdening."

Amber nodded, hoping the unburdening wasn't going to involve details of bedroom acrobatics with Sukie. The row with Zillah sounded a bit worrying though. Lewis and Zil seemed very close. As someone who could count the number of times she'd fallen out with her own mother on the fingers of one hand and still have some left over, Amber had every sympathy with that one.

The park, municipally cloned, was noisy with children; older people sat on the wrought-iron seats in the shade of municipal limes; lovers lay entwined on the parched cropped grass, blissfully unaware of anything or anyone else.

The paddling pool had standing room only, and was filled with shrieking kiddies in neon bathing costumes, but the ice-cream van was there, and after queuing for ages while Lewis found a reasonably quiet, reasonably shady spot, Amber emerged triumphant with two 99 cones.

248

She smiled to herself, watching the young mums lusting over Lewis with their doe-eyes. He, bless him, was so lost in introspection that he had no idea at all.

"Thanks," he took the ice cream. "And sorry for being a grumpy bastard."

"Sounds as if you had every reason." Amber sat beside him on the edge of a municipally-cloned rockery and tried to lick the melting ice cream from her fingers without it looking too suggestive. "So, go on — I'm all ears."

She listened. She really listened. She loved his voice, the soft rise and fall was musical. Magical. She wanted to cuddle him, but of course resisted the temptation.

"OK," she said eventually. "For what it's worth, firstly I think you should apologise unreservedly to your ma. No — really. Maybe you think she's been in the wrong for keeping everything hush-hush for years, but you don't know anything about the circumstances, do you? She must have had her reasons. Wanted to protect you. You going off all half-cocked and snarling wasn't very fair on her. She's done a great job as a single mum — and you said you didn't want to know about your father anyway —"

"Of course I bloody do!" Lewis finished his ice cream, licking away the last melting drops with a very pink tongue. "But I've always had to go along with the pretence, haven't I? I've always wondered who he was. Why she left him. I'm nearly thirty — and there's always been this huge gap."

"Maybe it wasn't like that. Maybe it was the other way round? Maybe he left her? Maybe it's just too painful for her to talk about it?" Amber sighed, feeling slightly guilty now about asking Cassiopeia to intervene on this particular subject. "Once you've made up with Zillah, maybe, if you give it a bit of time, she'll tell you the truth. But I don't think you should rush things. You've waited this long. Give it a bit longer. And be tactful, for God's sake."

Lewis nodded, wiping his fingers on his jeans. "Yeah, OK. I can do tactful. And I hate falling out with her — but I said some awful stuff to her — she'll probably never forgive me."

"She's your mother. Nothing's that unforgivable with your mother. Once she's got over the anger and the hurt she'll be OK. You'll see. And as for my part in the Timmy thing, I'm really sorry about that. I sort of gathered that it wouldn't go down too well — but what else could I do?"

"Not a lot, as I told Ma. Don't worry about it — she'll have told him no by now. But she might still have some tart words for you."

"I can take tart," Amber suddenly grinned. "I'll have to apologise to her, too. Look — shall we change the subject? I've got something that might take your mind off your problems for a bit — you'll never guess where I've just been . . . And I know you probably don't want to hear about my irrelevant girlie stuff, but honestly, today has been so funny . . ."

"Go on then," he said. "You've listened to me. And it helped. Thanks for that. I can see you're bursting to tell me and I could do with something cheerful."

250

Lewis, seemingly mildly disinterested at first, eventually started to smile as she told him about the HHLL, then he laughed. A lot. And he carried on chuckling as she told him about Freddo, too.

"So —" she looked hopefully at him "— as I've been invited to watch The JB Roadshow perform at a party, I wondered if you were free . . .?"

"Are you asking me out?"

She shook her head quickly. "Nah. Just to come with me as a mate. And I'd really welcome a second opinion about this band — before I persuade Fiddlesticks to take them on for Harvest Moon. So, if your diary is free of Sukie or anyone else a week next Saturday . . .?"

"I'll check and let you know." Lewis stood up. "But right now it sounds perfect. I can't think of anything better than gate-crashing some party to listen to a batch of wrinklie-rockers who were failures the first time round."

"Is that a yes, then?"

"With one proviso."

"Oh?"

"That you agree to make it a threesome."

Amber's heart sank. Sod it. She really, really didn't want to share either Lewis or the JB Roadshow with Sukie, the Irish witch.

Lewis grinned. "Take it or leave it."

"Maybe I'll leave it."

"Whatever. But Jem'll be really disappointed to miss it . . ."

CHAPTER
TWENTY

Under the Moon of Love

For Amber, the next few days passed in a sort of blur: the temperature soared, days and nights were heavy, hot, humid and headachy; the Fiddlestickers grew ever grumpier about the lack of rain and the lack of sleep; Hubble Bubble became a daily solo routine because Mitzi was now the burstingly proud grandmother of a little boy, Sonny, and spent every spare minute getting under the new parents' feet; Fern was lit up with love; Zillah wasn't.

As for Lewis, Amber hadn't seen him at all since the soul-baring in Winterbrook.

"If it's like this for Plough Night," Gwyneth puffed early one morning as she fed and watered Pike in the shady bit of Moth Cottage's back garden, "we'll all be out in our swimsuits."

Amber, having collected eggs, given the cats their breakfast, and made a pot of tea to go with their porridge — "Don't matter what the weather, duck, you can't beat a bowl of oats to start the day off proper" — set the table under the trees, and sank into one of the deck chairs. There was nothing but the sound of the birds, awake for hours as Amber could testify, still chirruping their multitudinous choruses to the new day.

She exhaled. Despite only wearing the minimum to preserve her modesty — a pair of white shorts and a midriff-skimming yellow vest — she was already extremely hot. She'd been about to say they could do with a good storm to clear the air and stopped herself just in time. That might be a Fiddlesticker homily too far.

She watched Gwyneth stroke the cats and fuss Pike again. Gwyneth was so lovely, always doing things for other people, never grizzling about anything. And after the successful kitten rescue mission — the kittens all being looked after and waiting for rehoming with the local Cat Protection lady — she and Big Ida's next animal welfare sortie involved a pet shop in Winterbrook with, they felt, inadequate caging facilities for their rabbits and guinea pigs.

Having made sure her beloved animals were eating up, Gwyneth toddled up the garden and beamed at Amber. "You OK, duck? Not too hot?"

"I'm fine — but even I'm beginning to think rain might be a good idea. Didn't you and Ida make some sort of early plea to Leo?" Amber spooned up porridge and golden syrup — something she'd never have touched in a million years in her previous life — with enjoyment. "For a storm?"

Gwyneth slid into her deck chair, practically disappeared from view, and had to haul herself back to the edge before she could tackle her breakfast. "We was going to, yes. But it don't do to tamper with the right dates or traditions really, duck. See, there's plenty in the village as'll curtsey to a sickle moon and ask for rain

— but not me. I'd never ask the moon for rain unless she had 'er five misty-rainbow rings round 'er." She shovelled porridge into her mouth with relish. "Asking for trouble, that is. Same as trying to invoke Leo's Lightning afore 'e's ready. Dangerous stuff. More tea?"

"Please," Amber passed her cup across the table. She wasn't going to venture an opinion on anything celestial. Not this morning and probably never again. After what had happened with Fern and Timmy following the Cassiopeia-wishing, she'd be very careful to mock anything she didn't understand.

Was it astral magic at work? She had no idea, but there was absolutely no rational earthly explanation for Timmy's volte-face. It was totally inexplicable.

Arriving back from that amazing day with the HHLL and Freddo and Lewis, and prepared to turn herself inside out with apologies to Zillah for her part in the love-nest search, Amber had found Chrysalis Cottage empty and had approached The Weasel and Bucket with trepidation.

Late afternoon, the pub had been closed for at least an hour and the trestles were deserted. Zillah, she knew, usually stayed behind to help Timmy with the clearing and cleaning and preparation for the evening's onslaught.

It might be a good time to try and justify her actions — at least she could apologise without an avid audience.

Surprisingly, it was Fern, her face glowing, her curls awry and wearing a melon grin, who had bounced through the beer garden to greet her. "Hiya! Can't stop! Got to go and collect Win — but you'll never guess what's happened!"

It being Fiddlesticks and this being Fern, Amber wouldn't even try to hazard the wildest conjecture. It was bound to be wrong. "Go on then — I can see you're bursting to tell me."

"Can't. No time." Fern glanced at her watch. "But Cassiopeia is a star. A real star. Oh, God — Amber! I'm soooo happy."

"Jesus, Fern — you can't just leave it at that. What on earth's happened?"

"Earth's got sod all to do with it." Fern waved her arms towards the sky. "This miracle is all down to the heavens."

"Have you been *dabbling*? Taking Win's medication? Sniffing something?"

"Nah — I'm high on love. High as a kite. As a star . . ."

"You're bladdered, aren't you? Have you been indulging in after-hours drinking? Why are you in the pub this late in the afternoon, anyway?"

"Nag, nag, nag," Fern had giggled. "I'm not here to drink. I'm here for a far, far more important reason — and no, can't say any more. Win needs collecting. Catch up with you later. 'Byeeee!"

And still beaming, Fern had skipped away in the direction of Hayfields.

Amber had still been staring after her when Zillah had stomped out of the pub with a tray to collect the last straggling empties.

They'd looked at one another. Zillah had smiled first. It hadn't reached her eyes.

"I've — er — just seen Fern leaving," Amber said. "Is she drunk?"

"Only emotionally," Zillah had scooped up half a dozen empty pint pots by their handles and screwed up crisp packets with a deftness that came from years of practice. "Timmy's given her a part-time job — and yes, I know. I was gobsmacked, too. He's always said she'd be useless, and then with no reason at all, he's welcoming her in here like she's Barmaid of the Year."

"Blimey . . ." Amber had exhaled. "But — why?"

"Heaven knows." Zillah had bent down with lithe fluidity to collect some plates from the grass. "And she's as ditzy behind the bar as she is in front of it, but give her her due, she's tried hard and she's worked like a dervish. The customers love her, of course, which helps — and she's so unremittingly cheerful." She'd straightened up easily. "I'm afraid we're closed . . ."

"I didn't want a drink — I was looking for you, actually."

"Were you? Any particular reason?"

"I ran into Lewis this afternoon. In Winterbrook. I was — er — working for Mitzi and he was collecting Jem from the joinery," Amber had explained quickly in case Zillah thought she'd been stalking her son. "We had a chat."

"Did you?" Zillah's voice had been sharp. "And?"

"I know you've had a fallout, but that's none of my business —"

"No, it isn't."

256

"No, but I just wanted to apologise to you — about the Internet stuff . . . the holiday places . . . Timmy . . . Timmy asked me to do it and I couldn't say no, could I? If I could have I would have — believe me. I —"

Zillah had rested her hip against one of the trestles. Amber noticed that the hem of her long purple skirt was stained with damp and there were strands of dried moss clinging to her bare toes. Had she been *paddling*?

"Amber, what you know, or think you may know, about my relationship with Timmy again isn't any of your business. Any more than my private disagreements with Lewis, OK?"

"Yes, of course, I know that, but —"

Zillah had sighed. "Sorry, love. I sound like a right mardy cow, don't I? No, don't answer that. It's not been a good time for me. And thanks for trying to explain — but there's no need. Timmy seems to have changed his mind about taking me away for a — er — romantic break."

"He has?"

Zillah had nodded. "Don't ask me how or why? But from straining at the 'Let's Spend the Night Together' leash last night, he'd become Mr 'Let's Take This Nice and Easy' this morning. Hardly given me a second glance — been all over Fern."

"*What?*"

Amber felt as though someone had punched the breath from her lungs.

Ohmigod! It had *worked*! She'd made a merely half-hearted, jokey, celestial incantation to Cassiopeia — and it had bloody worked!

Never, ever again would she mock this star-wishing stuff. Maybe, just maybe, there was more to Fiddlesticks' astral-magic than met the eye?

Ohmigod!

"So?" Zillah had asked casually. "How was Lewis?"

"Uh?" Still stunned by the Timmy-Fern news, Amber had to drag herself back to the matter in hand. "Oh, tired. Very. Hot. Upset. Miserable."

And still heart-stoppingly beautiful and sexy and gorgeous despite it all, Amber thought, remembering how Lewis had looked — like some hippie love god, sitting mournfully on that boring, boring rockery — and how every other female in the park had clearly agreed with her.

Zillah had moved away from the trestle and sighed. "Poor boy. I know the feeling. Maybe I ought to give him a ring."

"Mmmm," Amber had nodded. "I think that would be a good idea. And, Zil, I'm sorry. For interfering . . ."

"Don't be," Zillah had smiled. Properly. "You've no need. None of this is your fault. I should be the one to apologise. And I do. Unreservedly. Friends?"

"Definitely," Amber had sighed happily. "And I promise never to meddle in your life again."

Staring down into Gwyneth's back garden from her bedroom in Chrysalis Cottage, Zillah grinned. Gwyneth and Amber, sitting in the deck-chairs having breakfast with Pike and the cats dancing attendance, were chatting and laughing together as if they'd always shared a home.

Amber had made so much difference to Gwyneth's life, Zillah realised. Amber had made a difference to Mitzi, and to Fern and to Jem. Maybe even to Lewis although he refused to be drawn on the subject and still never treated her as anything other than a casual friend.

She watched as Amber helped Gwyneth to her feet from the depths of the canvas chair and they hugged one another, giggling over something Gwyneth had just said. With a pang, Zillah wondered what on earth Gwyneth would do should Amber decide to move on at the end of the summer. Both Gwyneth and Big Ida, although ridiculously fit, were one day going to need someone younger to keep an eye on them. Zillah had always been more than willing to take this on — after all Gwyneth and Ida had taken her under their wing when she'd arrived in Fiddlesticks and it wouldn't have occurred to her not to repay the love. But how would Gwyneth cope without Amber in her life?

"I love her like me own, duck," Gwyneth had confided. "She's like a daughter and a granddaughter and a friend all rolled into one. A proper gem."

The proper gem, Zillah noted with a shard of middle-aged jealousy, had stood up and stretched unselfconsciously: slender in her skimpy second-skin clothes, beautifully tanned now by the sun instead of that awful spray-on salon orangeness that she'd arrived with, her untamed hair almost silver.

Zillah groaned at her own dimpled and wrinkled flesh reflected harshly in the mirror, and wearily accepting the unchangeable, continued to dress in her long Indian print frock with the glass beads and sequins zigzagged through the organdie. Pushing her hair into its combs and slotting in large multicoloured dangly earrings, she paused only for a quick final coat of mascara and hurried downstairs.

There was just time for a cup of coffee and a whisper of Radio Two in the garden before the daily routine kicked in.

This morning the early morning ritual of communal cottage tea-sipping had been abandoned. Big Ida was spending a couple of days with her godsons in Newbury, and Amber — free from Hubble Bubble duties for the day — was taking Gwyneth and Pike out in the van for a picnic at Christmas Common.

Zillah was delighted to have some time alone to think. There was plenty to think about.

Fern was still at the pub, learning quickly, enjoying herself. Timmy, amazingly, seemed delighted with her. And with her company. Timmy and Fern seemed to find any number of reasons to be in the cellar at the same time or grab the same beer pump, and grin soppily at one another. Timmy was revelling in it and Fern — well, Fern was like a teenager in love.

Surely, Fern didn't reciprocate Timmy's feelings, did she?

It was all most peculiar.

And — and, obtusely, Zillah still wasn't sure if she was entirely happy with the situation or not — Timmy seemed to have forgotten all about the sharing of the Fowey love-nest. In fact, he seemed to have forgotten that for years he'd been trying to persuade Zillah to share every aspect of his life. True, he was still charming and warm and friendly towards her, and seemed ecstatically happy. But he'd — well — sort of cooled towards her.

It was a relief not to be pursued so relentlessly, of course, but even so, a girl didn't want to be totally ignored.

Lewis, when she'd told him, had laughed uproariously and told her she was still a crazy mixed-up flower-child who didn't know on which side her bread was buttered.

Oh — she sipped her coffee as Radio Two played something wistful by Bread — whatever else was wrong with her life, it was lovely to be on laughing terms with Lewis again. The making-up, on that hot afternoon after Amber had talked to her outside the pub, had been one of the most difficult moments in their relationship.

"I was going to ring you later," Lewis had said, his voice weary, his eyes strained, opening the door to his Hayfields flat to her for the second time that day. "Come in."

Immediately after her chat with Amber, Zillah had decided to take the bull by the horns and apologise to her son. After all if Lewis, who was usually so guarded with every aspect of his personal life, had unburdened himself to Amber, their row must have hurt him deeply.

And yes, he'd said some awful things — patently untrue things — to her in the heat of the argument, but now, having had time to mull it over, Zillah had realised the fault was hers. All hers. If only she'd been honest with him years ago.

"We're just going to have dinner," Lewis had said. "Jem's cooking something that might or might not turn out to be jambalaya."

"I don't want to interrupt you. This won't take long," Zillah stepped into the flat. "Hi, Jem — that smells lovely . . ."

From the kitchen, Jem had waved a wooden spoon at her in greeting. His smile was edged with Cajun sauce.

The living-room windows had been opened to the early evening sun, and Hayfields' grounds undulated in tie-dye shades of green and gold. Several of the Hayfields residents were having a noisy barbecue on the lawn.

"Jem won't bother us in here," Lewis had said. "He's too immersed in his cooking."

"Shouldn't you be watching him?"

"You know he doesn't need constant supervision. I've done the stuff he finds difficult — lighting the gas, lifting the pans — he's on stirring. Stirring is one of his favourites."

"As is tasting?"

There was a flicker of warmth in Lewis's eyes then. "Yeah — he does tasting to Olympic standard. Anyway, I'm sure that discussing Jem's culinary prowess wasn't why you came to see me . . . Would you like a drink? We've got some cans in the fridge."

And Zillah had declined the drink and plunged in and apologised, a lot, and said it was her fault for making such a huge mystery about Lewis's father, but

262

— and then Lewis had interrupted and apologised for jumping to conclusions and for saying the things he had which he'd had no right to say, especially to her, and they'd talked over one another, and apologised again, and eventually laughed.

"So," Zillah had finished, "I don't blame you one bit for flying off the handle. We've always been such good friends and always been open with one another."

"Except about this," Lewis had said, but his tone had lost its harshness. "Oh, look, Ma — you must have your reasons for keeping it quiet. I just hope he wasn't some serial killer or something like that. My guess is that he was already married? God — you're bloody inscrutable when you want to be! Oh well, I've spent almost thirty years with 'father unknown' on my birth certificate — I suppose I'll spend the rest of my life in the same state. Get over yourself, as Fern would say. You're not going to tell me, are you? Not even now?"

Zillah had shaken her head. "No point, love. Truly no point. I wouldn't know where to begin — and no, he wasn't married but he will be by now and he'll have another family and, even if we could trace him, he'd probably die if you turned up on his doorstep wreaking havoc in his nice, settled, orderly life."

Lewis had stood up and walked over to the window, his back to her.

The spicy scent of the jambalaya and the shouts of laughter from the barbecue hovered on the stifling air.

Then he turned round and looked at her. "Please answer me one question, then. Did you love him?"

"With all my heart. And I still do. And I always will."

★ ★ ★

After that, Zillah thought as the morning sun moved round Fiddlesticks and the garden grew ever hotter and she drained her coffee, it had been more than OK and she'd cried and Lewis had hugged her and so had Jem and they'd all been covered in Cajun sauce. And she'd stayed to dinner and then they'd joined the others on the lawn and all got quite merrily drunk as the misty lilac dusk spread up from the river.

The radio was still warbling softly as she stood up to face another day.

"Superstar" by the Carpenters.

Zillah was just too late to stop the first, poignant line — about an old love — echoing deep, deep into her heart. She slammed her hand on the off button and burst into tears.

CHAPTER
TWENTY-ONE

Lovelight in the Starlight

"Excuse me," Amber tapped the woman chattering in the massive arched and studded doorway of Winterbrook's Masonic Hall gently on the shoulder. "I wonder if we could have a word with — um —" she looked down at Freddo's scribbled note on the passes in her hand "— Joyce or Brian? Just to check if they've been told we'll be here?"

Lewis had been all for them bluffing their way into the ruby wedding party and taking the consequences, but Amber *had* to see the JB Roadshow in order to persuade Fiddlesticks to pay for them, and didn't want to risk the embarrassment of being thrown out before she'd heard a single note played.

The woman in the doorway broke off her conversation and peered at her.

"Oh, you just go along in, dear. They'll be delighted to see you. You must be Joyce's friend Cissy's daughter's girl. But what on earth have you done to your voice? You didn't used to speak like that, did you? Have you had electrocution lessons? My, but you've really grown, dear — but then you must have been only six or seven when I last saw you. Can't believe they've been married forty years, can you?"

"Er — no . . ."

"And we all said it wouldn't last, didn't we?" The woman chortled. "Especially with Brian's little *problem*."

Amber trilled with laughter too. She didn't dare look at Lewis who was standing behind her. However, Jem, who was holding her hand, joined in silently, his body shaking with glee.

"Bless him," the woman glanced down. "Young Arty always enjoyed a good joke. You haven't changed at all, Arty, love. Well, have a good evening — no doubt we can catch up on all the family gossip later."

"Oh, no doubt," Amber smiled, praying they never bumped into one another again. "Through here, is it?"

She shoved Jem, who was showing every sign of wanting to continue the Arty discussion in his own inimitable flamboyant gesturing language, ahead of her with a warning glare. "Don't. Please don't. We're not supposed to be here, remember — so if anyone calls you Arty you just smile and nod and be nice. OK?"

Jem poked out his tongue and winked.

"She thought I was someone called Simon. Married to Lorraine. Divorced after eighteen months. Left her with two kiddies and another on the way," Lewis grumbled as he caught them up in the elaborately stuccoed vestibule and they pushed into the main hall. "Sounds like I'm a bit of a loser to me."

The hall, midnight dark with the curtains pulled against the brilliant evening sunshine, but fortunately massively air-conditioned, was awash with everything ruby. Candles, streamers, balloons, little table lanterns, hearts and flowers all glowed the colour of congealing blood.

"Looks like a satanic mass," Lewis said. "And that table must be the sacrificial altar. Mind you, they'll be hard pushed to find a virgin in Winterbrook."

"And whose fault's that?" Amber smiled sweetly.

Lewis and Jem both poked out their tongues.

The white-clothed table, admittedly overdone with red roses and candlesticks, stretched along an entire side of the vast room. Waiters and waitresses whizzed backwards and forwards with dishes covered in cling film. Amber felt sincere professional sympathy at the size of the catering task ahead.

Jem tugged at her hand and pointed at the food.

"Not yet, gannet," she laughed. "You'll have to wait. Look, there are loads of little tables to sit at — shall we go and find one while they're still free?"

"Near the bar, the food and the exit for preference," Lewis grinned at them both. "This could turn out to be a long night."

Tugging at Amber's hand, Jem headed immediately for the circular tables dotted round the outskirts of the sumptuously linen-folded and gilded room. He chose the one nearest the stage, beside towering banks of Marshall amps and speakers. If the JB Roadshow were as good as Freddo had promised, she probably wouldn't be able to hear herself think later, Amber reckoned as she pulled out Jem's chair for him, let alone speak.

There were further ruby candles and roses on each table, along with wonderfully generous heaps of deep-red star sequins randomly scattered across the white cloths.

Delightedly, Jem started to gather them together and spread them into small celestial ruby drifts.

Joyce and Brian's official guests, hundreds of them and mainly all of an age, were clustered at least eight-deep round the bar.

"Shall we?" Lewis raised his eyebrows.

"Why not, seeing as neither of us are driving," Amber nodded. They'd decided to indulge in the luxury of a taxi in case the whole affair became very boozy towards the end. "I'll have a G&T, please, seeing as this is a posh occasion."

She watched Lewis move with his easy, confident stride towards the bar. It was the first time she'd seen him wearing anything other than the tight faded jeans and T-shirts. She smiled. Even dressed smartly, as Jem was, in black trousers and a baggy white shirt, he still looked like a beautiful fallen angel.

Jem, having organised the sequins to his satisfaction and now transfixed by the splendid banqueting hall, was pointing at everything with delight. Beside them, massive dark-red velvet curtains were pulled in towering tightly-closed dusty folds.

At the appropriate moment, Amber thought, the stage would be revealed. And the JB Roadshow. Hopefully.

A banner — hand painted on a double bed sheet — above the stage read: "Joyce and Brians Ruby. Congrat's Mum and Dad. Hears Too The Next 40".

Amber flinched and averted her eyes. Lynne Truss would probably have demanded a rewrite.

As Lewis edged his way closer to the bar, she and Jem continued to take in the rest of the grandeur. Oh, bugger . . . there was a table piled high with cards and presents. She hoped no one would have noticed that they'd arrived empty handed.

Oh — and over there, propped beside a glittery twin-deck disco, "Frank's Funk Machine", was a huge blown-up photo of Joyce and Brian on their wedding day. How sweet they looked, how in love, how very young: Joyce in her sticky-out lampshade wedding dress with a short veil over her Cilla Black hair, and Brian in a collarless Beatle suit with a pudding-basin fringe. And eight, no nine, bridesmaids all back combed and white lipped in rigid nylon frocks, not to mention two small pageboys in kilts and the best man who clearly had a severe squint.

Jem leaned across the table and grinned as he pointed at the tiny wooden pentangle round Amber's throat. The colours of the various veneers went perfectly, she thought, with her short brown and gold strappy layered dress rescued from one of her Moth Cottage bin bags and carefully aired and ironed. It was probably over two years old — she'd only worn it once, and no one back home would have been seen dead in anything so outdated. Amber hadn't given any of that more than a fleeting thought.

"I told you I'd always wear your star —" she smiled at Jem "— and I will. It really is gorgeous."

Jem made extravagant gestures involving the pentangle, the ceiling, his heart, Amber's heart and finally Lewis still queuing patiently at the distant bar.

Amber frowned, putting it all together, then she groaned. "Oh, Jem! You didn't? On Cassiopeia's? That was your star-wish? That me and Lewis . . .?"

Jem nodded, grinning from ear to ear and rocking jubilantly on his spindly golden chair.

"It won't work," Amber said. "Sorry. Lewis has so many girlfriends and —"

Jem frowned and did a double thumbs down.

"And," Amber continued, "we don't feel like that about one another. We like each other and we're friends, that's all."

Jem pulled a face and shook his head.

"It'd never work," Amber said gently. "I'm probably not staying in Fiddlesticks anyway and —"

Jem slammed his hands flat on the table and glared.

"And, even if I did, we have to love one another. And we don't. Cassiopeia won't change that. Lewis doesn't love me and I certainly am not in love with him."

Jem's eyebrows rocketed upwards and he tapped his nose.

"I'm not lying, honestly . . ."

Oh yes you are, she thought suddenly. Oh, God. Oh, *God!*

"That was embarrassing," Lewis chuckled, as he placed two pints of beer and the G&T on the table.

Had he read her mind? Amber squirmed. Oh, pul-ease, no.

270

"Not only is the bar all paid for, which means we're truly freeloading on Joyce and Brian's hospitality," he continued, sitting down and passing the drinks. "But I met Lorraine's new husband and he wanted to fight me outside because of the way I left her with the kiddies."

Jem chortled.

Amber, still reeling from the love-realisation, exhaled. "Oh — er — and what did you say?"

"I said I was Simon's identical twin brother and I'd like to take him out too, for the way he treated Lorraine. I left them all wondering why they couldn't remember that Simon had a twin. I only hope I don't run into Lorraine. There's bound to be a row about maintenance payments. Cheers!"

They chinked glasses.

Lewis joined Jem in creating new constellations of red stars across the white cloth, with much laughter and friendly disagreement. Amber sipped her G&T and cursed inwardly. OK, so she was in love with him: the lusting, the fancying, the liking, the friendship had all slowly combined and then, without her being aware of it happening, rolled into a far deeper emotion.

OK . . . so what? He'd never know, would he? As far as Lewis was concerned, nothing had changed in their relationship, had it? She could cope with this. Well, for now, at least. Long term was out of the question. She couldn't live in such close proximity and watch him with other women. That would send her completely doolally.

She sighed. Leaving Lewis would mean leaving Fiddlesticks, leaving Gwyneth, leaving Mitzi and Hubble Bubble, leaving Fern and Jem and the place she now thought of as home.

Oh, sod it!

Fortunately at that point, there was a bit of a mêlée by the bar, and a simultaneous scrabbling behind the stage curtains. A plump man in a purple satin tuxedo and a bad toupee fought his way through the velvet and into the spotlight.

"Ladies and gents," he wheezed noisily through his microphone, "if you'd like to find a seat . . ."

Amber, deciding she'd have to think about the falling in love thing later, watched as the guests, all decked out in various degrees of party finery, streamed from the bar and noisily found themselves seats round the tables.

"Lovely," the microphone hissed. "All sitting? Good. Great. Now, we all know why we're here don't we?"

Everyone did and said so rather raggedly.

"Come on!" the microphone whistled. "We can do better than that, can't we?"

They could and did.

"Lovely! Now let's all put our hands together for the happy couple! Ladies and gents, friends and family — I give you — Joyce and Brian!"

The Masonic Hall cheered. All eyes were on the curtains. Nothing happened.

Jem nudged Amber and pointed upwards.

"No way, mate," Lewis grinned. "They're not coming down from the ceiling. Not this time. We —" he leaned disturbingly closer to Amber "— had a Hayfields trip to the panto in Reading last year. The Demon King was lowered from the ceiling in a blaze of light. Jem loved it."

The curtains twitched a bit more. The man with the microphone scrabbled at the join, lifting them aside. His toupee suffered.

Everyone cheered a lot more.

Eventually Joyce, looking very haggard and in her wedding dress dyed dark red, tottered out, losing her veil in the process.

Everyone screamed with excitement.

Brian, who had clearly gained about ten stone since the wedding day and lost all his hair, was also in red, his suit making him look like a sad Santa Claus as he stumbled out behind her.

As the assembled throng whooped and clapped, an unseen tannoy blared the ghastly Peter Sellers' version of "We've Been Together Now For Forty Years".

Joyce and Brian looked suicidal.

Flummoxed, the plump man drew his finger across his throat and the tannoy came up with a scratchy version of "Congratulations".

Joyce and Brian, clearly Cliff fans, simpered in the spotlight, while a small child of indeterminate sex with a sagging nappy waddled up to the stage, dropped a bouquet of forty red roses at their feet and immediately burst into tears.

Stepping over the child, the plump man, obviously Frank, abandoned his microphone and wobbled down the stage steps and across to his Funk Machine.

"Come on," he yelled. "Come on, Joyce and Brian! Down on the floor! Let's be 'aving yer! And can someone move that bloody kid!"

The howling child's mother, cigarette in hand and halfway down a Bacardi and coke, undulated across the floor to collect her offspring.

"That's it," Frank barked tersely. "Get it out of the way, love. Quick as you like. Now, ladies and gents! Let's hear it for the happy couple as they take the floor for the first dance . . ."

"Congratulations" was drowned out by "The Anniversary Waltz".

Joyce and Brian staggered self-consciously down into the spotlight and trotted round the floor, seriously out of time.

Amber, sniffing back tears of laughter, couldn't look at Lewis.

Jem, however, was clapping his hands and stamping his feet, loving every minute.

The evening rolled on in much the same vein. She and Lewis chatted about the Fern and Timmy thing, deciding it had to be celestial forces at work — that or Timmy was going through a mid-life crisis — and if it was some sort of temporary aberration on Timmy's part they both hoped Fern wouldn't have her bubble burst too harshly.

They also touched on Lewis's fallout with Zillah, the apologetic making-up and her reluctance to divulge anything further about his father.

"I'm going to leave it for a while," he said, destroying an entire cosmos of sequin stars. "I've waited this long.

I guess I can wait a bit longer. Although I do want to find out. Still . . ." he sighed, "at least I know she loved him now. That's something."

Jem reached across and hugged him. Amber really wanted to do the same.

Around them, The Funk Machine played suitable music, people danced, shrieked, laughed and argued, all the time drinking themselves silly at the happy couple's expense, and then much to Jem's delight, the food was made available.

"I'll go," Amber said, standing up. "I'm used to carrying plates of food. A bit of everything?"

Jem held up both hands.

"Double helpings? OK. Shan't be long . . ."

As she left the table she thought Lewis said "Please don't be" but she'd probably imagined it, and if she hadn't, it probably only meant he was starving.

The food, while not up to Mitzi's standards, was very good and plentiful. And despite their misgivings about the morals of using the free bar, they'd refilled their glasses several times. By the time Frank wobbled back to the stage, they were all feeling wonderfully relaxed and mellow.

"Laydees and gent-le-men!" Frank had been at the free bar too. "I know you've all had a great time so far —"

Much cheering.

"But now is the moment we've all been waiting for! I shall put my Funk Machine away —"

Desultory titters and one shout of "About bloody time".

"— and join you in dancing the rest of the night away to the UK's — no, to the world's — greatest soul band!"

Amber wondered if Frank was related to Freddo by hyperbole.

"Lay-dees and gent-le-men! Put your hands together for . . . THE JB ROADSHOW!"

CHAPTER
TWENTY-TWO

Stars!

There was a split second as the curtains swept back when Amber knew she was holding her breath, then, just as Freddo had predicted, the hairs on the back of her neck prickled and her flesh shivered.

The JB Roadshow, in a blaze of moving criss-cross lights and twinkling star-studded backdrop, exploded into "Sock It To 'em JB" their trademark opening number.

The sound was out of this world.

The drummer thundered out the famous James Bond rhythm as the other band members moved in synchro, side-stepping, rocking their instruments into the air as the singer strutted, shouting into the audience. Then the two guitarists, followed by the organ, took up the tune, which grew and roared round the hall. The band were now moving in unison as they played, the overhead star-lights cascading down on them.

The singer grabbed his microphone again and yelled out the James Bond film titles. The Masonic Hall joined in with gusto.

The guitarists moved together, their fingers sliding expertly over the strings, the volume increasing, as again the organist picked up the main thread while the singer, enticing and seducing his audience, swayed and stamped and socked it to 'em in a frenzied crescendo of noise. The beat pulsed into Amber's body. She could literally feel the bass line in her bones. Oh, it was spectacular. Real, live music by musicians who knew how to play — and then some. It knocked clubbing and mixing decks into an entire hatstand of cocked headgear.

She stared, transfixed at the stage, her body moving to the beat, knowing she was laughing. They were sensational. Truly, truly sensational.

And Freddo's photos hadn't lied at all. Well, OK, maybe the three brass players had slight paunches and the keyboard player had less hair than the others, but otherwise, considering they must be ancient, they were fantastically well preserved. All tall and lean and looking the real McCoy in tight black velvet flares and neon bright satin shirts, the JB Roadshow brought the Masonic Hall to its knees.

As "Sock It To 'em JB" came to its ear-splitting climatic end, everyone was on their feet clapping, yelling, screaming for more. The band had hardly broken sweat and, knowing they were great, smiled down at their adoring audience.

The singer, all dyed blonde hair and wicked grin, moved his body sexily towards the microphone and with the drummer and the bass player still quietly keeping the beat, introduced the band to massive rounds of applause.

"Our brass section — Monty, Pete, and Joey! On drums — Jezza Samson! On lead guitar — Berry

Knight! On bass guitar — Clancy Tavistock! On organ — Ricky Swain! And who have I forgotten?"

"Yourself!" screamed the Masonic Hall.

"Ah yes," he winked. "And I'm your vocalist — Tiff Clayton! Ladies and gents — get up on your feet, get on to the floor, put your hands in the air and welcome The-J-B-ROADSHOW! Let's hear it ONE-MORE-TIME!"

The Masonic Hall erupted.

The next number was the Bar-Kays irrepressible "Soul Finger", and within seconds of the gotta-move opening bars, the floor was packed. Everyone danced and waved their arms above their heads.

Again, on stage, the JB Roadshow thundered, stamped, clapped and played up a storm.

"Stone me!" Lewis yelled in her ear. "It's exactly, exactly like listening to my ma's records! This is what I grew up listening to. They are absolutely brilliant. She would have loved this!"

Oh, she will, Amber thought. Fiddlesticks will have the JB Roadshow for Harvest Moon even if it means I have to sell my body to pay for them.

Jem was on his feet, balancing himself against the table, clapping his hands and swaying with delight.

"Come on, Jem!" Amber bent down and shouted. "Dance with me!"

Grabbing both her hands, Jem grinned and moved out on to the packed floor. Finding a vacant patch in front of the stage, Amber held his hands tightly and they stomped and rocked to "Knock on Wood", followed by "Soul Man" then "Sweet Soul Music" — each one sounding better than the last.

"Call me a gooseberry if you like," Lewis yelled, moving between them and taking one of Jem's hands in his, "but I'm not missing out on this!"

"In the Midnight Hour" was followed by "Mustang Sally" and they danced together, grinning like children, singing the wrong words, elated.

Soul tune after soul tune, all perfect, roared and rocked from the stage. Amber felt she could have danced all night. She'd never felt so high, so alive.

"Ladies and gentlemen," Tiff Clayton caressed the microphone, with the last chords of "Hold On I'm Coming" reverberating round the hall, "we're going to take a break for twenty minutes. Then we'll be back — and yes, I promise you, for — er — Joyce and Brian and all you like-minded lovers out there, we'll be playing some slow and smoochy soul in our second set!"

Everyone clapped and whooped.

"In the meantime, get the drinks in, rest your feet and we'll see you again in twenty minutes when we'll sock it to you ONE-MORE-TIME!"

Still cheering and applauding, everyone made a beeline for the bar.

The noise was echoing in Amber's ears. She'd probably hear it all night, long after they'd left Winterbrook.

"I'll get some drinks," she grinned dazedly at Lewis. "Shall I?"

"I'm just going to take Jem to the gents — so, yeah, great — and I'll see you in a bit."

He smiled at her. Jem, still jigging, smiled at them both and winked.

By the time the second set started, they were all a little drunk. Amber, deciding that they'd probably never get served again, had got four of everything.

This time, the JB Roadshow opened with a shortened version of "Sock It To 'em JB" combined with "Soul Finger". Instantly, everyone was on their feet, albeit a little more raucously and unsteadily this time. Amber watched them on stage, feeling the music throb into her, the frisson of excitement tingle through her veins.

They were electric, exciting, noisy, talented, and very, very sexy.

"Come on," Lewis grabbed her hand as the band roared into "I Feel Good". "This is seriously good — come on, Jem."

They danced together again, holding Jem's hands, crushed by Joyce and Brian's friends as the soul music, song after familiar song, thundered up into the stucco and gilding.

This, Amber thought dreamily, is the best night of my life — ever.

"And now —" Tiff Clayton once again caressed the microphone "— we're going to slow things down a bit with a special request from Brian for Joyce on this very special day . . ."

The Masonic Hall went "Aaaah . . ."

"So let's see all you lovers out there smooch away to Brian's heartfelt choice: the late great Otis Redding's 'I've Been Loving You Too Long'."

Lewis and Amber looked at one another and spluttered with laughter.

As the slow, soulful opening bars started, Jem pulled them all closer together. Amber grinned down at him, shaking her head. Then they swayed slowly, the three of them, as Tiff Clayton growled out the bittersweet lyrics.

As the band moved on to "Private Number", Joyce and Brian appeared to be having words.

Jem pulled away from them, frowning, pointing down to his feet.

"What's up?" Lewis leaned close to him. "Have you hurt yourself?"

Jem shook his head, then placed his palms-together hands against the side of his face.

"Tired? You lightweight!" Lewis laughed. "OK — go and sit this one out. Can you manage OK?"

Jem nodded, and as he made his way carefully through the swaying couples he turned and winked at Amber.

It just seemed so natural, as the JB Roadshow slinked into the sultry "When a Man Loves a Woman", to move into Lewis's arms. As he slid his hands round her waist, Amber felt as though her flesh was on fire. She slowly put her hands onto his shoulders, knowing she was trembling, praying he wouldn't notice. They moved easily together, bodies touching, moving away, moving back again. Natural. Instinctive. Like lovers.

The JB Roadshow kept them in this delicious state through several more Otis Redding and Ben E King numbers, then Tiff Clayton spoiled it all by announcing they were having a further uptempo soul selection for the boppers.

As the band started their stepping and swaying routine and "Land of a Thousand Dances" screamed into the hall, Amber moved away from Lewis. "I think I'll join the lightweights," she said, her voice disappearing into the music. "OK?"

He nodded, still smiling, and followed her back to the table where Jem had rearranged the sequinned heaven again and was grinning from ear to ear.

"Yeah, OK," Amber hissed at him. "Very clever. It worked — but it was only a dance or two. Not a lifetime commitment. And I hope you've left us something to drink . . ."

Still beaming, Jem pushed the glasses across the table.

"Feeling better?" Lewis asked, as he sat down. "Good. And I think we'll have to rechristen you. Oh, no — don't look all innocent like that. You need renaming, and no, not Arty, you meddlesome sod. I think we'll have to call you Puck'n'Cupid from now on."

"I've already told him," Amber said lightly, "that it was only dancing."

"Exactly," Lewis drained half a pint of beer without stopping. "Only dancing . . ."

They sat back in their chairs, closer together now, relaxed. Amber, reliving every minute of his hands burning through her flimsy frock, his body touching hers, wondered if Lewis could still hear her heart thundering. Oh, bugger the love-thing. Why Lewis? Why, oh, why had she fallen head over heels for a man who, at best treated her as a friend, and at worst, seemed totally disinterested.

It had never been like this — heady, floaty, walking on air — with Jamie. It had never been like this, full-stop.

The party was coming to an end. Amber simply wanted it to last for ever.

The JB Roadshow hadn't flagged, each song was as fresh, as professional, as the one preceding it. It had been a truly amazing experience.

"Hi, Amber, duck," a cheerful voice chuckled above her. "You look good enough to eat. Everything OK? Enjoying it?"

"Freddo! How lovely to see you," she grinned delightedly up at him. "Thanks so much for this — it's been a brilliant night. It's — they've —" she nodded towards the stage "— been fantastic. Everything you said and more. I didn't think you'd be here . . ."

"Got to make sure my boys get their dues." Freddo put his glass on the table and pulled up a chair. "I always try and make the last bit of the act anyway to see how they've gone down and pick up any future gigs. All the boring management stuff, you know. Hi." He leaned across the table, holding out his hand. "I'm Freddo. Agent to the stars."

Amber laughingly introduced Lewis and Jem and everyone shook hands.

"So." Freddo cocked his head on one side. "Will they suit, duck? The boys? For your moon gig?"

"Absolutely. Definitely. They're just brilliant."

284

"OK, so when you've got the go-ahead from your people you just give me a bell — or better still, come along to see me in person and we'll firm up."

Amber nodded.

The JB Roadshow were winding down now, playing Aretha Franklin and Solomon Burke. The Masonic Hall was smooching madly. Joyce and Brian were dancing the last dance with other people.

Freddo pushed his chair back. "Give us ten minutes or so when the set's finished, then come round the back of the stage. All of you. Bring both your young men too, natch, duck. You can meet the boys, give them a bit more info about your gig. OK?"

"Yes, great, thanks."

"Just go up the stage steps there to the side, round the curtain, across the stage, and there's a little blue door straight ahead of you. You'll find us — no sweat."

Jem chuckled happily as Freddo said adios and pushed his way up on the stage and round the side of the heavy curtains.

"Is he for real?" Lewis laughed. "I thought you'd exaggerated. This has been a hell of a night." He leaned across the table. "Thanks, Amber. Thanks for all of it. I can't remember when I last enjoyed myself so much. It's been sheer magic."

Jem, filling his pockets with star sequins, indicated that he heartily concurred.

Twenty minutes later, with the Masonic Hall's clearing-up, saying-goodnight, mwah-mwah noises in the background, Amber, with Lewis holding tightly on to Jem's hand behind her, pushed her way into the backstage dressing room.

The room was smoky, and reeked of beer and cigarettes and a raft of different deodorants. A couple of pot-bellied, long-haired, middle-aged men were rolling up cables, wheeling amplifiers, and generally tidying up the necessary rock'n'roll paraphernalia.

The JB Roadshow, stripped of their on-stage glitz, were all dressed in jeans and T-shirts and slumped, exhausted on various bits of equipment swigging beer from cans. They still looked, to Amber, pretty damn hot for their age.

"Hi guys!" Freddo waved his can of lager across the room. "Come along in. I've told the boys all about you."

Tiff Clayton, the singer, more lined close to but nonetheless still extremely attractive, laughed. "He certainly has — but he lied. You're even more stunning than he said."

Everyone laughed then. Amber blushed.

Freddo stretched. "I've told them all about your weird village thing, duck. I mean, being local, I know how strange these rural customs can be and Fiddlesticks is renowned for its moon-bayers — but even so, they didn't quite believe it."

"Believe it," Lewis nodded. "The place is mad. Barking. But they'll love you. You — all of you — were, are, brilliant."

"Thanks, mate." Tiff Clayton grinned, his face creasing into wrinkles. "We try to please."

Amber felt ridiculously shy now, being backstage with the band who were, after all, a bunch of tired middle-aged men who'd just finished work. Her ears were still ringing.

"Um —" she smiled at everyone, "I just wanted to say, well, what Lewis has just said really. You are amazing. I've never heard anything so fantastic in my life. Er —"

The band raised their cans to her.

"What I'd suggested to the boys just before you came in —" Freddo yawned "— is that if your people give the go-ahead, I'll come over and give the place a bit of a recce. I'd like to check out the venue for myself. I mean, being an open-air gig, I'll need to know we've got all services to hand, and the safety stuff — all the boring crap that has to be done these days — will that be OK?"

"Fine," Amber nodded. "Good idea. Look, if it's OK, why don't you come over on one of the other celestial festival nights?" She glanced up at Lewis. "When's the next one?"

"Plough Night — it's not anything spectacular, but yes, it'd give you a bit of a taster and you could get the lay of the land and stuff."

"Plough Night it is then," Freddo said. "And when's that exactly?"

"Middle of August — not long."

"Sounds good to me. So, Amber duck, you'll be in touch and all being well, is it a date?"

"Definitely," she smiled happily at the band who now looked as though all they wanted to do was sleep for a week. "We'll see you in the middle of August — and Fiddlesticks won't know what's hit it."

CHAPTER
TWENTY-THREE

What A Little Moonlight Can Do

"So —" Fern bounced up and down in the corner shop's already broiling early morning queue "— then last night he said that he couldn't understand why he'd never before realised that I was a woman."

Amber, who days later still simply couldn't get "Sock It To 'em JB" out of her head, frowned. "And you took that as a compliment, did you?"

"Naturally."

Fern bounced some more. Her chest was leaping up and down on its own. Billy Grinley and Dougie Patchcock, thumbing through what passed for Mrs Jupp's top-shelf mags, stopped leering over the rather demure centrefolds and leered at Fern instead.

"So, is it — I mean — are you — you know?"

"Together?" Fern giggled. "Nah — not yet. But I'm working on it. Oh, but it's so lovely after all those years of loving from afar to actually be able to talk to him, and laugh with him, and be with him, and share things. We —" she looked quite serious "— have got a lot of learning stuff to do, though. I mean, we don't really know each other at all. We're at that lovely stage where everything we say is all new and fresh and exciting."

Amber shook her head. It was inexplicable. It certainly sounded like love — well, maybe not the madly crazy, topsy-turvy, heart-punching, all-in-a-heap, out-of-nowhere love that she felt for Lewis, of course — but love nevertheless.

"And have you mentioned to Timmy that this — this bolt from the blue — occurred straight after Cassiopeia's Carnival? I mean, does he believe that it's astral magic at work, too?"

"Oh, yeah, definitely," Fern grinned as the queue shuffled forward. "He says he went to bed that night dreaming of whisking Zillah off to some Daphne du Maurier hideaway where he intended to propose — and woke up knowing it was the worst idea he'd ever had in his life. He said it scared him rigid. He thought he was going mad. And then he said, when he saw me outside the pub that morning, he knew, he just knew . . ."

"OK, I agree it all sounds pretty miraculous, but —" Amber frowned "— you can't move in with him, can you at the moment? You can't live together? Or work permanently at the pub? Or, well, be together as a couple at all, because of Hayfields and Win."

Much to Dougie and Billy's delight, Fern bounced even more. Amber fleetingly wondered if she should mention getting a good sports bra. No, possibly not. Anyway, whatever else she thought about the Timmy-Fern thing, even she had to admit that Fern's bosoms were absolutely made for bar work.

Fern spun round on one foot. Her chest caught up eventually. "Ah, but even that's going to be OK. See, my contract with Hayfields is up at the end of the year — I'm on short-term contracts. Different clients who are just passing through, or being assessed for other homes. It's not a lifetime one-to-one commitment like Lewis and Jem — because Win's leaving Hayfields in December. She's moving to Devon. To a similar sort of set-up but nearer to her family. She's really excited — she's been waiting ages to get a place down there. I was never going with her — sooo it'll mean I'll be absolutely free to be with Timmy for ever and always from Christmas. Magic, huh?"

"Magic . . ." Amber echoed weakly.

"Yes?" Mona Jupp peered over the bacon slicer. "Next?"

"Just these —" Fern pushed several bars of chocolate and a handful of iced buns across the counter "— please. The chocolate is for Timmy — he's got such a sweet tooth, bless him — and the buns are for Win. She's sitting outside on the bench. We're going to paddle in the stream to cool off and feed the ducks."

"Not with my best fancies, I trust." Mrs Jupp made a moue of annoyance as she bagged up the buns with a flourish and a twist. "They're fresh in this morning. Anything else?"

"No thanks." Fern paid for her purchases, and smiled soppily at Amber. "So — what about you? D'you want to come and feed the ducks with us and sit in the sun and talk about the meaning of life and love and the wonders of the cosmos?"

Amber shook her head. "Hard to resist, but sorry — I'm here to see Mrs Jupp and then I'm taking Gwyneth and Big Ida into Hazy Hassocks to do some shopping this morning while I go to work."

"Catch you later, then," Fern smiled beatifically as she bounced out of the shop.

Dougie and Billy watched her bosoms go with regret.

"Tell you what, though," Fern paused in the doorway and beamed at Amber. "Doesn't Fern Pluckrose have the most *gorgeous* Thomas Hardy ring to it?"

"Madness." Mona Jupp frowned at Amber. "Dangerous stuff, this flaming star-wishing as I've always said. It throws up the most unsuitable liaisons. We've just got used to Timmy drooping about all over the flaming place looking like a pathetic flaming mooncalf after poor Zil, and then — wham! — he's plighting his flaming troth to young Fern, she's besotted and the Lord knows where it'll all end."

"In bed and happily and for ever with any luck," Amber sighed.

"Dear God, girl," Mona Jupp snapped. "That's taken as flaming read! Cassiopeia don't take prisoners. What you asks for is what you gets — even if it does take more than one flaming incantation to get there. See, there must be all sorts of people asking her for all sorts of clashing matches at one time, if you gets my drift? Lots of love tangles. Star-crossed lovers all over the flaming show. That's what people don't understand — sometimes she can't make things happen instant, like — it takes her a while, maybe years, to untangle the threads. Now, whatever it is you want, I hope you're not going to try and pay for it with your flaming iffy Visa card."

Amber blushed, still embarrassed at the memory. "No — er, that is, I'm not buying. I wondered if I could have a word."

"Now?" Mona screeched. "Flaming now? Before nine in the morning? My busiest flaming trading period?"

"Well, yes, sorry. It's a busy morning for me too — but this won't take long. I just want to know if there's a fund or something to pay for all the celestial celebration stuff."

"And for why?"

Rapidly, horribly aware that Dougie and Billy had now turned their attention to her legs beneath the briefest denim skirt she possessed, Amber explained about the possibility of entertainment for Harvest Moon. Just to round the summer off nicely. To make the evening go with a swing, so to speak.

"How much would we be talking about and what sort of entertainment?"

Amber then explained about Freddo and the JB Roadshow and how wonderful they were and how they were exactly what Fiddlesticks needed. She'd thought the cost, at first, seemed quite high, but then there were eight of them after all, and the roadies and Freddo, so really it was very reasonable, wasn't it?

"And they're good, are they? Suitable for all ages?"

"Wonderful. Amazing. True stars. Out of this world. Brilliant. Real family entertainment."

"Ah, good. Not sleazy? Not like that flaming Eminem girl that Goff keeps going on about?"

"Not like her — er, him — at all, no."

292

"And value for money?"

"Oh, absolutely. Worth every penny."

"And could we charge for people to see 'em, do you think?"

"I'm sure you could," Amber said, not having a clue, but much encouraged by the fact that Mona Jupp hadn't screamed and said no-flaming-way.

"As it 'appens, we do have a bit of a pot for festival extras," Mona said. "We raises money at the Christmas Fayre and the bring-and-buys and we allus have a raffle every third Sunday after Goff's taken the family service. We haven't spent any decent amount for years and years. We must have a tidy sum by now. More'n enough to pay for your bit of a band, that's for sure."

The whole shop was now riveted by this high-powered financial discussion. They clearly hadn't seen such entrepreneurial wheeler-dealing in Fiddlesticks for years.

"And who'd have to make the final decision?" Amber asked. "Is there a committee?"

"Lord, no. Committees only mean everything gets talked about and nothing gets done. Me and Goff deal with it. Well, I say what goes and Goff does the books. Now, as it happens, I'm mightily partial to a bit of music — and if we can charge people to get in to listen to 'em and have a bit of a dance, then why not? I'll tell Goff it's all done and dusted. The flaming pot has enough money in it, so yes, I say let's flaming go for it."

Amber wanted to hurl herself across the bacon slicer and kiss Mrs Jupp. Fortunately, the realisation that such an extravagant gesture would mean the revealing of her knickers to Dougie and Billy meant that sanity prevailed.

"Thank you!" she beamed. "So, can I tell them, or at least their agent, that it's a definite?"

"Why not? Yes, do." Mona Jupp fluttered her sparse eyelashes. Sukie, the Irish witch mobile beautician, clearly hadn't got to grips with them yet. "Actually, I've always missed having a bit of live music at our little festivals. It really hits the spot for a gel, if you know what I mean. And, I'll let you into a secret — I was a bit of a groupie in my early days, you know."

"Really? I'd never have guessed . . ."

"Ah, I once threw my vest at Frank Ifield."

Still absolutely walking on air, Amber dropped Gwyneth and Ida off at Big Sava, and skipped along Hazy Hassocks winding High Street, keeping in the shadows thrown across the mishmash of shopfronts by the line of towering sycamores, towards Mitzi's shed.

"Oh, blimey — fancy meeting you here," Zillah emerged from the library, her arms full of romantic novels. "You look very chirpy."

"So do you," Amber said. "And that's another gorgeous Boho dress — your wardrobe is a dream. Oh, please don't tell me you came into Hazy Hassocks on that bloody mad bus. Didn't Gwyneth tell you I was bringing them in this morning for their big shop? I would have happily given you a lift, too."

"Lewis did —" Zillah shifted the books "— on his way to Winterbrook with Jem. But thanks for the retrospective offer — I may need to take you up on it one day. Just off to work with the Proudest New Grandmother in the Western Hemisphere?"

Amber giggled. "Yes. You off to the pub today?"

"Eventually. In time for the lunchtime grazers, yes. I must say —" she grinned suddenly "— that it's far less emotionally exhausting these days, now that Timmy's decided that our future isn't going to be a joint one."

"It must be — although I suppose you now have Billy and Dougie and Slo and Goff all thinking their luck's in?"

"They can think what they like," Zillah chuckled. "And I can handle them — they're just playing at being would-be lovers; they'd run a mile if I gave them the come-on. Whereas with Timmy it was the real thing and so very wearing. And I didn't want to hurt him because he's such a lovely bloke. Whether it was someone's Cassiopeia-wish working for Fern and Timmy, or not, I don't really care. Not now I've got used to the idea. It's taken a weight off my shoulders, I can tell you. Timmy's lovely and will always be one of my best friends. I only hope Fern's up to the task of coping with all that undying devotion."

"I'm sure she'll handle it." Amber said. "Zillah, honestly, it's lovely to see you looking so happy."

"Happy might be an emotion too far, love. But yes, I am feeling more at peace with myself. Strange, because nothing, apart from Timmy's defection, has happened to really alter the situation." She laughed again. "I can only imagine that someone put in a plea to Cassiopeia to make something happen to cheer this miserable old bag up a bit."

Amber hoped she wasn't blushing.

"Anyway," Zillah continued, "I understand you had a great time the other night? At the Masonic? Lewis said it was fantastic."

"Oh, it was. Amazing — the best night out I've ever had. The JB Roadshow were just brilliant. I'd never seen or heard anything like them. I was obviously born far too late — missed out on real live music from real talented musicians without the interference of synthesisers or computers or any other artificial tampering. I wish you'd come with us —" Amber stopped and paused for breath. "No, really. You'd have loved it. And it wasn't just me and Lewis, you know, as a couple. It wasn't like that at all. And we had Jem as a chaperone."

"Matchmaker, you mean." Zillah grinned. "Jem always makes his feelings about Lewis's girlfriends very, very clear. Mind you, I do wish I'd been there — I still hanker after the old days of live bands in every village hall every Saturday night . . ." She stopped for a moment, lost it seemed in wistful recollection. "Er — sorry, love. So? This band — the JB Roadshow? Are they local?"

"No, I don't think so, but their agent is. Anyway, you'll be able to hear them soon. It looks as though they'll be providing the music for Harvest Moon. Mona Jupp has just given me the go-ahead."

"Really? Oh, wonderful. That'll liven the village up a bit. I'll have to get my dancing shoes out of mothballs. Mind, I'll probably be the only one in the whole village who knows all the words to all the songs."

296

Amber shook her head. "Mona Jupp might just challenge you on that one. She used to chuck her undies at Frank Sinatra."

"Did she? Really? I didn't know Ol' Blue Eyes had played Bagley-cum-Russet Village Hall."

"Well, it may not have been him, then. Maybe it was Frank and his Funk Machine? Frank Someone anyway . . . oh blimey, look at the time! I really have to go. Mitzi will go spare if I'm late. See you. Take care . . ."

"You too, love," Zillah swept away with her armfuls of happy-ever-afters. "Have a lovely day."

Amber was humming "Sock It To 'em" as she pushed her way into the Hubble Bubble shed.

"Sorry I'm late, Mitzi. I met Zillah and we got chatting and —"

"That's OK. We've got plenty of time and I'm all organised, although it's far too bloody hot for what we've got on today," Mitzi sighed, standing as close to one of the blurring whirring fans as she dared. "A funeral and a kiddies' birthday party. Both biggies, so we'll both have to be at each one. Anything smaller and we could have split up, taken one each. Still, I wasn't going to turn them down, was I? Oh, let me show you these . . ."

Amber sighed. Ever since Sonny's birth, Mitzi had turned up with a new batch of grandson photos every day. As they seemed to been taken merely seconds apart they were all much of a muchness. Amber had learned very quickly to study them for exactly the right amount of time and how to make all the right oohing and aahing responses.

Amber handed back the sheaf of photos with the correct amount of deference. "He's gorgeous. Really gorgeous. So, business booming?"

"Very much so." Mitzi filed the photos away, smiling. "Oh, and the HHLL have booked us again for every one of their meetings for the foreseeable future, so they can't have objected too much to the all-in female wrestling."

"Probably gave them the most fun they've had in years," Amber laughed. "So, are we double booked today, then — or is there a gap?"

"The funeral is at eleven and the kiddies' party is booked for lunchtime. So, if we get to the wake at half-eleven, it'll mean being away in time to get to the party by one . . . They're both here in Hazy Hassocks, thank goodness, but we're still going to be cutting it fine to get from the wake, back here, rip off the black stuff, dress in less scary clothes for the children, reload the van, and make it to the party on time."

"So why don't we take the kiddies' stuff with us?" Amber asked. "And our party clothes? The food will all keep OK in the cool boxes, and we can surely manage to strip in the van without causing a public decency offence?"

"Good thinking," Mitzi said happily. "I knew there was a reason I employed you. Are you ready to load up, then?"

Amber nodded. "Ready and waiting — oh, er no, I'm not — could I just make a quick phone call?"

"Of course, but why on earth don't you get your mobile sorted out? It'll save you so much time."

"I know," Amber said blithely, squinting at Freddo's card and dialling the number on the Hubble Bubble shed's phone. "I used to think my life would come to an end without it — now I don't even know where it is, but yes, you're right, I must — oh, hi — Freddo? It's me Amber — yes, it's all systems go. Yeah? Brilliant. And you'll come over on Plough Night to suss everything out, will you? Yes, yes — there's a pub. About seven? You know the date? Great — yes, look forward to it . . . Bye."

And grinning delightedly at the way everything was working out so perfectly, she skipped into the kitchen and helped Mitzi in the routine loading of the van.

Constance Motion was pacing up and down the pink-blocked drive when Amber screamed the Hubble Bubble van to a halt.

"Where the devil have you been?" Constance snapped, her black veil sticking to her lacquered curls in agitation. "The mourners are all in there, waiting. Perpetua and Slo have had to entertain them for heaven's sake, to take their minds off the lack of food."

"We're not late," Mitzi said, scrambling from the van behind Amber. "Slo said the funeral was at eleven, which means even with the briefest of send-offs, they wouldn't be back here until half past and it's not quite eleven now and —"

"The funeral," Constance said in spectral tones, "was at nine-forty-five. Slo booked you to start the wake at ten-thirty. And don't try to blame him this time, Mitzi Blessing, because I was there when he made the call."

Amber, frantically dragging the boxes from the back of the van and hoping her black skirt wasn't too short for the occasion, pulled a face. Ooops.

Since Sonny's arrival, Mitzi had been a bit ditzy about everything. There had been several minor errors in bookings and some of the recipes had been, well, a little odd. But she seemed to have got to grips with things again now.

"Oh, right — I'm really, really sorry," Mitzi said apologetically. "No, honestly. I wouldn't have had this happen for the world. It's unforgivable of me — I hate being unprofessional, Connie, you know that. And I'll admit I have been a little — er — distracted lately. It'll never happen again. Are the poor mourners devastated?"

"Not about the loss of their Uncle Michael, no." Constance sniffed. "About not getting their mitts on to the grub, yes."

Mitzi smiled. "Right — so double helpings of Weeping Walnuts and Tansy Tears, is it?"

"Whatever you've got to make 'em gnash their bloody teeth and stop grizzling about their bloody stomachs." Constance flicked at her veil which had now stuck to her harsh slash of lipstick. "And quick about it!"

With Mitzi in hot pursuit, Amber hurtled into the house with the boxes, unloaded them, handed round plates and napkins — black and guaranteed not to run — tried to wear her most miserable expression, and winced at Slo and Perpetua who were doing a sort of John Travolta and Olivia Newton-John routine in the corner of the living room to the consternation of a couple of dozen bemused bereaved.

"You've been so long they've run out of dirges and sad odes," Constance hissed. "The *Grease* thing is what they do at the Evergreens Christmas Party."

"You're the one that I want . . ." Slo warbled, shimmying towards Amber with a strange expression. "Whoa-whoa-whoa-whoa — yeah."

Amber shoved a Tansy Tear in his mouth.

"Right," Mitzi puffed. "Push as much weepy food into them as possible and let's get out of here. If I've mistimed this one I've probably mistimed the kiddies' party, too."

Amber nodded and trotted briskly through the ranks of mourners, piling their plates with lashings of Teardrop Explodes and Weeping Willow Waffles whether they wanted them or not.

"That should do it," Mitzi nodded in satisfaction. "And it'll shut the Motions up, too. There's enough grief-inducers in that lot to have Uncle Michael's non-mourners blubbing and howling and rending their garments for weeks to come. The whole place'll rival the Wailing Wall within fifteen minutes. Now, grab the van keys, and let's bugger off to the Broughton-Pogges."

They arrived at the Broughton-Pogges' mock-Tudor with minutes to spare.

"No time to get into our less scary clothes," Mitzi said. "We'll have to pretend we're Goths."

"Crikey," Amber blinked as they slithered from the van and started to unload the goodies. "Posh or what?"

"Not as posh as it looks. Harrods money, Pricerite taste. Makes Tarnia Towers look like Buckingham Palace. And they aren't married — Broughton-Pogges is an amalgamation of their surnames. Father — Jason Broughton — plays football for Reading or Oxford or Swindon or somewhere like that. Mother's the Pogges. A vacuous ex-lap dancer called Lezli. Ready to roll?"

They rolled.

"If you're the caterers for the twins' party," a tinny voice screeched through the intercom as they rang the bell, "the trade entrance is round the back. And you're late. My husband and I will not be in attendance. Nanny is in charge. Nanny will let you in and show you to the refectory."

Exchanging raised-eyebrow looks and trying hard not to giggle, they hefted the party food round the side of the house, their feet slipping and sliding on several tons of multicoloured shingle.

"Like trying to run a bloody marathon on Brighton beach," Mitzi puffed, as they finally reached the back door.

A very pretty Eastern European nanny with green hair and purple nail varnish and a lot of love-bites hustled them through acres of bad taste into a long, much-windowed room set out with about fifty child-sized chairs and tables, and decorated with balloons and streamers.

"That's fine," Mitzi gulped at the nanny. "Thank you. We'll only need a few minutes to get everything ready."

302

"Good," the nanny shrugged. "When they eat it means I can have some time off. Please keep them in here as long as possible. I am at the end of my tether."

"Difficult, are they? The twins?" Amber asked sympathetically, as she and Mitzi darted round, setting out the rainbow plates and bowls and finger food in jewel-bright colours.

"They are bastard bitches from hell," the nanny said, stalking away. "I hope you poison the little shits."

"Nice to find someone happy in their work," Amber giggled. "Jesus!"

"What?" Mitzi paused in sprinkling hundreds and thousands on top of a Bagpuss cake.

"Have you seen the banner? 'Happy Eighth Birthday Fantasia and Heliotrope!' Poor little sods. They're probably known as Fanny and Helly. Who in their right mind would want to call their kids something as outrageous as — er — um — whoops, sorry — I forgot . . ."

"It's OK," Mitzi said loftily. "My daughters have never had a problem with being called Dolores and Tallulah. Well — not much. Well — OK, point taken . . ."

They grinned at one another again.

"Right — let's go and put Nanny out of her misery," Mitzi said. "And if Granny Westward's recipes work she should have a nice peaceful afternoon."

"God, Mitzi — you're not going to sedate them with this lot are you?"

"No, of course not. These are some of Granny's specially-adapted-for-children dishes . . . just a few concoctions using catnip, celandine, marjoram, meadowsweet, quince — and a liberal sprinkling of pomegranate seeds. Together, they're all guaranteed to bring happiness, harmony, euphoria and glee to the most miserable child. They should be chuckling their little heads off in no time."

They stood back as the miniature hordes of Ghenghis Khan roared into the room.

The noise level was terrifying, as were the table manners. Cutlery was used as weapons as they crammed as much of everything into their mouths as they could with their fingers, talking all the while.

Fantasia and Heliotrope, dressed in matching Kylie Minogue stage outfits, punched each other and their guests as they ate, standing on the tables, kicking over chairs, food oozing from their clenched fists, spitting out anything they disliked.

"Nice," Amber muttered, pressing herself back against a window. "Remind me to make a sterilisation appointment the minute we're out of here."

Horde of locusts wasn't in it.

Within minutes the tables were left with only debris. The Bagpuss cake was sliding down one wall. There wasn't much sign of euphoria, harmony or glee.

Fantasia and Heliotrope stopped yelling obscentities, looked at one another, made a half-hearted attempt to tug one another's braided hair, then burst into tears. Falling into a clearly one-off sibling hug, they sobbed snail-trails of body glitter down each other's tiny shoulders.

For a second the room went silent, then, as one, the fifty tiny guests started howling and sobbing and prostrating themselves with inconsolable grief.

"Hell's fire!" Nanny poked her head round the door. "What you done to them? This is so good! Mega! Er — I fetch the bloody parents!"

The din grew worse. The weeping and wailing grew louder. Above it all Mitzi's mobile rang.

"Hello?" she screamed above the mass keening. "What? *What?* Oh, holy shit!"

"What?" Amber yelled above the cacophony. "Mitzi? What the hell's going on? And what are you doing?"

"Running," Mitzi laughed. "Come on! Leave everything! Let's get out of her before Jace and Lezli arrive on the scene. That was Slo on the phone — Uncle Michael's mourners have tripped out and are currently executing a laughing conga up the High Street! In the rush, we've mixed up the cool boxes, Amber! Bloody run!"

CHAPTER
TWENTY-FOUR

Once Upon a Star

"And now they've introduced a bloomin' hosepipe ban," Gwyneth sighed, as the Moth, Chrysalis and Butterfly Cottage occupants, minus Amber, sat outside in the already scorching sun enjoying their early morning cuppa. "Me runners are hanging as limp as an old whatnot as it is."

Zillah giggled. She kept giggling these days. It was really odd. She hadn't giggled for years. And she had this feeling of — she wasn't sure of what exactly — but of some sort of tingling anticipation . . . She put it down to being free of Timmy's full-on adoration. What else could it be? Nothing else had changed. Nothing else was ever going to change.

"We could still do a bit of a rain incantation tonight," Big Ida was saying. "I know we've discussed it before, and I know it ain't right on Plough Night and the moon's not even in the right quarter, but needs must. We ain't seen a spit of rain since I don't remember when."

"May, or maybe April," Gwyneth said, puffing as she bent down to pat a panting Pike on the head. "This is like living in Arundel."

Big Ida and Zillah peered at her.
"Arundel?"

"Ah, that cowboy place in America. All scorched dry and red-dusty with big cacti."

"Oh, *Arizona!*" Zillah chuckled. "And I don't think we're quite as hot and dry as that."

Big Ida adjusted her sunhat. "Won't be long, you marks my words. Bloody global warming — I blame it on them people as takes their holidays in foreign climes and brings the tropical 'eat back 'ere with 'em instead of leaving it where it belongs. It ain't natural. I can't remember a summer like this one."

Zillah could.

The year Lewis was born. The year she came here to Fiddlesticks, frightened, alone, lonely, heartbroken.

It had been a scorching summer then, too. Day after day of relentless blue sky and broiling sun. And she'd felt so ill through her early pregnancy, and Gwyneth and Big Ida had helped her settle into Chrysalis Cottage, the only place that had been cheap enough to rent far enough away from anyone who knew her, and they'd been so very kind. And she'd known they'd been shocked that she was pregnant and unmarried and without a partner even in the background, but they hadn't shown it, hadn't uttered one word of censure.

The rest of the village had, she'd known, regarded her as some sort of loose woman, but Gwyneth and Big Ida had shielded her from the worst of the hurtful remarks. They'd been kindness itself, and helped her turn damp, dirty, deserted Chrysalis into a home.

And in the late autumn it had rained at last, and Lewis had been born, and she'd loved him with an intensity she thought she'd never feel again, and some of the heartbreak had eased and she'd vowed that the rest of her life would be spent in making him happy and secure, and that not having a father around would never be a handicap for him.

And, she felt, she'd achieved that, hadn't she? Lewis had grown into a rounded, positive, fulfilled man: happy through school and college, with lots of friends, great exam results, a stupendous social life, a job he adored.

She'd done her best for him. She'd made up for her mistakes. There were no regrets.

No regrets? Zillah sighed and ran her flip-flops through little runnels of dust. Not quite true. There was still one. Only one.

"Zil? Zil, duck?" Gwyneth was peering at her. "Wakey-wakey, duck. You was miles away. Ida was just saying we ought to make a rain incantation to Leo tonight come what may. What do you reckon?"

"What? Oh, yes — why not?" Zillah smiled, not caring one way or the other. "I don't suppose the celestial gods and goddesses will object too much. Plough Night, Leo's Lightning, they're both much of a muchness, aren't they?"

"Zil!"

Big Ida rocked with indignation at this blatant heresy.

Zillah chuckled. "Sorry, Ida. But honestly, Plough Night is always a bit of a damp squib, isn't it? All that dreary stuff about nature's bounty and plentiful crops and things. Nothing exciting ever happens on Plough Night, does it?"

Amber was outside The Weasel and Bucket the minute Timmy unlocked the doors at 6 o'clock.

"Crikey," he grinned at her. "Has living in Fiddlesticks turned you into a lush at last?"

"You wish! No, I'm meeting someone," Amber said, walking into the warm, musty, yeasty pub. "Didn't want to be late. And to be honest, Gwyneth is taking this hosepipe ban thing so seriously that she's decided we all have the same bath water. I didn't want to go in after Pike," she joked, "so I was given the five o'clock slot. I've been ready for ages."

"And very nice you look, too." Timmy made an extravagant bow. "Even more gorgeous than usual. This someone you're meeting — is it a date? Lewis?"

"Thank you. No and no," Amber clambered onto one of the high bar stools. "Although hopefully Lewis will be here sooner rather than later, too."

As he poured her a large glass of house white, Amber told Timmy about the JB Roadshow, and about Freddo coming to give the facilities a once-over before Harvest Moon.

"Ah, yes, Zillah told me about that. Should be great. I like a good band. And it'll bring the punters in here in droves." Timmy exchanged wine for money. "Plough Night's OK, but because it's more generally focused on the land rather than the heart, it doesn't generate quite so much excitement."

"So I gathered," Amber sipped her wine. "It sounds like a sort of school harvest festival without the veg."

Timmy laughed. "Hmmm . . . that's not too far off the mark. Mind you, we can't ignore its importance — specially round here. We're still very agricultural: lots of working arable farms and nearly everyone has an allotment or at least a vegetable patch. No, Plough Night is as important here now as it was hundreds of years back."

Amber took another mouthful of wine. Plough Night truly didn't seem to promise much by way of excitement. Not like St Bedric's or Cassiopeia's or even the rumours she'd heard about the breakaway Andromeda-faction. Even Leo's Lightning was supposed to produce something spectacular — and as for Harvest Moon — well, if she had her way it would be the best thing Fiddlesticks had ever seen.

No, she had to be honest, the only reason she was looking forward to Plough Night was because it meant she'd spend time with Lewis.

What was that sad quotation? They'd done it at school. Something about love being everything in the life of a woman, but only a minority interest in the life of a man?

Dear, oh, dear . . . She stared through the pinpricks in the darkly ivy-covered windows. Was she seriously in danger of turning into one of those sad, love-sick, obsessive, needy women who wiped out every other aspect of their lives, existing only for the moment when the object of their desires deigned to bestow a few minutes of their precious time?

Was she hell?!

310

Well — OK, maybe she was edging in that direction, but she could do something about it, couldn't she? She was still in control of her faculties, her emotions, her life.

Timmy broke rudely into this deep introspection. "Er — is Zil on her way over, do you know? She's due in at half-six and she was really strange at lunchtime. Very flippant and giggly. Haven't seen her like that for ages. I had the feeling she might have something on her mind . . ."

"Sorry? What? Oh, Zil? No, sorry, haven't see her," Amber muttered, thinking Zillah's new freedom of spirit had a lot to do with Timmy — but probably not in the way he wanted to hear. Not even now. It might still hurt his feelings. "But she's usually on time, isn't she? I'm sure she'll be here. And isn't Fern working tonight, too?"

"She's on Hayfields duty." Timmy looked bereft. "I'm going to pop over to see her later, when we've shut. Look, Amber, you don't think I'm making a complete prat of myself, do you?"

"Over Fern? No way! She's loved you for years. It just took a bit of astral magic to sort it out. You two will have the archetypal happy ending."

Timmy beamed again. He looked, Amber thought, like a fat cat that had fallen into a vat of cream. How very weird this love thing was. Still, at least one of the tangles had been satisfactorily unravelled. Cassiopeia would probably take hundreds of years to sort out the others.

As if by magic, the pub, one minute silently warm and deserted, with dappled sun patterns across the polished floorboards, was filled with hot and thirsty people.

"Sorry I'm late." Zillah, looking anything but, grinned as she floated through the throng and ducked behind the bar. She was wearing the beautiful rose-sprigged dress and had long rosebud earrings dangling through her curls. "I was listening to some of my old records while I was getting ready. Lost all track of time. OK, who's next?"

Amber watched Zillah as she served customers, laughing, exchanging the necessary few words. Timmy was right: she looked so much more relaxed now. Happier. It must be so nice for her, Amber thought, to be able to get sexily glammed up for work at last without Timmy thinking it was all for his benefit.

Lewis suddenly appeared through the throng, and grinned at Amber. "Your long-haired lover from Winterbrook is outside."

She tried really, really hard not to tingle at his appearance or the grin. "Freddo? Already? Brilliant — but why didn't he come in?"

"We arrived at the same time, so he's grabbed a table and is chatting to Jem while I get the drinks. It's too hot to be inside anyway. Oh, hi Ma — when you're ready . . ."

"You wait your turn," Zillah said cheerfully. "Being family doesn't mean you can jump the queue. Next!"

"I'll have a house white if you're buying, ta." Amber slid from the stool. "I'd better go and rescue Freddo —"

"He won't need rescuing from Jem." Lewis looked affronted. "Surely, you know that by now?"

"Of course I do. I wasn't worried about Jem. Jem'll be the perfect host. It's the rest of Fiddlesticks I'm concerned with. They don't often see people like Freddo round here, do they?"

Her worst fears were realised as she forced her way into the beer garden and blinked in the glare of the sun spiralling on the western horizon. Freddo, his hair even more bleached and wild, his skin even more perma-tanned, his wrists and neck covered in rap-master bling, was surrounded by curious Fiddlestickers, most of whom knew, thanks to the village jungle drums, why he was there but still felt the need to offer him advice.

"Hi, duck. My, you get prettier by the day." He looked up at Amber in relief as she elbowed her way through Goff and Mrs Jupp and Billy Grinley and the Motions. "This is a quaint little village," he dropped his voice to a whisper, "but the natives are a bit odd."

"Tell me about it," Amber smiled, kissing Jem and shaking Freddo's hand before she sat down. "Mind you, rumour has it that they're even weirder in Bagley-cum-Russet."

"Oh, yeah. I heard that, too. Haven't been out to any of these villages for years," Freddo said. "Spend every waking minute on the agency: out on the road or in the Winterbrook office. Too little time, too many villages — you know how it is?"

Amber nodded. "When I first arrived here I thought I'd be bored to tears. I simply couldn't imagine what people in the countryside found to do all day. I was itching to get into Reading for shopping and nightlife —"

"And you haven't?"

"Not once. Too busy to even think about it," Amber grinned. "Far too occupied here to even give it a second thought."

"I could take you out in Reading one night, if you liked." Freddo made an expansive take-it-or-leave-it hand gesture. "Round the clubs, take in a few bars. I've got some good contacts in the best venues. Nothing heavy."

"What about Mrs Freddo? Wouldn't she object?"

"Hardly, duck. Mrs Freddo was my receptionist."

"The one that went to lunch in 1998 and didn't come back?"

"The very same."

They laughed together. The assorted Fiddlestickers, who had been hanging on every word, joined in.

"I think Timmy's doing half-price drinks about now," Amber said softly to the hovering crowd. Then she leaned towards Slo and lowered her voice even further. "And Lewis was flashing the fags around like there's no tomorrow when I left him . . ."

"That got rid of 'em sharpish," Freddo said in admiration as the throng melted away. "What the hell did you say to them?"

"Simply what they wanted to hear. All untruths I'm afraid, but by the time they've argued the toss in the pub they'll hopefully have forgotten about you and we can get some peace."

"Cool, duck. Look, are you sure you don't want a job with me?"

"Couldn't stand the pace," Amber grinned. "And thanks for the offer of an evening in Reading, but I'll pass on that too, if you don't mind."

"Someone else doing the squiring, is there, duck?"

"No," Amber shook her head, "but I live in hope."

Jem took her hand and placed it on his heart, then held up his hands, crossed at the wrist and gestured towards the pub.

Amber laughed. "Jem lives in hope, too, apparently. I think we're both probably going to be disappointed . . . Oh, look — right on cue . . ."

Lewis, looking even more like a hippie love-god, with the sun radiating in golden splendour behind him, carried the glasses over to the table.

"Is anyone going to let me in on the joke?"

They all shook their heads, still smiling.

"Sod you, then," he said affably, sliding his long legs on to the bench alongside Amber. "So, what's next on the agenda?"

"We were hoping you could tell us," Amber said, nodding towards the village green where large crowds were already gathering. "What exactly goes on at this Plough Night thing?"

"Firstly, it's nowhere near as much fun as Cassiopeia's," Lewis stretched his legs under the table. His trainer rested against Amber's sandal. Neither of them moved. "Although I think there'll be a lot of off-the-record rain-wishing tonight." He moved his foot slightly, closer, not away, and smiled. "However, the main idea is to ask the Plough, when the constellation appears in the sky, to bring rude good health to the villagers and prosperity to their undertakings, and of course, a hearty crop to their gardens and fields. Goff does the public incantations as usual, and then we have a lot to drink and usually something earthy like jacket potatoes to eat and that's about it . . ."

Amber returned the pressure of his foot. "So when would be the best time to show Freddo around?"

"Sooner rather than later," Lewis said, looking innocent. He moved his foot away. Slowly. "As soon as we've finished these drinks — if that's OK with you, Freddo, we'll go and take a stroll."

"Fine by me," Freddo drained his pint of Hearty Hercules in record time even by Fiddlesticks' standards. "It's only on the green, isn't it? The others will be able to find us?"

"Others?"

"Ah, the band's been playing a couple of local gigs. They're free tonight, staying over in Newbury. I issued an open invite to any of them that are sober enough to make it — hope that's OK?"

"The more the merrier," Lewis grinned, finishing his own pint and standing up, helping Jem to his feet. "As you can see, there aren't any restrictions."

They wandered across the green, bathed in the last spectacular pink-gold glow of the sun as it disappeared behind the Hazy Hassocks hills, Jem holding Amber's hand.

She looked up at Lewis as they crossed the rustic bridge. "What was all that about — the footsie thing?"

316

"What footsie thing? If your size eighteens got in the way back there then it's hardly my fault, is it?" He ruffled her hair fleetingly. "Seriously Amber — I'd never play games with you."

Feeling suddenly very hot, Amber looked down at the parched grass. Was this a seminal moment? Was it —?

Bugger.

Sukie, the Irish witch, along with several of her friends, was skippetying towards them through the crowds.

"Hi," she flashed white teeth at Lewis as she passed. "We must get together for that drink sometime."

"Yeah," Lewis grinned. "We must. I'll give you a ring."

Jem frowned at Sukie and then at Lewis and squeezed Amber's hand very tightly. She squeezed it back. She really wished she could squeeze Sukie's neck.

Fortunately the murderous moment was interrupted by a familiar voice.

"Amber! Amber — over here! Look who I've brought to see you!"

Mitzi and her family were out in force, and Amber, leaving Jem with Lewis and Freddo, spent ages cooing over Sonny, delighted to see him in the flesh at last, and chatting to Mitzi's two pretty daughters and their partners and exchanging north-western banter with Joel, the to-die-for dentist.

"Jace and Lezli phoned this afternoon," Mitzi said. "The Broughton-Pogges. Apparently Fanny and Helly, the nightmare twins from hell, have been extremely subdued and dutiful since the party. They added a bonus to our fee and have asked us to go back and cater for their wedding party next year. As we seem to have done very well out of our — er — my recent mistakes, maybe getting the ingredients wrong should be something we make a feature of in future recipes . . ."

"Please, no," Amber laughed. "I don't think I could take it."

She ran to catch up with the others. Freddo was in deep conference with Goff Briggs.

"They're just deciding the best place for the stage and the power cables and the security and safety stuff," Lewis said. "And Jem's sulking."

"Why?"

"Because Sukie said she wanted to go for a drink and because I said I was going to ring her, I gather. I've tried to tell him I was using polite-speak-code for 'I had a great time with you, and I like you very much, but I won't be seeing you again'."

Amber suddenly did mental handstands across the green.

"I also told him that I have so many girls' numbers in my little black mobile that I'd never settle for just one."

The handstands collapsed in an undignified heap.

The rest of the evening passed in the usual Fiddlesticks manner: lazy conversations with friends, raucous laughter, and a fair amount of drinking.

As the sky eventually darkened, Goff, his neck garlanded with woven corn like some ancient pagan leader, stalked towards the centre of the green, a potato in one hand and a clump of earth in the other.

The crowds parted to allow him through until he reached the little hillock beside the rustic bridge. Much to Jem's enjoyment, several children, rather unwisely in Amber's opinion, trotted behind him and stood on either side of the stream, holding blazing torches aloft like miniature Olympic flames. She supposed, should the worst happen, the kiddies could always be dunked quickly in the water to douse the resulting inferno.

Over to the right, just visible through the willows in the deepest gloom, Gwyneth and Big Ida were furtively holding their own little ceremony involving a watering can, a few runner beans, a candle and a length of hosepipe.

"This is truly scary shit, duck," Freddo muttered beside her as Goff started his nature's bounty spiel. "Spooky. Give me a nice bit of transcendental meditation any day. Now that I understand."

"Do you want to go back to the pub?" Lewis asked. "Get a head start in the queue for the jacket spuds?"

"No way," Amber said. "Sorry Jem — I know you're probably starving, as ever, but I'm sure there'll be plenty. No, if you don't mind, I want to watch this . . ."

Goff was now holding the potato and the clod of earth aloft towards the skies. The majority of the crowd seemed to be mumbling.

"He's offering them up and asking the Plough to give Fiddlesticks a plentiful crop," Lewis informed them. "Those with a vested interest in farms and gardens make their own earthy-fertility wish now, too."

"Stone me," Freddo shook his head. "I'm getting spooked and no mistake."

Amber giggled.

Lewis moved nearer to her. "Can you see the Plough? Up there?"

Call her a pushover, but she loved this bit of the astral ceremonies. The standing close and pointing.

"Trixie dog, you mean?"

"I told you it was best not to mention that," Lewis laughed softly. "And certainly not here and not now. There are those who may think you were mocking."

"Would I mock? Moi?" Amber squinted upwards at the deep purple sky, now alight with scattered silver sequins. "Um — yes, I think I can see it. Yes — yes, I can — I think. Over there, isn't it? Oh — but what's the other one? The smaller constellation right next to it with the really, really bright star?"

"Actually," Lewis said, his face close to hers, his breath warm, "although I hate to say this, your thing about the Plough looking like a dog isn't that far out. The Plough is also part of a larger constellation called the Great Bear. The bright star you can see is the Pole Star, which is part of the Little Bear —"

"Only needs bleeding Goldilocks to round the fairy story off nicely," Freddo muttered.

Lewis laughed. "Legend has it, that there once was a beautiful princess — what? Yeah, Jem, *just* like Amber — well, Juno, who was queen of the gods, was so jealous of this princess that she turned her into a bear. Juno's son was out hunting and was about to shoot the princess-bear when Jupiter, the king of the gods, turned

320

him into a bear as well and swung both animals up into the sky by their tails — the reason both constellations have long trailing stars — so they could live together safely and happily ever after."

"Bugger me," Freddo sighed. "I wish I was smoking what you were smoking. I haven't heard anything quite so trippy since 1969 . . . oh, hi guys! You found us then. Isn't this the weirdest set-up ever? Our gig here's going to be a blast."

Amber turned to see a smattering of the JB Roadshow — the singer, and one of the guitarists, and the drummer, or maybe it was the keyboard player — standing beside them in the musky darkness looking totally bemused.

Everyone exchanged pleasantries, and Jem, scenting jacket potatoes, tugged at Amber's hand and gestured impatiently towards The Weasel and Bucket.

"Yeah, OK," Lewis laughed, ruffling Jem's hair with the same brotherly affection he'd used earlier in ruffling Amber's. "The show's all but over. Let's go and find the food. And there's still time for some serious drinking."

Freddo and the JB Roadshow residue — still looking, Amber reckoned, *very* fit for their ages in their faded denim and surfer-boy shirts — perked up considerably at this, and they all made a beeline for the pub. It did her ego no end of good, Amber thought, being seen in the company of such a bevvy of male beauty.

The JB Roadshow members — Tiff Clayton, Clancy Tavistock and Ricky Swain, as Freddo had reintroduced them — were all very complimentary about the village and the forthcoming Harvest Moon booking, and diplomatically polite about the strangeness of the Plough Night celebrations.

"I like all the old traditions myself," Tiff Clayton said to Amber, giving her a practised look from beneath his dyed blond fringe as they crossed the rustic bridge. "Like kissing under the mistletoe and the best man getting first dibs at the bridesmaids."

"Don't listen to him," Clancy Tavistock, who was walking just ahead of them with Freddo and Lewis, turned and grinned. "He's all talk and no action these days."

"Ah, maybe," Tiff sighed. "But I've still got my memories and my dreams."

"Dreams, perhaps," Clancy laughed over his shoulder. "The memories have all been embellished by age or eroded by recreational substances."

The others laughed. Ricky Swain was walking on the other side of Amber, humming a tune, explaining scales and riffs to an adoring Jem.

They were nice blokes, Amber thought as they crossed the road towards The Weasel and Bucket. Nice blokes, immensely talented, and pretty damn cool.

"This is my shout," Freddo said, as they forced their way through the beer-garden throng. "What's everybody having?"

Despite the majority of Fiddlestickers still being out in force on the green, the usual suspects were perched at the bar. Timmy was obviously in the kitchen cooking up a veritable storm of jacket potatoes, and Zillah,

322

looking radiant in the rose-sprigged dress, her hair all tousled, smiled across at them as they walked in.

"Is it all over, then? Fiddlesticks guaranteed healthy crops for the next twelve months? I thought Goff looked a bit of a twerp in his — oh my God . . ." Zillah clutched the bar, her heart going into overdrive. Taking huge gulps of air, she tried to steady herself, but the pub and the customers were growing dark and swirling dizzily round and round and round.

"Zil? Zillah?" Billy Grinley slid from his stool and ran behind the bar, rapidly followed by Dougie Patchcock. "Quick, Lewis! Quick! I think your ma's fainted!"

CHAPTER
TWENTY-FIVE

I Was Born Under a Wandering Star

It was Zillah's final year at university. A year in which her tutors and her parents confidently expected her to get an upper second, if not a first, in history. A year in which she realised she wanted to be free.

Free from studying, free from being the model student, free from being a dutiful daughter, free from doing what everyone else wanted and expected, free from conforming, free from — oh, just *free*!

It made not a jot of difference how many times her friends, all diligent students, told her that once the finals were over she could be as free as she liked. Once the finals were over, and the three years of hard work had resulted in a qualification that would enable her to take whichever path she chose, she could let her hair down, take a year out, anything. Anything she wanted. Only a few more months to go.

A few more months! A few more days would have been too long.

What she wanted was to be free. Now.

Dropping out was all the rage, of course. But all the dropouts from Zillah's college seemed to have wealthy, indulgent parents who really didn't mind what their offspring did and who looked on university as simply three years of socialising; or were born into inherited silver-spoon money; or had family firms which would suck them up after they'd returned from wandering the hippie trail, turning on and discovering themselves in Marrakech or Kashmir.

Zillah's parents had nothing. Just a bursting pride that their only daughter had made it to Oxford — a word they always spoke in hushed and awed tones, and somewhere they'd never visited because they didn't have a car and the train fare from their Cornish fishing village was way, way beyond them — and was the first in the family to ever go on to further education, let alone to one of the most prestigious universities in the world, and would probably become a school teacher.

A school teacher was the most respected of professions as far as Zillah's parents were concerned. It was what they wanted for her: to come back to Cornwall with her degree and teach history at one of the girls' grammar schools in say, Truro or Bodmin. To pass on her knowledge and education and enthusiasm to other local girls who then might have the same academic opportunity, thanks to Zillah. It was their dream.

It had never been hers.

And now, weary of studying a subject she no longer enjoyed; exhausted from hours and hours of reading words that simply floated through her brain; tired — oh so tired — of the academic life; mentally battered and physically shattered, Zillah wanted to be free.

Her head was crammed with facts, her brain bursting with sifted, selected, assimilated information. Blackwells Bookshop and the Bodlian Library became her places of daily worship. Facts, facts and more facts. The only fiction was in her weekly letter — there was no phone at home — to her parents.

"Give it a little break," her tutor advised. "You've no need to cram, Zillah. You're an excellent student. You have a natural intelligence, a gift for learning, a talent for imparting all that you know. You'll gain an extremely good degree. You've studied hard, worked hard ever since you arrived — don't burn out now. Take a couple of weeks for yourself, go home, relax . . ."

Zillah didn't want to go home. If she went home she'd never return to Oxford. Never get away again. Going home wasn't the answer.

"Well, have some fun, then," her tutor laughed. "Go out and party. Dance 'til dawn. Enjoy yourself. Goodness — this is the antithesis of what I normally have to tell my students!"

But Zillah had done parties and dances and punting and Commem Balls; she'd not been overwhelmed by the hectic and varied social life on offer in Oxford — it simply hadn't really interested her. And after getting drunk a few times in The Eagle and Child and The Turf Tavern and several rowdy nights where Town and Gown mixed in the sinisterly dark corridor of White's Bar, Zillah had resumed her studies, her essays, her total immersion in her history course.

None of it was what she wanted.

"You haven't been made to feel — well — unwelcome?" her tutor enquired kindly. "There is an awful lot of snobbery here and however hard we try to stamp it out . . ."

And Zillah said, no, her soft Cornish accent and humble background had not once been a problem. She'd found the students, all the students, accepted her as she did them. Class, colour, creed — none of those had ever been an issue.

"And there's no man involved? This isn't an affair of the heart gone wrong?"

Zillah shook her head. There was no man. There had been boys, several boys, fellow students — and they'd had fun, and exchanged kisses and inexpert fumbles, but that was as far as it had gone. There had been no lover. Not ever. Her virginity, like her heart, was intact.

"Well, my dear," her tutor smiled gently. "I can only advise you to take things easy for a while, enjoy yourself, forget about the finals."

And Zillah had.

She would never be able to explain the blissful freedom she felt on that spring morning, leaving Oxford, everything she needed for her new life packed into a single haversack, her hair, like her skirt, long and blowing wildly in the breeze.

Walking away, with no regrets, from everything everyone had ever wanted for her.

She told no one she was leaving; hadn't left a note. Just tidied her room in her digs, stacked up the few belongings she couldn't take with her, left enough money to pay the residue of her rent, and walked away from the dreaming spires' stifling prison.

With no idea where fate would take her, she reached the outskirts of the city and stuck out her thumb.

The first driver took her as far south as Winchester. Students hitching lifts were normal, there were few questions asked, and no danger. Solitary drivers were simply pleased to have some company.

After Winchester, where she'd had coffee and a doughnut, Zillah hitched a further lift. In a lorry. This one took her towards the New Forest, stopping at the Cadnam roundabout.

Zillah watched the lorry drive away and lifted her face to the sun. Ahead the New Forest spread in wildly glorious green and gold splendour, the wind-born scent of broom and ferns and mouldering pine needles, a balm. Ahead lay the future: a nebulous future — no longer shaped by rigid timetables and other people's expectations. A future in which she would, for the first time, take control of her life.

Skirting the road-wide cattle grid, the ground mossy and yielding beneath her feet, Zillah walked slowly south, sticking her thumb out as she heard vehicles approaching. The morning air was soft and warm, and for the first time in her life she felt her spirits rise with the soaring bird song. The primal forest, organic, surrounded her, cloaking her safely, giving her a true hippie feel of being at one with nature.

This was what she wanted. To be alone, unfettered, free to make choices, free to be herself instead of the model daughter, the model student.

A blue transit van pulled up on the left ahead of her and the driver stuck his head out of the window.

"Want a lift, darling? Bournemouth any good?"

Zillah nodded, gathered her skirt up and ran, pulling the passenger door open, scrambling inside.

"Hi."

The van was crowded with boys of her own age, seven very attractive boys, with long silky hair and long slender be-jeaned legs and logo'd T-shirts. They all looked very tired and fairly uncomfortable, as crammed in with them were all manner of bags and musical instruments and huge black speakers and rolls of cable.

"Make room for her in the back," the driver called over his shoulder. "Budge up a bit."

They budged, and Zillah, after only a fleeting moment of doubt about the wisdom of accepting this lift, and her haversack had tumbled over the three boys in the front seat and into the back.

The boy sitting next to her, the boy with the huge dark eyes and the high-cheekbones and the sulky-beautiful mouth, smiled. "OK? Not too squashed? Let me help you . . ."

She fell in love with him then. There and then. At first sight.

"No . . . I'm fine. Thank you . . . This is very kind of you."

"Our pleasure," the driver said, selecting first gear and indicating to pull away. "Where have you come from?"

And Zillah told them. All of it. Because she'd spent years and years of lying to everyone, especially to herself, and this was like the best confessional in the world.

And they listened and offered no censure at the cavalier way she'd binned her glittering academic future, but said they hoped she'd made the right choice, and congratulated her on her decision to take control of her life. And they shared their Coke and cigarettes and chocolate with her as the New Forest rolled by outside, the bracken a green carpet and the myriad oaks a latticed green canopy.

"And you — you're a rock group?"

"Soul band, yeah," one of the boys in the front seat said. "We've got a rented house in Kilburn that we share, but we're rarely there. We're on the road most of the time. One town after another. It's cool."

Zillah shook her head. She had never before known anyone who lived an itinerant life. How wonderful it must be travelling, playing music, packing up, moving on. No set routine, no one day the same as the hundreds of others on either side.

Perfect freedom.

The beautiful boy beside her introduced the others, six of them in the band, and the driver who was Stan, their roadie, chauffeur, general all-round good geezer.

"And I'm Clancy Tavistock, bass guitarist. Collectively, we're Solstice Soul."

"Zillah Flanagan," Zillah said, wondering if Clancy Tavistock could hear her heart thundering. "And I'm sorry — but if you're famous, I've never heard of you."

They all laughed, the laughter drowning out Jimi Hendrix on the radio.

"We're quite well known on the club and festival circuit," Clancy said, stretching his long, long legs over the seat in front, easing his back. "But the Beatles, we're not."

Zillah watched his unconsciously sensuous movements, aching to touch him, shocked and slightly ashamed at the intensity of the wanting.

"We've just got a record deal," they told her. "UK soul is very hot at the moment. Everyone is after white soul boys. We're not kidding ourselves that we're going to be the next Ram-Jam Band — but we've got bookings as far ahead as the eye can see, and we're making decent money at last. Mind you, we've always had fun — money or no . . ."

And as they headed nearer to the south coast and the sky grew huge, silver washed in the sun, they chatted easily and Zillah learned that they all came from London, had been in various bands since they'd been at school, been together professionally for eighteen months.

Zillah's musical knowledge was shaky to say the least. She preferred the Stones to the Beatles, loved American soul singers like Otis Redding and Eddie Floyd, could sing along with most of the Top Twenty, but the years and years of studying had interfered with the keeping up with current trends.

"We could educate you if you like," Clancy said. Then he'd laughed. "Always supposing education isn't a dirty word, of course."

They were going to Bournemouth to play a gig. At a biggish venue. Staying for a couple of nights in a guest house — one of the perks, they told her, of having a proper management structure, it beat kipping in the van hands down — then on to a booking in Christchurch, then inland again to Dorchester, then back to the coast, Southampton followed by Brighton.

"If you haven't got anything planned," Clancy said, passing her another can of Coke, "you could hang out with us tonight. Watch the gig, stay at the guest house, sort out what you want to do, where you want to go, tomorrow."

"That sounds great, thank you. If you're sure I won't be in the way . . ."

And so for the first time in her life, that night, Zillah had been "with the band". They'd checked into the guest house, a few roads back from the sea front, and they'd kindly rearranged the rooms so that Zillah could have one on her own, and had refused her offer to pay.

"This is all on our management account," they told her. "Make the most of it. We do."

So, Zillah had sat beside the stage and watched entranced, as Solstice Soul slammed their brilliantly talented way through the classics like "Soul Finger" and "Knock On Wood", and various ska and reggae and Motown tunes, looking even more sexily gorgeous in their tight black flares and their satin shirts, making the girls in the packed non-stop-dancing audience scream.

And she knew this was what she wanted; where she wanted to be.

And later, much, much later, after they'd packed up and found a chip shop open and shared an after-midnight supper on the black, deserted sea-front where the strings of coloured lights danced like a fallen rainbow on the undulating water, they wandered back to the guest house, all still on an adrenaline high.

In the largest of the bedrooms they had all shared a bottle of Canadian rye whisky laced with dry ginger, drinking from the tooth mugs, and Clancy Tavistock had slid his arm round her shoulder and kissed her.

And that night he'd shared her bed and told her that he loved her too, and Zillah didn't believe him, neither did she care. She was in love and her body was on fire.

The next morning, at breakfast, the landlady served them a full English, and grinned wickedly at Zillah, and Zillah grinned back, sharing the woman-to-woman knowledge, and not feeling ashamed as she'd always imagined she'd be — as her parents had told her she would if she ever did anything like this — but liberated and floating and happier than she could ever remember.

And when Solstice Soul played Christchurch that night, Zillah was still there, and when they moved on, it was as if she'd known them and been in love with Clancy for ever.

She wrote home, explaining everything to her parents, telling them that she was happy, safe, having fun — and not to worry about her. She apologised about abandoning her academic studies, but knew they'd understand — which was more or less what she wrote to her tutor too.

And then, for nearly two halcyon years, she and Clancy Tavistock were inseparable. She believed him now when he said he loved her; no one was in any doubt of it. They were made for each other, blissfully happy, good friends as well as lovers, sharing everything.

Clancy was kind, funny, intelligent, good tempered; they talked about anything and everything, arguing good-naturedly, challenging one another's views. Zillah took odd bar jobs while the band was on the road and more permanent ones when they were back in London where she shared Clancy's room in the rented house, pleased to be able to pay her way.

She loved him as he loved her, with an intensity that defied description. Together, they were magical, and everything around them became star-spangled. Never once did she regret leaving her other life behind. This was her life now, this had been preordained.

She still wrote long weekly letters to her parents, or sent postcards from whichever town the band was playing, but they never replied. She wasn't particularly worried — they'd never been the greatest correspondents, and as long as they knew she was safe and happy, they'd be OK.

The band and Zillah continuously toured the country, then they spent time in the recording studio laying down "Summer and Winter" which went into the album charts and made them more in demand than ever.

There was a management takeover, and the new bosses arranged a tour of Germany, Italy, France. Six months. And no women.

The rest of the band had transient girlfriends, and didn't mind too much. Clancy said if Zillah couldn't go then neither would he.

Zillah had told him not to be stupid, not to even consider wrecking his career as it was reaching its zenith, for her. Six months apart would kill her, too, but she'd still be there when he came back. They'd be so busy the time would just fly. She'd stay on in the rented house in Kilburn, find a permanent bar job, they could write all the time — and think about the getting together session they'd have when he finally came home.

So, he left, and they both cried, and as she made her way back to the house from the airport, Zillah felt her world crumbling around her. Six months. How could she survive for six months without him? Of course she trusted him, and even if there were groupies throwing themselves at him, so what? He'd come back to her, wouldn't he? But how on earth would she survive until then?

The next cataclysmic events all rolled in on one another like an inexorable gathering tide of disaster.

The new management stopped paying for the Kilburn house — after all, it had never been part of their deal and the band were away touring Europe; they also refused to tell Zillah where exactly Solstice Soul were at any one time, nor would they pass on letters or messages; as she couldn't afford to stay on in the house and the bar work didn't pay enough for her to stay living in London, she decided to go home until Clancy came back to the UK. He hadn't written — but he would, she knew he would.

Anyway, she'd be able to contact him then, through his record company, surely? And then he'd write to her and give her a forwarding address abroad. It would be OK. But, oh, she missed him so much. The days and nights without him, without their carefree, wild, itinerant, hippie, happy life, were an aching physical pain.

Zillah wrote to her parents, telling them she was coming home for a while, and on the same day as she posted the letter, the thing she'd feared for some weeks was confirmed: she was pregnant.

She'd hitched down to Cornwall, feeling sick and lonely and more than a little frightened. But she was going home. And Clancy would be back before the baby was born, wouldn't he?

"You're not stopping here," her dad said, opening the door just a crack. "You've broken your mother's heart. You clear off back to where you came from. You're no daughter of mine."

Stunned, Zillah had tried to speak to her mother.

"We had such dreams for you, Zil. We gave up our lives for you. You went to Oxford — you were coming home to be a teacher — and you let us down." Her mother's eyes were flinty. "We were a laughing stock. And you've ruined your own life, my girl. No, your Dad's right — you made your bed when you gave up your studies — now you bloody well lie on it."

"But, Mum," Zillah choked on her tears. "Mum — I'm pregnant."

"And so you're a whore as well, are you?" her mother had spat, slamming the door. "Go away, Zillah. We never want to see you or hear from you again."

It was the local vicar's wife, sniffily disapproving, who took her in overnight and found, through the church network for fallen women, the cottage in Fiddlesticks. Berkshire, it was considered, would be far enough away for Zillah not to be any further embarrassment to her family.

And Zillah had arrived there in the middle of a scorching summer, lonely, frightened, heartbroken, and clearly labelled as "one of them girls in trouble". As she had to pay the rent for the cottage herself, she'd taken a bar job at The Weasel and Bucket, and despite all her frantic efforts to contact him, never heard from or saw Clancy Tavistock again.

CHAPTER
TWENTY-SIX

Midnight Moonlight and Magic

"I'm fine . . . no, really . . . oh . . ." Zillah blinked muzzily.

She was sitting on the kitchen doorstep of The Weasel and Bucket, her head being pressed down towards her knees, a glass of iced water slopping on to the lap of her frock.

"Honestly, I'm OK now. Don't know what came over me. Must have been the heat . . ."

Lewis and Amber and Jem were all staring down at her, their white faces matching in shock and concern.

She wriggled round a bit to see who was pressing on the back of her neck.

"Timmy, let me get up — honestly — I'm fine now. Get back into the bar — you'll be so busy — all those potatoes to dish up . . ."

"They're all cooked and out there on the hot trolleys. Billy and Dougie are holding the fort."

"Doesn't matter. Timmy, please. Go. For me. Please. There's no need to make a fuss. I'm okay."

Eventually, still looking worried, he went.

Zillah sighed, sipped at the water and took a deep breath of cool night air. Her head was clearing, her heart resuming a normal rhythm.

There. She was fine. Truly.

She looked up at Lewis. "Sorry, love. That must have been a bit scary for you."

He squatted beside her, holding her hand. "Do you want an ambulance? Or I could run you into the Royal Berks in no time. Ma — you're ill, aren't you?"

"Sweetheart," she squeezed his hand. "I'm not ill. I'm ridiculously fit. And no, I don't need to go to hospital or anywhere else. I just fainted. I'm feeling a hundred per cent again now."

"You never faint. I've never known you faint. Ma, please let me take you to the hospital — just to get you checked over."

Zillah laughed rather shakily. "No, honestly, love. I don't need a check-up. Give me a couple of minutes and I'll be back at work."

"You will bloody not," Lewis hugged her. "You're going home. Now. And I'll stay the night. Amber can take Jem back to Hayfields. Martha will sit in with him. And tomorrow I'm going to make a doctor's appointment and —"

"Lewis, love, stop right there." She smiled gently. "Listen to me — I'm absolutely fine. All I need is a couple of minutes."

To do what? Zillah exhaled. To explain to Lewis that she'd been foolish enough to think that a stranger in the bar, a beautiful tall man with glossy hair falling over his big dark eyes, a man with high cheekbones and a sulky-sexy mouth, was his father?

That this man, who had clearly only come to Fiddlesticks for Plough Night and no doubt had a wife and kiddies waiting in the beer garden, was Clancy Tavistock? The only man she'd ever loved?

She laughed to herself. Tell him that and he really would think she was ill — and not just physically.

And it wasn't as if it had been the first time. God, no. Over the years she'd imagined she'd glimpsed Clancy Tavistock in all manner of peculiar places and her heart had gone into overdrive and she'd had to stop and steady herself — although she'd never passed out before, which must be down to the stifling heat — and when she'd looked again it had been a complete stranger and part of her had died.

Amber stooped down. "Zil, if you're really feeling better, I'll take Jem back through to the bar, shall I? I think he was pretty scared when you keeled over. He'll be better out of the way."

Zillah nodded. "Good idea — and he's probably hungry, aren't you Jem?"

Jem, clinging to Amber's hand, nodded. He'd been crying.

"Come on, then." Amber led him away from the back door. "Let's see if Timmy can put a whole mountain of grated cheese on your spud, shall we? Or would you like baked beans? Or maybe both?"

Jem nodded happily and trotted out of the kitchen with Amber.

"She's very good with him, isn't she? They get on really well."

"What? Oh, yeah," Lewis nodded. "And he loves her to bits. Ma — I don't want to talk about Jem or Amber right now. I want to know —"

"Good lord, Lewis," she smiled gently at him. "What will it take to convince you that I'm absolutely OK? Do I have to turn cartwheels or something? Look, I'm going to stand up and prove to you that there's absolutely nothing wrong with me at all. Not even the slightest wobble. There! OK?"

He grinned at her. "Yeah, OK — but still, people don't faint for no reason and —"

"Lewis?" Timmy poked his head round the door, "Jem needs to go to the loo. Amber can't take him obviously and I'm all tied up and . . ." He looked at Zillah. "You're looking a lot better, love. Get yourself off home as soon as you want. I'll walk you over the green and make sure you're OK."

"No you won't," Lewis frowned. "I will. I've already told her —"

Zillah shook her head, laughing. "I'm going nowhere. Lewis, go and see to Jem. Timmy, get back to your spuds. Both of you, leave me alone and stop bloody fussing!"

In the bar, the crowd jostled and roared: Plough Night was being critically analysed with Paxmanesque acidity; potatoes were being eaten at the speed of light; Zillah's "funny turn" was no longer the hot topic it had been half an hour earlier, now being put down to the heat, summer flu, the change, or a fad diet, depending on who you listened to.

Amber, sitting round the table with Freddo and the JB Roadshow, was simply relieved that whatever had caused it, Zil was OK now and everyone had stopped flapping. Lewis had taken Jem to the gents and Timmy, Dougie and Billy were behind the bar, frantically busy. Fiddlesticks life was back to normal.

Clancy Tavistock stood up. "Excuse for a minute, will you — and yes, I know it's my round next. I'll be back in a moment. There's just someone — er — something I need to do . . ." And he disappeared through the crowd towards the bar.

"Is he after a woman?" Tiff Clayton ran his fingers through his bleached hair.

"Surely not." Freddo frowned over his pint. "He's gay isn't he?"

"No! Is he? Really? Do you know? Or are you guessing?"

"Well," Freddo blustered, "I've never seen him with a wench, never heard him talk about one, never . . . I just assumed."

"Clancy's all man, all right," Ricky assured them. "But he's never bothered much with women in all the years I've known him. None of his girlfriends have become permanent fixtures. He always says he's looking for the perfect woman."

"Daft sod!" Tiff Clayton roared with laughter. "The imperfect ones are always the best!"

Ricky drained the dregs of his beer. "Clancy seems to prefer his own company, that's all."

"What a waste," Amber said idly. "He'd be a great catch. Even at his age, he's pretty damn gorgeous with those eyes and that hair and that body and the way he smiles and walks and —"

They were all looking at her.

"Oh, blimey Moses crikey O'Reilly!" she muttered, using one of Gwyneth's favourite expressions, as the realisation hit her like a ten-ton truck. "I would think that, wouldn't I? They're so much alike! Why didn't I notice it before? Oh-my-God!"

"Want to share?" Freddo leaned across the table. "Fancy our Clancy, do you?"

Amber shook her head and looked quickly round the bar. There was no sign of Clancy Tavistock.

Oh, hell's teeth — what on earth had she done?

What had she so flippantly asked Cassiopeia for? For Fern and Timmy to get together — sorted; and for Zillah to find happiness with the man she loved; and for Lewis to be reunited with his father.

She gulped, feeling very, very sick — Cassie had scored a double-whammy with the last two, then.

How else could it have happened? It had to be astral magic. It would take a trillion-to-one chance for it to happen by sheer coincidence.

Oh-my-God!

Zillah, who had refilled her glass of water, was standing in the back doorway, watching the bats sweep and dart in the velvet darkness, listening to the moths fumble clumsily against the outside lantern, enjoying the peace.

"Zillah."

She froze. Every part of her skin was ice cold and red hot at the same time.

"Zil?"

She exhaled. She wasn't going to faint. Not this time.

She turned round slowly, willing it not to be him. Wanting it to be him so badly that it hurt.

"Hello," he smiled at her with tears in his eyes. "You haven't changed one bit."

"Neither have you." Her voice was croaky. She cleared her throat. "Um —"

She was trembling so badly that the glass tumbled from her hands and shattered on the tiles. She watched the iced water trickle in rivulets round her feet.

He didn't move. "When we came into the pub earlier, I just caught a glimpse of you behind the bar and I wondered — I thought — but then, I've spent the last thirty years thinking that I've seen you on buses and trains and in supermarket queues and —" He stopped and took a breath. "And I knew, of course, that tonight it wasn't going to be you again — then you weren't there and they said you'd been taken ill and it wasn't until just now, when they mentioned your name . . ."

"So, if I'd been called Susan or Ann —" She tried to laugh but it sounded like a sob.

"Zil," he took one step forward and stopped again. "Did you see me? Did you know it was me?"

She shook her head. "*Thought* it was. Might be. For a fleeting moment. That's all."

"And you fainted? Really? I mean — you're OK? I mean — oh, Christ, Zillah — I don't know what I mean. Don't know what I'm saying. Don't know what's happening."

She looked at him and swallowed the lump in her throat. "Neither do I. And yes, I passed out because,

because — well, you know why — and I'm perfectly OK now — and — and I can't believe this is really happening."

They both took a step forward and hesitated.

"I went mad trying to find you," Clancy said, pushing his hair away from his eyes in the old familiar gesture that had haunted Zillah's dreams. "When you didn't answer my letters . . ."

"I didn't get any letters. And you didn't answer mine."

"I didn't receive any either. And I tried ringing the house in Kilburn as soon as we arrived in Munich and someone said you'd gone and hadn't left a forwarding address and —"

"I had to leave Kilburn within two days of you leaving the UK because the house was being sold. I wrote to you, care of your management offices, asking for the letters to be forwarded. Telling you where I was, what was happening."

"I didn't get them," he said again.

And then they were both talking at once, and eventually managed to unravel that the new management company must have destroyed both sets of forwarded letters, strictly enforcing the "no women" clause in Solstice Soul's contract. These days there wouldn't be a problem — but back then all musicians had to be seen to be young, free and single by order of their managers. It meant, they believed, that the fans would think they were still in with a chance of one day capturing the heart of their particular favourite. Even the Beatles had had to deny their wives, hadn't they?

"I thought you'd found a nice scholarly professor with whom to spend the rest of your life."

"No way. I just thought," she said shakily, "that you'd found someone else on tour."

"How could I? I loved you so much, Zil. I — I thought you'd forgotten about me and gone back to university."

"No, I never went back. And I tried to contact you everywhere — but even the record company said they had no information."

"Solstice Soul split before we'd finished touring Europe. It wasn't the same with the new management — fights over money, too many drugs, too much of everything. It stopped being fun. I walked out on them and the record company were furious because we'd broken our contract. I knew they'd try and sue for the breach, so I gave them no information at all."

Zillah tried to work some saliva into her dry mouth.

Clancy shrugged. "When I got back and found you'd disappeared off the face of the earth, I rang Oxford — tried to find your old college, your home address, anything. It was like trying to squeeze state secrets out of James Bond."

Zillah wanted to cry for all those wasted years.

"I never forgot you, but after a while I stopped trying to find you," Clancy continued softly. "I assumed you didn't want to be found."

"Me too. I searched for a while and then — well — just shut you out of my life. Of course, it would be so much easier now, wouldn't it? With mobile phones and texts and emails and friends-bloody-reunited . . ."

Clancy nodded. "So — are you married?"

She shook her head. "Never. You?"

"No. Various relationships. None of them particularly successful."

"And now?"

"No one." His eyes were tired. "You?"

She shook her head. "No. And are you happy?"

"Mostly," he shrugged. "I've had an OK life — well, eventually. I've done lots of different stuff — session musician, teaching guitar, some studio work, then I went back to playing live music about ten years ago. The JB Roadshow are a great bunch. We've always been in work. We make a good living. I suppose I'm happier now than — well, than at any time without you. What about you?"

Zillah sighed. "Much the same. I've lived here for thirty years. Worked in the pub. Life's been OK. Good, really."

"I'm glad."

"Do you still live in London?"

"No — I stay there when I have to, but it's not where I call home. I tend to drift. I own a flat in Henley, by the river, bought with the money from Solstice Soul years ago. I let it out mostly, but sometimes I stay there . . . I suppose that's more my permanent home than anywhere else."

Zillah ran her fingers through her hair. She felt very tired. Drained. In all her fantasies she'd imagined that if she and Clancy ever found each other again they'd fly into each other's arms, lovers again, and simply pick up where they left off. But how could they? They'd had a lifetime apart. They were virtual strangers now. Different people.

Clancy leaned against the table. "Zil, I'm not dreaming this, am I? I mean — this has been my dream for as long as I can remember and I'm so bloody confused now. I don't know if I'm awake or asleep. How did this happen? Tonight? Now? After all this time? How?"

Zillah took a deep breath. She thought she might have a good idea.

"Do you believe in magic?"

He grinned at her. "You mean you're a witch and this is the result of some voodoo spell? Nah, Zil — I'm not buying that."

"Astral magic," Zillah said. "I didn't really believe in it either, but now . . ."

"You've lived here too long," he said gently. "Freddo was telling us about all the star-wishing that goes on here — you surely don't really think . . .?"

"I don't know. I honestly don't know. No one here knows about you . . . about us. I didn't make any sort of starwishes if that's what you mean, but maybe someone else did. On our behalf?"

"Why? Who else would know about us? Who else would care? No — that's all too silly for words. Mind you, if they did, then I'm very, very grateful to them whoever they are." He took a deep breath. "So, what happens now? Where do we go from here?"

"I've no idea."

The silence was interrupted by Amber appearing in the kitchen doorway.

"Er — I'm really sorry to barge in, but they're getting a bit restive out there because it's Clancy's round and Freddo wanted to come in and haul him out and Tiff thinks that he's missing out on some assignation and they all want to know where he's gone and I sort of guessed — er — and Lewis and Jem are back from the gents and I thought it was better if I came in rather than Lewis because . . . because . . ."

Zillah shook her head. Lewis! Oh, God!

"OK, love." She nodded at Amber. "Clancy's just on his way out and —" She stopped. "What did you say? What did you mean about you sort of guessed?"

Amber scuffed the tiled floor with the toe of her sandal. "Er — well, I knew Clancy hadn't gone out of the pub or to the loo and I knew you were still in here and so I guessed he was in here with you and — oh, hell, Zillah! He is, isn't he? You know . . ."

Zillah, trying to crank her brain into gear, nodded. "Look, Amber — if Clancy goes out to the bar to get his round in, can you ask Lewis to come in here please. Preferably without Jem. We need to talk."

Clancy frowned. "Now you've really lost me. What am I? And I thought Lewis was Amber's bloke? Isn't he? God, Zil — he's not your toy boy, is he?"

"I've been a toy boy on several very enjoyable occasions in the past —" Lewis stuck his head round the door, laughing "— but even in this kissing-cousin village I'd draw the line at —"

"Lewis," Zillah cut in quickly, "I need a word." Or several million. All impossible.

"OK — Amber can keep an eye on Jem for a minute, can't you?"

"Yes, sure . . ." Reluctantly, Amber disappeared back into the bar.

Zillah looked at them — Lewis and Clancy — standing so close together and wondered why neither of them could see the resemblance. Lewis had inherited so many of Clancy's features, so many of his mannerisms, he'd always been so like his father.

Clancy moved away from the table. "I guess I'd better go too. Freddo can get quite unpleasant if anyone skips their round —"

"No, please stay," Zillah muttered, her blood roaring in her ears. "Just for a moment."

"Are you all right?" Lewis's eyes were filled with concern. "You're not feeling faint again, are you? You've gone really pale. God, Ma —"

"Ma?" Clancy frowned. "*Ma?* You mean, Zillah is your *mother?*"

"Yeah. Why?" Lewis looked at Clancy. "Jeeze — you didn't really think I was —"

"Lewis," Zillah held up her hands. "There's no easy way to say this to either of you but —"

"You are ill!" Lewis exploded. "I knew it! But —" he shook his head towards Clancy "— what's he got to do with this? You've only just met him — why is he in here anyway? I mean —"

Zillah's eyes filled with tears. "Lewis — listen. Clancy is your father. Clancy, meet the son you never knew you had . . ."

CHAPTER
TWENTY-SEVEN

Moonlight And Roses

Two weeks later, Fiddlesticks was still a-buzz.

The Zillah + Clancy = Lewis revelations had rocked the village to its dry and dusty foundations.

Sadly, Gwyneth and Big Ida's early rain star spells hadn't produced the goods. The sky remained resolutely clear, the sun scorched from dawn to dusk, and the hosepipe ban was still firmly in place. Even the stream had dried to a thin sluggish ribbon, with small children standing in it, wearing floppy hats and suncream and nothing else, looking despondent. Everyone was wilting and praying tonight's collective Leo's Lightning incantation would bring at least a dribble of water to the parched village.

Fern and Amber, sprawled under the willows wearing as little as possible, far more interested in the Zillah-Clancy stuff than the weather, had been over and over the implications.

"So, what are they doing now? Zil and Clancy?" Fern's tongue protruded from the corner of her mouth as she concentrated on constructing a daisy-chain. "Making up for lost time? Shagging like rabbits?"

"*Fern!*"

"Well, wouldn't you be? After all those wasted years apart? And he is bloody gorgeous — even though he must be ancient as hell."

"Pot-kettle-black?" Amber sniffed. "After all, aren't you slipping between the stripy flannelette sheets of someone who also belongs to the tea, toast and Terry Wogan brigade?"

"Timmy has a duvet and Wogan is cool . . ." Fern began, and then laughed. "Oh, I get it. Joke. Sarcasm does not become a laydee, my dear — so sod off. And we're not discussing me here, we're discussing Zil and the wrinkly rocker — so give."

"Nothing to tell. And if there was, I wouldn't. So there."

Actually, Amber knew no more than Fern. As far as she was aware, Zillah and Clancy had been seeing each other on a sort of getting-to-know-you basis. Discreetly meeting away from the village for their dates, there had been no sign of Clancy sneaking in or out of Chrysalis Cottage. Even Gwyneth and Big Ida, delighted by the reunion, hadn't been able to shed much light on any developments.

"Just so long as she's 'appy, duck," Gwyneth had said, her eyes misty, "that's enough for us. That gel 'as been like a daughter to me an' Ida. She deserves some real happiness at long last. And she's just glowin' now — proper warms the cockles of your heart, it does."

It did, Amber had to admit, and it had also lifted her huge burden of guilt over the affair. She'd decided, however well things had turned out, to stay forever silent about her involvement. To be honest, the whole

Cassiopeia manifestation love-wish thing had scared her rigid.

She'd never, ever mock astral magic again.

Then there'd also been the question of her own future to consider. Should she go or should she stay? Ever since Plough Night, Amber had been more than occupied with Hubble Bubble, with dozens of bookings coming in, and Mitzi — absolutely delighted about the Zil-Clancy reunion — had not only made her a permanent member of staff, but also press-ganged her into signing up for the college course.

"I don't know if I'm stopping here, yet . . ."

"Of course you're stopping!" Mitzi had been scathing. "Where else would you go, for heaven's sake? This is your home now — and I for one couldn't manage without you."

Her parents, happily settled in the Andalucian goat shed, with both Coral and Topaz in love with someone called Carlos — whether it was the same someone called Carlos, Amber wasn't quite sure, but knowing Coral and Topaz's cat-fighting prowess she sincerely hoped not — had been delighted. However, Jemma and Emma and Kelly and Bex had been scandalised when she'd told them she was going to be staying on in Fiddlesticks for a while longer. And even more scandalised that there was no man involved in her decision.

Lewis.

She hadn't seen Lewis at all.

She was sure, after the shock of being introduced to his father, he'd chosen to keep very much out of the way. After all, it must have turned his whole world upside down. It was an awful lot to come to terms with. Fern had reported that he seemed OK at Hayfields, and that Jem was ecstatic that Lewis now had what he considered a proper family, but that no one had actually been brave enough to broach the subject with him.

"We'll see him tonight, though." Fern rolled on to her back and placed her daisy chain tiara on top of her curls. "He'll be at Leo's Lightning. Wonder if Zil will bring the Rock'n'Roll Love God?"

"Like you care," Amber snorted. "I've seen you sneaking out of The Weasel and Bucket in the misty hours of dawn looking like someone who hasn't spent all night discussing the alcohol percentage volume of the various beers."

Fern gurgled. "Oh, Timmy is sooo good. I'm having the best sex ever."

"Far, far too much information." Amber pulled a face. "But I'm glad you're happy."

"I'm not happy — I'm ecstatic. So, that's me sorted, and Zil, so who does that leave?"

"Bog off. Don't even think about it. I've told you a million times, Lewis and I are friends — nothing more. Even if — big, big if — he did decide he wanted it to be more, I couldn't cope with being just one of many. Been there, done that, no intention of repeating the experience."

"We'll see." Fern rolled on to her ample stomach and started plucking more daisies. "I'll monitor the progress, or otherwise, tonight. Win is going to be with all the Hayfields crew for Leo's, so I'm working behind the bar. I'm practising for my rest-of-life role: Fern Pluckrose, Landlady and Bon Viveur. Bet you're really jealous, huh?"

Amber stretched on her back, the sun sizzling down, and sighed.

Zillah walked barefooted on to the balcony, her long lilac dress soft against her skin, and leaned against the white railings. Below, a myriad boats moved silently through the burnished river. The sun-ripples reflected in kaleidoscope prisms all around her. It was elegant and luxurious, cool out here compared with the searing heat of the day, and so blissfully peaceful.

Clancy's Henley apartment was wonderful. Spacious, comfortable and decorated in cream and pale green and dove grey; it almost seemed part of the river. They'd spent a lot of time here in the last two weeks, talking, crying, laughing, catching up.

It seemed to Zillah that the years had all concertina'd together. Before, there had been the Clancy years and the non-Clancy years: now those non-C decades seemed to have passed in a flash. Not that she felt the years alone had been wasted: she'd raised Lewis, and kept a roof over their heads, and had a life. No one could ever have replaced Clancy in her heart, so why should she have ever considered settling for second best?

Today they'd driven out to Marlow for lunch, invisible amongst all the other summer diners, and come back to Henley and strolled by the river. There was still much to say, so much to talk about, but now it didn't matter. Now they had forever to do it in.

The years had simply rippled away.

"OK?" Clancy walked out onto the balcony and stood beside her, close but not touching, leaning on the balcony rail. His feet, like hers, were bare. The sun had turned his skin to butterscotch, and streaked his hair with gold. His jeans were faded and his T-shirt showed his in-shape body.

He was still the most beautiful boy in the world.

"More than OK, thanks. It's been a blissful day. I'm really enjoying this . . . this — whatever it is we're doing."

"Courting?" Clancy grinned. "Or is that too old-fashioned for words?"

"Courting sounds lovely to me. Walking, talking, getting to know each other all over again, simply going out together — dating . . . After all, we didn't do any of it before, did we?"

Laughing, Clancy shook his head. "Love and lust at first sight didn't leave us much room for the formalities back then, did it? I didn't even know your surname for three weeks — and we'd spent most of those in bed."

Zillah giggled. "Great, wasn't it?"

He nodded, smiling. "The best."

"Mmmm." Zillah shivered with the delicious memories, then leaned further over the balcony, watching a couple trying to moor a punt, laughing together. "Do you know, I just don't understand how you can ever bear to ever leave this place. It's so perfect."

"It's just a shell," he sighed. "Or at least it has been. A pretty nice shell, granted, but empty, soulless, lonely — like me. OK to come home to when the travelling has become too much, but otherwise I'm happy to rent it out on short terms, and sometimes used to think I never wanted to see it again."

"I think I expected it to be full of soul band memorabilia." She smiled at him. "You know, photos of gigs and wild celebrity parties, and the platinum disc for "Summer and Winter" framed on the wall of the downstairs loo, and a spare Gibson Les Paul or two suspended from the ceiling . . ."

"I tried that. It didn't work. It was just pretentious — and whatever else I am, I don't think I've ever been that. Anyway," he said cheerfully, "my letting agent told me I'd got to keep the flat as straight and impersonal as possible if I was intending to rent it out to visiting businessmen and their families who might just think it was some sort of rock'n'roll den of iniquity."

"That was the house in Kilburn, wasn't it? Wild, or what?" She laughed. "And I played the album again this morning. I haven't played it for years — not ever really, not since . . . but it's never off the turntable now. I'm in danger of wearing it out."

"Actually, it's being reissued on CD in the autumn — to tie in with Soul Survivors, a big nationwide soul band tour. They're bringing over some of the really big names from the States to tour the UK for six months. Every promoter in the country is jumping on the soul bandwagon. Freddo was talking about us cutting a quick JB Roadshow album to throw in as well."

357

"I'd buy it," Zillah grinned. "Then I'd have two to drive the neighbours insane with. But however good it is, it'll never be the same as Summer and Winter."

"Do you really still like it? Does it still sound good?"

"Better than good. It's brilliant — and so much more than that. It's us, our life, back then. Vivid. Every song has a memory attached. A place, a town, a beach, a party . . . us, together. Do you — will you — as the JB Roadshow, be playing the same stuff?"

"At the Harvest Moon gig?" He shrugged teasingly. "You'll have to wait and see. You'll probably think we're pretty crap now — after all, you heard it all first when it was young and fresh."

"Mmmm. Like us? Still, we've worn pretty well, haven't we? No reason why your music should have gone downhill, is there?"

"No reason at all," Clancy said, his eyes, like hers, drowsy with memories.

They stood in relaxed contemplation for a while, watching a pleasure cruiser glide past beneath them, the tourists all sunburnt and laughing, trying to feed the swans, pretending to topple overboard.

Clancy broke the silence.

"How's Lewis?"

"Doing OK," she said slowly. "Getting his head round it, was how he put it. He likes you very much — you know that, and is delighted to know about his background at last, and says as long as I'm happy then he's happy."

"But?"

"I didn't say there was a but."

"You didn't need to."

Zillah laughed. "You always could read my mind. Oh, it's not a huge but. I think, now he knows the truth about everything, that I wasn't a floozy and that you didn't do a runner because I was pregnant, he's much happier — but he's scared."

"He's not the only one." Clancy pushed his hair away from his eyes. It immediately fell back again. "I'm absolutely bloody terrified."

"Are you?" Zillah looked at him. He still had freckles on his nose. She used to kiss them. "Why?"

"You know why. Lewis isn't the only one having to come to terms with the father-son thing, is he? I'm eaten up with guilt about all that. Thinking of you, on your own, having a baby — our baby — and me not knowing, and you thinking that I'd stopped loving you, that I'd left you . . . And now, our baby is a man — a really great bloke to boot — and I've missed so much, and I don't know how to handle it. Where to start."

"We can't change the past. We can't go back, so regrets are pointless. Oh, I've always regretted losing you — but I've never once, not even for a nanosecond, regretted leaving college and doing what we did. And you're doing just fine with the present. So is Lewis." Zillah smiled gently. "You're very much alike."

Clancy shook his head. "He does look a lot like me, yes. I don't know why I didn't think about that before — but he's got your brains, going to uni, doing the job he does, and your compassion and your sense of humour and —"

"Your charm and patience and gentleness."

Clancy laughed. "Pretty good so far — so why is he scared?"

"Because he thinks you'll leave me, I guess. Because that's all he's ever grown up with: me alone, him not knowing about you, not being sure why — I mean I know you both sort of understand why I decided not to tell him — what was the point when I thought you'd dumped me? That would only hurt him more. And now he's scared that just when he's found the final piece of his jigsaw, this — this perfect bliss will end."

"And will it?"

"How do I know?" Zillah traced the outline of the tiles with her bare toe.

Clancy sighed. "You see — that's what I'm scared of too. Losing you again. I'd die. Honestly. I thought I was going mad, going to die of a broken heart the first time, but now, having found you again and — well, there simply wouldn't be any point in going on. Zillah — I want to spend the rest of my life with you."

She didn't say anything. A family of ducks paddled past in the glittering river below, leaving a perfect V wash in their wake.

"Zil? Oh, hell — I haven't got this all wrong, have I?"

She turned to him, shaking her head.

"Are you crying? Oh, Zil . . ."

Then she was in his arms, for the first time in thirty years, and he kissed her and her body dissolved with lust. Oh, God . . . it felt absolutely wonderful.

Just like the first time.

"What time's this rain-dance thingy?" Clancy stretched lazily. "Have we missed it?"

"Don't think so." Zillah opened her eyes. "It's still daylight — unless it's tomorrow already, of course. I've kind of lost track of time."

"Me, too."

They giggled together.

The river reflected in shifting watermark shadows on the ceiling of the dove-grey bedroom. It was still stifling despite the soft whirr and best efforts of the colonial fan. The white sheets, a tangle of Egyptian cotton, had long since fallen to the floor. A slight breeze wafted through the open balcony doors, shivering softly through the long white voile drapes.

It had been amazing.

The years had fallen away. They'd surely never been apart.

Naked almost before they'd left the balcony, unashamed of their bodies, they'd made love with all the passion, all the intensity, all the pent-up longing and wanting, all the sheer, perfect love of that first time.

Zillah, worried at first about her flesh no longer being velvet smooth, tight, unblemished, had simply melted at his first touch. She'd trembled beneath his fingers. Nothing mattered. He was beautiful and told her over and over again that she was, too. The most beautiful woman on earth.

And now she was.

Tumbling together, familiar and yet new, they'd rediscovered each other's bodies with an urgency and tenderness that had made her laugh and then cry with pleasure.

"Zillah . . ."

She'd turned her head on the deep pillow. "Mmmm?"

"I love you."

"I love you too. And I think I'm dreaming."

Clancy had stroked her hair away from her face. "Then let's hope we never wake up."

She'd rolled towards him, the soft river air cooling her heated body. "I've wanted this for so long, knew it would never happen, thought that maybe I'd imagined how it used to be . . ."

He'd pulled her into his arms, kissing her again. "Me too. Oh, God, Zil . . ."

And that had been hours ago and since then they'd repeated the experience a couple more times, more slowly, more tantalisingly, just to reassure themselves that it hadn't all been a figment. Now, sated, happy, drowsy with love, neither of them really wanted to get up and shower and get dressed and go back to Fiddlesticks.

"Remember when Solstice Soul had time off and we used to stay in bed all day?"

She sighed with pleasure. "Mmmm. And we'd stagger downstairs to grab another bottle of wine and go back to bed — and then, when we got hungry, we'd sneak off in the small hours to that all-night shop on the corner and eat curry in bed and fall asleep just as the dawn was breaking . . ."

They held each other, smiling, remembering.

362

"We could do it all again." He ran his fingers down her body. "Unless you really want to go back to Fiddlesticks and dance in the rain."

"We did that before, too. Remember? Somewhere in the wilds of Shropshire, wasn't it? After a gig? In the middle of summer at about two in the morning? Naked."

Clancy laughed. "God, yes . . . And then we made love. And we were like drowned rats and afterwards we couldn't find our clothes, so we ran back to the van without them . . ."

She took his face between her hands and kissed him. "I don't think Fiddlesticks will miss us tonight, do you?"

CHAPTER
TWENTY-EIGHT

Dancing in the Moonlight

"If it don't rain tonight," Gwyneth puffed as she and Big Ida trudged across the village green in the rapidly falling darkness, "I'm going to shrivel up like me veg. And Pike hates it being hot like this. So do the hens. The cats now, they're still enjoying it, but us humans ain't meant to go without water for this long."

"Ah, it's like being in the Gobby Dessert," Big Ida affirmed. "Lovely weather for camels."

Amber, walking with them, smiled in the gloaming. She was so pleased that she'd decided to stay in Fiddle-sticks. How could she ever leave it now? Loving Lewis was a bit of a bummer, of course, but hey, no one had ever promised her that life would be perfect, had they?

"It'll rain," Big Ida tipped her head back. "Count on it. Leo's Lightning will see to that."

Amber also looked up at the sky. It was perfectly clear, with a lemon-slice moon and a sheen of stars. If it was going to rain it'd be some sort of miracle.

"We'll see you later, duck," Gwyneth said. "When Leo's in the right place and we do the rain dance. Me and Ida are booked to spend the evening with Mona Jupp and the Motion gels."

"Rather you than me, then," Amber giggled. "Have a nice time."

She paused on the rustic bridge and pushed her hair away from her damp face. The temperature didn't seem to have dropped since midday. The air was motionless, humid and oppressive. The majority of Fiddlestickers were, like her, still dressed in vests and shorts.

Leo's Lightning she'd learned, didn't involve the usual eating and drinking extravaganza. It all sounded far more pagan, with the entire village gathering together to ask for rain.

"Even if you've had a really wet summer?" she'd queried. "Wouldn't that be a bit pointless?"

Gwyneth had looked shocked. "Leo don't just make it rain at the drop of a 'at, duck. It ain't hit and miss. He knows exactly what we needs and when. If we've 'ad a wet summer, then 'e 'olds back on the old waterworks until we do need it. See, Leo's there to guarantee we gets what we needs to make the Plough Night wishes for good crops come true."

Amber had nodded, still slightly sceptical. "But, how? I mean — what about meteorology and weather forecasts and climate change and global warming and stuff like that?"

Gwyneth had shaken her head sorrowfully at this glaring gap in Amber's education. "All rubbish. Leo is in charge of the weather, duck, not the likes of that Michael Fish or those dopey girls with long fingernails and no command of the English language what you gets on the telly these days. It's preordained in the heavens. In the lap of the gods. If you asks him proper, Leo measures out exactly the right amount of rain from one Lightning Night to the next. Garn — I thought everyone knew that."

Amber had looked shamefaced and said she must not have been concentrating on that day at school.

She smiled to herself in the sultry darkness now. Poor old Leo was going to have to rip the skies apart to keep the Fiddlestickers satisfied tonight.

Amber scanned the crowds sitting late-night picnicking on the parched grass, knowing she was looking for Lewis. She could see most of the familiar faces — but not his.

The Hayfields mob, out in force, were sitting on tartan rugs, laughing. She could see Win amongst them, and oh yes, Jem, chuckling and eating — so surely Lewis wouldn't be far away?

"Looking for someone?"

"Yes — no — sort of . . ." She smiled at him. "And how do you do that? Always manage to creep up on me out of nowhere?"

"Years of practice, having learned to sneak silently away from jealous lovers."

"Show-off."

He laughed. She hoped he couldn't hear her heart. Oh, God — he was sooo gorgeous. Was she ever going to be able to simply look and not touch? Would she turn into another Zillah, resigned to accepting lifelong celibacy because no other man would measure up to the only one she ever wanted and couldn't have?

She'd give it a try. She could do no more.

"How are you?" she asked. "I haven't see you for ages. Not since — I didn't like to —"

"No, I needed to be on my own. To have time to myself. Just to sort stuff out in my head." He looked at her. "I appreciate you keeping your distance. You understand me really well, don't you?"

"I've learned quite a bit about you, yes." Amber felt ridiculously flattered. "Enough to know that when you wanted to talk to me about it you would, and if you didn't, you wouldn't. And, especially after our chat in the park at Winterbrook, I know what this — what Clancy appearing like he did — must mean to you. Too much to take in?"

"Far too much," Lewis sighed. "But I'm getting there. He's a really nice bloke. He's taking it easy too with the absent-father stuff — at least he hasn't suggested he takes me to the zoo or football matches or bloody McDonald's."

Amber giggled. "And Zillah is so happy, isn't she?"

"Yeah," he nodded. "She is. Really happy and carefree for the first time in my life — which, at first, totally pissed me off, but then I thought that was bloody selfish of me. I've always been secure. I know how much she loves me. The love she felt — feels — has always felt for Clancy, is different."

Amber really, really wanted to cuddle him. She managed not to. "And you always wanted to know who he was, and why he wasn't around — and now you know everything."

"More than I ever imagined. It would make a great weepy film, wouldn't it? All that time they wasted, loving each other, unable to love anyone else — and I never knew Ma had been to Oxford or any of that. She had a whole secret life. How amazing is that? Christ! So much stuff has come tumbling out of the closet . . ."

"But you're OK with it?"

"Getting there." He looked at her. "I can understand now, that with a secret as huge as that, the longer you leave it to talk about, the more impossible it becomes. I suppose if Ma had told me about it all when I was little, it would have simply become part of my life. I'd've accepted it and not thought too much more about it. But she didn't — and then there was never going to be a right time."

"I think she's been amazingly brave," Amber said. "And the way she was with me when I arrived — it all makes sense now. Gwyneth and Ida and everyone, including me, thought she loathed all your girlfriends and was pathologically jealous of them, whereas all she really wanted to do was protect them from you."

"Cheers."

Amber shook her head. "No, sorry — badly put — but you know what I mean. She knew you looked like Clancy and obviously thought you were going to behave like him, too. Or at least how she *thought* he'd behaved. Which in turn made her fiercely protective underneath all that dreamy sadness, and no one really knew why."

Lewis nodded. "Yeah — you're right. And most of it has fallen into place now. But I've always been dead proud of Ma, doing what she did for me, giving me the life she did — now I'm more than proud. And if this doesn't sound too wet for words, it is a truly romantic story, isn't it? Ma and Clancy? They really were made for one another."

"Yes, they were," Amber said, with a lump in her throat. "I hope they spend the rest of their lives making up for the lost years and being happy. Do you think he'll move into Chrysalis with her?"

"No idea. He's got a place in Henley, which isn't that far away. Maybe after all those years of living apart they'll just sort of move between the two? It'll be strange for them both, I guess, living together after all this time of having their own space. Whatever they decide, as long as it's what they want and they're together, I'll be happy."

"Honestly?"

"Yeah, honestly," he nodded. "Mind you, I have told him that if he ever hurts her, then I'll kill him."

"Right — OK — and what did he say to that?"

"That if he did, then I'd have every right, but that he never, ever will. And I believe him. He worships her. Adores her." Lewis laughed. "It sounds odd, doesn't it? Like suddenly I'm the parent, the carer, the protector, anxious that my beloved offspring should be making the right life choices?"

"I think it sounds as if you're a thoroughly nice man, who has been brought up exactly right, with a fair set of values, and a caring, compassionate and generous heart — which is, after all, why you do the job you do at Hayfields so brilliantly."

"Christ!" Lewis laughed. "And that makes me sound like the most boring paragon on the planet!"

"Oh, no — you'll never be that."

"There is one thing I do regret about all this, though," Lewis said wistfully. "Just one."

"What's that?"

"That along with all the other obvious stuff I've inherited from Clancy, I haven't got a bloody musical bone in my body. I could have made a fortune — not to mention the groupies . . ." He sighed, then grinned at her. "Anyway, enough about all that for tonight — there's something I want to show you."

He held out his hand but she didn't take it. Couldn't. She simply followed him along the side of the stream, skirting the crowds, past the bridge, ducking under the willows, until they reached a clearing.

"Lay down."

"What?"

"Lay down," he grinned at her. "Just do it. Please."

"OK, but I didn't think we had this sort of relationship. And I'll have you know I'm not the kind of girl who —"

"Amber —" he was laughing "— shut up and lay down. On your back."

Giggling, she did and he lay beside her, mere inches away, so that she could feel the warmth of his skin, smell the lemon of his shampoo and shower gel mingling with the scent of the crushed thyme and baked earth.

"There," he pointed upwards. "Isn't that sensational?"

She stared up at the sky.

It was a vast, never-ending canopy, the deepest blue-black, and the stars, millions of them, were a

370

giant's throw of glittering, brilliant, three-dimensional diamonds.

"There's nothing — or almost nothing — more beautiful than an August sky," Lewis said softly. "Nature has all the best shows."

Amber didn't speak. It was enough to simply stare upwards at the celestial glory with him beside her. She felt as though her body was floating towards the sky, that she only had to stretch out a hand and she'd be able to catch the stars in her fingers. It was as if time and space no longer existed. It was simply stunning: primeval and wondrous and out of this world.

"Leo is the August constellation," Lewis said, also still gazing upwards, "both in astronomy and astrology. He's also, conveniently, the god of the elements which is why we have Leo's Lightning tonight."

"It's wonderful," Amber whispered. "Do you know, I've never looked at the sky like this before. Never seen it. Just taken it all for granted."

"We all do that with familiar things. It's only when you start to peel back the layers and look at what you've got that you realise . . ." he stopped. "Yes, well, you know what I mean."

Amber turned her head to look at him. He was smiling at her, his eyes gentle.

She took a deep breath. "Lewis —"

"Sorry to break up the party," a wheedling voice hissed from above them, "but I don't suppose either of you has got a spare fag?"

"Bugger off, Slo!" Lewis groaned, rolling over and sitting up. "And no we haven't."

Amber sat up too, the moment of astral enchantment shattered.

"Do you think Martha or any of the Hayfields lot will have a fag?" Slo looked twitchy. "Those bloody do-gooding cousins of mine have found the stash in the Weasel's lavs. Flushed the lot. Mean witches."

"No one at Hayfields smokes," Lewis said, picking dried grass out of his jeans. "But if it's any good to you, I do know Goff keeps a few cigars tucked away for special occasions."

"Does he?" Slo frowned. "Sly old fox! I never knew that. So, 'e has them on him, does he?"

"Oh, yes. Carries them all the time."

"Thanks, young Lewis, you're a pal." Slo beamed, marching purposefully away into the darkness.

"He doesn't, does he?" Amber chuckled. "Goff, I mean. Keep a few choice Havanas about his person?"

"Probably not," Lewis agreed cheerfully. "But he might — and it got rid of Slo, didn't it? Now, where were we?"

"I don't know where you were —" Martha, the Hayfields housemother, bustled up in a matronly way, looming over them like a beomoth in the gloom "— although I can probably hazard a pretty good guess, but they're just about to start the Leo's Lightning thing proper and Jem won't do it without you." Turning on the heel of her sturdy Mary-Jane's, she gave Amber a cursory glance. "Sorry, love — duty calls."

372

"Sometimes," Lewis grumbled, standing up and brushing the remaining grass from his jeans, "I really, really hate this place."

Amber, itching to join in the jeans-brushing but managing to resist, also stood up. "You don't mean that."

"No," Lewis grinned. "I don't. What about you?"

"Me? Oh, I hate it so much that I've decided to take up Mitzi's offer of a permanent job, start the day-release course at college in Winterbrook, stay for the foreseeable future . . ."

"Really?" Lewis's face was inscrutable. "That's great news — Jem will be ecstatic."

They slithered towards the main throng, everyone standing up now, almost visibly twitching with anticipation. Amber could see the entire village gathered in the blackness and then some.

All except Zillah and Clancy.

Lucky so-and-sos, she thought. Bet they won't need any celestial incantations to bring on the fireworks tonight.

The sky was still huge and clear, the stars a trillion twinkling sequins, the moon perfectly unshrouded by even the merest wisp of cloud. There was still no breeze, no hint of any to come, nothing to relieve the thumping, sticky humidity. In fact, no chance whatsoever, Amber thought, of Leo coming up with the goods.

They plucked a beaming Jem away from the Hayfields crowd, and each holding a hand, made sure he didn't stumble.

"What do we do now, then?" Amber asked.

"Skip," Lewis said, straight-faced.

"What?"

"We all hold hands and skip."

"You're having a laugh." Amber frowned up at him. "Aren't you?"

Jem shook his head, grinning hugely.

Amber exhaled, thankful that no one who knew her from her trance and house days in the northern nightclubs could see her now. *Skipping?* Holding hands and *skipping?*

With a lot of scuffling, and swapping places, and several small arguments, the throng seemed to eventually organise themselves into two huge circles, one inside the other. Somehow, in the organising, Jem was now between Lewis and Billy Grinley and Amber found herself rather disconcertingly holding Dougie Patchcock's hand on one side and Lewis's on the other.

Sod's law, she thought, that the first time they had any sort of physical contact it had to be in the company of about 8,000 other people and when she had exceedingly sweaty hands.

However, the tingle when his fingers laced with hers was well worth the wait.

They seemed almost ready to go, everyone practically quivering to let rip, when a small mêlée in the inner circle halted things.

Slo and Goff were rolling over and over on the ground, scuffling like badgers.

374

"He was trying to mug me!" Goff yelled indignantly, glaring malevolently with his one eye. "He had his hands in me pockets!"

Amber sucked her lips together to prevent the shriek of laughter escaping and didn't dare look at Lewis. She could feel him shaking.

Once Constance and Perpetua had broken up the fight and Slo and Goff, still glaring at one another were sulkily forced to hold hands like sworn enemies at a children's party, they were off.

The concentric circles skipped in opposite directions, faster and faster, like a manic game of The Farmer's In His Den. Amber's feet seemed to have left the ground as they ran and whooped and skipped, round and round, increasing in speed until the faces were a blur.

She really hoped she wouldn't be sick.

Just when she felt she really couldn't keep up the pace any longer, and wondered how on earth old people like Gwyneth and Ida managed to cope with the G-force, and if Jem's pentangle would have her eye out, everyone started singing:

Leo's Lightning
Nothing Frightening
Send us rain
Send us rain
Bring the storms, bring the gale
Bring the thunder, bring the hail
Leo listen
Let rain hissen

★ ★ ★

It would never make the charts, Amber thought dizzily, although it might go down a storm on Eurovision.

Then as quickly as the Fiddlestickers had started the mad skipping, they stopped.

Several people fell over. Amber, now suffering from a severe case of vertigo, staggered to a halt, pulling away from Dougie Patchcock but still managing to hold Lewis's hand.

"Jesus . . ." she muttered groggily as the village green continued to spin.

Jem grabbed her free hand to steady himself, gurgling happily.

"He loves Leo's night," Lewis said faintly, still swaying. "Loves the skipping and the singing. Although, personally, I'd prefer to feel like this after thirteen pints of Hearty Hercules and a kebab . . . What?" He looked down at Jem. "Oh, yeah. Nice."

Billy Grinley was being discreetly sick on Perpetua's sandals.

The Fiddlestickers, all tottering, slowly began to disperse towards The Weasel and Bucket. Right now, Amber thought, alcohol was surely the last thing they needed. However, she was delighted to see that Gwyneth and Big Ida were amongst them, still on their feet.

"Is that it?" She blinked at Lewis. "All over?"

"Actually, I think it's only just begun."

She thought she'd misheard him. Her inner ears weren't back on track. Surely he didn't mean . . .? Hadn't meant . . .? No, of course not. Get a grip. Don't fall for it. Don't become a bedpost notch. Don't become another Lewis Flanagan conquest. Fight it. You're friends — it's better than nothing. Far better than the alternative.

Impatiently, Jem tugged on her hand and pointed at the sky.

"What? Yep, the stars are fabulous." Amber pulled herself quickly together. "But Jem, sweetheart, much as I know this will probably get me burned at the stake round here, I'm feeling very queasy and right now I've had just as much of stars as anyone can take — so . . . bloody hell!"

The Fiddlestickers had all paused on their wobbling pubward journey. Everyone was looking upwards.

The sky was no longer blue velvet with a drift of diamonds: it was dark and angry, the moon being swallowed up by billows of heavy, towering clouds. Black on black.

The willow trees started to shiver as a breeze rustled across the green. The temperature dropped a few degrees as the first heavy raindrops fell.

Amber shook her head. "No way. Absolutely no way — oh, flipping heck!"

The skies literally opened. It was as if some giant hand had ripped the clouds apart.

The rain fell in a blinding torrent, bouncing from the parched ground, shuddering and thundering through the trees.

The Fiddlestickers screamed with delight, most running towards the pub, a few simply standing, heads tipped back, allowing the downpour to sluice away the weeks of heat.

"Come on," Lewis shouted, holding her hand more tightly. "We'll shelter under the trees. No, trust me Jem — it won't thunder and lightning. At least not yet — the trees will be safe . . . Come on!"

They ran, the three of them, slipping and sliding across the now treacherous green, the rain drenching them in seconds, towards the nearest of the willows.

Beneath the tree the noise was amazing: a roaring waterfall, gushing past them, drumming, pounding, as the rain dragged the sweetest perfume from the baked earth.

Lewis, his hair plastered to his head, pulled Jem against the trunk, his arm round him. "OK mate?"

Jem, grinning delightedly, nodded, catching raindrops in his hands as they flowed from the tips of the branches.

"And you?" Lewis looked at Amber. "Are you all right?"

"Me?" She wiped the rain away from her face, and blinked drops from her eyes. There were mud splatters up her legs, her clothes were saturated and her hair was in rat's tails. She looked a wreck. "Do you know, I don't think I've ever been happier in my life."

CHAPTER
TWENTY-NINE

Shine on Harvest Moon

"Shine on Harvest Moon . . ."

In the bar everyone took up the chorus even though it was only early evening, and although growing dark outside, the moon was still nowhere to be seen.

September already, Amber thought, as she helped Mitzi with the final cling-filming in The Weasel and Bucket's kitchen. Where on earth had the time gone?

September — still warm, but fresher now since the welcome rain of the last month, with its brilliant blue and golden mornings and hazy purple dusks. The trees just starting to change colour and the promise of darker nights and crackling fires and cosy Christmas to come.

September — the end of her fourth month in Fiddlesticks and she couldn't imagine ever living anywhere else.

Fiddlesticks, and the villagers, and, yes — the star ceremonies, she'd accept that now — had changed her life.

They'd changed her, too.

"All done?" Timmy popped his head round the door. "Enough to feed several armies?"

"Absolutely," Mitzi nodded. "And all the proper stuff — nothing too OTT. All very suitable for tonight's 'all is safely gathered in' motif. The best of Granny

379

Westward's harvest home recipes. Loads of banana and tomato — although not together because I tried that and it looked like vomit — and pea and ginger, and carrot and grapes and olives, and peaches and marrow and pomegranate and —"

Timmy held up his hands, laughing. "Stop right there. It sounds like something Fern concocts and calls a curry."

"Look at you," Mitzi grinned. "You only have to mention her name and you're all gooey-eyed. Going well, is it?"

"Blissfully," Timmy sighed ecstatically, drifting out again to serve yet another can't-wait-a-minute-longer customer.

"Right — that's us done, love," Mitzi said, patting Amber's hand. "You've been a godsend. Or maybe that should be a St Bedric-send?"

Amber laughed. "Crikey — that seems so long ago. But yes, maybe. I mean — this — all this, is what I asked him for with my first very sceptical green-cheese wish."

"Mmmm, but don't forget what I've always said about this practical magic stuff: you've got to know how to use it. True, some of the manifestations are totally inexplicable, but I still maintain the magic — herbal or celestial — only gives you a shove in the right direction. Yes, it makes things happen — I don't doubt that for a minute. Not any more. But when it does, the rest of it is up to you. And you —" Mitzi smiled "— have used it wisely. Anyway, I'm off for a shower and a cuddle with Joel — if I'm lucky and he's not wrestling with a wisdom tooth — and we'll no doubt see you later. I can't wait for this Harvest Moon festival. Having a real, live band will make it one the village'll never forget."

Amber sincerely hoped so.

The night was closing in as she left the pub, and she smiled proudly at the activity still taking place under massive arc lights on the village green. It was as if the circus had come to town. The Fiddlesticks kiddies had never seen anything like it, and were crowded round the huge festival-type stage, getting in the way of umpteen electricians and sound men and lighting and special-effects experts who were all beavering away getting things spot on for the JB Roadshow.

Goff, Billy and Dougie, bristling with importance, were checking off tick-lists with the police, a whole host of security and parking personnel had been recruited, and it looked, Amber thought happily, exactly like a mini Glastonbury.

Only an hour or so to go until darkness proper fell; just enough time to get ready for the biggest party Fiddlesticks had ever seen.

She felt a shiver of excitement. It was magic. Sheer magic.

In fact, since Leo's Lightning, everything had seemed — well — bewitched.

Lewis and Clancy were getting on really, really well. They'd spent hours together, talking and explaining and catching up and simply getting used to their new and unexpected relationship. So far, it seemed to have worked out better than either of them could have hoped, although Lewis said he'd never be able to call him Dad. Clancy apparently hadn't minded at all and had promised never to call Lewis "me laddo", or at least not in public.

Zillah, of course, was simply on cloud nine — Amber couldn't remember ever seeing anyone quite so happy; Gwyneth and Big Ida were merrily planning planting their autumn gardens, their winter keep-fit programme and their next animal-rescue sorties; Fern and Timmy were so loved up it was becoming embarrassing — which only left Amber.

Well, she was enjoying the challenge of her college course, and the Hubble Bubble job was wonderful. So — everything in the garden was rosy, wasn't it?

Well, yes, almost.

There'd been no major Lewis-developments to report since the snuggling-up under the wet willows, although Amber thought they'd become closer in a friendly way. There was no longer the remote disinterest in his eyes when he looked at her, and although she ached to touch him, to hold him, to kiss him, she'd accepted that friendship was all she was going to get.

Ah, well.

It was, Zillah thought, sitting on Clancy's guitar case, in the noisy, overheated, backstage bustle, exactly as if they'd turned back time.

She'd met the other JB Roadshow members several times since her reunion with Clancy, of course, but she'd never heard them play. Now, with Clancy, amongst all the paraphernalia, it was exactly as it had been all those years before with Solstice Soul.

The laughter, the growing tension, the good-humoured jibes, the panicky loss of plectrums and drumsticks, the drinks and last-minute cigarettes, and run-throughs of tunes they'd played a million times before.

"Unbelievable out there." Tiff Clayton, his hair newly bleached for the occasion, beamed lecherously at her. He was like Billy Grinley all over again only with a bit more showbizz pizzazz. "Full house. The whole green is packed as far as the eye can see, and people have got candles and picnics and it's mind-blowing."

"Pretty hot totty, too," Berry Knight, the lead guitarist grinned. "Just right for you, Tiff. There are at least three chicks of pensionable age but still under eighty in the front row."

Clancy bent down and kissed her. "OK? Not nervous?"

"Of course I'm nervous." She touched his cheek. "I was always nervous before a gig, wasn't I? It's no different now."

"Yes it is. Everything's different now."

She giggled. It was. Nothing would ever be the same again. And she loved it.

"Right boys," Freddo strode into the mayhem, his hair flowing, his bling sparkling. "The crews are all up and running; sound, lighting, special effects all A-OK. The security boys are happy and everyone's ready for —"

"Blast off?" Ricky Swain, the organist asked.

They all laughed.

Freddo shrugged cheerfully. "Whatever. So — are you all tuned up? Tuned in? Turned on? Amps tested? Guitar strings —"

"Shut up!" They howled at him.

Clancy pulled Zillah to her feet and kissed her. "Are you going to watch from the green?"

"Yes, Amber and Lewis and Jem are saving a space for me on their front-row blanket." She slid her arms round his neck. "I'll be bursting with pride. You're going to be great."

"Going to be?" Clancy raised his eyebrows. "I thought I'd been great on several memorable occasions recently?"

"Too much information!" the rest of the band yelled, chucking empty beer cans.

"Um, right!" Freddo clapped his hands. "I'm going to be making a little announcement, in my role as MC on stage when I introduce you — but there's a teeny extra bit of news I need to impart now."

They all stopped and looked at him. Zillah felt her heart sink. Surely not a management change? Not when Clancy's second-time-around career was going so well?

"As you know, there's been a big resurgence of interest in soul music, and some of the biggest names are coming over from the States for the Soul Survivors nationwide tour and —"

"Yeah, yeah," Jezza the drummer made wind it up movements with his hands. "We know. And you said we'd cut a quick album to tie in . . ."

384

"Which you will," Freddo said. "Studio is booked next week — and we don't have much time so you'd better be bloody good. Anyway, the great news is that we've been booked on the tour too as a support act."

The band all whooped and stamped their feet.

"Which means," Freddo yelled above the din, "that you'll be on the road for six months, playing some of the biggest venues in the country, and as none of you are spring chickens, I suggest you all start taking mega doses of Sanatogen and Wincarnis right now."

"And loads of Viagra for Tiff," one of the brass players shouted.

They were ecstatic.

Zillah simply wanted to cry. Six months! Just when she'd found him again. How could she be parted from him for six months? It was just like the last time — and she'd lost him, hadn't she?

"Zil?" Clancy looked at her. "What's up? I thought you'd be thrilled. It's stupendous news for us. We'll have an album out and be on the same bill as really, really famous soul bands."

"I know —" Zillah tried to smile "— and yes, it's great news. Wonderful."

"It'll be just like the old days."

Zillah nodded. "Clancy, honestly, I'm thrilled for you. It's just what you, the band, need. And this time I'll still be waiting where you left me when you get back. Promise."

"*Waiting? Left?*" Clancy frowned at her. "Do you think I'd go anywhere without you? Zil, darling, this is now — not back in the dark ages! Do you think I could bear to be apart from you for six minutes — let alone six months? You're coming with me. This is for us, Zil, not just me."

"Really?" Zillah felt as if she'd swallowed sunshine. "Really? Oh, wow. You mean . . . Oh, wow! Six months of touring . . . Together. All the time. Being on the road . . . Different towns, different places — I've hardly been out of this village for thirty years . . . oh, wow!"

She kissed him and he kissed her back and the years dissolved.

"Ahem!" Freddo coughed. "If you two could just hold back on the full-frontal stuff, we do have a show to put on."

The harvest moon, a huge golden orb, hung in the navy sky like a painted backdrop.

Sitting on her blanket with Lewis and Jem, Amber felt a fizz of excitement. The stage was massive and snaked with cables, and the towers of amps promised blood-tingling noise, and the banks and banks of lights warmed the slight chill of the evening.

Gwyneth and Big Ida and the Motions were at one end of the row, with Mona Jupp and Goff and the other pub regulars at the other. Behind them, all the Fiddlestickers and hordes of people from Hazy Hassocks and Bagley-cum-Russet and even Winterbrook, were cheek by jowl.

Everyone was waiting, anticipating, the tension almost electric.

"Look at Zil," Amber nudged Lewis as Zillah appeared from backstage and made her way down the makeshift steps towards them. "She looks amazing. Like the archetypal hippie rock-chick . . ."

Lewis smiled proudly, as Zillah, in a long black skirt and a silver bustier under a black shawl, her hair all tousled, her long silver earrings catching the light, picked her way towards them.

She sat beside them, leaning across, kissing them all, her eyes sparkling.

"Amber." Zillah squeezed her fingers. "Thank you. For this. I don't know how you managed it — how it happened — but I'll never be able to thank you enough."

"That's all right," Amber said gruffly, squeezing Zillah's hand back, suddenly afraid she was going to embarrass them all by a bout of emotional girlie crying. "I'm just so pleased for you. And for Clancy and for Lewis and — Oh-my-god — Zillah!"

But before she could say anything else, with a fanfare of unseen trumpets, Freddo bounced onto the stage.

The audience whooped and yelled and cheered as he picked up the microphone and strode up and down the stage, waving.

"Does 'e sing?" Constance Motion piped up. "Is 'e the turn? Is 'e like Val Doonican?"

Freddo raised his hands for silence and ran through his introductory spiel, telling everyone about the JB Roadshow and announcing the great news about their forthcoming tour.

The audience screamed and yelled and clapped a lot more.

"Get on with it!" Slo shouted. "I wants to ask young Gwyneth for a waltz!"

Amber leaned towards Zillah. "Quickly — before they start — is that what I think it is?"

"And there's one more thing to tell you," Freddo bawled, still stalking up and down. "Today, it was my great pleasure — probably the greatest pleasure of my life —"

Zillah and Lewis were now exchanging conspiratorial glances across Amber.

"— to witness the marriage of our sensationally talented bass guitarist, Clancy Tavistock and your very own, very beautiful, very, very sexy, Zillah Flanagan!"

The audience exploded. The applause was thunderous. Gwyneth and Big Ida were laughing and crying. Everyone was staring at Zillah, beaming.

Amber hugged and kissed Zillah. "I *knew* that was a wedding ring! I knew it! Oh, Zillah! Congratulations — I'm so pleased for you — delighted — it's amazing — but . . ."

"Lunchtime. Winterbrook Registry." Zillah looked as though she was going to burst. "Freddo and Lewis as witnesses. No one else. We didn't want a big do. Quiet as possible. We wanted to keep it a secret. I made Lewis promise not to tell anyone — not even you and Jem — until we'd finally done it."

Jem, having worked out the implications of Lewis now having what he'd always wanted, kissed everyone.

Lewis grinned. "It was the most romantic thing ever. I bloody cried — but at least I didn't have to wear a bridesmaid's dress . . ."

"And —" Zillah leaned towards Amber "— there's something else."

"God — you're not pregnant are you?" Lewis pulled a mock-horror face.

Zillah punched him. "I'm going to be touring with Clancy — I'll be away for six months. My only problem will be Gwyneth and Ida and Chrysalis, so —" she beamed at Amber "— I'd like you to move in as my house-sitter and geriatric-reprobate-minder, love. Would that be OK?"

OK? *OK?* Living in that fabulous retro cottage, still able to be with Gwyneth, having her own space? Having privacy to — to do her own thing, entertain . . .? OK?

"Zillah — oh, yes. Yes — thank you. Oh, blimey," Amber hugged Zillah again. "Now I really am going to cry."

But there simply wasn't time.

With a whoosh and a crescendo of unbelievable noise and a blinding blaze of lights, the JB Roadshow, in their velvet flares and bright shirts, swarmed onto the stage, and Tiff picked up his microphone.

The noise was incredible as they thundered into their opening "Sock It To 'em JB" number and as one the audience was on its feet, swaying and clapping, already dancing.

Clancy looked down at Zillah and blew her a kiss.

The Fiddlestickers roared some more, the roar lost in the raw, raunchy, explosion of soul.

They were, Amber thought giddily, as she clapped her hands above her head between Lewis and Jem, even better than they'd been at Winterbrook. And Clancy was sooo gorgeous.

Lucky, lucky Zillah.

The band rocked on, perfect, professional, sensational. Fiddlesticks had never seen anything like it.

"Holy shit," Lewis laughed as the JB Roadshow launched into "Soul Finger", "Mrs Jupp has just thrown her knickers at Tiff Clayton."

CHAPTER
THIRTY

Catch a Falling Star

It really had been the best night Fiddlesticks had ever known.

Everyone had danced and sung all night, screaming their enthusiasm, refusing to let the band leave the stage until they'd played an extra hour of encores. It was the early hours of the morning before the last high-as-a-kite villager staggered away across the green.

Now, unable to sleep and still on an adrenaline buzz, Amber sat alone outside Moth Cottage in the darkness. Gwyneth was sleeping soundly with Pike and the cats curled on her feet, and in Butterfly and Chrysalis Cottages, the dimmest of lights glowed. Big Ida was definitely snoring. Zillah and Clancy definitely weren't.

It must be about 4 o'clock, Amber reckoned. Everywhere was still, with only the noises of the night creatures disturbing the silence. And warm, too, for September, the darkness sweet-spiced by wild garlic and thyme and grass crushed beneath hundreds and hundreds of stomping feet.

The Harvest Moon still hung in the sky, the silver of the stars dwarfed tonight by its golden majesty.

It had been a wonderful, wonderful night on all counts.

She suddenly stiffened in the darkness, her ears, now accustomed to the country sounds, picking up something . . . someone . . . crossing the green. Holding her breath, Amber listened. Definitely footsteps. Probably a late-night reveller still staggering home. She shrank back into Moth Cottage's shadows.

The footsteps came nearer. Then stopped. So did her heart.

"Amber?"

"Lewis?"

He paused at the gate. "What are you doing?"

She smiled in the darkness. "And shouldn't that be my question?"

"Couldn't sleep. Jem went out like a light. I simply couldn't settle."

"So you thought you'd stroll round the village, did you? In the wee small hours?"

Lewis shook his head. "I'm not sure . . . and no I'm not drunk. I just wanted . . . needed . . ." He looked at her. "Do you fancy a walk?"

"Oh, yes, nothing I'd like better. I always wander around Fiddlesticks at this hour. No, sorry . . . OK." She joined him at the gate, smiling up at him in the moonlight. "And what the heck are you carrying?"

"Oh, this," Lewis, looking slightly embarrassed, let a handful of shingle trickle to the ground. "Er — I actually thought I might chuck them at your window . . . oh, sod it, Amber. I needed to see you. To talk to you."

She tried to rein in her beam. Fairly unsuccessfully.

They walked slowly, side by side, across the road and onto the green. The stage still loomed in the distance, but everywhere was silent.

"Today," Lewis said, "has been amazing. With Ma and Clancy getting married, and then the show tonight and yet . . ."

They'd reached the rustic bridge. Amber leaned against the flaking woodwork, listening to the rush of the now refreshed stream gurgling beneath them. Her earlier beam faded as rapidly as the stars at sunrise.

Lewis didn't look at her. "We — we never have any time to ourselves, do we? Not to say anything much? Just snatched conversations. There's always something, someone, else making demands. And I do need to say this to you. Now. While we're alone."

Amber was relieved that he couldn't see her face. She'd been dumped before; she knew the signs. She'd cope. Hopefully. It was, however, desperately galling to be dumped by someone she loved more than life but, sadly, wasn't even going out with.

"Look —" she decided to make it easy "— I know what you're going to say. And I do appreciate you doing it now, privately, without the usual Fiddlesticks audience. And I promise I won't be a pain. I know, because I'm staying in the village, you might find it difficult — but I promise I'll leave you alone and —"

Lewis frowned. "I'm not sure I understand. Are you telling me —"

"That I'm fine with just being friends," Amber nodded. "Yes. Right from the start, when you collected me at Reading station, I knew you weren't interested. I knew, and OK, maybe I —"

"Amber," Lewis interrupted, "when I saw you waiting at the station I thought you were probably the most beautiful woman I'd ever seen in my life, but —"

Amber sighed. There it was. The but bit.

". . . but," he continued, "you were so — so well, cloned. Oh, God, I don't want to insult you. But your clothes, all the make-up, the bone-straight hair — you looked like a million other girls. Like a uniform. And gorgeous, glamorous women like that, like you, like I thought you were, only want celeb lookalikes, to be a footballer's wife or something . . ."

"Excuse me?" Amber frowned at him. "I've never wanted to be a footballer's wife — or any other wife come to that —"

Not strictly true, but what the heck.

"No, no — but what I mean is, with me being a bit of a hippie throwback, and a social worker to boot, I thought —"

"Dangerous thing, thinking," Amber said softly. "Try asking sometimes."

"What? Well, yeah, OK — but you see, over the weeks, as I got to know you, I realised that the outside gloss wasn't you. You were — are — feisty, intelligent, kind, funny — all my misconceptions were just that. And you didn't need the slap and the fashion stuff — and well, like now — just jeans and a sweater and your hair all natural and you, individual, the inner you, shining out . . ."

Not sure if this was a compliment or not, Amber shrugged. "I think I get your drift. But yes, you were wrong about sticking a label on me. I haven't changed — although my life has, and I've learned since being here that there are more important things than celeb crap, and being an identi-kit woman, and false glamour. Fiddlesticks has brought out the best in me. People like Gwyneth and Ida with their caring about animals, and Zillah being so brave, and yes, you with Jem — you've all shown me that there's much more to life than I'd ever thought. And it's rubbed off — I guess there was always this me, underneath . . ." She stopped and looked at him. "But — er — Lewis, what exactly are you trying to say?"

He looked away from her for a moment. "I wondered — if we could sort of move the relationship on a bit. From being friends to — er — going out together? Properly. As a couple?"

Oh, whoopee! Amber's mental gymnastics had a blissful workout. Then, right in the middle of the back-flip, they stopped. She couldn't cope with being another Sukie — one date — then passed over for the next pretty face.

It would simply break her heart.

"I don't know. I mean yes, I'd love to go out with you — you know that, or at least you should. But as we're being painfully honest, you have got a terrible reputation, haven't you? Look, I'm not asking for lifetime commitment here, but you've made the love 'em and leave 'em thing an art form, haven't you?"

"Because of Jem." Lewis looked at her then. "My commitment to Jem is lifelong. His lifespan may not be as long as ours, but while he's alive — and God, I hope it's for a long time — he is my sole responsibility. I've never, ever met any woman who could cope with that. With sharing me with him."

"I love him."

"He loves you, too," Lewis swallowed. "Which is why I had to be sure that you wouldn't leave him — us — me . . ."

Amber took a deep breath. "Are you saying . . .? I mean . . ."

Lewis nodded. "I can't stand this any longer. Amber —"

Suddenly the dark sky sizzled with silver.

"What?" Amber grabbed Lewis's arm. "What on earth is that?"

"Shooting stars," Lewis said softly. "Real astral magic. Nature's firework display."

Amber gazed in total awe as the stars shimmied and sped across the dense velvet, vivid pinpricks of light leaving a dusting of diamonds cascading in their wake.

"It's beautiful . . . Amazing . . ."

"So are you," Lewis said softly. "Oh God — I love you. I love you so much, but I come with so much baggage."

"As long as it's Luis Vuitton, I'll be happy," Amber giggled. "No, sorry, sad fashionista joke. Oh, God —"

And then she was in his arms and her body melted with wantonness as he kissed her.

396

And ages and ages later, bathed in the light of the harvest moon, they still clung together.

She giggled, thanking her lucky stars for bringing her to Fiddlesticks and Lewis. In fact, thanking her lucky stars for absolutely everything.

"Mmmm," she sighed blissfully, wriggling against him. "Whatever else Cassiopeia and the other celestial gods may have fixed for everyone else, she didn't have a hand in this. I didn't ask her for this."

"No." Lewis smiled, kissing her again. "But I did . . ."

Also available in ISIS Large Print:

Love Potions

Christina Jones

H. E. Bates for the 21st Century — Katie Fforde on Hubble Bubble.

When aromatherapist Sukie Ambrose starts using her cottage garden for inspiration — and raw ingredients — for her products, she thinks she's just hit on a good way of saving money while offering her clients a way of de-stressing and relaxation. However, Sukie lives in a village where strange things have been known to happen ... She discovers that her new improved lotions and potions are making her massages distinctly magical — and producing more star-crossed lovers than Shakespeare could ever dream of.

Sukie has only one lover in her sights — the delectable Derry Kavanagh. Sadly, Derry is dating Sukie's house-mate and is therefore definitely a no-go target for her home-brewed love potions. Or is he ...?

ISBN 978-0-7531-7784-6 (hb)
ISBN 978-0-7531-7785-3 (pb)

Welcome to the Real World

Carole Matthews

Pub singer Fern Kendal has the voice of an angel but her talent is wasted. Like millions of others, all she needs is a break, but in the real world she knows that'll never happen.

Evan David's exquisite tones have enthralled opera buffs throughout the world. People pander to his every need. But what Evan needs now is a break — from it all.

When Fern is picked to be Evan's PA their two worlds collide. Neither one is prepared for the effect they will have on each other. For something happens when they are together — and it's more than just music . . .

ISBN 978-0-7531-7794-5 (hb)
ISBN 978-0-7531-7795-2 (pb)